She felt the strong, warm hands sliding up her spine, into her hair.

The familiarity of the contact made her breath catch—and then the hands were gone. The cold that surrounded her, the loss of that odd anchor, left her breathless.

She looked up. Stared into a pale gaze, golden and hot. Caught another flash of light in those eyes, though it only lasted seconds.

"Are you hurt?" murmured the man. Rikki shook her head, unable to speak—too rattled, too consumed. She heard her name shouted and tried to turn. Her knees wobbled, making her stagger, but those long arms slid around her waist, holding her against a hard, lean body. He was hot as hell; an invading heat, soaking through skin to bone. For one heartbeat she felt safe in that warmth, that embrace—utterly protected—and it was such a foreign, startling feeling, she almost forgot what had happened.

Or why feeling safe could never again be possible.

By Marjorie M. Liu

Marjorie M. Liu

The Last Twilight

A DIRK & STEELE NOVEL

AVON

An Imprint of HarperCollinsPublishers

AVON BOOKS
An Imprint of HarperCollins*Publishers*
10 East 53rd Street
New York, New York 10022-5299

First Avon Books mass market printing: June 2011

ACKNOWLEDGMENTS

I would like to thank Dr. Sai-Ling Liu for the gracious use of her time as I peppered her with questions about being a physician and practicing medicine in Africa. Many thanks to my agent, Lucienne Diver, and my editor, Chris Keeslar.

When you arise, alive, tomorrow, you'll be someone else:
but something is left from the lost frontiers of the night,
from that being and nothing where we find ourselves,

something that brings us close in the light of life,
as if the seal of the darkness
branded its secret creatures with a fire.

PABLO NERUDA, from "Sonnet LXXXIII"

PROLOGUE

THE monkeys began dying at dawn. Only the children noticed. They were playing a game of soccer, just within sight of the refugee camp. The river was nearby, the jungle wall thick and hoarse with crying shadows. Birds jammed the air.

The soccer ball was made of cowhide, rough-stitched and brown and stuffed with grass and dried elephant dung. No proper bounce, but it was good enough to kick. The children had been playing since the first hint of light in the sky—at least an hour—and they were hungry and sweaty. So hungry, for such a long time, they hardly noticed anymore.

The children were playing on the road. It was flat and dusty. No traffic, though the boys took turns standing on a rock to keep watch. Not for other refugees, but for men carrying guns, or trucks with an unfamiliar shape or growl. Between the five of them, they owned a whistle, a gift from one of the doctors in the camp. The boy on the rock had it now, held tight in his fist. He was ready to blow the whistle, just in case.

The soccer game got rough. One hard kick, and the ball

flew into the jungle. The boys threw up their hands, shouting, pointing fingers. The littlest one was responsible; he was shoved, unwilling, toward the thick brush and towering trees. He protested loudly, tripping over knotted vines, falling on his knees. Smaller than the ferns, or the twisting roots angling out of the ground; swallowed by shadows that radiated a thick wet heat that buzzed with stinging mosquitoes.

You are easy food for a snake, laughed his friends. *Watch out.*

The child watched. He glanced over his shoulder as the leaves closed behind him, shutting out the dawn light. It would be hours before the sun rose high enough to pierce the upper canopy. Until then, a constant twilight, fit only for leopards and spirits; cries of birds, echoing.

He heard a thud, off to his left. Heavy, like a melon falling. Or a body. He turned to run and his bare foot touched something hard and leathery. The ball. He had been standing beside it the entire time. He scooped it up, still ready to flee, but before he could take a step something fell from the trees in front of him. He screamed.

The other boys crashed through the bush, calling his name. He did not answer them. His attention was on the ground. He pointed as his friends arrived, and all of them fell silent, staring at the twisted body of a monkey sprawled in the dried leaves. A white stripe cut across its brindled forehead, and its tufted ears were yellow. Blood dotted its nose and the corners of its eyes.

The monkey was not alone. Other bodies lay on the ground; little lumps of dark fur that blended well with the shadows. The eldest boy whistled, rubbing his palms against his stomach as he stepped close and touched a limp haunch with his bare toe.

"Still warm," he whispered.

"This one fell," said the smallest, still clutching the ball. Another crashing thud, out of sight on their left, made them jump; they looked up and saw shadows swaying unsteadily in the branches, eyes blinking in the forest twilight.

"They are so quiet," someone said.

"We should go," murmured another, backing away.

The eldest stooped and picked up the dead monkey by its tail. The boys hissed at him, but he straightened his shoulders and flashed his teeth. "Aren't you hungry?"

The smallest shook his head. "We are not allowed to take bush meat."

"It was already dead." The boy started walking, slinging the monkey over his shoulder. "Come on. If the *mondele* give us trouble, we will show them this place and prove we are innocent." His grin widened, and he patted his flat stomach. "We will do that anyway, I think."

The other boys looked at each other. Another monkey swayed and fell from the tree. It almost landed on top of them. Dead, with blood in its eyes. Like it was weeping.

The children ran from the jungle, calling after their friend who was already racing down the road toward the white tents of the refugee camp. The monkey bounced against his back. Blood dripped from its eyes into the dust, against his calves.

The boy was fast and his legs were long. He had a strong heart, the promise of meat in his belly; the sweet anticipation of seeing his mother smile. For that, anything.

He was dead by sunset.

CHAPTER ONE

RIKKI Kinn was in Brazzaville, stuck in an arm-wrestling match with a drunk Congolese soldier, when the CDC in Atlanta called her cell phone. She knew who it was without looking at the screen; they had a special ring tone: ABBA's "S.O.S."

"You give up now, you buy us all beers, eh?" said the man across the table. His navy beret sat askew on his head, and sweat dribbled down his ebony face. His eyes were red-rimmed, and he swayed, just slightly.

His grip was strong but not painful. Rikki smiled through gritted teeth. "Maybe *you* want to give up, Jean-Claude. Before I beat you *again*." She puckered her lips and kissed the air. The men gathered around the table laughed and slapped Jean-Claude's shoulder. The cell phone kept ringing.

Muscles burned; her arm quivered. Rikki glanced at one of the soldiers and he plucked her cell from its clip and placed it in her left hand. Congo pop music, full of sharp beats, threaded through the open door of the stifling corrugated shack she was sitting in.

She flipped open the cell. "Doctor Kinn speaking."

"Rikki, it's Larry. Get ready to move. We've got a Hot Zone. Level Four."

Jean-Claude slammed her hand into the table. Rikki did not notice. She closed her eyes, dizzy and breathless. "Where?"

"Between Bumba and Lisala. Mack is already there. He'll fill you in when you arrive."

"Fill me in now."

"Not on this line." Larry's voice was cold, hard. Rikki knew that tone. She clamped her mouth shut and glanced at the soldiers. Only Jean-Claude met her gaze, and he no longer appeared quite so drunk. Rikki pushed back her chair, dug into her pocket and pulled out a twenty-dollar bill. She tossed it on the table and moved to the door.

"Transport?" she asked, staring out at the gates of the dock, which was crowded with yet more soldiers, all of whom were trying to control the endless bottleneck traffic of bodies: bare backs bent under loads of burlap sacks and bushels of sugar cane; uniformed porters stumbling beneath the immense luggage and wares of Zairean businessmen in loud suits and gold jewelry. Wheelbarrows pushed by gaunt men passed Rikki, along with scooters and creaking carts piled with clothing; castoffs from America, no doubt. Shouts slammed the air, as did fists; everyone wanted to be on that ferry idling on the river's edge, and the only way to get there was to push and shove and fight for every step.

Rikki heard an odd clinking sound on the other end of the phone. Like glass. "Mack said you were in Brazzaville. Can you make it to Kinshasa by the evening?"

"Sooner. I'm already at the ferry."

"Good. Colonel Bakker will meet you on the other side, and he'll put you on one of the UN planes headed for the affected area. Questions?"

Rikki snorted, scuffing her shoes against the dirt floor, kicking debris into a stagnant puddle outside the door. "You just told me I can't ask any."

"Rules of the game," Larry said, and then, softer: "Be careful, kid. This one's trouble."

"Story of my life," she replied, and flipped her cell phone shut. Tried to imagine, for a moment, what she was headed for, but her mind stayed blank, and all she could do was watch as sunlight cut skeins through the dust and blue exhaust, the air thick and damp and hot. Her entire body was slick with sweat; she was glad she had cut her hair before this last trip to Africa. Short, like a pixie.

Tinkerbell, her daddy would say. A slip of a thing: his princess, his little Thumbelina. Small, but with a punch.

The soldiers were watching her. Rikki schooled her expression into something cool and easy; a well-oiled mask. Her second skin. The twenty had disappeared from the table, and in its place was a deck of cards. Jean-Claude stood only a foot away, his reddened eyes thoughtful. "What is wrong?"

Everything, Rikki thought, but she put a smile on her face and said, "Duty calls. You want to help me get on that ferry?"

Jean-Claude knew her too well. His eyes narrowed, so sharp, but he reached behind the door and picked up his rifle. He gestured to the others. "Of course. What are friends for?" And then, bending close, he whispered, "I would have beat you this time."

His breath smelled like beer. Rikki shook her head and grabbed her backpack. "In your dreams."

"Not without my wife's permission," he replied easily, and stopped her, just outside the shed. "You are going to a sick place?"

She hesitated. "Yes."

Jean-Claude nodded, sucking on the inside of his cheek. No words, though. He turned on his heel, grabbed her arm, and pulled her toward the heaving crowd. The other men from the shed pushed ahead, clearing a narrow path that Rikki and Jean-Claude squeezed through. All of them were rough; brutal, even. People fell getting out of their way; packages were dropped and trampled. Rikki was almost knocked down herself, but Jean-Claude's hand clamped tight and he hauled her upright, almost carrying her against his side.

The immigration official stomped out of his post as they passed. He was as tall as Jean-Claude, but twice as wide; he towered over Rikki and tried to grab her other arm.

"Vos papiers!" blustered the man, but Jean-Claude rattled off a long stream of words in their native language, and pushed him away. No stamps in her passport this time around. An illegal departure from the country, but nothing that would land her in too much trouble—for the right amount of money. If she were caught.

The ferry's metal ramp appeared, crowded with bodies, wares, and livestock. Another immigration official lay in wait at the top; Jean-Claude said a few more hard words, leaned in close—his rifle butt poking the man's chest— and escorted Rikki past him. She heard her name shouted, and turned in time to catch a wave from one of the young soldiers who had been in the shed. She held up her hand, nodding, but Jean-Claude pushed her away from the rusted rail toward the other side of the boat, not letting her stop until the crowd thinned and they could see the smoky edge of Kinshasa looming on the opposite bank of the muddy Congo. Dirty steel and stone, cut from the jungle like a scar.

Jean-Claude still gripped her arm. His fingers squeezed hard, and in a low voice he said, "Make an excuse. Do not go."

Rikki glanced down at his hand and raised an eyebrow. "Two years we've known each other, and you've never given me advice."

His gaze flickered to her breasts. It was not a sexual look, but Rikki knew exactly what he was remembering, and it made her want to cover herself. She kept steady, though. Too much time spent building herself up to crack the mask now.

"Jean-Claude," she said. A low sigh escaped him, but he lifted his gaze and looked her in the eye—which was almost worse. She could not stand his pity.

Or his words. His voice was too gentle, as though he was trying to soothe some wounded animal; rabid, wild. "I have never given you advice, because you were in no state to take it. Not then. And by the time you healed—"

"No." Rikki finally had to look away. "No, Jean-Claude. Please."

"Please," he echoed. "Do not go to the sick place. Make an excuse."

"You know I can't do that."

His hand tightened. "Rikki—"

"Let go of me, Jean-Claude."

He did, holding up his hand, and glanced away; first at the slick metal deck, and then the swirling waters. "I hear rumors coming out of Zaire. More and more stories every day. The new government has changed the name of its country, but the people are still the same." He gave her a hard look. "The UN will not be able to protect you."

"I've got bigger worries than the rebels."

Jean-Claude shook his head. "I was not speaking of the rebels."

Around them a shout went up, accompanied by a ringing bell and a rough announcement that the ferry would be leaving at any moment. Goats bleated; a baby squalled; somewhere nearby, a woman crooned. A breeze licked the sweat from Rikki's face, but she could not savor it. Jean-Claude backed away, holding his rifle against his chest.

Rikki swayed after him. "Spit it out. You have something to say."

"No." He stopped, wetting his lips, holding himself stiff. He looked uneasy, and the fleeting smile that appeared on his face was pained, sickly. Not him. Not like the man who had once saved her life. "Next time you come around, we wrestle again, eh?"

"Jean-Claude."

"Be careful," he whispered—and turned, practically at a run, driving himself hard through the crowd, slipping around carts and stacked bushels of grain. Rikki pushed away from the rail, calling his name, but he never looked back. She lost him in moments.

The bell kept ringing; a black cloud of smoke coughed from the stern, burning Rikki's nostrils. The ferry heaved, shuddering, and a low groan filled the air, followed by the chugging hack of the engines as the ferry finally pushed from shore. On her way. No turning back. She tried not to think of Jean-Claude's words. Or that look in his eye. No telling what to make of his warning, either, which was . . . really crappy.

He was scared for you. Be grateful someone cares enough to be scared.

Hell, *she* was scared. All the time. She just hid it better than most people. Rikki preferred being a hard-ass to having no ass at all. She thought her father would approve.

But here, now, there was nothing that could be helped,

nothing to do but take a little care. Same as always. Rikki focused on her breathing. Watched the river and the people around her. Staying present, in the moment—savoring, while she could, the kind of solitude only a crowd could offer. Peace, among strangers. No demands, no ties. No shoulders but her own to lean on. Which was all she could trust to keep and hold. Lesson learned, hammered home. More times than she wanted to think about.

Friend to everyone. And friend to none.

A nearby man held a full-length mirror in his arms. It had been wrapped in cloth at some point, but pieces of fabric were slipping free. Rikki caught a glimpse of herself. Short brown hair, sharp brown eyes, a small face red with heat and slick with sweat. No make-up, but with lashes black as soot; a full pink mouth and cheekbones high and round. Natural born, her father had always said. Just like her mother.

Rikki felt like she was looking at a stranger. Tore her gaze away fast.

The ferry ride lasted only thirty minutes. No one approached her, though she heard the occasional murmur of *"le blanc"* behind her back. Made sense. She was the only pale face on the ferry, and they were headed for Ngobila Beach. The Gauntlet. Hell Ground. No one went to the Beach unless they had to, and she would be an easy target for the soldiers. Good thing she liked trouble. Good thing those men knew it, too.

Up close, Kinshasa boomed with twisted shacks and spires, smoke that curled through the haze of humid air. Somewhere out of sight, dogs barked. Behind her, voices got louder; a buzz of excitement, fear. Rikki steadied herself.

Ngobila Beach held no surprises. Crazy, business as usual.

It took a while for the ferry to dock, and she used the time waiting to study the crowd below, the forefront of which consisted mainly of screaming soldiers in green uniforms, and beggars missing limbs. Rikki watched one young woman utterly without legs drag her torso across the rocks, her hands wrapped in colorful rags. She had a bag slung over her shoulders, the canvas bulging with sharp-edged objects. The maimed woman glanced up at the ferry and zeroed in on Rikki. Stared into her eyes with a hollow intensity that was hard to shake off. But not impossible. Rikki had seen worse. She would be swimming in it by the end of the day.

People began pushing each other down the ferry ramp to shore. Rikki let herself be carried by the surge, pressed tight on all sides by tall strong men carrying grain sacks on their heads—men who flashed her friendly smiles when they saw her looking. They tried to make room; Rikki was almost half the size of everyone around her, and being short in such a crowd felt like moving in a furnace, a stifling pocket of trapped air that smelled like sweat and excitement and fear. Close to being trampled; closer still to suffocation.

Congolese soldiers waited at the bottom of the ramp. Black berets and green fatigues; handguns and rifles and AK-47s brandished like charms. One of the security officers stepped forward and grabbed Rikki's arm. His breath smelled like beer and his teeth were white. Sweat rolled down his face. Rikki slid her hand into the top pocket of her cargo pants.

"*Bonjour, Docteur.*"

"*Bonjour,* Simon." Rikki smiled and slipped a fifty-dollar bill into his hand. The officer's eyes crinkled and he palmed the cash to his chest, slipping it inside his shirt where no one could see it. He slung his other arm around her shoulders and gestured to the men with him, who began clearing a path through the crowd, much as the other soldiers had done for her at the Brazzaville dock.

He led her past the immigration office—a place that Rikki had learned, some years back, could be avoided in its entirety with one phone call and a well-placed bribe. Corrupt, yes; immoral, maybe. Rikki had taught herself not to care. Passports had a way of getting lost in that place; same with people. And she was always on a deadline.

"You have a guest waiting for you," Simon said, as they passed through open iron gates into a quiet area free of the crowd. "He is a very frustrated man."

"Most men are," Rikki replied, and Simon laughed out loud. He was still laughing when they turned a corner in the dusty yard and Colonel Bakker came into view. His pale blue beret stuck out like a piece of sky.

Simon stopped and said, *"Au revoir, Docteur."*

"Until next time?"

He patted his chest, winking. "It would be my pleasure."

Rikki smiled, fairly certain it reached her eyes, and turned to walk away fast, fingers mentally crossed. There was always a risk to the games she played at the borders. Simon could change his mind. Arrest her.

Rikki's neck prickled; she fought the urge to check and see if the officer still watched, and instead focused on Colonel Bakker, whose hard gaze was not on her, but a spot over her shoulder. He looked unhappy.

"Bastards wouldn't let me meet you at the ferry," he muttered, when she was close enough to hear him. "Got worried."

She glanced over her shoulder. Simon was gone. Bakker said, "You need to be more careful."

"I'm always careful," Rikki said, thinking of Jean-Claude's warning. "But I have different ways of protecting myself. You know that."

Bakker grunted, and she wondered if he, too, was remembering. Probably. Seemed to be a lot of that going around today. Two years was obviously not enough time for some memories to fade.

But the colonel did not look at her breasts, and his eyes were clear and without pity as he said, "Don't know how you do it. Those soldiers won't give me the time of day, but to you . . ." He stopped, frowning. "Must be a girl thing."

"Must be," she said dryly.

Bakker was a big man, broad through the chest, his fatigues drenched in sweat. Well into his fifties, his skin was too fair for the sun; his face and neck were red, peeling, his blue eyes bloodshot. He was rubbing them even as she held out her hand in official greeting, and he muttered, "Damn dust."

She retracted her hand, just slightly. "Not pinkeye, is it?"

He gave her a dirty look, made rather less menacing by the fact that he was still knuckling his eye socket like some ten-year-old on the verge of tears. "Smart-ass punk."

"Grumpy bear." Rikki grinned, and this time it was all her—no mask, no illusion. "You need a hug?"

Bakker glanced askance at the man waiting for them inside the jeep. "Try and I'll shoot you."

"Bet your wife loves that line."

"Why do you think we're getting a divorce?"

Rikki placed a finger over her heart and made a hissing sound. "Very nice, Colonel."

He grunted, pointed at the Jeep, and she obliged with a smile. Relaxed, for the first time in a week. Jean-Claude knew her better than Bakker, but Bakker reminded Rikki of her father, and there was something warm and gruff about his face and voice that she couldn't resist. Like having a shot of home.

The ride to the airfield took less than thirty minutes. They drove past twisted metal slums and palm trees. Bakker sat in the front passenger seat while one of his men drove. He mopped his sweaty face with the back of his hand and said, "Larry fill you in?"

Rikki closed her eyes and leaned back against the seat. The air-conditioning felt good. "He said the lines weren't safe. That Mack would do the talking when I got there."

Bakker made a small noncommittal sound. "What were you doing in Brazzaville?"

"Coordinating with some folks from the Red Cross. Trying to get some better drugs from the pharmaceuticals instead of the usual expired shit." Rikki frowned, opening her eyes. "Why?"

Bakker gave her an odd look. "You didn't tell anyone when you left."

"Didn't know I had to."

"Things have changed."

Something about his tone reminded her of Jean-Claude. Rikki straightened. "What's happened?"

"Nothing." Bakker rubbed his eyes. "Nothing but talk."

"Seems to be a lot of that today."

His mouth slanted into a scowl. "Do tell."

"You first."

Bakker's gaze flickered to the driver, then back to Rikki. *Not here,* his eyes seemed to say, but there was something more than caution in his expression. Her concern deepened.

"We're almost there," said the young man behind the wheel. Rikki watched his gaze jump to the rearview mirror and linger there. A furrow formed in his forehead. She turned, gazing out the back window of the Land Cruiser, and saw a black truck, polished to a mirror shine. Expensive. Unusual. Bakker also twisted in his seat. His eyes flinched.

"Speed up," he told the driver, and touched the gun clipped to his belt. His other hand reached for the radio set into the dash. Behind them an engine roared. Rikki looked back and this time glimpsed the truck's driver; pale skin, dark sunglasses. He seemed to be looking right at her.

He was not alone. Men suddenly stood from behind the cab of the truck. They leaned on the shining metal roof with goggles strapped over their eyes, dust and wind kicking up brown hair. Kevlar vests hugged their broad torsos, and in their hands—guns. Big fucking guns.

Rikki's breath choked. "Bakker."

"I see them. Get down on the floor."

"Bakker."

"We're getting you to that village," he said in a hard voice, still looking at the truck pressing close behind them. "Now, *down!"*

Rikki unbuckled her seatbelt and slithered to the floor. She put her head down. She breathed in and out, in and out, heart hammering.

It happened fast. The Jeep rocked forward, metal shrieking. A second impact sent her head into the door. Pain splashed. Blood roared. Bakker shouted, but Rikki could not hear him over the piercing grind of the two cars slamming together. She was thrown again into the door, and she covered her head, using her legs to wedge herself tighter into the small space.

The back window shattered. She heard popping sounds. Gunfire. The Jeep swerved. Bakker was still screaming directions, interrupted by the crack and hiss of a voice over the radio also shouting, until suddenly Rikki felt a hand tap her lower back and Bakker said, "We're here. Get ready to run."

The side window shattered; the young man at the wheel grunted. The Jeep swerved again, wildly out of control, then stopped so hard she thought they might flip. Bakker swore and opened his door. He said, "Go."

Rikki fumbled for the handle, shoved open the door, and fell out on all fours. The cement burned her hands. Hot air washed over her. Straight ahead she saw a white plane with the UN logo stamped on the side. Peacekeepers were kneeling, rifles raised, aiming at the truck behind her.

Bullets ripped the air. Bakker shouted her name. She glanced up and saw him leaning against the hood of the car, gun in hand. His eyes were wild, every vein and tendon in his neck strained and popping.

A bullet slammed into his chest. He dropped. Rikki threw herself over him, pressing her hands down on the wound. Bakker was still conscious; he whispered, "Run."

Blood leaked from beneath his body; the bullet had gone straight through. Rikki glanced over her shoulder; the peace-keepers were waving frantically at her, but the men from the black truck still had not given up. Barricaded behind their own truck, they were still firing.

Rikki peered into the car. The young driver was slumped over the wheel; blood covered his seat.

"Rikki," Bakker murmured, eyes fluttering closed.

"Shut up," she muttered, and hooked her hands under his armpits. Dug in her heels, putting her back into it. She dragged Bakker toward the plane. He had to weigh almost two hundred pounds and she barely hit ninety, but her old training still carried true, and she was able to move his dead weight. A long smear of blood followed them. Bullets whizzed past her head, but she kept her focus narrow, concentrating only on taking that next step backward.

She did not notice when the gunfire stopped. She did not hear her name shouted. She did not let go of Bakker, even when the peacekeepers finally made it to them. One of the men was an emergency medic. She saw his kit and her hands finally uncurled, let go, reaching instead for tools, the weapons of her trade.

They worked frantically to stop the bleeding. Bakker kept breathing. One of the peacekeepers tried to get Rikki to leave him—it was not safe, *not safe*—but it was not until the UN medical unit arrived that anyone could convince her to stop.

She fell backward on the burning cement, watching as men and women strapped Bakker to a stretcher. Hands touched her shoulder, her arms—hands that helped her stand. Rikki barely noticed. She looked around for the first time, saw the Jeep, empty now, and behind it that black truck riddled with bullets. The windows were shattered. Bodies slumped inside the front. Men hung over the back, dripping blood.

She stared, trying to make sense of it all—and when she was done trying, and failing, she looked back at Bakker, only to find him gone. Borne away by the medics in their van, which she saw in the distance, blue lights flashing.

Bakker. Her chest felt hollow. Her scars burned. She wanted to cry, but that was wrong, so wrong. She'd cried herself out years ago.

Someone got her on the UN plane. Someone else retrieved her backpack from the battered Jeep. Rikki sat in a jump seat near the pilots, who solemnly shook her hand

and assured her that the flight would be easy breezy. Rikki merely raised her eyebrow. The men got the hint and stopped talking. Within minutes they were in the air.

She always felt queasy when flying, but this time was worse. There were spots of blood on her arms. She had worn latex gloves while working on Bakker, but they had not protected everything. She touched her hair and felt glass.

Rikki took a deep breath and stared out the window. Below, the Congo River wound through the rainforest like a thread of quicksilver. She saw settlements cut into the green, as well as farmland and roads. People, surviving. People, dying.

The UN will not be able to protect you, Jean-Claude had said. *Be careful.*

Rikki smiled grimly. Careful. Right.

Two hours later they landed in the Hot Zone.

CHAPTER TWO

EIGHTY-NINE hundred miles away, a cheetah ran through the streets of San Francisco.

It was three in the morning. Empty sidewalks, quiet shadows; a breeze that was cool and sweet. A good neighborhood, with good homes. A view of the sea.

No one saw the cheetah. He was fast and kept to the shadows. Larger than others of his kind, with black roses on his body and soft teardrop lines that curved from the corners of his golden eyes. Lean, narrow muscles flowing with restless liquid grace. Wild, on the loose. A predator, prowling.

Reciting Shakespeare in his mind.

This thing of darkness I acknowledge mine, thought the cheetah, gliding through the gloom, the pavement wet beneath the rough pads of his feet. It had rained. The air still smelled fresh with storm. Too much to resist for someone who needed to stretch his skin.

He ran for an hour before returning home. He had never owned a house before coming to America, but he earned a good deal of money now, and had bought his home the year before; a cottage at the end of a cul-de-sac. The real estate agent had called it a Tudor, but the cheetah did not care about names, only that he liked the dark lines cut against cream, the flow of the roof and walls. He liked the windows, which faced the south. He loved the garden, which was large and covered in trees and thick hedges, bluebells and roses.

The cheetah approached his home through the backyard—now wild with tall grass and unruly flowers—pausing for just one moment before he parted the hedges with his nose.

Men waited for him by the kitchen door. One of them was young, pale, with black wavy hair and eyes older than stone. He smelled like fire. His companion was taller, his face half hidden by the turned-up collar of his leather jacket. His eyes were closed, mostly covered by a sweep of brown hair. He leaned against the house, hands shoved into his pockets.

The cheetah continued to linger in the shadows, tasting their scents. There was only one reason these men would come here, like this, and though he did not begrudge their presence, he did not want this night to end. Such a lovely night.

"Amiri," said the tall man softly. His eyes remained closed.

The cheetah pushed through the hedges. Golden light swept over his fur. His joints popped, twisting and growing as every bone in his body stretched to accommodate his second skin. No pain, just a sensation of becoming liquid, hot like lava, pouring and reforming into fingers and arms and legs, fur sliding away into some invisible twilight; a ghost, a beast, the shadow of his soul; like poetry, a dance.

The cheetah shrugged off his body and became a man. The golden light seeped into the night, falling around his naked shoulders like a cloak. He stared at his hands for a moment, taking in his ebony skin, which glinted with hints of gold. Flexed his long fingers, imagining claws. Wondered, as he sometimes did, which was real. And if he had to choose, what that choice would be.

"Amiri," said the tall man.

"Yes." He stopped looking at his hands, and smiled. "Come in. I will make us some tea."

AMIRI DID NOT OFTEN ENTERTAIN GUESTS, THOUGH HE certainly had enough cups and chairs to accommodate the two men in his kitchen. They sat at the small dining table, holding their mugs of tea; relaxed, easy, tossing sugar cubes into the steaming liquid. Books surrounded them; on the tabletop, stacked on the chair between the men, on the gleaming checkered floor. Some were new, most bought used from a small shop only a mile down the road, which Amiri frequented on the weekends for hot chocolate and the sweet smile and conversation of the elderly woman who ran the register. She always appreciated his choices in literature, had a word or two for every book.

Max had his elbow resting on Chinua Achebe, with Octavia Butler beneath his wrist and some Dickens perilously close to falling in his lap. "You need shelves, man."

"I have them," Amiri replied, buttoning his shirt. "But they are full."

Max smiled against his teacup. "I guess I know what you do in your spare time, hiding away from the rest of us. Bets were on you having a girl."

Amiri shook his head, only slightly amused. A tabby cat, scarred and huge, entered the kitchen. He chirped once, slashing the air with his tail. Amiri took the hint. Poured him a little milk. The young man named Eddie reached down to stroke his back.

"I didn't know you had a cat," he said, voice soft, young

as his face. His eyes looked tired, and up close the scent of fire, ash, was even stronger. He radiated heat.

Amiri shrugged, rolling back his cuffs. "He began living in my garden last month. A week ago he invited himself in. Who was I to discourage him?"

Max raised an eyebrow. "He's not fixed. He'll spray."

"We have an agreement." Amiri smiled, showing his teeth. "He knows what I will do if he ruins my home."

The cat stopped lapping the milk, gave him a long hard look, and stalked from the kitchen, bowlegged. Max shook his head, the corner of his mouth twitching, and set down his cup. His coat was still on, his face mostly hidden. Even in the light, it was difficult to see his eyes. He smelled like coffee, like he had been drowning in it. "Something's come up. Roland tried calling, but—"

"I was out," Amiri finished, and tilted his head, considering his words. "It must be important, if you are here. I have not seen you in over a year. You were unwell then, if I remember."

Max tapped his forehead. "Too many people. I had to go away for a while."

"And now?"

"Now Roland wants a favor." Max hesitated, glancing at Eddie. "He's sending us to Africa. Zaire. We take the plane tonight. He wants you to go, too."

It took Amiri a moment. He was quite certain his hearing was damaged. He had been listening to rather loud music, of late. Rocking out, as his friends might say.

"Could you . . . repeat that?" he asked, slowly.

Max winced. "I'm sorry, man. You heard me the first time."

"Ah." Amiri went still; feeling, as he did, something empty inside his chest, a void seeping from his heart to his

toes. The world felt fuller than he did: floors creaking, fau-
cets dripping, the wind sidling against the kitchen window;
the faint scent of old paper and ink; and his dinner: raw
steak and asparagus, with a drip of honey on his tongue for
dessert. Full. Simple pleasures. Safe.

And then the void disappeared, and in its place was a
hard bitterness. Memory. Loss. He turned away, bracing
himself against the sink. "He wants me to go, does he?"

"It's urgent."

"No doubt."

"He thought you would understand."

"Then he is no mind reader," Amiri replied. "And neither are you."

Max fell silent. Eddie might as well have been a ghost.
Amiri wished he could be so insubstantial. Memories had
teeth. Biting hard with gasps of sunlight, the sensation of
heat. Feet digging into hot earth, the clean scent of some dry
blowing wind. Racing antelope. Drowsing with elephants.
Crying lonesome music with the screams of eagles wing-
ing low over the golden rolling grassland. That last day, that
lovely foolish day. Leaving the city for the wild to shed his
human skin. Believing in safety. Taking freedom, *secrets,*
for granted.

And for that carelessness, nothing but needles and machines and that doctor with his smile.

Max sucked in his breath. Amiri cursed himself, turning. "I am sorry."

"No." Max pinched the bridge of his nose. "It's my fault
I can't stop hearing what people think."

Eddie studied both men like they were breaking beams
holding up a bridge; serious, sober, watching the world fall
down. Amiri fought himself, wondering what his own face
must look like. "Why Zaire?"

Max looked away from him. "Roland has an old army buddy who works at the CDC. A guy named Larry Coleman. He called last night and asked for Dirk & Steele's help with his operations in Central Africa. Off the record."

"And what are we to do for this man?" Amiri's voice sounded cool inside his ears; distant, calmer than the quickening beat of his heart. The cheetah stirred within his skin. Claws idled beneath his fingernails.

Max's jaw tightened. "Investigate. Protect. Coleman is afraid that one of his people is in danger. A doctor named Regina Kinn. Rikki, for short."

"What is the threat?"

"No specifics. Coleman didn't want to share too many details. We're supposed to learn more once we reach our target."

"I don't like that part," Eddie said quietly, playing with a sugar cube. "We'll be running blind."

"Roland wasn't happy, either. But he trusts Coleman. Owes him."

I do not owe him, thought Amiri. "If he thinks the woman is in danger, he should bring her home."

"Already suggested that. Was told she's needed there. Maybe that makes her a target." Max hesitated. "Neither of you have to go, you know."

"No," Eddie said, tossing the sugar cube into his cup. Amiri remained silent. It had been almost two years. Two years since he had been kidnapped from Kenya, his native land. Nearly two years since he had regained his freedom. Not that it mattered. Even when opportunity and time had conspired to make travel a possibility, he had not returned to the continent of his birth.

Zaire is not Kenya, a small voice whispered. *And you cannot stay away forever.*

"Amiri," Max said softly.

Amiri ignored him, glancing down at his hands, momentarily overwhelmed by homesickness, heartache; for the sun, the hot stiff winds, his little flat in that charming Nairobi slum that probably no longer existed. Worse, his students. Those shining eyes, voices chiming. Little hearts straining to learn, and him . . . him, just as eager to share his knowledge. No better than a child, himself. The human world, still new and fresh and lovely.

Good memories and bad. Nothing that could be returned to him. That life, so carefully constructed—nourished from nothing—murdered. In more ways than one.

"Why us three?" Amiri asked softly. The cat walked back into the kitchen, flopped down on the tile, and proceeded to clean himself—noisily, leg rudely lifted; in public, no less. He would need to call someone to watch the cat. Perhaps Elena or Aggie. He had few female friends. Married women. Safe women. Like that sweet elderly clerk at the bookshop. No temptation.

Max gave him a long thoughtful look. "I asked Roland. He said he had his reasons."

"Reasons." Amiri closed his hand into a fist. "He is a telepath. He should know *my* reasons."

"Amiri—"

He cut Max off with a hard stare. "No. I will go. But you and I both know this should have been handled differently."

Face-to-face, with Roland himself. He was their boss, in the loosest sense of the word—their coordinator, the center of the agency's worldwide dealings. Not its founder, though he spoke for them. Roland was a powerful man. Dangerous when cornered. Amiri respected that.

But this was not right. It was not time. Amiri was not

ready to face what he had lost. What he might lose again. He had a new life now. Delicate, quiet, anonymous.

Your friends need you. They need you more than you need your fear.

Such a little thing, fear. So irrational. Amiri almost laughed at himself, though it would have been a bitter sound.

He slung the cat over his shoulder, needing something warm and living to hold. Taking a book with him, he left the kitchen to pack.

IN THE TWO YEARS THAT AMIRI HAD BEEN WITH THE DIRK & Steele agency, he had done little that could be spoken of in an open manner. As far as most people knew, Dirk & Steele was nothing more than an internationally respected detective agency, and while that was true on paper, and though the agency's mission to help others was heartfelt, its public face was simply a cover for the truth: that the men and women of Dirk & Steele were remarkable for reasons entirely separate from their skills at sleuthing—and that, indeed, not all of them were completely, definitively, human.

But they are home, Amiri reminded himself. *Home and family.*

Mysteries, living riddles—psychics and gargoyles, mermen and shape-shifters, creatures beyond legend—hiding in plain sight, mingling with humanity. And, oh, how miraculous not to be alone. Even if Amiri so often was.

The three men flew out on a private jet, a concession to Max, who found the packed quarters of a commercial airliner and all the minds within too much to bear for any extended period of time.

Amiri, too, disliked air travel. The scents were always bitter and cold, the people worse, stress rolling from skin to rub against his nose like sandpaper soaked in sweat. Breathing through his mouth never helped; his tongue could taste the ugliness. It reminded him of a cage. But he endured, in the relative comfort that only money could buy, and twenty-four hours later, he found himself back in Africa. Not Kenya, but close enough.

The Kinsangani airport was a mess. Crowded, hot. The immigration officials wanted bribes, which were paid; taxi drivers and beggars mobbed the outer doors of the terminal. Chaos, with a voice. But Amiri ignored it all the moment he stepped outside. Warmth washed over him, soaking into his muscles. He did not shield his eyes when the sun burned his face. He gazed up and up, staring into the white burning bloom.

A dusty dented van pulled alongside them and a dark-skinned man with even darker freckles peered out the window. He motioned with his hands and yelled, "From Larry, yes? I am Duna, his liaison!"

Amiri, Max, and Eddie got in, and were blasted immediately by a rattling air conditioner that sounded less gentle than a chain saw. Amiri slammed shut the sliding door, nearly taking off fingers as the crowd surged around them, banging on the windows. Duna shouted. Eddie looked concerned and Max simply winced. Amiri closed his eyes and put his head back, listening to the babble of voices. A rainbow of sound. He had forgotten what that was like.

"They want money before they let us leave," said Duna, but a tight grin passed over his face and he put the van in gear, gunning the engine. The vehicle rocked once, then pushed through the shouting crowd like a fat slug squeezing through a keyhole. Amiri glimpsed moving hands, the glint of steel tire spikes, but the van lurched free before its wheels could be turned into flapping rubber and he gripped the seat as they careened onto the road, narrowly missing an oncoming flood of bicycles and motorbikes.

"Jesus," Max said.

"Eh," shrugged Duna, and flung his arm back, nearly jabbing Amiri in the eye as he pointed toward the rear of the van. "Gifts. With Larry's best regards."

Amiri shared a quick look with Eddie, and bent over the seat. Pulled back a blanket. Stared at an open crate filled with AK-47s, several handguns, and a bin filled with Band-Aids.

"Huh," Eddie said.

"You're not a typical assistant," Max added.

Duna merely shrugged. Amiri reached down and fingered the Band-Aids, which were an astonishing shade of purple. He bit back a smile. "For bullet wounds, I assume?"

"Blood does stain, after all," Duna said, slyly.

"How very true," Amiri replied, and patted Eddie on the back as he began to cough.

Duna did not take them far—hardly more than a mile off the narrow freeway, down a rough side street where he parked beside a billboard covered in hand-painted French. Advertisements for a film development service, antiques, and Jesus. A chicken scratched the dust, and nearby in an open red shed, Amiri saw a barbershop—men on chairs staring into cracked handheld mirrors while shears clipped and danced. He heard laughter, American rap blasting through stereos, the murmur of women, the brush of their clothing and the slosh of water in the buckets they carried on their heads.

Amiri listened, and watched, and felt like a stranger. Not Kenya, true—but he wondered if it would matter, whether too much time had passed. He had always been an outsider;

his father had seen to that. But this was different. The pain, different. He had never truly learned how to be human—not until he was more man than child—and he felt that now more than ever. The lack of connection. Isolation, loneliness. Stranger. Strange land. All because of his blood. Because of bad luck, bad timing, his own stupidity.

The cheetah rumbled. Amiri chided himself. *No self-pity. Do not dare. You are alive. You are strong. You have friends. You have purpose. Nothing else matters.*

Nothing, except the hole in his heart. Nothing, except the quiet knowledge that he could never go home again. And oh, he had not felt this way in years. Too occupied, too content with his new life. But being here brought it back, all the very worst and best.

Duna reached beneath his tattered seat for a manila folder. He passed it back to Amiri and said, "This is Doctor Kinn."

Rikki, he remembered Max calling her. He held the file in his hands, uneasy. Occupied with his thoughts. It was only when Eddie began reaching over did he flip open the file. He was uncertain what to expect, but he got his answer, fast. Found himself struck hard, unprepared for yet more heartache.

It was a photo of a woman. Still young, but no girl. A body shot, a candid photo that could have been taken from a personal album. There were potted flowers behind her, and the edge of some corporate building, all steel and glass. Impossible to tell her height, but she was slender, compact, with short brown hair and a dark gaze so intense it was like looking down the barrel of a gun. Her face was shaped like a heart, her skin the color of pale Saharan sands—blindingly warm, shifting colors of cream—and her smile was fierce as a lion's grin, wry and sharp, with a brilliance to it that was breathtaking in its sincerity. She was a woman who made promises with her smile. A woman who broke hearts with it, as well.

Amiri liked her face. He liked the spirit shining there, as though there were sunlight beneath her skin, bright and breathtaking, burning. Bold as fire in a bowl of ice. He could not stop staring.

Not for you, whispered a dull voice. *She is not for you.*

Bitterness crawled up his throat, as well as an ache so close to loneliness he clutched for something, anything, to fill the gaping hole in his chest. He chose pain. Dug his nails into his palms, cutting himself. No one seemed to notice—except Max, but that was to be expected. Amiri trusted him to keep a secret. He had no choice.

"She's cute," Eddie said, peering over his shoulder. Amiri forced down a growl. Cute was not an accurate description. Beautiful, maybe; utterly unattainable, perhaps.

Dangerous, whispered that same deadened voice, which was his father now, and hateful. *Human women are dangerous. Use them, leave them. Do not trust them. Do not love them.*

Or they will pay the price, recalled Amiri, and against his will, suffered yet more memories: Ebony skin damp with sweat, rolling soft under his hands. A husky voice, whispering his name with pleasure.

And later, fear. A woman's awful, terrible fear.

He took a deep steadying breath and forced himself to look past the photograph to the documents underneath. There was little to find, other than a description of Rikki Kinn's education and degrees, as well as some personal observations cobbled together by someone with a very colorful opinion.

Demanding, read Amiri. *Stubborn as hell. Occasionally makes shit smell good.*

"Sounds charming," Max said, leaning over to read. "So, why is she in trouble?"

A loaded question. Giving Duna direction, focus, something that Max could eavesdrop on. Amiri watched his gaze turn distant, contemplative—then worse: startled, horrified. Never a good sign.

Duna hesitated. "One thousand people are dead. Killed by disease, all in one night. Ebola, we think. Deep in the Congo."

Amiri's stomach dropped. "We have not heard anything."

"Of course not." Duna turned and slammed his hands down on the wheel. "We have worked hard to keep it that way. All the secrecy and games? Done to prevent a panic. It is bad enough when only a handful die of that disease, but now? If word got out, even by accident, there would be chaos."

"And Doctor Kinn?"

"The CDC's lead investigator in this region. She is at the camp even now, trying to determine what happened." Duna rubbed his head and leaned against the wheel. "There are very few left with her capabilities. Other doctors have gone missing. Locals, no one foreign, but prominent in their fields. Only a handful of physicians have ever encountered these particular hemorrhagic fevers. And now, in all of Central Africa, there are only two. Doctor Kinn, and another CDC employee, Mackenzie Hardson."

Max sat back, closing his eyes. "Why isn't this Hardson guy on the protection list?"

"I do not know. Larry was only concerned about Doctor Kinn." He grimaced. "Some peacekeepers have disappeared as well. Just . . . gone. This is not out of the ordinary, you know. Rebels are not above a bit of ransom, or leverage."

Amiri glanced again at the photograph in his hands;

those eyes, that smile. "Is this conjecture, rumor? Or has anyone actually threatened Doctor Kinn?"

Duna did not answer, but Amiri was not looking at him. He watched Max instead, and when the man stiffened, eyes turning cold and hard, no words were necessary. Any fool could see the answer.

Max's hair fell over his eyes. "You have something to tell us."

Duna faltered. He looked uneasy, and Amiri did not think it was entirely because of what he had to say. "Yesterday morning, foreign mercenaries attempted to intercept Doctor Kinn. The attack was brazen. She was in the presence of UN peacekeepers when it occurred."

The men stared. Amiri dug his nails deeper into his palm, fighting to maintain his calm. It was difficult, which was a surprise. He was good at containing himself. Had a lifetime of practice. Strong emotions were always ill-advised. Passion was dangerous. Anger, worse. Repression as a means of survival was an important lesson for any shape-shifter.

But even so, Amiri could not fathom himself the depth of his rage at the idea of that shining woman at the end of a gun. It made him sick.

Max glanced at him. "You should have told us. Called us in transit. Made it clear what happened the moment we got in this van."

"It would have changed nothing. You are still here to protect the doctor."

"Is she well?" Amiri nearly had to repeat the question; his voice belonged to a different man—low, hard, more growl than speech.

"She is fine," Duna said quickly, giving him a worried look. "But one of her escorts died and the other is in critical condition."

"Fuck," Max muttered. "Rebels are one thing, mercenaries another. Those guys don't get called in for cheap shit. What else do you know?"

Duna studied Amiri's closed fist, which was beginning to drip with pinpricks of blood. "Rumors. Politics. The war machine continues to turn. Corruption has ruined this country, and foreign scavengers sniff at the borders, trying to broker deals for Zaire's minerals. Mercenaries are used to . . . persuade people. And to pave the way for enterprising businessmen who travel the interior, making their own deals with those self-proclaimed local warlords who hold military power over valuable areas."

Amiri looked again at the woman's picture. He wanted very much to take it with him, and felt irrational for that desire, for the hunger he felt when staring into her eyes. "What does any of that have to do with her? Or those other doctors?"

"We do not know. That is the problem." Duna tapped his watch. "Time to go back. The UN convoy will be departing from the airport in two hours. Larry arranged for you to travel with them. We must not be late."

Not enough time. "I thought Mr. Coleman wanted subtlety. Traveling with others will expose us."

"Subtle is slow. It gets you nothing."

"And lies are just as easy," Max added, giving the man a sharp look.

Duna's expression never changed. "The soldiers you will be traveling with do not know you are providing extra protection for Doctor Kinn. Only that you are independent security specialists hired by the CDC."

Eddie frowned. "We just came from the airport. Why did we even bother?"

"It was at Larry's request. Too many wagging ears."

"Whatever. What you've given us isn't enough to do shit, not even to pretend." Max gave Eddie and Amiri a thoughtful look. "You'll have to leave me behind."

"No," Eddie said, straightening.

"Yes. There are two major cities in Zaire. This one, and Kinshasa. If mercenaries have been hired to kidnap people—specifically, our doctor—this is where they, or someone who knows them, will be spending their downtime. I'll poke around, do a little eavesdropping, see what I turn up. Meanwhile, you and Amiri can play bodyguard."

"I cannot guarantee your safety," Duna protested. "And this is not a good city for outsiders. The rebels, even the soldiers—"

"I've been in worse," he interrupted. "I can handle myself."

I do not like this, Amiri thought at Max, and then for Eddie's sake, added, "There are too many unknowns."

"It stinks," Max agreed. "It stinks so bad I can't stand it. That's why I need to stay. Unless you want to wait for someone to get killed before we start asking questions."

Amiri frowned. Eddie began to argue, but Max held up his hand and gave him a sharp look. The young man grimaced, fingers digging into the van seat. The temperature jumped another several degrees. Amiri understood how he felt. They both stared at Max, but all he did was mutter, "Mother hens," and reach behind his seat for the weapons Duna had brought. He gave Eddie a handgun, which was quickly stashed in his backpack.

Amiri refused to take a weapon. Max did not push. He slipped the gun into the back of his pants, under his T-shirt. Amiri folded Rikki Kinn's photograph, and placed it in his pocket. He caught Eddie watching him, but the young man gave him a faint smile, and that made Amiri feel less a fool.

Their return to the airport was quick. Duna took a different road around the terminal, heading directly to the airfield. They were stopped at the entrance by a UN guard, but their names were on a list. Duna drove through and parked three hundred feet from a cargo plane being loaded with supplies stamped with the Red Cross logo.

"One more thing," Max said to Duna, as they left the van. "Why *did* Larry call in outside help? Why not rely on the UN to protect her? They managed it yesterday." When Duna hesitated, Max's expression darkened and he said, "Never mind. Wait for me, okay? I'll be back in a minute."

The three men from Dirk & Steele walked to the airplane. Eddie watched his feet. Amiri gazed up at the sky, patient.

"You two would be good in a monastery," Max muttered. "Vows of silence, and all that."

Eddie smiled. "And?"

"And it's a fucking mess. Duna doesn't know shit. Nothing we can use. Coleman left him hanging dry for our arrival. Regardless of the guns."

"The timing is peculiar," Amiri mused.

"Yeah. It also bothers me that he's been so secretive. People go missing, you tell someone. You don't bury it."

Eddie jammed his hands into his pockets. "Coleman held out on Roland."

"Roland is not easily deceived," Amiri said.

Max grunted. "As soon as I get out of here, I'm calling him. Maybe he can pry something useful out of his old *buddy*." He clapped Eddie on the shoulder. "Stay out of trouble, kid. Don't burn down the rain forest."

Eddie said nothing, just nodded, giving Max a look so solemn that Amiri wondered if there was more amiss than he realized. The young man backed off and walked away. Max sighed.

Amiri said, "Something else is wrong."

"It's nothing. Really."

"Max."

"Amiri."

The two men stared at each other. Max's scent shifted into something hard, bitter. He did not blink. Amiri moved in close, feeling the cheetah rumble beneath his skin—finding himself, too, in the odd position of standing on the other side of trust. He did not know what to do.

"There's nothing *to* do." Max dropped his chin, his gaze hidden beneath his hair. "We all burn, Amiri."

"Then we burn together." Amiri held out his hand. "Or what is the use of having friends?"

Max said nothing, but after one long moment slapped his hand against Amiri's and squeezed hard. Leaned close, whispering, "Like you should talk."

Perhaps, Amiri thought, raising an eyebrow. "But I am certainly no worse than you."

Max blew out his breath. "Focus on the woman. Tell her anything you want, but make sure she lets you stay close. Things are going to get ugly. I can feel it."

"And you?"

"I'll be in touch, one way or another." He backed away. "Take care of each other."

Take care of yourself, Amiri thought at him. Max nodded, turning quickly on his heel and marching back to Duna and the van. No looking back. Amiri gave him the same courtesy.

Eddie waited by the loading area. A tall young man wearing army fatigues and a blue beret stood with him. Red hair—what little Amiri could see of it—stuck to a pale sweaty face covered in freckles. Blue eyes studied his approach, with an expression entirely too trusting for the responsibility of playing soldier.

"You must be the other American specialist," the boy in the beret said, before Amiri could introduce himself. His accent was Swedish; crisp, curling, cold. "My name is Patrick. We will be leaving soon."

"He was just telling me what we should expect." Eddie glanced over Amiri's shoulder at the departing van.

"Ah, but you're also from Africa right?" Patrick nodded, smiling. "Eddie mentioned that. You probably already know everything I could tell you."

Amiri made a noncommittal sound, but before he could point out the obvious—that not every place on the continent was the same, and therefore he was just as lost as anyone else—Patrick pulled an envelope from the pouch at his side and handed it over.

"Funny. Someone brought this around to one of our guards not ten minutes ago. Said it was for the black security man coming from America. That's you, I suppose."

Amiri frowned, and took the envelope. It was flat and brown. His name had been written in neat script on the outside, along with delivery instructions. He felt odd holding it.

"Please give us a moment," he said to Patrick, and the young man ducked his head, backing away. Amiri turned, and despite the people surrounding him, brought the envelope up to his nose to smell. His tongue flicked the paper.

Eddie stepped close. "What is it?"

"I do not know." Amiri tasted the scent. It was nothing he could place; too many people had been in contact with the paper. But there was something . . . bitter . . . that made a shiver run up his spine.

He opened the envelope. Inside were pictures. Amiri

almost dropped them, but Eddie reached out fast, pressing his hand on top of the images. He exhaled hard, eyes wide. Amiri simply stared.

The photographs were of him. Not him as a man, but him as a cheetah. No mistake about it, either. He knew what he looked like, even as an animal. He knew his eyes.

But the last picture—at the very bottom—was no simple animal. It was him, caught in the act: standing on two legs like a man, but with all the fur and features of the cat. An alien creature changing, caught in limbo. Someone who should not exist.

"I know this," Amiri whispered, looking beyond the still shot of his shifting body to the photograph's background: dry grass, acacia trees, a blue horizon. Kenya. He remembered the day. These were the pictures that had ruined his life.

"There's a note," Eddie said, hoarse. He held out a folded slip of paper. Amiri hesitated, and took it. Swallowed hard. Looked down.

Welcome home, he read. Two words. No signature. More than enough.

Max was right. Things were going to get very ugly, indeed.

CHAPTER THREE

Two days after the outbreak, and they were still fishing bodies out of the river.

It was night. Stars in the sky, ribbons of them, with light enough to illumine wet bodies, skin that glistened as the shore of the river thickened and heaved and the waters filled with blood.

Rikki waded, thigh deep. Biohazard suit on, surgical mask and goggles firmly in place, three layers of latex gloves secure over her hands. Hot as hell. Her head swam. Sweat poured from her hairline, down her back. She needed a drink. Soda, vodka, orange juice—anything wet that was not this river, not the fluids leaking from the eyes and ears and noses of the men, women, and children sprawled and floating on the shore and in this shallow inlet, which had offered some protection from the raging dragging current just beyond.

The flashlights were not enough. Rikki said, "Oh, Jesus. Oh, Mack."

"Shut up," muttered her colleague, hoisting a small body into his arms. "Shut up, please."

Rikki kept walking. Earlier, men had screamed at her to

get out. Men had yanked on her arms and tried to carry her. Crocodiles had already killed twenty people in the aftermath of recent floods; the bodies here would be an easy lure, despite the crude nets anchored around the affected area.

Bodies in the water. No way to stop the contamination.

Her worst nightmare. If Ebola—assuming that was the killer—could be transmitted in semen up to twelve weeks after clinical recovery, then water would be little different. Everyone—everyone who depended on this river—was royally screwed.

Teams had already gone downriver by pirogue to check the health of local fishermen and farmers, as well as look for any dead monkeys like the ones in the forest surrounding this place. A small military force had also been called in, as well as the Red Cross and any other international organization that could keep a secret. So far, no one had turned up a thing. No sign of another outbreak.

Not yet, she thought. The virus could still be incubating. For many, the Congo River was a means of livelihood as well as the only water source for miles. No one would be able to stay away for long. Not without the wrong questions being asked.

She turned and watched Mack hand the dead child to another aid worker. There were less than a hundred volunteers in camp, not nearly enough to handle the deceased, but all they could gather in a short time—and the only people they could trust not to get themselves killed. It took a certain kind of person to work with Ebola victims. Control freaks were the best.

"You know," Mack said, catching her eye. "I've been thinking about those notes the doctors left behind. The river makes sense."

"Yeah?" Rikki shone her light across the water, illuminating her colleague as he moved close. Doctor Mackenzie Hardson was a big man, and underneath his gear all gray—gray hair, gray eyes, gray T-shirt. Only his skin had color, but not much. He was pastier than rising bread dough, and almost as soft.

His goggles were foggy with condensation. "Think about it, Rikki. The excessive fever, raging thirst—complaints from patients that they felt like they were on fire, that their blood was boiling. The medical clinic was overrun. People would have come here as a last resort to bring down their fevers. Problem is, they were too far gone to get out."

It did, indeed, make sense. Rikki briefly closed her eyes. "You wanna know something else, Mack?"

"Not really."

"This is worse than Ebola," she said, feeling cut, sick. "You know it is, Mack. The amount of hemorrhaging alone proves that. Usually only a third of victims bleed out, but I haven't seen a single body in this vicinity that isn't soaked in blood. And those symptoms the doctor noted? No mention of vomiting or diarrhea. Not once."

"Rikki—"

"I'm telling you, Mack. The virus has evolved . . . or this is something entirely new."

"Rikki—"

"No survivors," she added, ignoring him. "Not one, not in over *one thousand* people. The camp doctors called you in at the first sign, and by the time you got here everyone was dead. That is unprecedented, Mack. Ebola is deadly, but someone always survives. *Always.*"

And it did not kill so quickly. According to the notes Mack and his team had discovered upon his arrival—including messages to the living that Rikki found heartbreaking—death had occurred less than six hours after the first sign of symptoms. Usual containment methods had proven useless.

No one in the camp had stood a chance. A massacre at the end of a machine gun would have been kinder. Something Rikki knew all about.

Mack still stared at her. She said, "What?"

"What, nothing," he replied darkly. "Except that I think you made me pee pee myself." Rikki sighed. Mack shook his head. "It's almost time for us to check our temperatures. You feeling anything weird? Hot? Tired?"

She gave him the finger. "You?"

"Shit. I could collapse at any moment."

She would have laughed, but that would have involved vomiting up her spleen or sobbing out her guts. She had never worked an outbreak of this magnitude—never imagined, in her worst nightmares, that she would have to. And it was worse, so much worse, with no one left to save.

No one but themselves.

Without waiting to see if Mack followed, she began slogging through the water toward shore. Floodlights had been set up, the brush hacked back. Rumbling generators drowned voices, the nightly jungle chorus. Everyone wore biohazard suits, even the peacekeepers, some of whom had put away their weapons to help load bodies into bags. Rikki only hoped someone had told those men that touching a body dead from Ebola was as dangerous as handling a live grenade.

There but for the grace of God, thought Rikki, struggling to contain her terror: a hard hot stab of liquid heat that traveled straight down to her knees and made her wobble. She had to stop for a minute—pretended to survey the water—and remembered that she was wearing a mask. A real mask, goggles and all. She did not have to be strong.

She could be scared. She could show it on her face and no one would be the wiser.

The idea brought Rikki no relief whatsoever. She had no time for fear. Not now, not here. She had things to do. Maybe later, when this was over. Maybe, or not ever.

You can't go on like this forever. Your heart can't take it.

Yeah, whatever. And whiners burned in hell. According to her old coach, anyway. Besides, it didn't matter what her heart felt. She'd gotten by for years on true grit alone; hard, stubborn strength of will. No other alternative, nothing left back home. And here at least, she could make a difference.

Even if she wondered, sometimes, what it would be like to have another life. Something softer. Not so lonely. Not so alone.

The water swirled black and restless around her legs. Rikki took a step, then another, ignoring the burn in her eyes. Swallowing it down past the knot in her throat, she forced herself to look up. Head held high.

Two men on shore caught her attention. Again, she stopped walking. They were staring. Measuring. The men were swathed in protective gear, backlit by floodlights, but she noticed them because they were not working, because they were staring. At her. Goggles and masks might hide faces, but she still felt the weight of their gazes. That old survival instinct.

Years ago she would have shrugged it off. Even two days ago, she might have. Told herself they were aid workers, doctors, scientists. Mack and his team might be handling logistics, but Rikki was the virus hunter, the CDC's own little wild child, and for some reason that always made her a sideshow at these things.

But these men were different. They did not belong. It was their posture, their stillness. Like hunters, fighters. A more intense quality than the soldiers scattered throughout the camp. Rikki remembered the airfield, the gunfire. Bakker, taking a bullet to the chest. She slowed, wary, watching those men and their hands. One of them was taller than the other. Her skin prickled when she looked into his hidden face. Her heart hurt, too. Sharp, hard, like her ribs were made of knives. It was a lost, awful, feeling, made worse because Rikki could not look away, not even to blink. She felt as though she were seeing someone for the first time in ages; someone lost from memory, a dream. It made her breathless.

Rikki forced herself to move. Careful, wary. Sidling toward the peacekeepers. She had one foot on dry land, heart pounding, when the first scream cut the night. High, piercing, horrified. Every hair rose on her body like her skin was made of electricity. Water thrashed, something large pounding the surface like a torn drum.

Oh, damn.

Rikki had no time to turn. The tall man, that hidden masked man, began running toward her.

He was fast. So fast she couldn't even defend herself as he dropped, skidding, and grabbed her around the waist. Rikki cried out as he rolled them back into the shallow water—tumbled together like socks in the dryer—and she forgot how to use her voice as an immense set of jaws snapped at the air where she had been standing. Rikki saw teeth, a long, ridged snout, the shadow of a slit eye, primal and cold.

The crocodile lunged again and the man hauled back, sending them rolling. Something large and rough smacked against her leg, and this time when she went down it was face first in the river. Her surgical mask slid off. She swallowed water. Water that rolled down the inside of her suit and splashed into her eyes. A body bobbed nearby, leaking blood.

No, she thought. *Oh, God.*

Arms tightened—they were hard as rock, tense with terrible strength—and Rikki might have been a feather the way she found herself hauled out of the water; boneless, weightless. She turned her head just enough to see the man carrying her. His mask and goggles were gone. His face was dark, his cheekbones high and sharp, and his eyes . . . his eyes were *glowing.*

The world slowed down to pinpricks of sensation and sound: the harsh breathing of the man beside her, the heat of him against her back; her heart, hammering, the taste of blood in her mouth as she bit down on her tongue. His eyes, his eyes, his glowing eyes.

Cries cut through her. And then, the crocodile—it was so close she felt the sharp exhalation of its breath as it made another pass at her leg. The man pulled her away, but she kicked at the creature anyway, fighting hard, her voice hoarse, breaking.

She was still shouting when the crocodile caught fire.

Her voice choked; her legs pinwheeled into stillness. She stared, lost in stupefied horror and disbelief as flames erupted inside the animal's mouth, through its teeth, bursting across its head with such fury she wondered if there was accelerant on its skin. Heat roared through her biohazard suit, and her last glimpse of the creature as the man holding her turned them was of that massive scaled body writhing and submerging, again and again: drifting, twisting, almost dead. Rikki wished someone would shoot the animal in the head. End it quick.

Someone else had the same thought. A gun went off near her ear. One shot, then nothing. Silence rang dull in the fading echo; the air smelled like cooked meat. The water stopped splashing against Rikki's thighs. Those arms around her body relaxed, just a fraction. She wanted to see, she wanted to know, but as she began to look over her shoulder those strong warm hands stopped her, sliding up her spine, into her hair. The familiarity of that contact made her breath catch—and then the hands were gone and the cold that surrounded her, the loss of that odd anchor, left her breathless.

She looked up. Stared into a pale gaze, golden and hot. Caught another flash of light in those eyes, though it lasted only seconds.

"Are you hurt?" murmured the man. Rikki shook her head, unable to speak—too rattled, too consumed. She heard her name shouted and tried again to turn. Her knees wobbled, making her stagger, but those long arms slid around her waist, holding her against a hard lean body. He was hot as hell; an invading heat, soaking through skin to bone. For one heartbeat she felt safe in that warmth, that embrace—utterly protected—and it was such a foreign startling feeling, she almost forgot what had happened. Or why feeling safe could never be possible.

Again, her name was called. She managed to turn, just enough to see Mack stumbling toward her, accompanied by members of his team. Another figure stood near, the second man on shore who had been watching her. He held a gun. She could not see his eyes behind the goggles, but he was staring at the crocodile, which was drifting, smoking, sparks and embers still clinging to its leathery hide.

Mack stopped just out of reach—teetering on his toes, hands clenched into fists. He tried to say her name but croaked, his voice breaking on every syllable.

"I'm fine," Rikki said, but that was reflex talking and not the truth. She had just taken a bath in a soup made of death, swallowed it down into her body. Just like the man who had saved her life. His face was wet. His mask off.

Worse than Ebola. Not the same thing at all.

Rikki looked at Mack and saw it in his eyes. Horror.

"Isolation ward," she whispered. "Two beds. Do it now, Mack. Hurry."

But Mack said nothing, *did* nothing—staring instead like an idiot, all of his people blinking behind their goggles like owls. As though she were the crocodile, spinning and burning and dying. Rikki wanted to scream at them—she wanted to jump out of her skin and run until she died—and felt the beginnings of terrible nauseating panic swell hard from her heart to her groin.

No. No, *no*. Rikki dragged in a hard shuddering breath, and the hands at her waist tightened. The man. Rikki turned, meeting that long cool gaze, so calm, so steady; here was an anchor, safe in his unnatural stillness. For a moment it was just the two of them, no one else—and that was right, good, true—because it *was* just them. Same boat. Same death.

"We're a disease now," she whispered, shocked at herself but unable to stop; unable to curb the desperate haunting desire to make one last connection, to be seen, to be heard. "You and I are the only ones who will remember that we're people."

He stared, and in that moment the world began spinning again and the camp poured down upon them: bodies, voices, masked faces and gloved hands, all trying to pull her away. The man refused to let go. He held her close, tight, and she felt his lips touch her ear, his breath hot as fire.

"Then we will remember," he breathed, and his words, the unrelenting conviction in his voice, shot like an arrow down her spine. He let go and she reached for him—instinct, raw—but everyone moved too fast—finally, fast—and a wall of people swept between them before she could so much as graze his sleeve. She glimpsed him only once, still watching her over the sea of heads, and his gaze was focused and hard, and only for her.

Disconcerting, thrilling, heartbreaking. She could not look away, and when Mack stepped in front of her, blocking her view of the man's face, she could not say whether she felt relief or disappointment.

But she did feel alone. And for the first time in years, she hated herself for it.

THE FIRST ISOLATION WARD HAD BEEN SET UP WITHIN AN hour of Mack's arrival two days before. This was standard protocol at any outbreak site, as a means of quarantining and treating the sick. Problem was, no one had been sick. Just dead.

Three distance barriers covered the entrance to the ward, as well as a separate isolated exit, which held a contaminated-materials bin and disinfectant boot baths. A rough structure—the camp's former medical center—built from wood and canvas. Mack's team had duct-taped layers of plastic sheeting over the flimsy walls and across the dirt floor, sealing in the room except for small vents in the ceiling. A portable air conditioner run by a rumbling generator pumped in cold air. Rikki felt the chill of it race across her skin, then Mack pulled her to a curtained area just outside the ward. Floodlights burned. Mosquitoes buzzed.

Mack brought out a bottle of bleach. Rikki's heart jumped.

"We need to get this over with," he said. Rikki nodded, jaw tight as steel, and watched as he began diluting the disinfectant with water. He poured it all in a pump and screwed on the hose. Ready to spray her within an inch of her life and send every germ packing to hell.

"I'll do it myself," Rikki said.

"You can't reach everywhere," Mack replied.

"Still looking for an excuse to see my ass?"

The skin above his surgical mask reddened. "You know the protocol."

Yes, she did. She'd been the one holding the hose on several occasions, and this, she figured, was karma coming to kick her derriere. "Bend the rules, Mack. I'm trained. I won't miss any spots. I'll come out of here so clean I'll be raw."

Mack hesitated, then shook his head. "I know how to be impersonal. Let's just do it fast and get it over with."

Not the words she wanted to hear. Panic touched her throat. Walls, closing in. Rikki reached for the hose, but Mack pulled it away, out of reach. She tried again and he did the same, frowning. "Rikki. Let me."

"Jesus, what am I, five? I'm a big girl." She tried one more time to take the hose, but Mack stepped back, eyebrows furrowed in an obstinate frown. It was a look she wanted to wipe right off his face. Her hand closed into a fist. He gave her an even sharper look. Rikki did not care. She wanted to hit him. She was desperate to hit him.

Get hold of yourself. It's not his fault. He doesn't know. He wasn't there.

Just doing his job. Being thorough. Refusing to leave her the hell alone.

Rikki held her ground. She did not unclench her fist. Mack stared like he was seeing her for the first time, and she supposed he was. She just did not want him to see the rest of her.

The plastic curtains rustled. One of the nurses poked

her head in. Her name—RUTH—was scrawled in black letters on the forearm of her biohazard suit sleeve.

"The other man is prepped and ready to be disinfected," she said, talking slower and slower as her gaze darted between the two doctors. Picking up on the tension.

Rikki still held Mack's gaze. Her fingers uncurled, painful. "Take him first."

Mack's eyes narrowed. "No."

"Fuck you, Hardson."

"You first," he replied, so quiet anyone else would have thought he was being gentle—except for that edge, that soft edge. "Now get undressed. We have to get you clean. There's still a chance."

"I am not getting naked in front of you."

"Then Ruth."

"No."

"For fuck's sake, this is *serious*. You need help—"

The curtain rattled, interrupting him. Ruth—who had been shamelessly watching their exchange—yelped rather loudly as a long dark hand reached around her. It was the man. And he was naked.

Rikki tried not to look, but there was too much muscle and smooth rich skin, and his eyes—those eyes watching her like she was a prism burning rainbows—were so intensely hot she felt branded with his stare; cut, cocooned, pinned, and wrapped so tight she could hardly breathe. Goddamn, but she was sick. In the head, sick.

The man hardly glanced at Ruth and Mack. "Is there a problem?"

Mack frowned. "And *you* are?"

"Sent from Larry," replied the man shortly, giving him a piercing look. His voice was buttery, with a slight accent that was educated and refined. *The Naked Professor,* Rikki wanted to call him. Except that he held himself like a fighter, sleek and fast and hard. She still felt the branding weight of his arms around her body. That heartbeat moment of safety.

"Larry," she echoed, hoarse. "What the hell does that mean?"

"Never mind," growled Mack, with a look in his eyes that Rikki might have called uneasiness. "Clean first, talk later."

Rikki set her jaw and reached for the hose. Mack blocked her, still sharply disapproving, and a shot of pure despair raged so hard through her heart she wanted to cry—or smash his brains in.

"Please," she said to Mack. "Don't force this."

"I have to," he said, the expression in his eyes truly baffled. "For God's sake, Rikki, you're not that shy."

Oh, God, she wanted to tell him. *Oh, Mack.*

But there was nothing else to say, because the other man, that naked watchful man, suddenly moved. Reached out with one long arm to grab Mack's shoulder and pushed him past the curtain. Taking Ruth with him.

Mack was big, but he might as well have been made of cotton candy for all the fight he put up. He cursed. Ruth squeaked. The other man said, "Stay out."

"You're crazy," Mack said.

"Not yet," replied the man.

"Rikki—"

"I'm fine," she found herself saying, and then, more forcefully, "I'll be fine, Mack."

He stared at her like she was a stranger. She felt like one, even to herself. But she held her ground, even as Mack said, "I'm getting help."

"Do so," said the stranger. "See if it makes you feel safer."

Mack's eyes flinched. The other man dropped the curtain in his face. Rikki half-expected her colleague to burst back through, fighting, but he did not. She heard voices—another man, younger—and then footsteps, shuffling quickly away. Leaving her. Rikki wondered idly if she should feel abandoned, even betrayed, but she dug deep and found nothing of the kind. Just an odd terrible relief that was stronger than fear . . . and almost as confusing as the man standing in front of her.

Rikki searched his eyes, looking for that unnatural light. Nothing, only amber, gold, pale as honey. Too much to stare at for long. Like being scorched by the sun. An intense look, eerily intimate. It made her afraid, but she buried it. Made her uneasy, but she buried that, too. Never mind the man was a stranger, naked as day. He wore his nudity like it was nothing—another skin, another kind of clothing. Easy and proud. She envied him for that.

They stared at each other. Silence burned. Rikki remembered the river. She could taste it in her mouth. A chill burst over her body, but even so, just then, a faint smile touched the man's mouth, heart-stopping, and she forgot for one moment that they were both dying, alone, strangers. She did not mean to—her own mouth curved faintly—and she felt the roots of that smile curl up from her heart.

Cut short. His gaze lost its steadiness and something flickered hard in his face; it looked suspiciously like grief. Rikki swayed toward him, caught up, and the man turned away, facing the curtain. "Hurry."

She was losing her mind. "I don't understand."

"I am buying you time," he said harshly. "And I will make certain no one sees you."

Rikki froze. "How—"

"I heard you talking. Here. Out there." He glanced over his shoulder and his gaze was raw. "I listened."

Listened. Such a small thing. But this . . . what he was doing, unasked, without her needing to explain . . .

Saving you again.

Rikki pressed her palm against her gut, steadying herself, staring holes into the back of his head. "Thank you."

"Hurry," he said again, and Rikki did. She was careful as she stripped down. Had to talk herself through the act of peeling off her tank top and bra.

The man never turned. After a time, she began to relax enough to trust his word. His unspoken acceptance of what she needed.

She blasted herself with the hose. The water was lukewarm. The bleach burned her nostrils. She began to shake after less than a minute. Violent tremors, uncontrollable. Not from cold. She could not stop looking at the man.

"What's your name?" she managed to utter.

"Amiri," he said.

"Call me Rikki."

"As you wish," he replied softly, not turning, and Rikki closed her eyes. She closed her eyes and did not think about anyone watching her. For the first time in years, she touched her scars in the presence of another living person.

And she was not afraid.

CHAPTER FOUR

BATHED, dressed, inside the isolation ward, Rikki sat on a cot. She wore loose green scrubs, still damp. A new pair of tennis shoes were on her feet. Ruth had left clothing outside the curtains during the wash, and Amiri had passed a set over his shoulder. Mack had still protested afterward—promised to send a formal complaint to Larry—but that was fine. Let him. Just as long as he left her alone, unprofessional hypocrite that she was.

Amiri had not attempted to look at her body. No words of comfort, either. There was not a sound as Rikki had hosed him down with disinfectant. He had submitted with quiet dignity, certainly more than she possessed, and no trace of that broken grief she had glimpsed in his eyes. She might have blamed her imagination, if she had one.

Amiri sat across from her on another bed. Cross-legged. Eyes closed. A stranger, her rescuer; a dark Buddha, maybe. Serene and unaffected, his face nothing but a smooth mask. Rikki envied him. She could still taste the river in her mouth.

Stay clinical. Stay detached. Her mantra. Her prayer. Not that it helped. She needed another distraction. Her nostrils still ached, and bleach burns covered her body. A dull throb gathered at the base of her skull. She thought of that bad afternoon two years past. Friends dead. A gun jammed in her mouth. Knives flashing.

A certainty of death, she told herself. Her father's face swam to mind. His gruff smile, his gnarled wrists bound together in handcuffs. That last wink before the bailiff took him away. Always trying to make her feel better.

Rikki could use some of that now. She dug her hands into the mattress and glanced at Amiri. There was no way to tell how he felt. She wanted to poke him in the chest, rattle his chain, start a fight. Make him show something other than that deep damn calm.

"Amiri," she said, breaking the silence between them.

He looked at her. In this light she could see that his eyes were a true gold, like a cat. She remembered them glowing. Told herself it was a trick. Eyes did not glow.

The rest of him was singularly elegant: that chiseled face, the long lean body; strong arms and tapered fingers. Every movement—the turn of his head—preternaturally graceful. Beautiful. Predatory. Rikki felt like she was staring at someone who was only pretending to be human. It made her feel strange, like she was losing her mind.

"Amiri," she said again when still he did not speak, regarding her instead with those uncanny eyes: farseeing, dangerous.

"Doctor Kinn," he replied. She liked how her name sounded in his mouth, as though she were a lady. Soft and gentle. Something she had not felt for a long time.

They stared at each other. Rikki said, "I never thanked you."

"I believe you did."

"Not about the river."

"Ah," he said. Then, after a brief pause, "I would rather you did not."

"Oh." She felt stupid. "Of course. I'm sorry for what happened."

"Sorry," he echoed, frowning.

"It doesn't mean much, I know," she told him, trying to keep her voice empty, flat. "You saved my life. You *helped* me. And this is what you get."

His frown deepened. "You misunderstand me. Thanks and apologies are unnecessary. I did *not* save your life. Quite the opposite, given our current circumstances."

Rikki hesitated. "The crocodile might not agree."

But Amiri shook his head, as though it meant nothing. Like crocodiles were small things. She wished she could feel that way. Teeth still filled her head. Teeth and fire. Swallowing water fresh with bobbing bloody corpses.

Raw memories. Rikki tried to hold it together, but it was not her night. A violent shudder tore through her body, shaking her from head to toe. Filling her with a chill so profound she imagined her bones were knitted from ice cubes. Her teeth rattled. Fingers dug into her thighs. She could not stop quaking.

Amiri watched. Rikki forced herself to meet his gaze, daring him to say something. She hoped he would. All she needed was an excuse. Any excuse. Maybe then she would stop finding him so mesmerizing.

But he surprised her, again. She watched, suspicious and confused, as he slid off his cot and walked to one of the large plastic tubs stacked against the sheeting. He peeled back a lid and pulled out a folded blanket. Shook it loose, and before she could protest, was at her side, throwing the soft cotton over her shoulders like a cape. He tucked the edges around her legs.

Rikki never felt the weight of his hands. A light touch, delicate; it was in sharp contrast to his size, the strength she remembered so well, sharper still to the heaviness of his golden gaze, which held an odd mix of melancholy and determination. Hooks in her heart; like an echo resounding. His eyes were a mirror. All Rikki could do was stare.

Amiri's fingers grazed her jaw. "I should call for someone."

Hot. Each breath felt hot. Her lungs burned. Rikki stopped shaking, but only just. She clutched the soft blanket closer. "It's nothing. But thank you."

He shrugged and sat back on his cot, watching her carefully. "Are you warmer now?"

She nodded, mute, and he looked away. Seemed to hesitate, to hold his breath. He sat so still he hardly seemed human. His face and body were too perfect, warm and dark and shimmering with gold. But then he sighed, and the spell broke, and Rikki blinked, hard, fighting herself as he said, "You believe we are sick."

"Yes." She could not lie.

His calm never faltered. "And that we might die?"

"It's possible."

"How much time do we have?"

"Not enough."

"So, it will be fast. When it happens."

"It was for everyone else, as far as we can tell."

Amiri gave her a long, assessing, look. "You have seen this before?"

"Not this." She hesitated. "Maybe I'll take notes."

"Ever the scientist?"

She felt a smile creep on her face. "Just bored."

He laughed—a low sound, almost a rumble, a purr. "You are too intelligent for boredom."

Heat suffused her face. "And you?"

"I am quite intelligent," he replied, slyly.

Rikki mock-kicked him, still trying not to smile. "That's not what I meant."

Amiri leaned away, holding up his hands. "Boredom is a state of mind I have never attained. It is too much like deep meditation. Mindless. Ineffectual. Reading is much better."

"There are no books here."

"Ah." He tapped his head. "But there you are wrong."

Rikki bit her bottom lip, but it was no use. Something was bubbling inside her chest, something bigger and fiercer than fear, and it was full of sunlight and warmth and some deep song that rumbled and rumbled and pulled her under, tumbling her, softening her, soothing her cold heart with a gentle, gentle, hand. She smiled. She smiled like she meant it, and she did. It was the best damn smile she had felt in years, and it was natural, easy.

But it did not last. Not for her, and not for him. Amiri's mouth hardened, becoming somber, contemplative; and in his eyes, a sharp restlessness. Even discomfort. Regret.

"Forgive me," he said, finally. "Please, forgive me. I was sent to protect you. And I failed."

Rikki was silent too long. His jaw tightened; his gaze intensified. "I told you. Larry sent us."

"Yes," she replied unsteadily. Her fingers twitched, but her cell phone was gone, bagged with all her other personal belongings. Not that it mattered. Reception did not exist outside the major cities. "When did he contact you?"

"Recently. We moved fast to reach you."

"If this is because of yesterday—"

Amiri held up his hand. "Foreign mercenaries were sent for you. That is no small thing."

Bakker. Jean-Claude's vague warning. Rikki briefly closed her eyes, trying to focus. The threat of infection made everything else feel like child's play; she had no stomach left to think about alternatives. "Coincidence. Some random attempt at cutting a deal for ransom. Happens all the time. No one was *sent* for me."

"Other doctors have disappeared. Local physicians, anyone experienced in dealing with Ebola. You are not the only target."

"Impossible."

"I am not deceiving you."

"I never said you were. But it's a small club. I know all those doctors. Someone would have told me if they were in trouble."

Amiri hesitated. "You did not know?"

Rikki stared, incredulous. "Know? I . . . you're serious, aren't you. They're really missing?"

"I have no reason yet to doubt the source."

She stopped breathing. Amiri's hand jerked once, balling into a fist. He pressed his knuckles against his thigh, and she stared at the lines of his curled fingers, the sinew of his wrist. Trying to focus on anything but the faces swimming in her vision.

"I was certain you would know," she heard him say, voice dim, distant. He sounded angry. "Someone should have told you. Warned you."

"Yes." She had the intense desire to punch someone's brains out of their ass. Starting with Larry. "How many doctors? How long have they been missing?"

He watched her carefully. "I do not know the time line, but according to Mr. Coleman's assistant, you and a Mackenzie Hardson are the only physicians left in this region with any related experience."

"Bullshit," she muttered. "There are nurses, scientists. What the hell is he playing at?"

"Excuse me?"

"We work in teams," she told him absently. "And for every Ebola outbreak, there's more than just doctors swarming. To take everyone who had experience with this disease would be impossible. There must be another factor. You've been given the wrong facts."

Or you're a bald-faced liar. Which, to her amazement, was harder to swallow than the idea that she was a target of kidnappers. Or that her boss had lost his mind.

She almost forgot that she might be dying. "So, because other people have disappeared, *Larry* thinks I'm in danger. Do you know why? Who's responsible?"

"We are investigating."

"Just like that?"

"Just so." His gaze was far gentler than his words, which made it difficult for her to remain angry. Again, she stared too long—and felt odd for it, warm. Or maybe that was the disease. A lovely thought.

"What are you?" she asked, and for a moment his gaze faltered. "CIA? Special Ops? Where did Larry find you?"

Amiri exhaled, slowly. "I am not a member of any military. I am an . . . outside contractor."

"Outside contractor. A mercenary. Just like those other men."

"No. I am nothing like them."

I believe that, she thought, but kept her mouth shut and lay back down on the cot, hands folded behind her head.

Bodyguard. Hired protection. Nothing like the other men Larry had tried to saddle her with. Brutes. Male chauvinists. Alpha dogs with their dicks hanging so far out it only took a word to bruise their egos. None of them had lasted a week. Not a one had wanted to risk their lives for her—not after she was done with them.

Deliberate. Calculated. Larry accused her of having a death wish, but that was a lie. Rikki was not against help. The right kind. Whatever that was. Something she had not found yet. No good hands she could trust.

She peered at Amiri, peripherally. He lay on his back, hands clasped over his stomach. She remembered his naked body, the lines of his back. How he had given her what she needed, without asking.

She tilted her head so that she could see his eyes. "It's been a long time since Larry insisted on protection."

Amiri studied her openly, with a precision and depth that was startling, even intimate. "I suppose he trusted you to handle yourself."

He said it like he meant it, which made Rikki smile, somewhat bitterly. "No. Never."

"But—"

"A girl can only change the man-diapers for so long before it's time to send the gun-toting behemoths home to their mommies," Rikki interrupted smoothly. "Bunch of whiners. I'm sure *you* won't be like that."

"I would hardly dare," he said. "Though I suppose if we should both begin to *die,* you might make an allowance for a complaint or two. Rest assured, I will change my own diapers."

"Fantastic," Rikki muttered, and closed her eyes. Cot springs creaked. She imagined Amiri, long and lean and hard. Graceful. Wild.

Enough. She tried to ignore his presence. Listened to everything but her thoughts: bullets, blood, combustible crocodiles; the liquefaction of her vital organs; the sight, imagined or otherwise, of a man's eyes glowing in the night.

Sounds from outside the tent were muffled. Like being in a plastic cocoon or a bright wide coffin. Another kind of prison. It reminded Rikki of her father and the old trailer park. The hospital in Johannesburg and those nurses with their pious pity and cold hands. For the first time in years she wanted a cigarette.

She fell asleep. When she woke, groggy and uneasy, Mack was in the room. Big man in his protective gear, sealed tight as a mummy. Ruth was with him. She took Rikki's blood pressure while Mack attempted to stick a needle into Amiri. The man resisted. Firm, but gentle.

"I do not want my blood drawn," he said.

"We need to," Max replied.

"You are mistaken."

"Are you a doctor?"

"I am a man of common sense," Amiri told him, dryly. "And whether I live or die cannot possibly depend on what your test tells you. There is no cure."

Mack said nothing. He grabbed Amiri's arm, attempting to hold him down. Like trying to restrain water; the other man slipped out of his grasp, eyes narrowed. "Do not."

"Come on. It won't hurt." His tone was all Mr. Doctor, patronizing, as though talking to a child. Rikki wanted to shake her head in shame. That, and hold on tight. Looking at Amiri—right then—felt like a hurricane coming, and she watched him give Mack a long hard stare of withering disdain. But her colleague was an idiot. He reached out again. Confident, self-assured.

Amiri slapped his hand away so hard the sound was like a gunshot. Ruth flinched, eyes wide behind her goggles. Rikki tried to control her own face. No emotion. Just anticipation. She knew the strength in those arms, and that had not been a gentle blow.

"You asshole," Mack breathed, as the skin above his surgical mask mottled scarlet. Amiri's expression never changed, not even slightly. Carved in stone. But the look in his eyes was worse than the mouth of the crocodile: sharp, chilling, deadly. But still calm. Still a gentleman—in the most brutal, effective, way possible.

"Next time I will break you," Amiri said.

Mack swayed, his hand cradled to his chest. His breathing was loud, his eyes narrowed. The syringe lay on the ground between them. "Fuck you. All of you and your damn beliefs. Primitive, superstitious—"

"Mack." Rikki did not raise her voice, but it was enough.

His mouth snapped shut. He turned on her, staring. "This man needs the test. You know how important it is."

She knew. She had made her career on taking blood from the infected, hunting live viruses. But she had never bullied her patients. Never forced anyone to take the needle.

Rikki looked at Amiri. He met her gaze, and it was like electricity—some live current, hot in her blood. She had never met a man who was so confident, so quietly self-assured, and it had nothing to do with excess; not even a hint of arrogance. This was a man who could handle things. Handle anything. And he knew it. He knew the cost of it.

Just like Rikki did.

It would take a fight to make him give blood. It would take more than Ruth and Mack. More than the peacekeepers patrolling this camp. Rikki had a feeling there was not a force on earth that could make this man take part in anything—*anything*—that he did not want to do. God help anyone stupid enough to try.

Rikki was not stupid. And even though she knew she should be frightened by the hard coolness of his gaze, she was not. She felt like she stood in the eye of the storm—his eye, his storm. Safe. Untouched. Hidden in plain sight.

I am buying you time, Amiri's voice echoed in her mind. *I will make certain no one sees you.*

They might as well have swapped blood—his gift was as strong a bond. And whatever his reasons might be, the least Rikki could do was show him the same courtesy. She had no choice.

"There are alternatives," she told Mack, and held up her hand against his protest. "Do a spot check with his saliva. The virus will be present there. Hell, do the same with me."

"They won't be as thorough."

"But you'll know for certain. We all will."

He stared at her like she was crazy, and she was—it was bad science, against protocol, her own rules—but Rikki stared him down, unwilling to bend. Unwilling to contemplate how and why she could take a stranger's side over Mack.

He almost didn't back down. She could see it in his eyes. But after a long silence, cut with the fidgeting squeak of Ruth's heavy breathing, Mack leaned down to scoop up the dropped needle. He tossed it into the infectious materials bin with enough force to make the plastic rattle.

"Careful," Rikki said, unable to help herself. "You might take an eye out."

Mack shot her a glare. Ruth also gave Rikki a dirty look. Amiri did neither, nor did he smile. Instead his gaze turned thoughtful, his skin crinkling, just slightly, around his eyes. Warm, so warm. Looking at him was like finding kindness, and that was as unexpected as the rough way Mack suddenly grabbed her arm, fingers clamping down too tight for comfort.

You don't have anything to prove, Rikki told him silently, but he was already tapping out her vein, and she forced herself not to protest as he jabbed the syringe so hard into her arm she imagined it hit bone. Hurt like hell, but she kept her mouth shut. Gave Mack a piercing look. He raised his eyebrow. Daring her. Rikki did not take the bait.

"Ruth, get that man's saliva." He raised his brow at Amiri. "You won't resist, will you?"

"This is more acceptable," he replied. No warmth in his eyes for the doctor; quite the opposite, if Rikki was any judge. He spat into a vial for Ruth.

Mack rolled his eyes. "There's an anxious young man who wants to see you. Would you like me to pass along a message?" Each word was clipped, forced.

"Vigilance," Amiri said.

Mack gave him a long look, but made no comment. He withdrew the needle from Rikki's arm and swabbed her skin with alcohol. Said, quietly: "Neither of you are displaying symptoms. That's some reassurance."

Rikki glanced at Amiri. "Anyone else sick?"

Mack hesitated, also taking a quick look at the man. "Maybe we should discuss this later. There are . . . confidentiality issues."

Amiri arched his brow. "Shall I go stand in the corner? Plug my ears with my fingers?"

Rikki tried not to smile. "Spill it, Mack. Or else there might not be a later."

Mack briefly closed his eyes. "No symptoms in camp. Reports from downriver are clean, too."

She tried not to think about what it would feel like to pull an *Exorcist* moment with her vital organs. "It's been two days since the initial outbreak. The people who died in the river have been in the water that long. We should be seeing symptoms by now."

"Our best guess is that the delivery system diluted the virus. That, or the sick aren't reporting themselves."

"The virus itself could be different."

"No live samples yet." Mack held up her vial of blood. "I'm hoping not ever."

"Liar," Rikki said gently, and that was enough to soften his mouth. But only for a moment. His expression turned pained, as though he looked at her and saw only death. Giving up already. Simply pretending otherwise. It made Rikki angry, but only because she had looked at other people the same way, in other isolation wards.

Work for the best, was the motto. *Work for the best, assume the worst, and never, ever, let your heart get broken.*

Easier said than done. Mack and Ruth turned to leave. Rikki said, "Hey, have you heard from Larry? Any word about people going missing at the regional hospitals?"

He raised an eyebrow. "No. Why?"

Rikki hesitated. "Nothing. Forget about it."

Amiri shot her a hard look. "Do not forget about it. Ask others. See if anyone has heard rumors. And if strangers should come into the camp, people who do not belong—"

"Like you?" Mack interrupted. "Larry's 'security specialist'? Some job *you* did."

Amiri's jaw tightened. "Be alert. That is all I ask."

"Of course. Anything less gets you dead." Mack's gaze flicked back to Rikki, but she stayed quiet. There was nothing left to say.

Mack and Ruth departed. Through the clear plastic walls, Rikki watched them bypass the disinfectant tubs. Her instinct was to call them back to hose down, but she kept her

mouth shut. They were not venturing into a clean environ-
ment. Just outside to the refugee camp. Later, when they
wanted to eat, or sleep, or use the restroom—*then* dumping
their gear would be a trial. The risk of infecting themselves
would be at its highest.

"Sloppiness is death," Amiri said, also watching them
leave.

She felt like apologizing again. "Just part of the job.
Helping people is dangerous work. I suppose you know
that, though."

"Life is dangerous," he said simply. "It is what you
make of it that matters."

Her arm still hurt. She watched Mack leave without a
backward glance, and felt very much alone. "So what do *you*
make from something like this? What's the price of a good
life? That's what you get paid for, right? Making people
dead, people hurt. Is that worth the risk of helping someone
like me? Being a hired gun? Cash make the wheels go
around?" She glanced down at her hands, trying to imagine
herself dying, gone, dead. Been there, done that, though this
was almost preferable. No fighting. No screaming. No pain.
Not yet.

Amiri did not answer. Rikki looked, and found him with
his head tilted, eyes unblinking as he stared at her. Her
cheeks warmed, but she did not lower her gaze.

"You are better than those questions," he said finally,
quietly. "And so am I."

She had no comeback. He was too dignified. It was like
having a not-so-peace-loving version of Gandhi call her a
snot, and the result was an acute sense of *Twilight Zone*-
itis; like she was floating in some alternate universe where
strange men could affect her with nothing but a look and a

word—make her regret, when with anyone else she would already be moving on.

Her face burned. "I apologize."

Amiri made a sweeping motion with his hand. "And you? Why are you here?"

She had to take a moment, still wrapped up in his hold over her—how one of his looks could be so powerful. It bugged her, but not enough to run from. Curiosity would kill her yet.

"I hunt viruses," she told him. "I chase outbreaks to find out what causes them. Others handle containment, but my job is to find the source."

"Dangerous work."

"Like you said, life is dangerous."

"But that does not answer why we do it."

Rikki stared at him. "Where *did* Larry find you?"

His eyes warmed—that singular warmth that made her gut twist, hot and unsettled. "You will have to ask him that yourself after we leave this place."

"Optimistic."

"As are you. I suspect your job requires it."

She shook her head. "Are you sure you're a bodyguard?"

"I never said *that*. Only that I had been sent to protect you. The two, I assure you, are quite different."

"Huh." She lay on her side, cushioning her head on her arms. "But here you are."

"Indeed," he said, and for a moment it was easy for Rikki to forget where she was, what had happened.

But not for long. She fell asleep again, and dreamed.

Her old coach was with her, a shouting man made of muscle turned to lard, stout and pockmarked and a genius at his craft: Markovic, former Olympic gymnastics champion. He was yelling, chasing her. Rikki did not know why he was angry, but it frightened her and she tried to run. Not far, though. She tripped. All grace gone, no strength left. Drained into the earth, like blood. Blood, on her hands. Blood, everywhere, from so many dead. Dead, all at once. *All at once.*

Bad dream. Rikki woke with a question on her lips, a nagging sense that something was wrong. Her fault. She had missed something obvious.

The lights in the tent were off. It was very dark. That was also wrong. She began to sit up and a hand caught her shoulder. Amiri. He was sitting on her cot, shadows gathered around his body. She imagined, once again, a faint glow in his eyes.

"What?" she whispered, but as soon as she spoke she heard shouts in French outside the tent. Hoarse voices, full of fear. Sweat beaded against her skin, and it was suddenly hard to breathe. Hot, suffocating. The air-conditioning had gone with the lights.

Gunfire made her jump. The *rat-tat-tat* of automatic weapons. Shouts became screams and Amiri dragged her off the cot and pressed her to the ground.

"Rebels," he murmured. And just like that, things got worse.

WESTERN MEDIA LOVED THE ENTIRE AFRICAN CONTINENT like some good crack, but only the parts that were hurting. It was what had surprised Rikki the most during her first six months on the job. She had seen the images, read the newspapers with their sad doomed stories—people starving, women raped, poverty and corruption and destruction—but the reality was stark, different, dusty and full of sunlight and laughter and enterprise—kindness, music, intellectualism; a rambling babble of diversity and

uncommon languages and culture, mingling and scrabbling
and making joy. Fifty-four countries, nine hundred million
people. Modern to rural, rich to poor. Folks working hard
for a living. Just like home.

Except for the rebels and wandering militias, scattered
throughout the Congo and adjoining countries. Except for
the politics that backed those men, and the genocide that
accompanied them. That much was true. Rikki had the
scars to prove it. A lot of women did, in this region, though
she had been hurt less in some ways, than others. No rape.
But what had happened was almost as bad.

She squeezed shut her eyes. Her scars ached. Like some
storm-burn in an old woman's joints, more frightening than
bad weather. She wanted to run. She wanted to hide. She
wanted to pick up a gun and start blasting into the night:
heartless, efficient, effortlessly brutal. Better than the alternative.

Screams cut the night. Amiri's arm tightened. Rikki's
heart pounded so hard she felt sick.

"This area's been quiet," she muttered tightly, trying not
to vomit. "But I heard rumors in Brazzaville that the rebels
and militias have been moving east out of Kivu. It's why
this camp was established. To take care of the folks running from their homes."

"It makes no sense," Amiri murmured, but he stopped,
squeezing her closer as the rough shouts got louder, accompanied by wet sobs and desperate pleading. Rikki did
not recognize the voices, but she wanted to run to them.
Faces flashed—old friends, dead—and she shuddered as
she remembered, with perfect clarity, her body dragged
through dirt and stone. Hands holding her down. Those
damn knives.

Bodies hit the ground outside the tent. Rikki bit her bottom lip, fighting like hell to keep from shuddering, but that was a joke and she felt Amiri's mouth touch her ear. He whispered something she did not understand, again and again, but just as the words took shape inside her dull ears, gunfire exploded. Bullets ripped open the plastic sheeting, razing the cots and monitors, kicking metal into cutting shards. Amiri wrapped himself so tight over her body he felt like a second skin. The fingers of his right hand dug into the floor like claws.

The hail of bullets did not last; in its wake came deafening silence. Amiri slithered off her body. His hand caught her wrist. She moved with him, breathless, straining to listen. Men spoke. She heard a patois of French, Lingalese, some other Bantu language. She imagined she heard her name.

Amiri did not stop moving. He pulled her to one of the plastic tubs that had been scored and knocked over by bullets. Scrubs had spilled out. Amiri pointed, then pushed down on Rikki's shoulders. She resisted. There was no place for him to hide. She tried to tell him that, but he covered her mouth and shook his head. He forced her to crawl inside the plastic tub. She was just small enough. Amiri pushed the clothing around her body.

"Stay," he breathed, and then he was gone: melting out of sight, utterly silent. Rikki wiggled forward, trying to see. It was too dark. She could hear, though—and after several breathless moments the low murmur of voices drifted from the entrance of the tent. Not many, but enough. Rikki took three quick breaths, forcing herself to focus. Trying to decide how long she could rely on Amiri before one of them was killed, or worse.

The voices got louder. The quarantine barrier rattled. Rikki heard uneasy laughter, a low crooning call. She tried to judge numbers, but it was impossible. Stacked odds, either way. Amiri was unarmed. She took another deep breath and nudged forward, just slightly. Looking for a weapon, anything. She found syringes. Spilled on the floor, just out of reach.

The quarantine sheet pushed inward. Rikki froze. Her hearing dimmed to nothing but heartbeats, the roar of blood. She was dimly aware of distant wailing screams, gunshots. People dying. None of it mattered. Only that plastic wall and the men behind it.

Then, not even that. Amiri exploded upward from the floor.

Rikki knew he was fast, but what she saw in that moment verged on inhuman—a blur, too quick to follow. He plowed through the quarantine wall and her ears could hardly keep up with the answering crack of bones, grunts, muffled cries. Furious, unrelenting. She slithered out of the container, reaching for a syringe. Her hand closed around plastic.

A gun fired inside the tent. Rikki tore off the syringe's protective cap just as a large figure fell hard through the quarantine sheet. It was too dark to see his face, but the body was all wrong, too thick and hulking to be Amiri. She smelled blood.

The man saw Rikki. He lifted his gun. She lunged. Small, fast, desperate; she hit him hard in the chest and jabbed the needle into his face. Aimed for his eye, but his cheek was good enough. He screamed. Rikki tried to knock aside his weapon.

Amiri appeared. He grabbed the man's head and twisted.

Rikki heard a sound like cracking knuckles, then silence. The gun dropped. She snatched it up, safety off, grip sticky with blood. She did not give the dead man another look.

Movement flickered at the corner of her eye, just beyond the torn plastic barrier. She aimed, adrenaline high and wild, but kept her finger off the trigger. Focusing. Listening. Amiri stepped in front of her, facing the flimsy wall. She heard the sounds of a brief struggle, a distinctive pop—one loud shot—followed by a sharp intake of breath, a muffled curse that was suspiciously American. Rikki forced herself to breathe. The gun was slick in her hands. She heard distant screams and thought of Mack, the nurses, everyone who had come here to help. This could not be happening.

Amiri said, "Eddie. Over here."

Rikki gave him a sharp look. "A friend?"

"Yes."

The plastic sheeting to the quarantine section rattled. She felt light-headed, out of her mind. "He can't. He can't come in here. We're contagious."

"Doctor Kinn—"

Rikki took a step toward the barrier. "Stop, Eddie, whoever you are. *Don't move.*"

"I'm sorry, ma'am," said a young male voice, far too close for comfort. "Contagious or not, you don't have much of a choice. You have to leave. Now."

Amiri took hold of her arm and for a moment she forgot herself. Training took over. She fought, using all her strength. He lost his grip, grunting with what sounded like surprise, but he was faster than her and his arms clamped down. She tried kicking him and he only squeezed harder, pressing his mouth against her ear. He smelled like blood. His hands were slick.

"We must," he whispered harshly.

Yes, she thought, finally gazing down at the dead man beside her, neck twisted, syringe jutting from his cheek. *Hell, yes.*

But she could not say those words. She turned her head, peering up into Amiri's eyes. "If we contracted the disease, we are *contagious.* We will kill innocent people everywhere we go, anyone we come in contact with. I won't do that." Even if she was prepared to use the gun in her hand to defend her life. No conflict there. Shooting men intent on murder did not, in her opinion, count.

Amiri's hands tightened; he shook her, just slightly, and in a voice so low it was almost a growl said, "Eddie, are the peacekeepers evacuating?"

"Trying to," said the young man, still out of sight. "They were taken off guard. Some are trying to find the medical personnel, but it's chaos out there. That's why we have to hurry. I don't know how much longer the planes will stay grounded before someone panics."

"Indeed," Amiri murmured, and then louder: "Go and find us some biohazard suits. Make certain yours is secure."

Eddie pushed back through the barriers. Rikki began to protest, but Amiri covered her mouth with his hand.

"I am not ready to die," he said in a hard voice. "And while I live, so shall you. We are leaving here, and you are coming with us, even if I have to carry you."

Rikki pushed away his hand. "And if we hurt others in the process? Can you live with that?"

Amiri said nothing. He shoved Rikki across the isolation ward, and though she put up a fight, he was the strongest man she had ever encountered, and nothing she did broke his stride.

She could have played dirty. Part of her wanted to. But

there was another part, ruthless and fierce, that wanted to run with him. Run fast, run long, and never mind the consequences. High ideals be damned. Because she also wanted to live. She wanted to fight for every breath, even if it killed. Even if all she had left was a day or an hour.

Go, whispered a tiny voice. *Don't look back.*

She went.

CHAPTER FIVE

I T had been a long time. Too long, to discover how much of Amiri's father still lived within him. He was glad it was dark inside the tent, that Rikki Kinn had human eyes and nothing more; that she did not look down at the bodies so still on the floor of the tent as he guided her out and away into the shrill hot night. The first kill was always the hardest, and sometimes the second, but there was a taste that a man could become accustomed to, and it was not the blood or the fear or even the death itself, but the power that belonged solely to a good hard murder.

Beneath his latex gloves, Amiri's hands were sticky with blood. He could taste it in his mouth. He had taken liberties, in the heat of the moment; had wanted a sense of the enemy, to take them into his body and listen to the nuances of the flesh: roots and blood honey and the stone of bones.

But he had learned nothing. Only, that he was an animal beneath his human skin—and that his human heart could not abide what that drove him to do.

Outside, bodies sprawled everywhere, covered in blue tarps: transitional corpses, awaiting transport to a secure burial site. Some of the deceased, however, were more recent; they wore protective gear instead of plastic sheets, the white fabric of the suits torn with bullet holes and covered in blood so fresh he could feel the warmth of it through his clothing.

Rikki made a sound. He found her staring at two bodies sprawled against the isolation tent. A woman and a man. Their masks had been torn off, chests nothing more than red pulp. Amiri looked close at their faces and placed them as the nurse and the doctor, the angry man who smelled like cigarettes and a splash of whisky. Mack. Ruth.

Amiri squeezed Rikki's shoulder, forcing her attention from her dead colleagues. He was afraid she would fight him, but her eyes held no tears, no grief—just something so hard and glittering she might have killed with a look, cut and burned and buried. He had never seen such eyes in a woman—not in anyone—and he had to look away, quick. She was so different from the photograph. Better. Still shining, but with a harder edge.

And her scent . . . her scent was sweaty, anxious, angry; and beneath it all, sweet and spice, vanilla and pepper. Rolling, warm. Safe. *Dangerous.* He was too aware of her. Even now he could hear her heartbeat, and it felt too much like his own.

Amiri grabbed her hand, flicked Eddie on the shoulder, and guided them both away from the tent into the ramshackle maze of the shadowed camp; away from the structured heart of UN tents, large and billowing and white; farther out to the torn edges, where the shelters became rougher, put together with blue plastic tarps and sticks and string. Crude, but decorated with flaps of brightly colored cloth and clothes that had been left to dry; stiff in the still night air, holding the shapes of ghosts, lives lost, the evidence of which stretched as far as his eyes could see. The ground was treacherous with corpses.

Amiri kept Rikki close, careful not to let her fall, though she was agile enough on her own. Fast and small, good at keeping low to the ground. They both wore biohazard suits. The material felt like a coffin rubbing his skin, or the bars of a cage. He could not stand the sensation, the confinement—the target it made of their bodies. He could still taste the river in his mouth, mixed with the metal of blood. Dead, dying, hunted: it was all the same now.

He pushed up hard against a tattered tent, Rikki tucked into his side. At their feet were cracked plastic bowls and canisters of water, piles of clothing, sticks and cloth fashioned into dolls. Articles of life, adrift with the dead. Eddie stepped on one of the toys as he slithered close; he flinched as the wood snapped. Beneath the goggles, his eyes were strained, bloodshot, the rest of his face hidden by a surgical mask. The biohazard suit made him look like a ghost.

The wind shifted. Amiri smelled gasoline. Sloshing sounds drifted on the hot night air; closer still, shouts in English and French were punctuated by the crack of automatic gunfire. Peacekeepers, trying to round up survivors. Fighting for their lives. Somewhere nearby a man screamed—bloodcurdling, so high-pitched as to be freakish, inhuman. The sound cracked Amiri's skull, flashing him back into that old tight cage, the lab in Russia. Screams for help echoing off the tile walls. The dying, always unseen, but rich in terror.

Circle come round. He was back again.

"Eddie," he murmured, and instantly regretted it.

"I can't," said the young man, flashing him an uncertain look. "Not from here. If I could get close enough to see them . . ."

You would set their weapons on fire, thought Amiri. *You would choke them with smoke and heat. You would be forced to kill, again and again.*

And there would be killing enough, before this was over.

Rikki stared at both men. "You want to help? Search for survivors?"

Eddie said nothing. He looked at Amiri, waiting. Rikki also looked at him, but her eyes narrowed and she held up her stolen gun. "I'm willing," she told them, but her voice was breathless, and he remembered her body in his arms, shaking so hard he thought she would fly apart. Amiri did not think he would ever forget that moment: overcome, hunted by a visceral, overwhelming desire to protect, to make her part of him so that he could hide her in his skin. Keep her safe from harm.

He had never felt that before. Never anything so strong.

"Willingness is not the issue." Amiri forced his attention from her, as uneasy with her presence as he was the danger around them. Somewhere, the man had stopped screaming. Death, capture, or escape. He met Eddie's gaze and shook his head.

Your eyes are old enough, he wanted to say, and though Eddie was no telepath, he met Amiri's gaze as though he heard every word.

The young man cleared his throat. "We need to hurry."

Amiri touched Rikki's shoulder. "Are you ready?"

She shook her head. "What about the others?"

"If we find anyone on the way out, we will take them with us. I promise nothing else, not if it means compromising you."

"I've already been compromised. If I do have what killed these people, bullets aren't going to mean much."

It means everything, Amiri thought, and from the conflict on her face, he sensed she felt the same—even if she were unwilling to admit it. So stubborn. He reached out and took her hand. She glanced at him, startled; her eyelids fluttered, her expression hardened.

Voices cut the night. Low, conversational. Unnatural in their calm. Coming close, fast.

There was no time to run. Amiri yanked Rikki down and pushed her through the opening of the tent behind them. Grabbed Eddie and did the same. They tumbled inside and the air was tight and hot with death.

The three of them huddled on their stomachs. Amiri felt something uneven and yielding beneath him. A body not yet wrapped in plastic. His hand touched cold stiff fingers. His skin crawled right off his body.

"Shit," Eddie breathed, flinching. Amiri saw Rikki poke his shoulder and the young man's mouth snapped shut. Outside, the voices were close. Amiri listened hard. The language was unfamiliar. Not Bantu or Lingalese, nothing he could place, though the curl of the words felt familiar. Sharp tones, angry. He heard a clicking sound, like a fingernail clipper.

Amiri exhaled slowly and pressed his eye against a slit in the tent flap. He felt Rikki do the same, peering through a small hole.

He saw legs. A trim waist. Two brown hands. One holding a cigarette, the other a canister of gasoline. Both twitching nervously.

There was another set of hands. Large and capable, skin shadowed with olive undertones. Mottled, marked with burns. One sinewy wrist glittered with gold, a Rolex. And in the other hand he saw a metal clipboard with a silver pen held under a long thumb.

No protective gear. No gloves. Just like the men he had killed.

Amiri could not see their faces. He did not dare try. He focused on those hands, trying to capture scents, the stories in their crackling voices. In the midst of it all, he heard only one word that was familiar, a name that made him question his hearing.

"*Rikki*," said the man with the clipboard. "*Rikki Kinn*."

Everything inside him stopped. Rikki froze tight against his side. All he could hear was her name.

And then the clicking sound resumed. The pen was taken up, something quick written.

Nearby, a gun went off. The men did not flinch. Amiri heard a woman scream. The men did not stop talking. In the canister, gasoline splashed. Its bearer said something loud, laughing nervously. His companion did not respond; he took the pen and stabbed the other man.

Amiri did not see the impact, but he heard it. Rikki recoiled. He grabbed her hand, squeezing—listening as that sharp throaty cry died to a high whine of pain. The man fell to his knees in front of the tent. Amiri glimpsed the crown of a bald head, a chiseled cheek. The pen jutted from his shoulder. His attacker said a few harsh words, and the man nodded his head, babbling. Making promises, no doubt. Trying to make up for whatever had just caused this stroke of punishment.

Amiri heard a clicking sound. The pen was ripped out. Its silver shaft was cleaned on the shuddering back of the wounded man. Then his attacker turned and walked away— back into the bullet-riddled chaos, like he belonged there. Amiri glimpsed long black hair, glossy as silk. Listened as that odd *click click click* faded away.

The stabbed man kneeling in front of the tent still held

his cigarette. His hand shook as he raised it to his mouth. He smelled like blood, death; bitter as poison. Mixed with the hard fumes of gasoline.

Which, after rising, he then proceeded to splash on the tent in which they were hiding.

It was so shocking that for a moment Amiri could not move—listening as the man upended the canister over the plastic sheeting and the ground around it—hearing those grunts of pain as the fuel rained down, soaking everything, seeping between the flaps.

No mistake about his intentions. None at all. There was only one reason a person doused something in gasoline.

Instinct took over. Amiri exploded from the tent, claws ripping through his gloves. He rammed his fists into the man's throat and wounded shoulder, slamming him into the ground with a crushed windpipe. Fast, efficient. There was no chance to shout for help. The cigarette slipped. Amiri knocked it back into the man's gasping mouth. Safer there. No fire. Gasoline continued to pour from the dropped canister.

Amiri sensed movement on his left, bodies in shadow. Guttural shouts pocked the air, along with the crackle of gunfire. The fumes from the gasoline rolled over him like smoke. His nostrils felt scalded.

Amiri danced back, the cheetah rising up through his skin. Fur brushed against the inside of his biohazard suit. His claws retracted, just barely, through the remains of his latex gloves. He could not fight the beast; it coiled inside his chest, screaming. He clamped his mouth shut tight and reached behind, grabbing Rikki as she pushed through the tent flaps. Eddie rode her heels. Amiri smelled fire, ash, felt an aura of intense heat radiating from the young man's body.

"Take care," Amiri whispered to him. "The petrol."

Eddie nodded, peering deeper into the distant shadows where the clipboard man had disappeared. Flashlight beams cut a swath through the night, and the movement of light solidified on tiny figures, slender enough to be children, an army of them. It took Amiri a moment to reconcile the sight. Those *were* children. Small boys, loaded down with guns and gas canisters. Stumbling, clumsy. Emptying out the fuel with awkward haste. They worked in a line, methodically moving over the wrapped dead with quaking intensity. Some adults stood with them, but they did little but shout and hold flashlights.

Rikki muttered something. Her words were muffled beneath her mask, impossible to understand. She stared at the armed youths.

Eddie said, "Come on. We can slip around."

"No," she said, still watching the boys splash the dead with gasoline. "Oh, my God."

Eddie went still. Amiri set his jaw, following her gaze, studying the children, concentrating solely on their actions. Their diligence. Their disregard for anything but those canisters in their hands, and those deadly diseased bodies at their small unprotected feet. He smelled the gas. Listened to it slosh, and in such amounts as to be part of the river wild on the other side of the camp.

He thought about the men. What he had just witnessed.

Amiri squeezed her hand. "You think they came here to burn the bodies."

Rikki looked at him. "I think they came to burn us all."

He stared, but there was no time to respond—a mechanical howl filled the air. The children stopped pouring gasoline over the dead and a shout went up.

"The plane," Eddie hissed. The UN plane. Their one way out.

Amiri hauled Rikki close, forcing her to run. He kept one hand on her shoulder, guarding her back, his muscles bunching from human to cheetah. Gunshots rode the air, sharp voices. A figure in bright orange and white lurched from the shadows between tents, gloved hands clutching a rifle. Eddie raised his own gun, but stopped at the last moment. It was Patrick, the young peacekeeper who had helped them in Kinsangani. Mask off, hood down, goggles hanging around his neck. He was wild-eyed, flushed, covered in dirt and blood, and running so deep on instinct that for a moment Amiri thought the young man would shoot them on sight. But then his eyes cleared, his teeth flashed, and he gestured fiercely.

"Not that way!" Patrick shouted, but it was too late; they'd already been seen. Bullets hailed down. Eddie whirled, shooting back into the darkness. Heat rolled off his body, pressing through Amiri's protective gear like a rush from an open oven.

Patrick still shouted. Amiri tried to listen, but this time it was Rikki who pulled, and he had no choice but to follow. They ran. Cut themselves away from the tents onto an open plain carved from the jungle. Airfield, runway, with only one cargo plane on the ground. *Reinforcements coming* had been the word on the flight from Kinsangani, though Amiri had paid little attention. Too many distractions. Memories of photographs, which were now nothing more than ash.

The airfield was crowded with the dead: a sea of body bags, stacked and tagged and ready for disposal. No scent of gasoline—not yet—but the smell of death was overwhelming. Amiri swallowed down the urge to vomit, and he set himself on Rikki, making certain she stayed close. Her scent cut through the carnage; wild, sharp, sweet.

A gunfight surrounded the plane. Amiri's eyes shifted

deeper into those of the beast and he found peacekeepers sprawled on their stomachs, peering through the aft loading bay of the cargo plane, shooting indiscriminately into the night. Amiri guided Rikki and Eddie closer to the body bags, searching for cover . . . and realized there were men there, too. Guns and faces were huddled amongst the bundled dead. They were firing on the plane.

But it was all wrong. His eyes were wrong. Those men could not be the enemy. Those uniforms . . . the colors . . .

Patrick shouted again. Amiri whirled and found the young soldier standing on the edge of camp. He waved frantically, beckoning them away from the airfield with furious, terrified, gestures.

"What—" Eddie began, but Patrick jerked, stumbling to his knees. He dropped his gun. Fell face first. Behind him, three men appeared. Men without biohazard suits, wearing light blue berets and camouflage gear. They were European in appearance; pale skin, dark hair.

Peacekeepers. Or men dressed as such. One of them nudged Patrick with his boot and laughed, while the others settled their gazes on Amiri and Eddie.

There was no place to hide. Amiri pushed Rikki behind him, but not before the men saw her. She was bundled tight, protective gear strapped over her face, but nonetheless the men stared, then glanced at each other with narrowed eyes. They raised their guns, taking careful aim. Behind, the assault against the plane continued; the massive engine roared.

Betrayed. They had all been betrayed.

The tallest of the men bared his teeth and called out in French; then, after a moment, guttural English. He was heavy with muscle, the tufts of his eyebrows furrowed over dark eyes that examined Rikki with an intensity that made

Amiri want to kill. He smiled and said, "Come, *mademoi-selle*. Come here now. We will keep you safe, yes?"

"Fuck you," Rikki shot back, the weight of her stolen gun briefly touching Amiri's back. He did not reach for the weapon, only watched as the interest in the Frenchman's eyes turned into a startling recognition. The man's smile disappeared. His finger rubbed the trigger of his weapon.

"Doctor," said the man softly, taking a step closer. *"Doctor Kinn."*

Rikki went still. Amiri said, "Eddie."

Fire exploded. Fire in their hands, against their guns, beneath their feet. The men screamed, dropping their weapons, dancing backward. Flames licked their clothing. Rikki gasped.

Amiri pulled on her arm as the men dropped, rolling, stamping out the fire. The UN plane had begun to move, but the gunfire hailing upon it only increased, pinging the metal surface with sparks and hot bangs. He shouted once again for Eddie, and the young man whirled, eyes narrowed, expression hard.

A wall of fire erupted around the body bags, an inferno that swept inward, so high and thick it blocked the sights of the men firing on the plane—blocked them, too, from getting a clear shot on Amiri, Rikki, and Eddie. He heard them shouting, the high crack of panic. He could still see them in his head—wearing peacekeeper uniforms. All wrong, askew, like they had been thrown on in a haphazard manner.

Amiri snarled, pushing Rikki and Eddie toward the moving aircraft. His muscles contorted, shifting; the woman was too slow and he swept her up in his arms, ignoring her gasp of surprise. Eddie was just behind, arms pumping, leaving a trail of heat in his wake. The plane kept moving. Amiri could see the pilots in the cockpit staring at them. He shouted, desperation making him hoarse.

The plane did not slow. Behind, Amiri heard movement, shouts, screams. Pursuit. Eddie stopped, turning with his hands raised. Heat scorched the air, rushing over Amiri's back with such force that he stumbled. Rikki gasped his name, arms clutched around his neck. He held her tighter, listening to the thump of her heart beneath the roar of the engines, smelling her fear beneath the miasma of death and fire.

"We're not going to make the plane!" Eddie shouted.

Amiri agreed. Unfortunately, no one was going to make that flight.

There came a high-pitched whine, and he glanced to the right just in time to see something long and bright rush into the air from the jungle's dark edge. It was like watching a falling star—a star in the shape of a missile—and it streaked through the night with a shriek.

"No," Rikki breathed, stiffening in Amiri's arms, flinching with a muffled cry as the missile slammed against the aircraft, tearing into it with a flash of terrible light.

Explosion. Shock wave. Shrapnel. Amiri took himself hard to the ground, covering Rikki with his body. Eddie fell against his side, also over the woman. The three of them huddled close, pressed so tight Amiri felt as though he was breathing for all of them. His ears hurt with the thunder and squeal of tearing metal, and the tremor of the air shook him as the plane ruptured again and again, passing from machine to nothing more than burning parts. His mask slid off, as did his goggles. He did not care.

He lost time, but not much. After the first terrible wave he lifted his head, just enough to see. Fires burned so bright it felt like daylight, and all around him was nothing but barren earth, hot metal . . . and just beyond, the jungle, waiting like some dark wet shadow.

Amiri staggered to his feet, dragging Rikki with him, holding out his other hand to pull Eddie up. They turned in a full circle, surveying the destruction. Sweat rolled down his body, pressure curling at the base of his spine, making his skin tingle.

Instinct. Someone was watching them.

He took Rikki's arm. "We go now. Fast."

She shook him off, staring. Her mask was gone, as were her goggles. Exposed, vulnerable, deadly. "This was murder. *All of this.*"

All of this. Her voice echoed inside his head, as did visions of the dead; a thousand corpses bloody and still and twisted in poses of agony. Amiri smelled burning flesh, the smoke of the massive funeral pyre.

Blood trickled down Eddie's cheek. His protective gear was torn, his face exposed. He did not seem to care. There was fire in his gaze: those flames, reflected. Burning. "Jungle or river," he said. "Those are our options."

Amiri heard distant shouts. The fire was spreading into the refugee camp, no doubt licking the edges of fumes and gasoline. Ready for another explosion, another consumption. The river was on the other side of it all, swift and safe. A sure thing.

But the jungle was closer, and he was good with shadows.

There was a path through the fire. Amiri did not know what lay on the other side, but it was better than remaining still. He pointed and Eddie wordlessly took the lead, running ahead. Amiri grasped Rikki's hand, but she pulled back again, still staring at the wreckage of the plane. He grabbed her chin and forced her to look at him.

She never blinked. He expected her to be distracted, terrified, but instead her gaze was clear, hot, her focus utterly striking. She looked at him like she could see straight through to his soul, and it stole his breath.

"We must go," he whispered, still holding her chin, his words tumbling into a growl. "We must live."

Rikki touched his face, her fingers trailing up his cheek to the corner of his eye. The contact was fleeting, but it sent a shock of heat through him that went deeper than the surrounding fires. For a moment he forgot himself, the danger, his convictions; the cheetah rumbled through his chest, responding only to this woman, her scent. His hand tightened. He swayed closer.

Eddie shouted his name. Amiri froze. His heart thundered, everything inside his body tight, hard. He could not believe what he had been on the verge of doing. So stupid, so thoughtless. Less than animal.

Rikki still studied his face, but there was a difference in her gaze that he could not bear to look closely upon. He turned, grabbing her hand. Rikki stumbled, but this time followed. They raced away from the fire, toward the jungle.

Eddie was waiting. Amiri felt a sliver of fear for the young man—for himself, as well. They had done too much tonight. All their secrets, everything they had to hide, was bubbling to the surface. In front of a woman with sharp eyes.

Exposed once, exposed again. The world is too small if you are not willing to hide.

The pressure at the base of his spine intensified; his hackles tingled. Just within the leading edge of the jungle he passed Rikki off to Eddie, and turned in time to see a man follow them from the flaming wreckage. Not a peacekeeper, not a doctor or aid worker. This man wore a pale suit and a pale tie. An incongruous sight; an illusion, perhaps. Amiri stared, taking in the tall lean body, the short blond hair. Sharp features, deadly eyes. A face that reminded him of someone. A presence that made him think of cages and steel and Russia.

The man was some distance away, but he looked directly into Amiri's hiding place and held up his hand. Waved, with a cold smile.

Amiri's chest tightened. He melted backward into the jungle, passing into shadow. The cheetah fought him; the beast wanted blood, could already taste it, bitter and keen. Amiri bit his tongue to satisfy the urge. No matter who their pursuer was, now was not the time. He had the woman to think of. And Eddie.

They were waiting for him deep within the bush. The air was hot beneath the night canopy. Amiri listened hard, but other than the low hoot of birds, he heard nothing to indicate other humans, or pursuit. Not that it would last. They had been seen.

"Remove your protective gear," he ordered, tearing his mask and goggles all the way off. There would be no hiding, no movement—not in this shambling outfit. He stripped away the latex gloves, hesitating for only a moment while he concentrated on maintaining the human appearance of his skin and nails.

Rikki and Eddie stared at him, unmoving. There was some light pushing through the trees from the burning airfield, but once they began walking it would be dark in the jungle. Only Amiri would be able to see, though Eddie, he thought, might have a penlight in his pocket.

"The disease," said the young man, tentative. "I thought . . ."

Amiri slowed his movements, glancing from his friend to Rikki, whose gaze was lost in shadows. He wished he could see her eyes; even so, he could not look away from her. His hands stilled. "There is more happening here than just a disease. Or am I wrong, Doctor Kinn?"

She stood very quiet, a far cry from the quivering fury he had spied on the burning airfield. Her silence was profound.

"Doctor Kinn," he said again, more gently.

"No," she said softly. "You're not wrong. But there's still a risk."

Amiri settled his jaw. "We have already been compromised. Even Eddie, with his torn suit. So we all die now or die later. I know what I choose."

"Yeah," she murmured. "But why do I think you always choose the hard way?"

Amiri smiled grimly, tearing off the rest of his suit. "Because for me, Doctor Kinn, the alternative has never existed."

CHAPTER SIX

WHEN Rikki was twelve years old, she'd found herself—in the span of one night—homeless on the street, with no money, no family, and no way up or out by any means other than what she could do for herself. Her father was in prison, and all the money saved from his days of trucking had been spent on a fat little lawyer who had done so little to help his client, he might as well have wiped his ass with Frank Kinn's freedom and flushed it down the toilet.

Twenty years later, Rikki felt like a kid again. It was not a good sensation.

The sky began to lighten not long after their escape. Slivers of it turned lavender, then peach, gasps of starlight fading. Birds screamed, lost in the dense canopy; monkeys howled. Rikki hardly noticed. Her legs burned, her throat hurt. A headache was building at the back of her skull. Adrenaline had faded. It was hard to breathe. She wanted to vomit.

Rikki did not blame Ebola, or any other disease. She refused to think about it. Or about the fact that she was a hunted woman. Not even the gun still held slick in her hand could compensate for that. Nor could the men who had saved her life.

Strangers. Mysteries. Amiri walked in front. He had taken off his shirt and tucked it into the back of his loose drawstring scrubs. His back was lean as a whip, his shoulders broad and sinewy, and though his skin was dark as rain-soaked earth, there were golden undertones that even in the forest twilight seemed to gleam in his sweat and in the play of shadows rippling against his hard muscles. He was tireless, quick.

But looking at him made Rikki's head hurt even worse. She glanced over her shoulder, desperate for a distraction. Eddie was behind her. She had barely gotten a look at the young man since escaping the camp. There was finally enough light to see the dark hair, the lean pale face. He was younger than she expected; young, with old eyes. Familiar, too. Startlingly so, which did nothing for her headache.

"Ma'am," he said quietly, catching her gaze.

"Hey," she replied, hoarse. Eddie reminded her of someone. Her brother. Dead at seven, but with that same dark unruly hair. Those soulful eyes. Uncanny, how much it seemed like him, if only older. The young man could have been family.

No, she told herself, turning away sharply. *No, don't go there. Don't you dare.*

But staring in the other direction was no help, either. Amiri was there.

Eddie wore a backpack. Rikki said, "Any water in there? Food?"

"I wish," he said grimly. "Aspirin, if you want it."

A root snagged her foot. She stumbled and Eddie almost stepped on her. She felt heat roll off his body. Too much heat. She turned, studying him more carefully, and the weak dawn light could not hide his flushed cheeks, or the brightness of his eyes. She forgot herself and reached

out to touch his forehead. Found him hot to the touch.
Burning up.

"You have a fever," she said. Eddie caught her hand and
pushed her gently away.

"No, ma'am," he replied. "I'm fine."

Rikki frowned, and glanced over her shoulder, intend-
ing to call Amiri. No need, though. He stood directly behind her, so close she could have touched him if she
breathed hard. Silent, silent, man. Rikki tried to keep her
voice steady as she said, "We need to stop."

"No." Eddie glanced at Amiri. "No, I'm fine. Really.
She thinks I have a fever."

"He's hot," Rikki protested. "And it's not from exertion.
It's internal."

Amiri looked at Eddie. "How do you feel?"

A tired smile touched the young man's mouth, and for a
brief moment the two men stared at each other with a weight
and gravity that made Rikki feel totally insignificant, a
stranger amongst friends. It made her wonder how they saw
her—if she was nothing but a paycheck. A burden.

That's what you are, *stupid. What else do you expect?*

Rikki didn't know, but either way, it cut. And that was
wrong. *She* was wrong, to want more. To desire even the
pretense of friendship. The security of it.

Amiri's shoulders relaxed, and he glanced down at her.
"He is fine, Doctor Kinn."

"Fine," she replied flatly. "Really."

"Ma'am," Eddie said gently. "It's nothing."

Her eyelid twitched. "I spent the better part of twenty-
four hours bagging bodies. You want to run that past me
again?"

He had the grace not to argue. Amiri turned away. "We
need water."

"A satellite phone would be better," she muttered, staring at his back. He said nothing. Kept walking. Rikki almost gave him the finger, but Eddie cleared his throat and that was reminder enough to act her age. So she shot *him* a look—the one usually reserved for drunks and circus clowns—and said, "What, oh paragon of health?"

The young man flushed a deeper crimson. "I just wanted to say thank you. For your concern."

"Oh." Rikki hesitated. "I suppose you didn't need it."

"Not now," he said easily, almost cheerfully, though she noted a soft aching fear flash through his gaze, an uncertainty that made her heart hurt.

Just a kid, she thought. He was too young to be out here. Too much like her brother, Frank Jr., what with that loopy sweet smile. She almost wanted to find a football and toss it at him, just for kicks. Which was . . . really pathetic.

She was silent too long. Eddie frowned. "Ma'am?"

"Rikki," she corrected him absently. "You make me feel old."

"Rikki," he said, with surprising gentleness. "It'll be all right. You can trust us."

Trust. She gave him a closer look. He met her gaze, square and true. Earnest, even sweet. Naive as hell, maybe, but she wasn't going to hold that against him. Not when looking at Eddie made her homesick for something she could not name. Rikki patted his shoulder. "Thanks, kid."

Eddie raised his brow, mouth twitching into a grin. "Kid?"

It was hard not to smile back, but it didn't last. The young man held her gaze without moving, those old eyes studying her with disquieting intensity. It made her uncomfortable, and just as she was about to say something he held aside some branches and gestured for her to precede him.

As she passed, he said, "Do you know why, ma'am?"

Rikki stopped. "Why what?"

Eddie searched her face. "Why would men want to hurt you?"

She stared, caught, but all she could think of was Bakker and Mack and every other person lost at that refugee camp. All she saw in her head were the flames and the dead: children, splashing gas on bodies; men in peacekeeper uniforms, men she should have been able to trust. Her scars ached.

Why, indeed?

Amiri appeared from behind the gnarled trunk of a massive tree, pushing aside a sweep of vines dripping from the canopy. His eyes were sharp. He did not need to say a word. He stared at Eddie and the young man flushed. Rikki glanced at him. "We were just talking."

"I asked Doctor Kinn why she's a target," Eddie said, with such simple honesty it was like looking at a choirboy— the kind with guns jammed in the back of his pants and spots of blood on his shirt. Rikki wanted to shake him around a little . . . or give him a noogie.

Amiri raised an eyebrow. "And?"

"And nothing," Rikki said. "What went on in that refugee camp last night was bigger than me."

Eddie shook his head. "With all due respect, ma'am, we weren't sent to protect a refugee camp. And even though it came under attack, it was your name those men knew."

"They knew more than your name," Amiri added softly. "They knew your voice, as well. The men at the airfield could not see your face when they recognized you."

"Someone prepared them," Eddie said. "Someone's been watching you."

Rikki closed her eyes, fighting for control. "We need to go back, you know. The camp is scheduled to receive a new influx of personnel and supplies. What's going to happen when they get there? More explosions? I assume they'll see the smoke if those fires haven't been put out, but that won't stop them from landing. And if those same people are waiting . . ." She thought of Mack. Ruth. "We have to send out a warning. There should be a radio left, some way of communi—"

"No," Amiri interrupted sharply, and then, softer: "No."

"More people will die."

"But not you," he said. "Not you."

Rikki stared. Amiri was an unflappable man, but last night she had seen a crack in the mask. Felt his hand on her chin, his heat; the way he had looked at her, hungry and dangerous with those fires burning all around them, in his eyes. His glowing eyes. Those impossible eyes.

His eyes were not glowing now, but the hunger was back, an intensity that rolled down to her bones, weakening her knees. So rough, so damn alluring.

Rikki shivered. Amiri blinked, relaxing his jaw. "You think I do not care about those people."

"I don't know what to think. Least of all, about you," she replied, and watched his gaze slide back into that cool mask; predatory, aloof. She wanted to tell him it was too late, that she saw right through him—that she could feel the echo of his emotions, the burning. No mask could hide that. And his calm did not make him any less intense. Not to her.

Eddie said, too quietly, "We should keep moving."

Amiri held Rikki's gaze a heartbeat longer. "Follow me. I found something."

MORE THAN SOMETHING, RIKKI REALIZED, MINUTES LATER, staring dumb and silent.

Tossed in the undergrowth were three aluminum cylinders

the length and breadth of her arms. Polished to a shine. Un-
marked. Missing caps. A fine white powder was scattered
on the ground around them. Not much, but enough to look
like someone had been playing with a chalkboard.

Eddie crouched, leaning close. He rubbed his nose, like
it itched. "Cocaine?"

Amiri frowned. "The scent is different."

Eddie reached down to touch the powder. Rikki snapped
back to herself and grabbed his wrist, squeezing her fingers so hard the young man winced. She did not know jack
shit about scents, but she recognized her own business
when she saw it. Even if it took a moment to register.

"Back away," she murmured, hardly able to speak.
"Don't breathe too deeply."

Both men froze, then turned slowly to stare at her. She
gave them hard looks, and tugged on Eddie's arm. They
moved. Rikki did not go with them. She stayed and stared
and looked for a big stick. Held her breath. Used a long
branch to push leaves and debris over the powder and canister. Hiding them.

When Rikki was done, she very carefully backed away.
She counted steps. She did not need to, but it helped her
focus. And not run screaming.

When they were all at least three hundred paces away,
very much out of sight and down a hill, Rikki braced her
hand—and gun—against her knees, and forced herself to
breathe.

"I take it that substance was bad?" Amiri said mildly.

"Shit," muttered Rikki, staring at her feet. "Fuck."

"Probably very bad," Eddie said, somewhere over her
head. "Like . . . we're going to die, bad?"

"Holy crap," Rikki said, and fell to her knees. "Jesus
Christ."

"Well, that's not comforting."

"Indeed."

"Think we should get down on *our* knees?"

"Humility and penitence?"

"No. Just tired."

"Ah." Amiri crouched beside Rikki. Eddie sat down on her other side. Both were dwarfing her, like trees to a sapling. She stared at them, looking into their eyes—golden, brown, both watching her with so much intensity, such fascination, she might as well have been a poodle in some tutu doing the cancan and singing showtunes.

"You two are insane," she said.

"No," Eddie replied, cheerfully. "We're terrified."

"Justifiably so," Amiri murmured. "What is it that I found?"

Breathe. Focus. Breathe. Rikki closed her eyes, swallowing hard. "First, did you touch anything? Before you came to get us? Did you get close?"

"No closer than we just were."

Rikki exhaled. "Good."

Amiri looked like he wanted to shake her. "Explain."

She rubbed the back of her neck, hurting. "Those canisters you found are sometimes used in the transport of biological materials. Airtight, waterproof, insulated, difficult to damage."

"They looked like thermoses," Eddie muttered.

"Ain't no coffee beans in that stainless steel," Rikki shot back.

Amiri frowned. "The powder? What is it?"

"No way to tell. It could be dozens of things. Drugs, or ground bone dust—part of some black market trade in human body parts. Pulverized animal bits, for sale in traditional medicines."

"Traditional medicines are not exactly terrifying."

"But anthrax is," she said, grim. "Smallpox. Biological agents. Deadly."

Eddie paled, staring at his hand. Amiri never flinched. "The same substance that killed those people in the refugee camp?"

Rikki's mouth clicked shut. He could have been reading her mind. But that question—that awful question—still felt like a steel-tipped boot in her gut.

And she knew what that felt like. Boy, did she.

Eddie stiffened. "I thought what happened there was natural."

Rikki said nothing. Neither did Amiri. They stared at each other, and she could almost hear his thoughts, turning inside his head. His eyes were piercing, intelligent . . . beautiful, if she could admit it—and she could, even if it were a secret she'd take to the grave.

"Hey," Eddie said. "I'm hanging here."

"I would need to run more tests," Rikki replied, looking at him. "But since I've got a snowball's chance in hell of managing that, better to be safe than sorry. No poking around anything white and dusty."

His face flushed. "Because it might kill me."

Rikki gave him the thumbs-up sign. He blew out his breath, rubbing his wrist where she had grabbed him. "What about the people who left those canisters behind? They didn't open by themselves."

Amiri rumbled, turning slowly to look behind them. Methodical, deliberate, thoughtful. Rikki stared at him. So did Eddie.

"What?" she said.

"I think I might have the answer to that question," Amiri replied.

"You hear someone?"

"No." He hesitated. "Something is rotting."

"Oh." Rikki pursed her lips, and thought about the open canisters. "*Oh*. Man."

"Exactly." Amiri raised his brow. "Both of you, stay here."

Rikki and Eddie looked at each other.

"You might need us," Eddie said.

"All for one, one for all," added Rikki.

Amiri's mouth twitched. "We are quite alone here."

"We're doing this for your protection," Rikki said, and made a shooing motion. "Go. Let's get this over with."

They took a circuitous route, and walked only a short distance before they came upon an area of rough damage—broken branches, undergrowth hacked, cold cigarettes littering the blanket of dead leaves and vines. Like Bambi's mother: *Man was in the forest,* and oh, it was time to run.

Amiri found the bodies. Four of them. Riddled with bullet holes. No blood appeared to have seeped from their eyes or ears, which provided only limited comfort, given that those parts of their bodies had already been eaten away by scavengers. Rikki was very tired of seeing dead people.

"Well," Eddie said, quite pale. "I guess that does answer my question."

Raises some more, too. Rikki kept a safe distance, peering at the decaying bodies. All four were men. Soldiers, from the look of things. Still wearing guns, practically bristling with weapons. Clothed in blood-stained olive-colored uniforms with good black boots.

"That's not natural," she said, thinking hard.

"That *is* generally the case with murder," Amiri replied, crouched with his fingers dipping delicately into the trampled undergrowth.

Rikki frowned. "What I mean is, no one ransacked their

bodies. Those are good guns. Expensive guns. And maybe the uniforms are ruined, but those boots look just-out-of-the-box, and in these conditions that's a miracle. Trust me. No gunman in this region is rich enough to *not* steal from the dead. Especially from someone you disliked enough to kill in the first place."

"She's right," Eddie said, with enough conviction—and experience—that Rikki gave him a double take. The young man blushed, and began to shove his hands deep into his jeans' pockets. He stopped and let one hand, the hand that had almost touched the powder, rest lightly against his leg. Almost as though he were afraid of doing too much with it.

Amiri brought his fingers to his nose and inhaled. "So, they were not killed for their belongings. Their murderers wanted for nothing except their deaths."

"A bit single-minded," she said, tearing her gaze from Eddie. "What *are* you doing?"

"Tracking," Amiri said.

"Huh." Rikki tilted her head, thinking of how he had found these bodies. Funny, how she had never doubted him. "You have a pretty good nose."

"Every sense is valuable," he said smoothly, and straightened to his full height. She craned her neck to look into his eyes. Wanting to say more, but unable.

Eddie stared at the dead men. "Shouldn't we bury them? It doesn't seem right to just . . . leave things the way they are."

Rikki hesitated, sharing a long look with Amiri. "We're drawing a lot of assumptions here. Maybe they didn't have anything to do with those canisters."

"Like two ships passing in the night?" He smiled tightly. "Somehow, I think not."

"Then we have to assume the worst."

Amiri tilted his head, tapping his fingers beneath his nose. His expression was troubled. "Agreed."

Eddie looked between them both. "So, what? You think they might have opened those containers? That they could be contagious? Covered in that powder?"

"Anything's a possibility at this point," Rikki said. "We don't have enough facts."

"Well," replied the young man, "I've already been exposed. At the refugee camp. From the two of you. Even maybe from that powder we found. So if those bodies *are* infected with something, how does it matter if I touch them?"

"It matters because it's not worth the risk," Rikki said sharply, thinking of how she had stayed to hide those canisters—these dead men possibly just as lethal. But bigger. Requiring hands. Proximity. "And maybe you're right. Maybe it wouldn't be a danger to bury them, but right now we're breathing and they're not. Sentiment never kept anyone alive" *And caution is better than regret,* she added silently, feeling like a coward for it. Hoping the scavengers acted fast.

Eddie gave her a hard, startled look. "Ma'am. With all due respect, just breathing isn't enough."

Rikki clamped her mouth shut. Amiri moved between them and placed his hand on the young man's shoulder, bending slightly to peer into his dark eyes. An odd sight, but only because he was so gentle; effortlessly so. Everything about him was effortless. The way he moved, his strength, his determination. His mystery. Rare, rare, man. It stole her breath away, at the oddest moments.

Like now. Bodyguard and counselor. Listening to his soft rumble as he said, "There is no shame in leaving those

men. It is not an act of desecration. You are not responsible
for their deaths."

Eddie's gaze never faltered. "Too many people are getting hurt, Amiri. Doesn't matter whether I'm responsible. I
don't want to get used to that."

Like you *have,* Rikki told herself. It wasn't entirely
true—the refugee camp had certainly rattled her—but it
was close enough to be disconcerting. She had a cold heart,
tough as rawhide, carefully nourished, watered with clinical detachment, isolation, raw science—and she had never
questioned why that might be wrong, even if it was a
single-mindedness confined only to her waking hours.

Rikki's dreams at night were another matter entirely.

She looked down at the gun still gripped heavy and
clumsy in her hand. Took a deep breath, and walked toward the dead men. She stopped halfway, staring. She did
not know them. She did not know why they had died.
Might have been for a good cause. Might have been bad.
She searched herself for even an ounce of compassion, and
managed to dredge up just enough to make her feel
ashamed of calling herself a doctor.

*"Doesn't matter whether I'm responsible. I don't want
to get used to that."*

From the mouths of babes and good young men. Rikki
knelt in the undergrowth, the thorny vines. Heat bore down
on her shoulders. Her throat was raw with thirst. Eddie and
Amiri shadowed her. She set the gun down.

Eddie knelt wordlessly and took her hand. He had hot
skin, like he was burning from the inside out.

Don't touch me, she wanted to say. *Don't touch me, I'm
dangerous.* But she thought again of those other men, at
the refugee camp, men and peacekeepers who had worn no
protection at all. Acting like they owned the place. And it

was too late, anyhow. All three of them had been breathing the same air, brushing up against each other. Touching.

She held up her other hand behind her head. Fingertips grazed her palm, twining slow and soft around her wrist. Amiri: warm, like holding sunlight.

Rikki smelled blood, the stink of dead bodies. Flies buzzed. She closed her eyes, and after some thought, said the Lord's Prayer, remembered distantly as the echo of her father's voice at the dinner table, and sitting on the edge of her bed. It was not entirely appropriate as a eulogy for the dead, for men who might not even appreciate the effort, but she had nothing else to offer. She did, however, try to find the meaning in every word that fell from her tongue, struggling to think of what her father would do—and finished, finally, with a quiet and heartfelt, "Amen."

Her companions did not say a word. Eddie kept his eyes downcast and solemn—so much like her little brother she wanted to look away and cradle her aching heart. Neither he nor Amiri let go of her hands; the young man stood and both of them pulled, lifting Rikki up to her feet, swinging her between them.

Eddie bent and picked up her gun. He offered it to her, but she shook her head and he slipped it into the back of his jeans, alongside his other weapon. Amiri, she noted, did not carry a gun.

She gave the dead a long last look, and felt the hairs on her neck prickle. Like someone was watching. She turned and saw nothing.

Amiri said, "What is it?"

"I don't know." She searched the undergrowth, which was spattered with sunlight. "Nothing, I guess."

Amiri touched her elbow and scanned the same area, eyes sharp as knives. "Come."

She did, but just as she turned away to follow him, she glimpsed a flash of green—brilliant, the fire of sunlight caught in emeralds—verdant and rich as spring.

Then, nothing. A trick of light. The forest, casting illusions.

Illusions, that for one moment, looked like eyes.

CHAPTER SEVEN

AMIRI found water on the craggy end of a buckle in the earth. It was a brackish pool that was hardly a hole in the ground, more mud than water. Rikki looked at it with unease.

"Worried?" Amiri asked, smiling faintly.

"Only because I don't have an IV of saline and a box of Imodium," she muttered.

Eddie also eyed the water like it had teeth. "I had a friend once who went camping and drank from a pond like this. He was stuck on a toilet for a week after."

Amiri crouched and dipped a finger into the stagnant pool. "And here, you forgot to bring toilet paper."

"Ouch," Rikki said.

"That's just mean," Eddie added.

A low chuckle escaped him. "Both of you, city people."

"And you?" Rikki replied, hand braced on her hip. Her face was flushed from exertion, her body sweat-soaked, but her eyes were bright and keen, and her jaw was set. So stubborn. Delightfully so.

Amiri's mouth softened into a smile. "Second nature,

Doctor Kinn. I am home, here. Home, where the wild things are."

"Ah," she said, with a bite. "And I suppose in your spare time you run around in a wolf costume, and conquer monsters with nothing but a look."

"Until they crown me king," he said, and took such pleasure in her startled expression that he almost laughed out loud. Instead, he settled for savoring her smile—a beautiful astonished smile that started small, then spread and spread until she looked at him with a child's delight, sweet and young and full of wonder. It made him breathless.

"Did I miss something?" Eddie said, glancing between them.

"Maurice Sendak," Rikki said, without looking away from Amiri. *"Where the Wild Things Are."*

"It is a children's book," Amiri added. "I have two copies."

"I have three," Rikki said. "In a box, somewhere."

"How sad," he replied. "They must be lonely."

"Oh, very."

"Must be a good book," Eddie said, looking between them. Much too thoughtfully. It made Amiri uneasy.

He rose, the cheetah stretching with him, just beneath his skin. "Both of you rest. I will go look for something we can eat."

"I'll go with you," Rikki said, surprising him. For one brief moment, he almost told her no. Instinct. Habit. He was used to being alone. He *should* be alone.

But he could not make himself say it. Not when every fiber of his heart wanted to be alone *with her.*

He glanced at Eddie, who nodded, shadows in his gaze. Trying to be strong, but haunted.

That changed when Rikki passed and chucked him on

the arm. Natural, easy, with open affection. The young man looked almost as surprised as she did, though Rikki covered it better, moving too quickly for Eddie to say a word. But he smiled at her back, all the trouble chased from his eyes, and *that,* Amiri thought, was another gift, all unto itself.

He held aside the undergrowth, guiding Rikki's passage, and when they were out of earshot, he said, "You like him."

She seemed to squirm, just a little. "Sure. But I even like you, for what it's worth."

Amiri inclined his head, not quite hiding his smile. "Eddie is young, hardly twenty. He has never been through anything like this. I worry about him."

"So why is he here? What possible experience could a kid like him have?"

"A great deal. More than he should." Amiri touched her shoulder, briefly. "It was good of you to give your respects to the dead."

Again, she looked uncomfortable. "What would you have done?"

"Truthfully?" He hesitated, casting for words. "I would have kept walking. The dead are dead. Life continues and must be preserved. Those men offered us nothing but the potential of trouble—and I owe nothing to strangers."

"Pragmatist."

"As are you, I think."

She said nothing for such a long time, Amiri feared he had misjudged her. But just before he could ask, she cleared her throat and looked down at her hands. Stared at them with such concentration he felt her mind was in some other place—and that her hands in those memories looked quite different, indeed. It made him uneasy for her.

"I am what I am," she said, enigmatically. "But it's been

a long time since I had to look into a mirror. Holding my-self up against Eddie made me wonder if I'm somehow . . . less . . . than I used to be." She tore her gaze from her hands, looked into his eyes, and for just one moment he saw something stark and vulnerable, something so quietly frightened that a shiver raced down his spine. "Do you worry about that, Amiri? Of becoming someone you never wanted to be?"

"All the time," he whispered. Soft words; soft, cutting, words. "But then I tell myself that lives ebb and lives flow, and that we are all less and more than we used to be. I prefer that to the alternative."

"Being dead." No hesitation, no question.

Amiri had to remind himself to breathe. "You understand."

"So do you." She smiled, grim. "What does that make us?"

"Dangerous," he said, without thought. "We are dangerous."

To ourselves and to each other, he finished silently, feeling his face heat. Talking to this woman was like cutting strings around his heart: too much, too fast, too soon. He was a fool. He was insane. This woman was not for him.

But then she smiled, that soft wondering smile, and he forgot that he should be wary, and he forgot that he should push her away, and all he could think was that he would be a lucky man if he could keep her by his side, even for an hour.

Rikki's stomach growled. She grimaced. "Pretend that didn't happen."

"I would, but my ears are still ringing."

She balled up her fist and he slid out of reach, taunting, beckoning her to follow. She did, eyes gleaming, and he led her on a slow merry chase, reveling in the heat of her presence, the sound of her breathing. All around them was a new world, green and lush and full of shadows, inviting the beast to run and dream. Not Kenya. Not home. But close, close, the continent beneath his feet the same as a star in the sky—the same for any eye, no matter how distant.

He followed his nose toward food, led them to a damp patch of earth where the ground was soft with decay. He pushed aside slick crumbling leaves, revealed fluted mushrooms the color of apricots. Rikki stripped down wide leaves to roll into a cone, a makeshift container, to hold them in. She ate one of the mushrooms. So did he. The taste was mild, earthy. He preferred meat.

"I would hunt," he said. "But a fire might give us away."

She chewed and swallowed. "You think they're still chasing us?"

"I am certain of it."

"The chances of anyone seeing us escape—"

"We were seen."

"Ah," she said. "Well, then."

"Yes." Amiri followed the curve of her cheek, the line of her throat. Sunlight dappled her face, bringing out the red and blonde in her short brown hair. More light yet was beneath her skin, as though she were another kind of shapeshifter, something far rarer than he. A small woman, a study in contrasts: She was delicately feminine, but radiating such raw strength in body and spirit that it was quite possible to imagine she could stop the world from turning just by the sheer force of her will alone.

He liked that about her. He liked many things about Rikki Kinn. "You live a dangerous life in Zaire. This is not a stable country, no matter your associations."

"No place is safe," Rikki replied. "I go where I'm needed."

"What inspired you to become a doctor?"

Her smile was slow, self-mocking. "Honestly? At first, only because it was a guaranteed job. Security. I didn't want to be a lawyer—I hate lawyers—but a doctor? Everyone needs a doctor, and they *help* people. That's the mission. Plus, there's money. Or at least, I thought there was."

"Somehow, you do not strike me as quite that mercenary."

"I'm not now. I've . . . matured. But my dad . . . he died when I was young, and the man who raised me after that didn't have much except heart and grit. Not that it mattered. Not until he got sick. And then . . ." Rikki stopped, shaking her head. "Markovic was a gymnastics coach. I was one of his students. We were going to go to the Olympics together. I was sixteen. We'd been preparing for years. But then he got lung cancer, and everything just . . . fell by the wayside. I started focusing more on school, on getting jobs to help pay the bills. Markovic insisted on college. He had coached the daughter of the Dean at the University of Kansas, and he used that to make sure I got in, with aid, scholarships, the whole nine yards. Just in time. He died a month after I started."

His heart ached for her. "And yet, you flourished."

"You fight or you sink. Just so happened I had a very good head for science. Don't know how or why. Chemistry was easy. Biology fun. I dug Calculus."

"And viruses?"

"Fascinating." Rikki's face relaxed into a smile. "Mysteries. Riddles. Living and nonliving, occasionally lethal, quick to evolve, almost impossible to kill. Something I fantasized becoming, when I was growing up."

An odd fantasy for a child, Amiri thought. "And now?"

Her smile turned faintly bitter. "Some dreams never really go away."

He could not argue with that, though he found it disturbed him, slightly, to hear her say it. "I suppose, here, you would have some cause to fear for your life. Most certainly, after last night."

"The rebels," she said quietly, looking away. "All that death."

"You have had dealings with them in the past?"

Her scent spiked, like a cushion of pins squeezing into his nostrils. Her gaze turned flat. "Some dealings. People have a saying now. *If you meet les forces négatives, c'est l'horoscope.* It's written in the stars."

Amiri made a small, noncommittal sound, trying to hide his distress at having upset her. "When I was young I did not believe in fate. Recent years have made me wonder."

"I don't wonder," she replied. "Fate is nothing but a coping mechanism. It doesn't mean anything."

"I would suppose it means something to those who need hope. Or explanations."

"I prefer to believe there are some things that can't be explained. That there's no good reason for having your life torn apart, just because someone else decided . . ." Rikki stopped and turned her face, but not before pure grief crumpled her features, so raw Amiri's heart twisted like a wrung cloth; wrenched, unbearable.

Your pain, mine, he thought, and had to look away, as well. "No one wants to believe in a destiny of cruelty."

"No one likes a whiner, either," she remarked, distantly. "Or a martyr."

Rikki blinked, focusing; then she burst out with a sharp bark of laugher. "What did you do? Before you decided to protect strangers for a living."

"Oh," he murmured. "It was a different life. Quieter."

"That's no answer."

He looked at her. "And do you always get what you want, Rikki Kinn?"

A faint, sad, smile crossed her face. "Not when it matters." There was no self-pity in those words, just the truth as she must see it.

Amiri captured her hand.

"Then we shall have to remedy that."

Rikki gave him a startled look. Amiri leaned close, holding her gaze—holding *her,* even as she tried to lean away from him.

"What?" she whispered, eyes large.

"I like whiners," he replied, gently. "One, anyway."

She stared. He released her hand. She did not move, or blink. Amiri could not help himself. He brushed his thumb across her lips, savoring their softness, the warm crush of pink beneath the darkness of his skin. Imagining what it would be to taste those lips.

She sucked in her breath, shuddering—with pleasure or concern, he could not tell. He did not let himself taste her scent. He drew back immediately, giving her space. Giving himself room to breathe. He thought of his father, and turned away. Started walking.

Rikki caught up with him. He forced himself not to look at her. But the silence was too much.

"You do not believe we are dying," he said. It needed to be addressed.

"You have your own doubts," she replied, and her voice was low, quiet. It was a dangerous, lovely voice.

Amiri steadied himself, studying the jungle walls, the shadows. He listened hard. "The men we encountered at the airfield were professionals. Peacekeepers or not, they knew what they were doing. They were too smart to enter the site of an outbreak without proper protection." He thought about the man with the clipboard, clicking and clicking. "When Eddie and I first arrived at the camp, we were not allowed off the plane until our biohazard suits were firmly in place, and until the attack I did not see one person who lacked that good sense. The caution, the *fear,* was too great. But those men who attacked us . . . *those men* . . . they were not afraid. Not of the disease. And that is unnatural."

"Unnatural," she echoed, untangling her ankle from a vine. "Fear is the common denominator between all people. Fear and hunger. Death."

"Love," he added gently. "Love, too."

Rikki looked away. "We could still be dying," she said. "But?"

"But those people at the refugee camp, every one of them, lost their lives within hours of each other. We have the notes to prove it, as well as the decay of the bodies. And *that* is unnatural. The transmission of a disease takes time. Some bugs are faster than others, but we're talking about a camp of a thousand. A regular outbreak would have started with just a handful falling ill. A Hot Zone of individuals. There would have been time to instill a quarantine, to warn others and put some kind of safety measure in place."

"But there was no time. Not in that camp."

"No. And no matter how virulent a disease is, that doesn't happen. Ever. It would require the infection of every single person, virtually at once."

"The water supply?"

"The water was pumped from the river, but as of last night no one downstream had become ill. They should have, if the contaminant was there." Rikki shook her head. "There were monkeys involved. They died first. That's what the notes said, what we found when we investigated the jungle near the river. Hundreds of dead primates, but only on the eastern edge of the forest. Other areas were clean."

"Someone could have eaten one of the infected monkeys. That might have started it."

"But slowly." Rikki hesitated, seeming to struggle for words. "That's what I missed, what I didn't think of until I saw all those bagged bodies on the airfield. Every one of us doctors were so caught up with the disease itself, we never stopped to think that *it might not be natural*."

Amiri thought of the canisters, of those dead soldiers. He could not tell her of the scents he had found, the numbers of men. Dull, days old; but still violent, dirty. He wiped the sweat from his eyes. "A weapon?" he suggested.

"Maybe," Rikki said. "But I'm making too many assumptions. It's not good science."

"You are following the only evidence you have. Logic does not require a test tube and microscope."

She sighed, hands tightening around the cone of mushrooms cradled against her chest, and continued to voice her thoughts aloud. "No rebel militia would destroy a UN-protected camp so thoroughly on their own. Not to mention those men in uniform were helping them. Which means they were paid, ordered. Working with someone—perhaps even someone on the inside. And if the people who ordered the destruction of that camp knew what to expect—if the disease *is* a weapon—then their actions imply the dead were no longer contagious. That whatever killed them did so fast, without danger of spreading. In other words, this is a disease with a shelf life."

"Is that possible?"

"I don't know. Anthrax isn't spread from human to human, but Ebola? Whatever this is, it scares the shit out of me."

It frightened Amiri, too. "The destruction was methodical. Dousing the bodies with gasoline in order to burn them. Destroying the plane to keep anyone from escaping to tell the story." He considered Duna, Max. "You are certain there was no media contact, no transfer of evidence to the outside world?"

"Mack and I *were* the outside world, the only people in that camp with a direct line to Atlanta. The Hot Zone was too big for media. We needed to keep the deaths secret in order to avoid panic. Or a frenzy. Journalists are hard to contain."

"And when should we know for certain whether we will take ill?"

"Tomorrow, the day after. Sooner, probably. What killed those refugees is *not* a subtle illness."

"A weapon," Amiri said again, almost to himself. "I still cannot imagine."

"Not many do. You have no idea of the value placed on live viruses. They're worth *billions* to the wrong people."

Amiri nodded. "And the woman who hunts them, who can identify them? What is *she* worth?"

Rikki flinched. "You can't be serious."

"Why not?"

"Because I have nothing to offer—not if they've already got what they're looking for. And if what killed those people in that camp is any indication, then they do. They really do."

"And yet, men were sent to kidnap you. Even last night, they would have stolen you away." Amiri stared at her. "Is there something you are not telling me?"

"No," she said, and he knew instantly that it was a lie.

Amiri waited, watching her cheeks flush an even brighter red. She was a bad liar. Even if her scent had not exposed her, everything else would have.

But he did not argue her deception. He looked away, jaw tight, hurt. Which was foolish. She did not know him. He did not know her.

Hairs curled against his neck; the air whirred softly with the chirr of insects, the flap of wings. He tasted something acrid on his tongue, faint, but alive with bitterness. Amiri turned, looking up, trying to see. The canopy was too thick.

Rikki shifted, swaying near. "What is it?"

"Smoke," he said. "I can smell it."

"The refugee camp?"

"Perhaps."

Rikki closed her eyes. "Do you think the rebels are still there?"

"You want to go back."

"People will be coming. Help."

"Help you can trust? You are a hunted woman, Rikki Kinn. Betrayed."

She hesitated. "You're saying the UN won't be able to protect me?"

"I am saying that you do not know who your friends are."

"And I'm supposed to trust you, is that it?"

His heart ached. "You want to make a difference. I understand that. You want to fight. I understand that, as well. But as long as you are alive, you are doing *something.* Those men knew your name for a reason—tried to *take* you for a reason—which means you are either a threat or a commodity. And now, a direct witness. Do you not see the value in that? The *importance?*"

"I'm not the only witness," she said quietly. Amiri opened his mouth, but whatever he was going to say died in his throat.

He turned, listening, felt bathed in heat, a cocoon of scent and sound, all under a domed shifting mask of green. He could hear every tick and whir of the world: insects buzzing, the whispers of leaves as some small animal snorted its way through the undergrowth—and the scents, the scents that were rich, lusty, wet, full of musk and loam and age; like twilight, shadows.

He could hear, too, the distant voices of men. The cracking of branches. Farther still, the scent of ash and fire and burned flesh. The world carried stories.

The cheetah inside went very still. Amiri did not. He grabbed Rikki's hand, momentarily blinded by a sea of sunlit green—the sun, the leaves; something more, like eyes, burning—and he blinked hard, shaking his head.

"Amiri," Rikki murmured.

"Men are coming," he growled, and gave her no time to ask. He pulled her close against his side, pushing them down the faint trail they had created, back to Eddie.

He was easy to find; Amiri glimpsed his white T-shirt through the trees. Down on his knees, he was drinking from the pool. His clothes clung to his lean frame. The air felt hot as a sauna, and smelled as though something had been cooking. Small plants drooped, wilting, and the water itself appeared different, too. It looked clear.

Amiri wanted to throttle him.

"What happened here?" Rikki turned, staring. Incredulous. Eddie did not answer. He looked at Amiri, face flushed.

Amiri took the wrapped mushrooms from Rikki's unresisting hands and handed them to the young man, using the close proximity to mouth one word: *Later.*

Then, "We will not be alone for long."

Eddie straightened. "Time?"

"Less than an hour."

Rikki knelt at the edge of the pool. She put her hands into the water and flinched. "Damn. It's *hot*."

Eddie stuffed a mushroom into his mouth. Amiri crouched, blocking her view of him, watching shadows gather in her gaze.

"Drink," he said. "You must."

"No," Rikki replied. "You're hiding something."

Behind him, Eddie went still. Amiri waited, searching her gaze, but she refused to budge.

Well. *He* was thirsty. He knelt low over the pool and scooped water into his mouth, drank heavily, feeling the burn of her gaze—and when he turned, finally, to look at her again, there was something wild in her eyes, as though she had caught him doing something not meant to be seen. It was an intimate glance, but instead of looking away, Rikki moved close and dipped her hands into the water.

She drank—hard, fast, like her life depended on it. Amiri imagined how the water must taste to her: clean and good and hot. When she finished, he did not look away, and she met his gaze with the same thoughtful intensity; sharp, all cheekbone and soft edges.

"Say it," she said.

"You must trust us," he replied, simply. "You must, or we cannot trust you. And all we have here is each other."

"Trust," she echoed. "I don't know you."

"It is no different for us."

"It's not the same."

"Because we are two men?"

"You can't force someone's trust."

"I know," he said heavily. "But I am asking for it."

She stared. "You're a hired gun. Why do you care?"

His hand shot out and grabbed her wrist. Rikki flinched, but all he did was place her palm on his chest. His heart thundered. Behind him, Eddie stirred, but he was hardly aware of the young man's presence. Only Rikki mattered.

"I give you my word," he whispered, with such intensity his voice broke. "You are safe with us, Rikki Kinn. You are as safe as my last breath. I promise you this."

He might have hit her. She looked as stricken as he felt. So much, he wondered if anyone had ever shown her kindness, how long it had been since she had relied on anyone.

Rely on me, he thought. *Trust me.*

"Why?" she whispered.

Amiri closed his eyes. He tried to find the words, but all that filled his mouth felt soundless and empty and hollow compared to what was boiling in his heart. He could not answer her. His reasons were too much, bigger than words. He could not fathom them.

He kissed her hand. Pressed his lips tight against her skin, pouring his answer into that one gesture—trying to give her all his desire and uncertainty—feeling like a fool with it. So much the fool, drunk on the fear and exhilaration that pounded through his blood. He could not differentiate the two. Like racing off the edge of the world, without anything to catch him. Losing his mind, losing his life. All the same.

Her scent rose—vanilla and pepper, rich and rosy and full of fire. Amiri loosened his hold on her hand, but instead of pulling away, he leaned in closer. His fingers grazed her chin, the high line of her cheek.

"Do you believe me?" he asked, hoarse.

"Yes," Rikki breathed, eyes wild. He did not stop touching her. She took a deep breath. "Are we done?"

"No, we are not." His hand dropped. The loss of contact left him cold. "Sometime soon I will ask once more why you are being hunted. I will ask if there is something you are hiding. And you will *not* lie to me. Not again."

Her face turned crimson, but she did not dissemble. "So ask me now. Get it out of the way."

A faintly bitter smile touched his mouth. "It would be better to give you time to know me first. So that when I do ask, you will trust me, and be too ashamed to lie."

He thought she almost laughed, and he held himself still as stone as she leaned in, so close her mouth brushed against his ear.

"Diabolical," she whispered. "But when you finally get around to asking me that question, expect some of my own. Like how Eddie managed to *boil a fucking pond*. Or why your eyes *glow*."

Amiri stayed frozen. Rikki pushed away and stood on unsteady legs. Watching him watch her. Gazes locked. Hiding nothing. He felt raw, cut open; the look in her eyes was little better. She held out her hand. Amiri did not need her help, but he accepted the gesture and stood. Her grip was gentle, firm, but the heat that gathered between their palms traveled to the bone.

Trust, he thought, aching. *Hypocrite. You, with your secrets. Expecting her to give you faith, when you have none for her.*

"We'll figure this out, somehow," Rikki murmured.

He thought it might be an apology—as much of one as he could expect, though he deserved nothing at all. Amiri tilted his head, and watched her with a stillness that he felt in his soul.

"Yes," he said softly. "I am afraid we will."

THEY HAD MINUTES, AT BEST, IF THEY WANTED ANY KIND OF head start. Rikki went to relieve herself and, when she was gone, Amiri turned to Eddie and raised his brow.

"You boiled a pond," he said flatly. "Was that entirely necessary?"

"Like you said," Eddie replied. "No toilet paper."

Amiri sighed, and the young man pulled the handguns from the back of his jeans. He checked the clips, replaced the weapons, and looked again at Amiri. His voice was less than a whisper. "How close are they, really?"

"Too close."

"And the plan?"

"Find the river. If we can reach a settlement, we can hire someone to pirogue us downriver to a larger town. Max needs to be warned."

"Sending help would be good, too." Eddie frowned. "Do you think we're sick?"

Regret flared, but not for himself. "I am not certain. There are inconsistencies. You know that as well as I."

"Yeah." Eddie glanced in the direction where Rikki had disappeared. "Those men who want her . . . they're not going to give up."

Amiri said nothing. Above the canopy, the high winds still blew in their favor; he smelled the lingering smoke of the fire drifting down through the leaves, as well as some bitter hint of man. He tasted Rikki's scent, as well. Covered in it; it branded his skin like an echo of fire.

It would have been easier if he disliked her. But in that, too, he was—to use the colloquial term favored by many of his friends at Dirk & Steele—utterly, miserably, screwed.

He heard Rikki coming back, and took another deep breath, steadying himself. "I will go and observe our pursuers. Provide a distraction."

Stop them entirely, he did not add. Eddie seemed to know, though, and began shaking his head just as Rikki appeared. She stared at them, and there was something dark and dangerous in her eyes.

"You try to leave and I'll bust your ass," she told him.

"You have good hearing," Amiri remarked.

"Cut the crap. You're no bait."

"But I am, as you say, a hired gun. This once, treat me as such."

Rikki flinched and looked away. Eddie stepped close. Blocked her from his sight. Face strained, flushed with more than heat.

"Go," Amiri whispered, forcing his hands to unclench. "I will travel back the way we came. If anyone is still following us, I will lead them away. It should not take more than the afternoon, but if I do not find you by evening, continue on. The river is to the west. Use the sun to guide you."

"I don't like this."

"You are strong enough."

"I'm not worried about me."

Rikki stepped around the young man. Amiri could not help himself. He moved close, bent down, and pressed his lips against her forehead. He heard her breath catch—or maybe that was his own—and he stepped back, quick. Shot Eddie a hard look. The young man's expression was inscrutable.

"Keep her safe," he said. "Remember what I told you."

Eddie said nothing. Amiri backed away. He did not look at Rikki again, though her presence burned at the periphery of his vision. He could not bear to see her eyes.

Amiri slid through the underbrush like a ghost. He heard his name called, but did not slow. He simply shifted his focus, forcing himself to concentrate on the task at hand. If he were going to do this, it had to be fast—done right.

Survival at any cost, he heard his father whisper with disturbing clarity. *Nothing else matters. Pride and honor are human constructs, meaningless. Accept them, and you accept the limitations of humanity. Become human in your heart, and you will die.*

Amiri wished he would stop hearing his father's voice. He blamed this place, blamed being on the old continent. Too close to memories. He had not heard his father inside his head for years, but this . . . this was like having him at his side, and that hurt too much.

He tore off his clothes, stashed them in the roots of an old tree, and entered the body of the cheetah. Bathed in fire, marrow and muscle melting, he molded into a shadow. Same heart, same mind. Hunter. Hunted. All around him, the scent of woman, clinging. Hot. Lush. Dangerous.

The cheetah ran. As a child, Amiri had dreamed long and hard of other lives, captured as he was by stories told to him by Wambui, his human nursemaid. His father, too, had tales, but these were morality stories laced with dire warnings against the world beyond and not quite as enjoyable as pirates and princes and men traveling through time. A shape-shifter, no doubt, could swashbuckle just as well as anyone else, even if he spent most days in the body of a cheetah.

Though Amiri was grown now, a man thirty-six years ancient, he still felt that child pulsing inside him as he ran through the jungle. Pushing him onward, filling him with a determination that was wholly pure in its focus, and sharp, so sharp. Dreams had always become his reality, and here, now, he was dreaming a way to survive.

It did not take him long to find the men: a loose squad of ten, armed with machetes and handguns, grenades, and AK-47s, dressed in lightweight olive fatigues. They smelled like smoke and death and gasoline. Their uniforms were covered in dried blood. One man had a necklace of ears hanging from his neck. Still fresh, a mixture of skin colors.

Amiri's belly scraped the ground. Invisible, he lost himself in the tangle, waiting in the underbrush, looking for opportunities. The men drank. The men ate. Some napped.

Then, with such casualness he almost missed it, one of the men pulled a photograph from his pocket. Stared hard, then passed it around. Amiri caught a clear glimpse of the picture from where he crouched and his body went stone cold.

It was Rikki. A black and white candid, a profile shot.

The photo was given to a man with a knife in his hand. He cracked a smile and made a slicing motion across the picture. Said something to the others—her name, followed by a string of words. A brief conversation ensued. One of the men patted his groin and grinned. Several men laughed. Amiri contemplated removing their tongues.

A radio crackled. The sound was crisp, clear, like a gunshot. The man who had first passed around the photo slapped his hand to a pouch at his belt and removed a small black unit that fit in the palm of his hand. He announced himself.

The voice on the other end spoke French. Amiri heard a clicking sound.

"Trouvé elle?" *You found her?*

"Non," answered the man, sharing a long look with his companions, some of whom shifted uncomfortably, even with fear.

"You have by sunset," came the swift reply, still in French, cold and sharp as nails left in a freezer full of clipboards and Rolexes and bloody pens. "I want her alive. Understood?"

"Yes, sir." The man waited for a response, but none came. Finally, with some hesitation, he slid the radio back into its pouch. Said some words in Bantu. The others nodded, but Amiri could taste the change in their scents. Fear. Anticipation. Adrenaline beginning to boil.

One of the men stretched, scratched his ribs, and ambled away from the group. Amiri followed, slinking low to the ground. He watched as the soldier found a spot out of sight from the others, tugged down his pants and squatted, plucking at the leaves around him.

Amiri came up from behind. Fast. Silent. He clamped his jaws around the man's neck, snapped his vertebrae. Crushed his windpipe. Tore out his throat.

The blood was hot. The cheetah liked the taste, but Amiri asserted control. He dragged the man deeper into the bushes, and shifted shape, just enough to regain use of his hands.

He stole a grenade. Prowled back through the brush, keeping low. Listening hard.

He pulled the pin, waited two seconds . . . and threw. No one had time to react. The explosion was horrifically loud. Monkeys screamed, hopping in the trees. Amiri shifted fully into the body of the cheetah. Smoke burned his nostrils, as did the scent of blood and viscera.

He crept into the crater left by the explosion. Five men were dead. Four were alive, but wounded. Those who lived, did so barely. Blood leaked from their ears, from blast wounds and burns. Eyes fluttered shut. There was no way to save them.

Amiri put them out of their misery. Not one had the strength to reach for a gun as he clamped his jaws over their throats and choked them to death. Clean, quick, painless. He felt some regret. His father would not have—a true cheetah, after all, did not know guilt—but human weapons were an unclean way to end a life, and none of these men had been given a fighting chance.

He kept the healthiest for last. The man was conscious, eyes open, breathing shallow. Little blood, but his body was limp. Paralyzed, perhaps.

Amiri crouched over him and shifted shape. He felt naked doing so—vulnerable—but the man would be dead soon. Amiri could only imagine the sight he made: a demon, some sorcerous apparition. He did not shift entirely into his human body, but instead kept the face of the cheetah, as much as he could.

When his vocal cords were restored, he dredged up what little French he remembered and rasped, "Why are you hunting the woman?"

The man's breath rattled. He squeezed shut his eyes, shaking his head. The scent of fear rolled off him in waves, and was so wet, so vile and purulent, Amiri wanted to gag. He wanted to run. He wanted to forget that woman who long ago had looked at him the same way, with the same scent, and called him monster. Monster.

For Rikki. For Eddie. Be the monster. Spare them the sacrifice of fighting for their lives.

Amiri repeated his question. Hard heart, hard voice. Thinking of Rikki, shaking in his arms. Those men, pointing a gun at her, talking soft as death. Eddie's old eyes. One thousand dead. He held up his clawed hand—black hooks curving wickedly from long furred fingers—and pressed them against the man's cheek.

"Tell me," Amiri whispered. "Tell me or I will make this slow."

"Paid," he mumbled, finally, coughing up blood. "We were paid to find the woman."

Amiri recalled the man with the Rolex, as well as the suited figure walking from the burning airfield. Waving at him, so casually. He remembered, too, the photographs.

"Why? Why her?"

"No. I cannot."

"Why?"

But he shook his head, terror sweating off his body. Amiri leaned in, trying to take advantage of that fear, but the man looked past him, gaze distant, and he realized that the horror he saw was not entirely for him.

"Tell me," Amiri rasped, hearing a clicking sound inside his mind as he read the man's fear.

"My family," gasped the man.

"Tell me about the woman."

"He will hurt my family."

"Why Doctor Kinn?"

But the man's eyes rolled up into his skull—he was choking, seizing up—and all Amiri felt was a deep low shame that did not weaken his resolve, but only made him hurt long and hard.

"More," he begged quietly. "Please tell me more."

But the man did not. Blood trickled from his mouth. His eyes closed. Amiri shifted back into the cheetah. The beast was ready, willing. He used his jaws, ended it quick.

He felt no satisfaction. Ten minutes, ten dead. Amiri slumped on his side, head bowed. Fur sticky. Smoke curled all around him. Some of the plants still burned, though the forest was too damp for the fire to spread. It was a smoke signal, though. More people would be coming. Amiri forced himself up, still in the body of the cheetah, and went to each of the dead men, scenting packs for food, water—searching for that radio. He found it, but the casing had shattered.

A breath of air stirred the ruff of his neck. In the dull burning silence, Amiri sensed movement, a whisper. He turned. Ready to fight.

And found an unpleasant, inexplicable, surprise.

A familiar man. Tall. Light brown skin. Brilliant green eyes. Tight black shirt and loose cargo pants. No shoes.

Time gentled nothing. Memories rose and died; soft,

spitting, brutal in their simplicity. Amiri looked at the man's hands—those monstrously strong hands—and felt them still, holding him down upon a cold steel table. Strapping him in while the doctor cut and prodded. That pitiless gaze, cool as cut stone. That body, bearing the wounds of Amiri's claws as though his flesh were made of air.

Amiri shifted, bones and muscles flowing warm into the shape of a man. No fear, no hesitation. No secrets with this man. He stood naked in the carnage, waiting and watching and staring into those unflinching green eyes.

It had been two years since he had seen this man. Not since the lab, Russia, the escape. So many memories, so many different people affected by that place. And by those who had imprisoned them there.

Now this. He could not imagine why. Why here, now.

"Rictor," Amiri said. The name tasted hard and old inside his mouth. He received no response. Not that he expected one. This creature was not made for words.

Rictor stepped sideways around a smoking corpse, and walked a slow circuitous path along the smoldering ring of the explosion; easy, graceful. He did not look once at the dead, nor did he seem to care that he moved barefoot through a bloody graveyard. His gaze remained on Amiri. "Long time," he said finally.

"Long enough." Amiri's claws threatened to push through the tips of his fingers. "You have been watching us."

"You hardly noticed."

"I was distracted."

"Yes. I saw that. Very sloppy."

Amiri tasted blood in his mouth. "Lectures?"

"I haven't done that in a hundred years," Rictor said. "No. I'm here for another reason."

"That does not provide me with the slightest comfort."

"No trust?"

"Do you?"

Rictor's smile was sour. "Only one. Me."

"And yet."

"Here I am." Rictor's eyes glowed briefly, and he glanced down at the dead. "Looking for prey and finding a hunter, instead."

Amiri's eyes narrowed. "Why *are* you here?"

"Obviously, to stare at naked men in the middle of the jungle. I have nothing better to do with my time."

"Rictor."

"Shape-shifters should really find a way to travel with clothes, you know." He ripped away a wide leafy frond from a low-lying tree and tossed it toward Amiri. "Here. Pretend it's a fig leaf. We'll go find your Eve."

Amiri batted away the leaf. "Answer my question."

"You're burning my eyes."

"Then close them."

Rictor shook his head and looked away. "Elena."

One name: all the explanation Amiri needed. Rictor's presence suddenly made sense. Mostly. "Elena asked you find me?"

His smile turned bitter, self-mocking. "She didn't need to."

Amiri regarded the man carefully. Elena was married to an agent of Dirk & Steele, and like her husband, Artur, she had . . . a gift. Her gift of healing had made her a target. All of them, even Rictor, had been held captive. Experimented upon, tortured, forced to endure impossible indignities. That was their bond. Strangers, working together to escape.

Rictor had been held the longest. Bound as a slave, compelled to obey every whim and command of his masters and mistresses, even those that hurt others. Not that such explanations made anything easier for Amiri. Rictor was a force to be reckoned with: incredibly powerful, human only in appearance—and perhaps not even that. Dangerous, unpredictable; sentimental about nothing. Except Elena.

Cold humor flashed over Rictor's face. "My kryptonite."

Amiri sighed. Smoke burned his nostrils, as did the smell of death. He wanted to leave this place. Rikki was waiting. He missed her face, her scent. Let Rictor read his mind about that, as well. He did not care.

"You should," said the man. "She's trouble. *You're* in trouble, for helping her."

"Apparently so," Amiri replied, and gestured lightly at the carnage seeping into the ground beneath him. "Are you here to help me with that trouble?" *In any way, help me. Please. For this woman.*

Rictor said nothing. Amiri nodded, not entirely surprised—not entirely without anger, either—and walked past him into the jungle. Arguments would gain him nothing. As Elena was fond of saying, *Rictor is as Rictor does,* and it was nothing more or less than that.

But Amiri glanced over his shoulder, anyway. Just in case.

Rictor was gone. Not even a scent to mark his presence. He might as well have been a ghost, some figment of the imagination. Which, in all honesty, was as good a description as any. Rictor guarded his secrets more fiercely even than Amiri.

Riddles and mysteries, he thought, and felt his muscles turn liquid, warm. He shifted into the cheetah, settling into his second skin with a relief that felt like coming home.

He did not follow the same path back to Rikki and Eddie. He wanted to—it was direct, fast—but he forced himself to circle back along the trail the soldiers had used, and then snake out from that, weaving silently through the jungle. He smelled the faint wet musk of elephants, padded through the territory markings of leopards, and just when he thought his instincts were being overly cautious, he stumbled upon the traces of men.

The footprints were hours old, and several miles from where he had found the first group. Downwind, they smelled of death, of fire and ash and blood; the scents of the dead, of the refugee camp, were cloaks of shadow. Westward bearing, as well, the men followed a parallel path to where Amiri had left Rikki and Eddie. Careful movements, with little destruction left in their wake. These men were silent. Quick. Professional.

And they were hunting.

CHAPTER EIGHT

Rɪᴋᴋɪ realized something was wrong several hours after Amiri left them. It had nothing to do with the harrowing run she and Eddie set themselves to, a flat throw-down with the jungle that left her breathless and bruised and quaking from exhaustion. Nor did it have anything to do with the fact that her nerves were rawer than a three-day-old slab of meat. No roadkill for brains, either, no matter how tired she was.

Instead, Eddie began to cough.

They were taking a brief rest, sitting on a pile of old dead leaves, sheltered and hidden by the claustrophobic clamoring undergrowth of brush and saplings and thorny vines. There was hardly room for people, and if they had been carrying anything more than the clothes on their backs, Rikki felt quite certain it would have taken a machete to make room for them both, even on the ground.

Eddie held sticks. He broke them, bent them, twisted their pliable forms into pretzels and knots. Quick hands, nimble fingers—though faint scars surrounded his thumbs and wrists. Burn marks, maybe. Small, round—like cigarettes had been put out on his body.

"You remind me of my brother," she told him, which she did not mean to say, though it slipped so easily free she did not regret the words, afterward.

Eddie smiled. "In what way?"

"Your appearance." Rikki pointed at the sticks in his hands. "The things you do."

"Keeping busy," he replied. "Where is he now?"

"Dead," Rikki said, without preamble or hesitation. No good ever came of either when saying that word.

To Eddie's credit, he made no gestures of solicitude, no sympathetic apologies. He blinked once, nodded slowly, and said, "How long did you know him?"

It was the first time anyone had ever asked that question. Rikki had to take a moment. "He was seven. I knew him seven years. I was nine when he died."

He looked at his hands, the burn marks. "And then?"

"My mother left." Rikki also looked at his hands. "Who did that to you?"

"Someone who left," Eddie replied, and gave her a faint smile. "Funny how that works."

Rikki fingered the edge of her shirt. "Yes, I know."

Eddie's smile faded. "Someone hurt you."

Her hand stilled. "What makes you say that?"

"I can tell. Takes one to know one."

She forced herself to breathe. "You're something else, kid. You should be in college, chasing girls and making fun of frat boys. What are you doing out here in the middle of nowhere?"

"Taking care of you," he said—so easily, as though it were the most natural thing in the world to care for strange women.

"I can take care of myself."

"Doesn't mean you don't need help. There's nothing wrong with that."

"Depends," Rikki said. "You're an idealist."

"Idealists are wishful thinkers," he replied, with surprising sternness. "I deal in reality. Besides, there's nothing ideal about being in trouble and not having anyone to watch your back."

"You're speaking from a point of luxury. You *have* friends."

"So do you."

"No," she said, unable to shut her mouth. "I don't have anyone like that." Except, perhaps, Bakker and Jean-Claude—but Rikki had done her best to keep them at a distance, and where were they now? Far away, and in a hospital. Bakker was hurt because of her.

Eddie's mouth settled into a crooked line. Rikki wanted to run from him, insult him, do anything but have herself laid out for him, but she stayed still, letting the young man study her.

"Well," he said finally, slowly, "Amiri and I are here now."

"Here," she echoed. She did not understand, could not interpret. His gaze said one thing—many things—but she was too practical, too afraid to accept the possibility he might actually intend something more than some naive kindness. "You're here, yes. But only because it's a job. Because you have to be. I don't appreciate it any less, but that's . . . that's not friendship."

Eddie gave her an inscrutable look, then turned away, focusing on the slender twigs in his hands. In a voice so quiet she hardly heard him, he said, "We don't trust you either, you know."

It took her off guard. Hurt her, too, though she deserved it. "I wouldn't expect you to trust me. We're strangers."

"Maybe." He did not sound convinced, which also surprised her. "But it makes things . . . difficult. You know?"

"Well . . . yes," she said slowly, not quite certain what he was getting at, but having her own sense that it was, indeed, a sticking point for all of them. Trust, it seemed, was a commodity they all valued—apparently to the point of distraction.

Eddie held out a twisty riddle of twigs: a bouquet of leaves and slips of wood. Rikki took it from him, twirling it between her fingers, and he said, "You thirsty?" The kid was all over the place.

"Yeah. You?"

He nodded and flashed her a weak smile. "I just wanted someone to complain with."

"Go for it." Rikki stretched out, closing her eyes. She tried not to think about their conversation, the isolation of it. *No friends.* She had no real friends, none that she had allowed herself—and not just in the last two years, but since her father and Markovic. Sooner or later, she always drove her acquaintances away—or lost them to death—and the absurdity of that, the tragedy, hit her hard.

You trust no one, she told herself, curling onto her side. *You're afraid of everyone.* Afraid of losing pieces of her heart. Afraid of judging wrong. Afraid of betrayal.

Afraid of being seen. Her hand rested against her stomach. Beneath the flimsy cotton shirt she could feel the ridges of deep scars that crisscrossed her ribs. She did not search out the rest; she knew where they all were. She remembered each cut that had made them.

And she was still here. Two years later. Still alive, still working, still living. Better than going back to Atlanta, where Larry had promised her a cushy spot in his office and lab. Better than running and hiding. She could do that here, in plain sight, and still pretend she was her old self.

But change always comes, she heard Markovic whisper.

Always, change. And be grateful, too . . . for when it stops, you are dead.

A person can die from too much change, she wanted to tell him, but had the old man been alive, it would have fallen on deaf ears. No whining was allowed. Eyes on the future. Adaptability, survival, determination: this was the golden triangle, the roots of a long life. Champions could not be weak. And neither could orphaned little girls.

I like whiners, Amiri's voice whispered. *One, anyway.*

Rikki heard Eddie stirring, felt a breeze against her cheek; she listened to the ghost calls of birds and tried to find peace. And for one brief moment, lost in the warm languor of the jungle twilight, she allowed herself a turn of fantasy; an escape. Stupid, impractical, but she let herself slip away, searching out the quiet, the old careful dream—of an embrace so tight, so warm, she would have no choice but to feel safe. As though a man could be home; a man she would have no need to hide from, who would turn her loneliness into some unimaginable myth.

It was a dream as ancient as her teens; romantic and droopy-eyed, conjured heroes in her mind. Knights, soldiers, scoundrels with hearts of gold sewn on their sleeves. Mysterious, enigmatic.

Eminently impractical. Rikki had gotten over those old fantasies, mostly. Bad relationships could do that.

But this time was different. Dream mixed with memory. Real arms surrounded her; warm strong arms, holding her close against a hard dark chest vibrant with heat and heartbeat and a low murmuring softness; promises of gentleness. A fantasy with a face, a scent, a voice. Eyes to stare into. Lips that pressed against her forehead, her hand.

Amiri, she thought, battling an insufferable ache. Un-

wanted feelings, which she did not understand—except that
there was something about him, the way he touched her, the
way he *looked* at her, his actions and words and even the
goddamn way he breathed, that made her feel like the tender
spot on a bruised heart. He made her feel too much, and
with nothing but a glance. He made her want to talk. He
made her want to trust.

Dangerous. Don't lose yourself. Don't let go.

Though what she had to let go of felt as much a mystery
as the one she had left behind in the refugee camp. Let go
of control? Let go of stability? She had pretended to have
both for her entire life, and it had kept her alive. But not
happy. She was not happy, had not been happy even *before*
the first attack, and the realization of that—sudden, sharp,
in her face—cut hard and deep.

No self-pity, she told herself. *You've got no time, no
place for it.*

Not when Amiri was alone, playing bait. Throwing himself to the wolves and without a complaint or hint of regret.
Whining? The man would probably sew his own lips
shut first. He was too dignified—had too much pride—for
anything else.

Beside her, Eddie made a low sound. Like he was clearing his throat. Rikki opened her eyes, thinking he was going to say something, but there was an odd expression on
his face and he swallowed like it hurt. She stared, thinking
hard. Then sat up, slowly.

"You okay?" she asked, trying to sound casual. Failing
miserably.

Eddie coughed, nodding. Smiling weakly. Like it was
nothing. Then he coughed some more. Small, at first, like
something was caught in his throat. He was fine for a

minute—long enough for Rikki to wonder if she was being overly cautious, but then his face turned red and his shoulders shook and he had to bend over. The cough that ripped from his chest made an ugly sound, closer to a gag, and it sent such fear down her spine she felt breathless.

"Lie down," she ordered, crawling to him. He shook his head, but she pressed on his shoulders and he was so overcome, trying to catch a break between those terrible shuddering coughs, he had no choice but to obey her. Rikki pressed her hand against his forehead. He was hot to the touch. Even through his T-shirt, she could feel him burning up. All that talk earlier about him being fine? Bullshit. She wanted to wring his neck.

"I don't have a fever," he muttered. "I'm warmer than other people, that's all."

"Whatever." Rikki cast around for something, anything she could use, and pulled the backpack over to her. She unzipped the bag, rummaging. Found a cell phone—useless, no reception—a white envelope filled with enough cash to be a personal ATM, and several passports bound together with a rubber band. At the bottom, a bottle of aspirin. And a photograph. Of her. Larry had taken it on her last trip to Atlanta, on the day after she cut her hair.

"You guys travel light," she said, voice strained. She tossed the photo aside and opened the aspirin bottle. She handed Eddie two. "Chew."

He did, grimacing. "Anything we need, we usually buy on the run."

"Too bad there's no mall in the middle of the Congo," Rikki snapped, and sat on her heels as he began coughing again. She thought back to the notes the doctors at the refugee camp had left behind, and the first thing she remembered was a hastily scribbled letter to a woman named Mary.

I love you. Remember that.

The letter, just like all the paperwork, was probably nothing but ash now. Mack was dead. Rikki was the only one left who had handled those notes directly.

Coughing was one of the symptoms. She remembered reading that in the notes. Coughing, raging fever, muscle weakness. Then blood. And death. The puzzle was, why now. Why him. If anyone should have been showing symptoms, it was her—or Amiri. Eddie had been in the biohazard suit far longer.

Except for exposure to the powder.

Eddie sat up, just a little wild-eyed. "Don't look at me like that. I'm fine."

"Yes," she lied. "But you need to rest."

"I don't," he protested, then stopped, whipping his head around to stare behind them into the jungle. His body shuddered, and he clapped his hand over his mouth to stifle another coughing fit. Rikki began to ask him what was wrong, but he held up his other hand and gave her a sharp look.

She listened . . . heard nothing—then realized that was part of the problem. No birds, no monkeys. Even the drone of the insects was gone. And in that silence, not so far away, she heard something snap. It was a metallic sound. Like someone was loading a gun.

Eddie shot to his feet and grabbed Rikki's hand. No hesitation. She slung the backpack over her shoulder and they ran, keeping low to the ground. The young man's hand burned with a heat she felt in her bones, searing like fire. She did not know where they were going, only that her heart pounded so hard she felt sick. Sick and terrified—and not just for herself, but for Eddie. Amiri.

It was happening again. Memory flashed: her team, her

friends, dragged from the Jeep, too stunned to fight, the sun on their faces, the thunder of the guns . . .

No, she told herself, squeezing Eddie's hand. *No.*

Rikki did not hear pursuit, but that was little comfort. Eddie's pace faltered. He began coughing again and she pulled back on his hand and forced him to rest. All around, the jungle twisted with vines and root clusters larger than her body. She saw a hollow near the base of several trees, shrouded on one side by thick vegetation. She tugged on Eddie's hand and pointed.

"Can you keep running?" she asked, knowing that if it was just herself she'd run right into the sunset and back again if it meant staying alive.

"I can keep going," he rasped, and past the youth of his face she saw once more the hard glint of those old, old eyes. Remembered the burns on his hands.

But it was too late. She heard another snap, almost on top of them, and they dove toward the hollow, scrambling into its moist darkness. It was just big enough for them both; it felt like a small cave, and the vines that curled over its entrance were thick, bruising with shadows. Eddie shoved Rikki all the way to the back, then huddled in front of her. His spine pressed against her cheek. Their breathing sounded loud, harsh. Her hands touched the guns at his waist.

Time passed. Rikki and Eddie did not move. Breathless, hot, drowning. Her scars ached, her legs began to cramp; something crawled along her neck into her hair.

Then, voices. Very quiet, hardly a whisper. Rikki stopped breathing. Eddie shuddered, stifling a cough. She placed her hand against his shoulder. Above them, clothing hissed.

And then, quite suddenly, a face peered into the hole. Asian, shaved head, eyes as cold as ice. A black vest, the edge of a gun in his gloved hand. He flashed teeth that reminded her of a shark.

"Come out," he said, softly. "Come out and play."

"No," whispered Eddie, and the man's feet exploded in flames.

It happened so fast Rikki hardly knew what to think, but the man's screams were no illusion and he danced backward, flailing. Shouts followed. Men raced into sight, brandishing guns. Not one of them had a chance to pull his trigger. Their feet caught on fire; their weapons burned red hot. They screamed and screamed, and it was the ugliest, most miraculous sight Rikki had ever seen in her life—just like that damn crocodile, only this time the distraction was too good to put the bastards out of their misery.

Eddie rolled from the hollow, taking Rikki with him. The moment they stood, gunshots rang out, bullets slamming into the ground around them. Eddie looked over his shoulder, eyes hard, and she heard an explosion, like a thousand matches striking at once. Heat rolled over her back, singeing the hairs on her neck, and she turned just in time to see a wall of flame rise ten feet high into the air, churning black smoke like a pyre in hell. Men still shouted, Eddie had out his gun, and she suddenly felt like some chick Rambo—missing a bandanna around her head and more muscles than God.

Eddie doubled over, coughing. Rikki pulled him into a stumbling run. She fell once; he yanked her up, and after that she lost herself—caught only in the desperate unbending desire to get the hell out of Dodge, fast, fast, fast. She kept expecting a bullet to slam into her body or some man to step into their path. Every branch that hit her chest reminded her of steel, every caw of some bird that old rough laughter. The sweat flowing down between her breasts felt

the same as hot blood, and her scars burned like the old
wounds were salted and open.

They did not stop until Eddie's legs finally buckled. He
went down hard, coughing and gagging, and Rikki fell with
him, too close to stop and tangle in his body. Her lungs
burned like she had been inhaling bleach, and only her
pure, stubborn, shit-stupid will to live was keeping her from
having a heart attack.

But she listened hard—or did her best—and heard no
screams, no sounds of pursuit. No gunshots.

"Oh, God," she muttered, rolling on all fours. She gagged,
puking up nothing but stomach acid, and felt Eddie touch
her back.

"We gotta keep going," he said breathlessly. "Come on.
At the rate we're going, we'll hit the river soon."

"Fabulous." She spit, wiping her mouth with the back of
her hand, and staggered into a quick walk that made her
head spin. Eddie did not seem to be faring well, either. His
cough—which she had thought could not possibly get
worse—shook his body like he was made of Jell-O, and it
was terrifying to listen to. She kept expecting to see blood
fleck his hands, and it did not pass her notice that Eddie
checked his palms each and every time.

*Six hours. According to the notes, each victim died only
six hours after symptoms began.*

She did not want to think about it. She did not want to
watch this boy die. Not when it should be her.

Or Amiri. Golden-eyed man. She wanted him to be here
more than she wanted to be safe, and that was some horrible
joke only she could play on herself. All of them, dying together. Bullets and disease. What a way to go. Down in a
blaze of glory.

Eddie was right: soon after, they found the river. They

stood on shore, staring out at the wild churning water, which was a color only slightly brighter than mud. On the other side, more jungle. No way to cross. Distances were hard to judge, but it had to be at least a mile, maybe more. Neither of them was up for a swim. Or maybe they just weren't that desperate yet.

"We need to find a boat," Eddie said.

"Amiri won't be able to find us if we do that. I won't leave him."

"I wasn't suggesting that," he replied, but he looked at her as though seeing something for the first time, and it was a quiet judgment that he passed, utterly inscrutable. It made Rikki feel odd. Like she had more to lose than just her life.

And then he started coughing, and they went to find a place to hide.

THERE WAS A FISHERMAN'S HUT A SHORT WALK DOWNRIVER, a squat structure made of sticks and mud that looked like it might wash away at the first hint of a hard rain. It was shelter, but they did not use it. Too obvious, in case anyone was still looking for them. Instead, they moved back toward the jungle, and hunkered down in the tall grass beside a stream.

Eddie plunged his entire head into the water and stayed there. Rikki watched him. Heat radiated off his skin, like he was on fire. Burning up.

It made her think hard—about a lot of things. But she did not ask. She also contemplated, briefly, the idea that he was contaminating the water supply with a possible illness, but hell, so much had happened already; if the refugee camp hadn't fouled the water with disease, one young man certainly wasn't going to.

"You know," he said, after coming up for air. "I think, maybe, I'm not feeling too well."

"Nah," Rikki said. "You're healthy as a horse. Young studs like you don't get sick."

He lay on his side, water streaming off his body. His eyes were bloodshot, gathering shadows. Only minutes ago he had looked nominally healthy, but his color was shifting from pink to scarlet, and that frightened Rikki so badly she had to kneel at the stream and drink, just so that he would not see her expression.

Eddie needs your best, Rikki told herself, and took a deep breath—sucking up every raw nerve in her body. She put the mask on her face.

But when she turned, his eyes were closed. She thought he might have fallen asleep, but he started coughing again, and rolled onto his back. Rikki knelt beside him, and after a moment's hesitation, smoothed his wet hair away from his face. She felt awkward, out of practice giving comfort to the sick. Most of the time, the people she dealt with could not be touched. Not like this.

She thought of her dad and Markovic. Amiri, with his golden eyes. "You have a girlfriend, kid?"

A faint smile touched his mouth. "I did. We're just friends now."

"Ah, the friendship deal. Not so cool, huh?"

"She has issues with guys," Eddie mumbled, shifting like his body ached. "Her father . . . was an asshole. He hurt her."

Rikki continued running her hands over his hair, trying to calculate the timing of his symptoms, the speed of escalation. "I bet you were her knight in shining armor."

He smiled again, weakly, his eyes still shut. Rikki said nothing else, letting him rest. She took his pulse, found it high and thready. His fever felt worse. Minutes ticking, his body breaking down. Faster than anything she had ever seen. This was no flu. Not some fluke.

Fuck, fuck, fuck. She wanted to scream.

Rikki lay down beside him. She tried not to think of her dead brother. Frankie. Little hands, his dark eyes. That smile.

Frankie had liked the *Transformers* cartoon. He'd enjoyed hiding her dolls and playing ball, or just poking her with sticks. Had curled in her bed at night and kept her back warm. Wiped his nose on her sleeve while they listened to their parents fight. Held her hand, telling her it would be okay when Mom and Dad used the word *divorce* and she cried.

She did not want to see Eddie die.

Rikki forced herself up and patted his stomach. "I need your shirt, kid."

Eddie did not ask, or argue. He sat up just enough for her to pull the T-shirt over his head, then slumped back down. Limp, boneless. Rikki dumped the white cotton in the stream, soaking it, then spread the cloth over his flushed body. She imagined steam, a low hiss, and ignored it all as she worked to bring his fever down.

I'm warmer than other people, she remembered him saying, and thought of fire—fire and heat and viruses. Those stubborn viruses. Biological infectious particles, evolved to survive in particular host environments. Affected by extreme temperatures. Sometimes. No one had ever experimented with exposing diseases to the internal extremes of a particular host.

"Eddie," Rikki said, rubbing his shoulder. "Eddie, I have to ask you some questions. I need to know if you can raise your body temperature without hurting yourself."

He peered at her, eyes bloodshot. It was easy to imagine blood seeping from them like tears. "Don't know what you're talking about."

Rikki frowned. "I know you started those fires."

Eddie's mouth tightened and he closed his eyes. She shook his shoulder. His skin was so hot. "Eddie, please, this is not the time for playing dumb. I don't give a shit how you do it. Question is, can you heat yourself up without frying anything vital?"

He ignored her. Rikki said, "Eddie."

"Don't ask me," he hissed, looking at her with an expression so piercing and haunted she rocked back on her heels; staring, tasting the fear in his gaze. Hard, desperate fear.

"I'm not going to hurt you," she whispered, horrified.

"You'll tell," he murmured, pressing his flushed cheek against the ground. "You're a scientist. You'll want to write a paper or something. Study us."

Us. More than one.

Amiri.

Rikki forced herself to take a deep breath. Then one more. She looked at her hands, then Eddie, and took the T-shirt off his body. She soaked it in the stream, splashing water on her own face. Brought the T-shirt back to Eddie and held it heavy and dripping over his mouth, squeezing water past his lips. He watched her as she did, and she watched him. Thinking of Frankie. Her little brother.

"Can you do it?" she said quietly. "Can you raise your temperature without hurting yourself?"

He judged her. She could see it in his eyes. Wheels were turning and turning, tasting her character. She let him, and did not blink.

"No," he finally whispered, hoarse. "I've tried."

"Okay," Rikki said, keeping calm. "We'll just have to stick with basics, then."

She began to move away, back to the stream. Eddie grabbed her hand. "You can't tell anyone."

"Tell anyone what?" she replied, sliding her other hand around him. She held him to her, comforting him in the only way she knew how. He stared, those dark eyes haunted, and Rikki tried to make him understand, tried in ways that words could not. She knew what it felt like not to trust. She knew fear.

And she also knew that if Eddie did not let go, if she did not hide her face for even a moment, he was going to see something he should not.

Rikki tugged, gently. Eddie let go, and closed his eyes. He did not look peaceful, but he did not look afraid, either. Resigned, perhaps.

Don't think too hard, she told herself, spreading the wet cotton over his flesh. She lay down beside him, trying to stay calm, and closed her eyes to shut out the sight of him.

She did not mean to sleep, but she did—dreamt fleetingly of knives and fire and men with sunlight for eyes. She woke with a bad taste in her mouth, a worse feeling in her gut, and lay very still, staring at the sky, listening. The sun had moved deep into the west, getting on into late afternoon. The wind blew softly through the tall grass, swaying it into a slow dance.

Somewhere nearby, stones crunched.

Rikki's heart shot so hard into her gut she almost puked. She inched up on her knees and peered over the grass. Just for a moment. Then she ducked down, fast.

Men stood by the river's edge. Only three, but she did

not trust her eyes. They were laden down with weapons, wore loose clothing. If they spread out, started walking upstream . . .

You are so screwed. Might as well pick your poison now and get it over with. Blaze of glory. Hoo-rah.

Eddie lay very still beside her. His breathing was shallow. Rikki pressed her fingers against his throat, and was not certain what disturbed her more—that he did not stir, or that his pulse was uneven. His skin was hot to the touch, frighteningly so, and she thought of fire and burning men. Herself, aflame. By accident, by direction. She did not know exactly what Eddie could do, but if he became delirious, lost control . . .

Stop. Right now, stop. Not when you know what it's like to be seen as broken. Don't you do that to him. Doesn't matter how strange things might be. He's still a human being.

And he was dying. She was going to die, too, but at least it was an eventuality she had prepared for. Eddie was just a kid. He had more hearts to break, more girls to play knight for. A life to live.

Rikki's eyes stung. She pressed her mouth against his ear. "Hey, kid. Can you hear me?"

His eyelids fluttered and he mumbled something incoherent. Rikki could not help herself—she kissed his forehead, smoothing back his hair. Frankie had liked it when she did that.

Stop it. He's not your brother.

But even so, Rikki could imagine Eddie filling that role and it hurt like hell. Two years spent fighting to avoid that kind of pain, and now . . . now she was being a fool all over again.

More rocks crunched. She tried to peer over the grass.

Her elbow nudged Eddie—by accident—and he took that moment to wake up. Coughing.

The sound was horrible, loud. Not so far away, she heard a shout. Eddie froze, covering his mouth, then looked down. There was blood in his palm.

He looked at her, stricken, and Rikki pushed him back, reaching beneath him with her other hand for a gun. "We've got company. I want you to stay here, out of sight. Okay?"

"No," he said, but there was no time to argue. She shoved him flat, using all her strength, and jumped to her feet in plain view of anyone who cared to be looking. And there were quite a few: men she had not seen before. Armed and staring.

Rikki ran, angling toward the river and the distant leading edge of the jungle, trying to draw the men away from Eddie. They shouted at her—one of them fired his gun into the air—but she slowed only enough to take a wild shot over her shoulder, which succeeded at nothing but making her stumble from the recoil and her frayed nerves. She caught her balance and kept running. She had to get far away, distract the men so much they wouldn't think to look for Eddie.

Stay down, she pleaded silently. *Kid, stay down.*

But it was too much to ask. She heard him shout, followed by another gunshot and a scream—and turned in time to see a glimpse of fire. But that was all. Something large rammed into her back and she went down hard, cracking her chin on the ground. Hands grabbed her waist, hauling backward, reaching over her to grab the gun still in her hand.

Just like before. Rikki went crazy. She twisted, screaming, using her elbows and legs, doing everything in her power to break free. Fingers dug into her scalp, but she rolled and scrambled backward, trying to plant her feet in the man's gut. He was big, red-faced, familiar—the man from the airfield who had called her by name. His eyebrows were thick as a moustache, creeping up his forehead like some awful wiry mat, and his breath smelled rancid, like garlic and rotting meat—with somebody's dirty crotch thrown into the mix.

His fingers crushed her gun hand. She bit back a cry and he grunted, eyes cold and angry, rearing back with his other fist, ready to slam it down into her face. Rikki steeled herself.

"Marco!" someone snapped. The man above her froze. He was breathing hard, almost shuddering with the effort not to land that blow. Rikki stared into his eyes, forcing herself to stay sharp. Ready.

"Marco," said that other voice, quieter now, smooth. "Marco, her gun."

Rikki tried not to let go, but the man dug his fingers into her nerves, and the pain was too much. He took the gun from her, and only then did he let go. She scrambled backward, breathless, trying to stand—

—and got an eyeful of nightmare. Eddie was crumpled on the ground, unconscious. A dart jutted from his shoulder. The metal reflected sunlight, making her eyes water. On either side of him stood two armed men dressed in black, big and husky with muscle, bristling with weapons. Blond. Hard eyes.

And in front of them, another man. Narrow, lean, with an angular face and short hair so pale it was almost white. He wore—of all things—a cream-colored suit and pale blue dress shirt, perfectly tailored and cut to his body. It was stained now, with sweat; his pants were covered in mud.

He turned slightly. Rikki saw a gun in his hand. Held with a delicate grip, finger on the trigger.

"Wild cat," murmured the man, staring. "Little Regina Kinn. What a pleasure."

Rikki bit down on her tongue. The man's eyes were cold, the color of old bone, and just as lifeless. Dead eyes. Same as those old prison guards who had watched her every time she went to visit her father. Like she was nothing, bait. Rikki had hated that. And she hated it now.

She pointed at Eddie. "What did you do to him?"

He seemed amused by her question. "I disabled a weapon."

"He's a *boy*."

The men behind him stirred, glancing at each other. The man in the suit smiled thinly. "I'm afraid not. Not *just* a boy."

Rikki swallowed hard. "Who are you?"

"A friend."

"Bullshit. Give me a name."

Again, that smile. "Call me Broker. Call me anything you like."

"Motherfucker," she said. "Get out of my face."

His gaze flickered. Marco slung his arm around Rikki's neck, jerking her against his chest. Her feet dangled off the ground. She began to choke. Broker moved close. He was all she could see. His eyes were cold, like ice. Not golden. Not warm.

"We will start first with you," he said.

CHAPTER NINE

E VEN before her father was sent to prison, there had been a sense in the Kinn household that things might get worse. Mother and wife gone, a child dead, money tight—the possibility of catastrophe was practically banging down the door. Not that Frank Kinn had ever let it get him down. He was a fan of Aunt Eller from *Oklahoma!* and of her one perfect sentiment: that people were about as happy as they made up their minds to be. It was something he never let Rikki forget.

Be strong. Don't give up. Don't lose your goddamn head.

But this was something that might have given even him, Mr. Pollyanna, a bit of pause.

She lay on the ground, on a clean white sheet under the failing afternoon sun. The material was soft and smelled fresh from the dryer, even though one of the blond men had shaken it loose from his pack. Eddie was nearby, on a similar sheet. He lay very still. His breathing was shallow. Blood flecked his nostrils and the corner of his mouth. The dart still jutted from his shoulder.

Broker sat beside her. No conversation. No explanations. Not even a cackle or some waggling of a sinister eyebrow.

Rikki would have preferred that. His silence felt like the grave.

Marco opened a small plastic box. Broker pulled out a pair of latex gloves. He snapped them on and flexed his fingers.

Rikki stifled panic. "What are you doing?"

"What I must." Broker looked her in the eyes. "Are you scared of needles, Doctor Kinn?"

Rikki said nothing. She glanced from him to the two blond men holding her down—and decided right then that if she ever saw another fucking bleach-bottle head of hair she was going to bite someone's face off their skull.

One of the men crouched over her shoulders. His fingers dug into her flesh, pressing down. He wore an earring, a diamond, just a pinch of a rock. The man at her feet had a tattoo of Elvis on his neck. The King was peeking out of his shirt.

"A Little Less Conversation" immediately began playing in her mind. She tried to move—managed to surprise the men—but Marco stepped in with a sharp foot to her gut, and she stopped. Mr. Earring shot the man a quick glare. Rikki tried not to wheeze.

"Marco," said Broker. "Go to Edward."

Marco did, shooting Rikki a dark look. His hands and arms were covered in white bandages. She did not like the way he stared down at Eddie. Or how he stroked the knife strapped to his thigh. He did not look exceptionally bright, but he made up for it in meanness.

"How do you know who we are?" she asked Broker, trying to keep her breathing steady as he removed a Vacutainer from the tiny plastic kit at his side. She saw several blood collection tubes embedded in foam, vacuum caps in an array of different colors—additive identifiers, for different blood work: toxicology, immunology, DNA studies.

"I make it my business to know many things," Broker replied. "Identities are one of the easier to come by."

Rikki looked again at Eddie. "He's been exposed to a disease. We all have."

"Of course."

"You're not worried about getting sick?"

Broker paused, staring at her. Then, very quietly: "Marco. Knife."

Marco knelt and unsheathed his knife. He placed the edge of the blade against the joint of Eddie's thumb. Rikki held her breath.

"I am going to draw your blood now," Broker said. "I am going to draw your blood, and you will not fight me. If you do, Marco will cut off Edward's thumb. He will cut off a finger for every time you disobey me."

"He's dying," Rikki said, numb. "What do I care?"

"Oh," breathed the man. "I think you care very much, indeed."

Hate swelled. "Leave him alone. I'm the one you want."

"Yes." Broker smiled, tying her arm. "But not the only one."

Rikki stared. He tapped out her vein and slid the needle home.

THE BLOOD DRAW WAS QUICK, RELATIVELY PAINLESS, AND utterly mysterious. Rikki did not dare ask questions, not with Marco looking so eager to slice and dice. Nor did she want to risk pushing the limits of what Broker called disobedience. His eyes were too cold.

Broker took Eddie's blood, as well. This time Rikki said, "You know what this disease is. That's why you're not afraid of getting sick."

The man raised his brow. "The boy must have breathed something. Perhaps at the canisters you found?"

Rikki almost choked. "How—"

"How nothing," he interrupted. "We've cleaned the spill. Destroyed the bodies."

"You're responsible," she whispered. "You made this thing."

"And how lovely that you did not take ill. How unfortunate, too, that this young man did." Broker sighed. "And Amiri? His health?"

Rikki said nothing. Broker smiled and finished drawing the last vial of blood. He gestured to the men. They tied her hands behind her back, bound her feet, and set her next to Eddie. The young man's breathing was slow and uneven. His face was red. Heat rolled off his skin. She tried to remember the notes, the recorded progression of the disease, but her thoughts ran up against static, the dull thump of her heartbeat.

"Hey," she whispered. "Hey, kid."

No response. Marco stood nearby, watching. Rikki met his gaze, straight and even, until the man with the earring stepped between them, seemingly by accident. He gave Rikki a look, though, and shook his head, just slightly.

A radio squawked. The tattooed blond slapped his hip and answered the call in perfect English, with a slight southern twang. A surprise; Rikki had been expecting something a bit more European, regardless of Elvis.

On the other end, words rattled in French. Rikki heard a distinctive—and familiar—clicking sound.

Broker held out his hand for the radio. "Yes?" he said, in English.

There was a brief pause. Then, from the radio: "Where are you?"

"Here and there," Broker replied. "My duties called me away."

Again, more silence. Then, "My men are not responding."

"How unfortunate."

"I think they are dead." The male voice on the radio did not seem especially heartbroken. "If we do not hurry, we will lose the woman, too. She cannot survive long in the jungle."

"No, I suppose not," Broker replied, meeting Rikki's gaze. "What would you like me to do?"

"I need replacements. Your men, this time."

Broker made his own clicking sound, with his tongue. "That is not part of our arrangement."

"The arrangement has changed." Flat, hard. "I want your men. You will give them to me."

"No." Broker's expression shifted into something so cold, Rikki found herself leaning back against Eddie's prone body for comfort, for that terrible heat.

"I will kill you," said the voice.

"And I will find your daughters," replied Broker. "I will find your wife. And I will sell them. I will give them to men who are skilled in unspeakable things. I will send you the pictures. Would you like that, Jaaved?"

"You would not dare." Rage. Shaking, terrible, rage.

"Your wife, then. Within the hour." Broker ended the connection and turned off the radio. He nodded at Marco, who pulled a massive satellite phone from one of the packs on the ground.

Rikki stared. "You're not serious."

Broker looked at her, and she suddenly wished very much that she had not spoken. "Jaaved will thank me, later. I could have chosen his daughters."

He took the phone and walked a short distance away,

Marco at his back. The man with the earring watched them go, then crouched near Rikki. He shared a quick glance with Mr. Tattoo, who grabbed water from the pack and brought it to Rikki.

"Eddie first," she said, trying to keep her voice steady. Rattled to the core by Broker's words.

The man shrugged and knelt. Placed the bottle against Eddie's lips and very gently tipped. Water went in, but most streamed down the sides of his mouth. He never stirred.

"You sons of bitches," she murmured. "He's just a kid."

"Never seen a kid do what he does," said the man, tattoo flexing. "We're all that's left. No one else can walk. All those men, and all he had to do was think hard."

He held the water bottle to her mouth. She thought about refusing, but could not see the point. As she drank, the man said, "You better watch yourself, lady."

She choked slightly. "Any other words of wisdom, Mr. Memphis Flash?"

The man blinked, then cracked a toothy smile. "Funny."

"I never make jokes about the King."

"Moochie," said the man with the earring, gaze flickering to his right. Marco was watching them. Broker still had his back turned.

"Moochie?" Rikki echoed.

"And he's Francis," said Moochie, screwing the cap back on the water bottle. "Got an opinion about that? Keep it to yourself."

"Right," she muttered, thinking hard. "You guys like working for psychopaths?"

"Good health benefits," Moochie replied dryly, and returned the water to the pack. The man named Francis said nothing at all. Behind them, Marco ambled close. He looked at Rikki, then Eddie. Studied the young man's face, bandaged fingers twitching. She thought of him at the airfield, dressed as a peacekeeper. Calling out her name. Screaming as the fire exploded around him. Obviously, not for long enough.

But these were the people in charge of the violence at the camp; she was sure of it. At least, they were part of the puzzle.

Marco brought back his foot like he was going to put a soccer shot high and deep. Rikki did not think. She threw herself over Eddie's body, caught the blow against her shoulder. It was hard and painful, but not as bad as knives. She heard a scuffling sound, men hitting each other . . . then Broker's voice, cutting through the melee.

"You told us you don't want them hurt," Francis said, breathless, somewhere above her head.

"Yes," Broker replied. "But at least he has the stomach for it."

Rikki felt cold. Fingers laced through her short hair and pulled back. Cold dead eyes stared into her face, but this time she swallowed hard and said, "You want to tell me why I'm so popular? Why you lied to that other man?"

"You know things," Broker said. "That is why Jaaved wants you."

She gritted her teeth. "And you?"

He smiled. "Because you *have* things."

She was afraid to know what that meant. Broker dragged her off Eddie's limp body. Behind him, Marco cradled a bloody nose. Moochie's knuckles were sticky red.

Broker tossed her down and looked at Francis. "Call the helicopter."

"No," Rikki found herself saying. "Why are you doing this?"

Broker ignored her. For one brief moment she entertained

the overwhelming desire to start screaming. Just because. Like some miracle would happen. Superman flying down from the sky.

But she kept her mouth clamped shut. There was no one who could help her. No one, except Amiri. And if, by some miracle, he were nearby and unhurt, she did not want him here. Not *anywhere* near here.

Francis got on the radio. Broker took the satellite phone and began dialing. Marco went with him, still holding his nose, his attention thankfully on Moochie instead of Eddie. One-track man. No imagination for multiple acts of revenge.

Rikki focused on Moochie, too. "Thanks."

But the man spit on his knuckles, rubbing them hard, and said, "Being nice isn't going to get you free."

"No," she replied. "But maybe you won't want to hurt me."

"Wanting and doing aren't the same things, lady."

"He paying you that much?"

Moochie glanced at Francis, who was eyeing them both. He finished talking into the radio and said, loudly, "ETA, ten minutes."

Broker glanced at him, covering the mouth of his phone. "The cooler and dry ice?"

"Coming," Francis said, but that was all. The edge of the jungle exploded.

Fire. Trees cracking. Black smoke billowing.

Everyone flinched, except Broker. In his eyes, an eerie light bloomed. Excitement. Anticipation. His mouth opened, just slightly, as though he wanted to taste the air, and he looked at the men. "Go."

Marco started running before he hardly had the word out of his mouth. Moochie followed, hugging an assault rifle to his chest. The grass came up to their waists.

Francis was slower. He paused by Broker. "Instructions?"

"Alive." Broker set down the satellite phone and took out his gun. He shot the device. One bullet, shattering the casing and components. Rikki wanted to kill him.

Francis stared, his expression inscrutable. Turned on his heel, walking fast. As he passed Rikki, he kicked a rock at her. It was flat. And up close, it was not really a rock. Not unless a stone suddenly had the power to transform into a very tiny pocketknife with matte black finish on the handle and blades. She looked at Broker, but he stared at the fire.

Rikki scooted forward, fingers scrabbling in the dirt. Her bindings were made of nylon cord. The knife fit nicely in her hand. It cut very well. She kept her hands behind her, and scooted backward, hard against Eddie. She curled her legs, fingers grabbing the toes of her shoes and pulling. Broker still did not look at her, but she suddenly had the terrible feeling that he knew exactly what she was doing.

And then, behind the man, the tall grass parted. Rikki met a familiar golden gaze: sunlight caught in amber, spinning heat and fire.

Then the world pulled back, and she realized that no, she wasn't seeing Amiri; she was looking at a cheetah. A big animal—too big, almost the size of a leopard—sleek and lean, muscles rolling with power. An unnatural sight. Cheetahs did not inhabit the jungles of the Zairean Congo.

The animal stared at her. Rikki stared back. Broker said, "Amiri."

She tore her gaze away to look at the blond man. He was smiling, ever so faintly, still staring at the fire. Rikki looked around for Amiri—terrified, relieved—but then Broker turned, slowly, to face the animal.

"Amiri," he said again, so softly. "Finally."

The man is crazy. Rikki began sawing at the bindings on

her ankles, no longer caring if he noticed. The cord snapped. She stood, swaying. Broker did not look at her. His entire focus was on the cheetah.

He drew his gun. Fast, his arm a blur—that gun flashed silver. The cheetah lunged, snarling. Their bodies crashed together. The weapon flew out of Broker's hand. He scrabbled to reach it.

Training took over. Rikki ran, tumbling forward in a tight roll that brought her up low and fast, almost on top of the weapon, perilously close to those flashing teeth and claws. Her fingers closed around cold steel and she did not give herself time to be afraid. She went nose to nose with that raging cheetah and slammed the weapon down, butt first, against the exposed side of Broker's head.

He was thrashing, and the first blow was glancing. She hit him again, double-handed, like holding a hammer coming down on a cockroach. The cracking sensation traveled up her arm. Broker grunted. Rikki held her breath. Slammed down the gun again—so hard she felt something squish. Broker went still.

Rikki fell back, shuddering. Her lungs could not get enough air. Her hands felt numb but she did not drop the gun. It was pointed in the wrong direction, but her fingers refused to loosen. She wondered if this was how her father felt, all those years ago.

You're in shock, she thought, again and again, as though it would cure her. She stared at Broker, at the dent in his skull and the blood seeping through his blond hair. He was dead. She could tell just from looking. She had never killed anyone before. She thought she might puke, and that surprised her. After all these years, she assumed she would have been harder, sterner, her heart made of stone. She had practiced enough murder in her mind.

The cheetah stepped lightly off the man. Rikki tore her gaze from Broker's head and looked into the animal's eyes. Golden, calm, elusive—and if she could ignore the fur, the face, if she looked only into that hot gaze . . .

Amiri, she thought.

It was insane; she knew it. But this—what had begun last night in the refugee camp—had crossed the line so far into crazy she did not know how to find her way back.

Same way you did before. The way you always do. Push on.

The cheetah did not move. Rikki stopped being frightened. She stopped caring. Her hands loosened and she placed the gun on the ground. Crawled back to Eddie. The young man was still, barely breathing, so deep in sleep it might have been a coma. His skin felt like fire to touch.

Another kind of warmth pulsed against her back; like sunlight pushing through a cloudy sky. Rikki did not turn. She held still, waiting, and when those strong dark fingers grazed her shoulder she knew who it was without looking. She closed her eyes. Forgot how to breathe and leaned into that touch. She did not understand—not why or how—but it was enough. She could suspend belief. She had done as much for Eddie.

Amiri's hand never left her shoulder as he moved around her. He was naked, long muscles rolling beneath his rich smooth skin. She was so damn glad to see him, she wanted to cry.

"He's dying," she said. Amiri smoothed back the young man's hair, his fingertips lingering on that pale cheek.

"Rictor," he murmured. Rikki frowned, wondering, but Amiri's shoulders stiffened and he stared up at the sky. She followed his gaze and heard, in the distance, an odd rough chopping sound.

"Helicopter," he said, and in one smooth movement grabbed Eddie's arms and hauled him over his shoulder. Rikki felt like she was having an out-of-body experience—floating, lost, her vision filled with stars—but she rose with him, grabbed the gun and the knife, and one of the packs.

She looked. Imagined movement on the edge of the jungle around the explosion, but no one shouted at her. No guns thundered.

"Rikki," Amiri growled. She hesitated, then turned around, frantically searching for the case holding the samples of her blood. She found it and undid the latch, upending them all. She stepped hard on the glass tubes. They shattered beneath her feet. Blood soaked the grass.

She looked up and found Amiri watching her. His gaze was raw, wild. Dangerous. Just like her heart. She saw the cheetah in his eyes.

She ran toward him. The helicopter was loud. Just as they reached the jungle's edge she glanced over her shoulder and saw the first shining edge of a black rotor. It filled her with fear, loathing; she felt again the *crack* of Broker's skull radiating up her arms; and worse, his eyes, his cold voice drilling down to her bones.

Amiri grabbed her hand. Behind them, in the clearing by the river, the helicopter began to land. Amiri shifted Eddie to a higher place on his shoulder. They did not wait to see who jumped out.

They slipped into the twilight shadows, running until all they could hear were the birds and trees, pounding hearts and roaring blood, and Rikki found herself like a ghost, lost between worlds, her only anchor the man in front of her.

A man who was not human.

CHAPTER TEN

THE grenade had been easy to carry in his mouth. Amiri had gone back, specifically for that. Found one more on the body of the first man he had killed. And then ran. Ran fast.

He was still running. Rikki was behind him now. It was getting dark. No sounds of helicopters, no voices of men. Amiri kept pushing. Taking nothing for granted.

He took them away from the river, deep into areas where the air was full with the rich scents of decay, so closed and hot it was like being inside a giant mouth—a place where the scents of men did not carry—and when he found a small clearing where the trees loomed, ancient and twisting, roots as thick as bodies angling into the earth, he stopped, and set down Eddie, and caught Rikki as she fell on her knees, gasping for breath. There was water in the pack she carried. They drank. They slept. Rikki, curled in his arms. Amiri, cradling her with his body. No words. No questions. Too tired.

Warm and safe. He had found her. He had found Eddie. They were alive. That was all that mattered.

* * *

THERE WAS A PROVERB FROM CAMEROON THAT AMIRI HAD been gifted with in years past, during a long bus ride along Nairobi's twilight roads, traveling home from a job of manual labor. His first job ever. He was tired and hungry and discouraged, a stranger in a strange land, still coping with the burden of making a life in the human city.

That night, he had found room on a hard seat beside a beautiful woman. A woman with cheekbones the color of polished obsidian; large sleepy eyes, high round breasts and smooth legs; long hair bound in ropey braids that touched his arm and smelled like musky skin and damp sheets.

Amiri remembered being twenty years old. Never having known a woman naked. Suddenly wanting *that* woman naked more than anything. His body instantly hard, cruelly indifferent to the embarrassment of knowing that everyone could observe his arousal, tall and strutting within his flimsy pants.

Now, years later, he could still see her—that sly smile—as she looked down at his groin and whispered, *"Careful. Thought breaks the heart."*

Too much thought. Not enough. Amiri had learned heartbreak well and good from that woman. Angelique Amubodem, an immigrant from Cameroon. Her body—two years after she had taken him into her bed, becoming his part-time lover—had still not, and never would be, found.

Thought breaks the heart. Words that whispered inside his head when he awakened in the night, drinking in the scent of another woman. Rikki.

She was no longer in his arms. She sat beside Eddie. Holding a water bottle to his mouth. Water dribbled past his lips. Something white and damp covered his forehead. A long sock.

Amiri sat up. Rikki smiled briefly, but it was tremulous.

She rummaged behind her in the pack and pulled out black underpants, which she tossed to him. Amiri did not want to wear the clothes of the enemy. But he looked into her face and could not protest. He rose, and dressed. Rikki did not say a word.

The night was soft and warm. Quiet as a coo. No breeze. Only movement would cause the air to stir, here. Nothing else. They were safe.

He sat down beside her. Their shoulders rubbed. He expected her to pull away. It was a test—he was testing himself, testing her. He did not know why, but he could not help himself and it terrified him, it terrified—but he did and he waited and she gave him his answer. And it was shocking.

She swayed close. Leaned into him.

Amiri held his breath. He hardly dared move. Her slow heartbeat sounded like music, some drumbeat primeval, searching out his soul. He wanted to press even closer. Mingle songs.

"Eddie," he said, hoarse. "How?"

"He got sick after you left. Went downhill, fast."

"I thought we were not contagious."

"Conjecture," she said. "But in his case, I blame the canisters. Based on something I heard back there, it sounds as though this disease is contracted through inhalation into the lungs. It's possible he breathed some of that powder we found. Unless he caught something at the refugee camp. Broker and his men certainly weren't concerned."

Amiri felt cold. "What did you say?"

Rikki hesitated. "Broker. The blond man that I . . . that you fought. That was what he called himself."

"Impossible," he murmured, but even as he said that word, he knew in his gut it was true. Broker. No one had ever found the man's body.

And those photographs he had received in Kinsangani suddenly made more sense.

Rikki turned. "Do you know him?"

Cold name, colder heart. "He is supposed to be dead, killed in Indonesia less than a year ago. He represents an organization with strong ties to organized crime."

"No surprise," she muttered. "But he also knew about the both of you. What you are."

Amiri's breath caught. Not because of Broker, but for the casual—even concerned—way she said those words. So easy, like it was nothing. He searched her gaze for fear, some cold awful horror, but Rikki looked at him, unblinking, and he saw little in her eyes but exhaustion and that same shadowed uncertainty that was a mirror of his own heart.

"And what do *you* know?" he asked, aware it was a stupid question, but unable to help himself.

"That you're both different," she said, just as carefully.

"Different," he echoed.

"Different," she said again, and raised an eyebrow. "Don't make me spell it out."

Amiri certainly would not. He tried to speak, caught himself, and cleared his throat. "You truly are not afraid?"

Rikki had to think about it for maybe ten seconds—which felt like ten hours, or ten days, or perhaps even ten lifetimes of trouble. "No, Amiri. I'm not. Unnerved, yes. Dismayed, totally. Ready to run screaming, you bet your ass. But not because of fear."

"You are handling it well," he said, feeling like a fool for such inanity. *Handling it well.* As though men shifted into animals most days of the week. Simple as American pie.

Rikki took a deep breath. "I'm a good actor."

"No," he said. "You are strong."

"Strong," she whispered. "I'm a scientist. Sensible. Rational. And I could be bullheaded and pretend that what I've seen is just . . . the product of stress. Delusion. Illusion. But I'm not that stupid. I'm not that blind."

Amiri struggled. "What will you do?"

She looked him in the eye. "What do you want me to do?"

He could not answer her. What he needed to say was too complicated; what he wanted, a matter of life and death. His life, the lives of others. His world, fragile as the truth, as one bad mistake. He had made that mistake. He had paid. He still paid.

Rikki said, "I made a promise to that boy. I promised to keep him safe. Do you think I'm a woman of my word, Amiri?"

He said nothing. She stared, then looked away, exhaling sharply. The hurt in her eyes cut him like a knife.

"Rikki," he said, but she held up her hand.

"No, I get it. I really do. You don't know me for shit. You don't trust me. Eddie said as much."

Amiri glanced at the boy, wondering just what they had talked about. "How much do you understand?"

"About you and him? Not much. Only that he can start fires with his mind. And that you . . ." She stopped, frowning. "Just what is it that you do?"

"I change my shape." His mouth felt numb. His words were hardly coherent. He could not believe he was admitting anything, but she had already seen too much. And he wanted to believe. He wanted to take that leap. Here, trust. Here, a friend.

Rikki stared, swallowing hard. "You . . . change."

"I become a cheetah," he added, trying to help her. Trying to help himself. "Only a cheetah."

"Why one animal? If you can shift your shape—"

"I do not know," he interrupted. "There are legends, myths, amongst my kind. That there was once a time when we were not constrained to one form, but free to choose as we wished. But other creatures became jealous, and so confined us, limited us. We became what we are. Shape-shifters, bound."

"There are more of you."

"There were many more, long ago. Now . . . our numbers dwindle."

Rikki closed her eyes. "And Eddie? Are there more people like him?"

"I have never met anyone like Eddie," Amiri replied, with a faint smile. "But there are others."

She leaned forward, out of his arms. Stared at him, then Eddie, whose face was red, his hair slick with sweat. Blood dotted his nostrils. He smelled sick, a bitter ugly scent, salty and filthy, acrid as old ashes. He was sleeping like the dead. A coma.

Amiri preferred to think of it as enchantment, waiting for a miracle. As long as Eddie lived, it was possible. He did not want to think of the alternative. The boy was his responsibility. His charge, to keep safe.

You cannot run faster than a bullet, Amiri heard his father whisper. *You cannot run faster than a friend, or a woman of ten thousand suns. Bring any of those into your life, and all you will find is suffering. Death.*

His father, the optimist—but speaking truth, after all. There had been bullets and friends, suffering and dying, and as for the woman . . .

She reached across his lap to touch the young man's hand. "It should be us."

"And yet," he replied, softly. Rikki's breasts grazed his

forearm. Her shoulder rubbed his chest. The urge to touch her was overwhelming, but he held himself back. Placed his hand flat against his thigh. Tried to control the response of his body, the quickening of blood in his loins. Found himself trembling with the effort.

Rikki looked at him. Her face was close, her eyes dark. "You're shaking."

"It is nothing," he said.

"You're sick," she whispered.

"No," he told her, but she twisted, rising up on her knees to press her fingertips against his cheek. Her scent rolled over him, warm as her body, and he could not help himself. He placed his hand over hers; trapping her, as gently as he could. Savoring the contact. Her skin.

Her breath caught. Amiri said nothing. He had no words, not even for himself.

You want her, taunted his father. *You want to take her. You want to mark her, make her yours. Your woman.*

His woman. Yes. He wanted that. He wanted Rikki Kinn beneath him, around him, squeezing him between her legs as he buried himself in her heat and scent. He wanted to mate—in the most primal way possible—and then make love, again and again, drowning her in pleasure. He wanted her to cry out his name. He wanted her to grow wet at the thought of him. He was not ashamed of that desire.

But what he felt went deeper than lust, and that . . . *that* was dangerous. His heart wanted her with a raw violence richer than blood, more profound than anything he had ever felt—and that was something he did not know how to reconcile. Or fight. He hardly knew her.

And as for trust . . . that was another matter entirely.

"You're so warm," Rikki said. She did not try to move

her hand. Her body was very still. Heartbeats, rocking inside her chest. Amiri's other hand crept up, sliding across her hip, around her waist. His palm fit perfectly into the lean curve of her spine, and he felt more than saw her thighs shift. Her scent changed, as well. He smelled spice, heat. Arousal.

"You think I have a fever?" he asked softly. "Am I so warm as that?"

"Burning," she murmured, and the barest hint of a smile touched her mouth, cutting him to the core. "You need a doctor."

I need you, he almost said, and the words rang so hard inside his head he had to catch himself to make certain he did not echo them out loud. For a moment, he thought he had; her expression faltered, her gaze growing uncertain, almost . . . afraid.

Demon. Monster. Angelique's voice, whispering across the years.

Everything inside him stopped. His heart froze. He let go of her hand. Stopped touching her waist. His skin felt cold; all of him, dashed with ice.

"You should rest," he said, looking down, away, at Eddie.

Rikki did not move. She did not speak. Her hand remained pressed against his face. His cheek burned beneath her palm; the only part of him still warm. He could not meet her gaze, and he waited, unable to speak.

She shifted, leaning close. Something warm touched his forehead. It took him a moment to realize it was her mouth. A kiss.

He looked up, stunned, but she was already sliding away, and he could not catch her gaze. She kept her head down as she stepped across Eddie, and he watched as she lay on the ground with the young man between them, curled on her side. She placed her hand on top of Eddie's chest, fingers splayed against it.

Dead woman, he thought. *She would be dead if my father were here.*

Like Angelique, or the handful of others who had crossed paths with the old cheetah. The price of being sloppy with secrets. Trusting those undeserving of the truth. Amiri had never had the stomach to solve his problems that way.

But he looked at Rikki, her small hand pressed so carefully on Eddie's chest, and her small kindness, that gentle comfort, were worth more than any promise.

He forced himself to lie down, and pressed his cheek against the leaves, listening to his blood, the blood of the earth, some low soft music of the night. He stared at Eddie's shoulder, willing his friend to wake. Praying silently for strength. Enough to see them through. Enough to keep himself safe from his heart.

"Amiri." Rikki peered at him over Eddie's chest. "You don't trust me."

"And you trust no one at all." He swallowed hard, closing his eyes. "Why is that, Rikki Kinn?"

She did not answer him for a long time, and when she did, her words were unexpected, chilling. "Broker took my blood."

He opened his eyes. She told him more. About Jaaved, the deception, his knowledge of the canisters and the disease. The help she had received from the mercenaries in Broker's employ.

"A double cross," Amiri mused. "What game was Broker playing?"

She said nothing. He watched her closed expression, the

way her fingers played with Eddie's shoulder. He said, "It is time for the truth, Rikki Kinn."

"The truth," she echoed.

"Tell me why these men hunt you. Tell me your value to them."

She hesitated. "If it's what I believe it is, then I'm in deeper trouble than I realized."

"Tell me," he said again, searching her eyes.

"I found something," she replied, looking away. "My entire team, not just me. Two years ago we were doing research in this region. There had been an outbreak amongst some chimpanzees, and so we went looking specifically for fruit bats in that vicinity. Trying to confirm findings that those animals were the natural reservoir for Ebola. Reports had already gone out to the media, but some of us thought it was premature." She closed her eyes, fingers going still. "So we're out there, and we're deep in the bush, and we find some bats. We run tests. Every single one of them comes up positive for the virus. Every one. Antibodies, viral genomes in certain organs. Isolation of the virus on sensitive cell lines." She took a deep breath. "That last bit was the mother lode. You can isolate the virus in living human subjects who are infected with the disease, but those samples are controlled like Fort Knox. Random, too. No way to predict when you'll get one, because outbreaks don't just happen every day. But those bats were a stable source. *Anyone* could get to them."

"Someone with an eye for making a weapon?"

"Exactly. We didn't tell anyone of our findings. We were afraid to until we knew more. The CDC, the military—people talk. They overreact. So we went back to map the area. To get a fix on just how big this thing might be. We told folks where we were going, just not why." Rikki looked down. Collecting her thoughts, he believed, until he noted a faint shudder. Amiri reached out and grabbed her hand. Rikki squeezed it, and kept on squeezing.

"We were attacked on the way there. Some rebel militia out of Kivu. There had been problems for some time, but we'd managed to avoid them. This was different. The UN convoy was running late, an hour behind us, and we were too eager. We left without them. We had some guns, but that was laughable. We were scientists, not soldiers."

"But you survived."

Something flat and empty entered her gaze. "I was the only one. The only reason I did was because that UN convoy was coming. The commander of the militia got afraid. Worried about retaliation. Thought it would be useful to have a hostage, someone to use as a bargaining chip."

Amiri controlled himself, barely. Fought for his voice. "How did you escape?"

"I almost didn't. I was close to death. One of the men we had hired to take care of us had also been running late that day. Another person we left behind. Jean-Claude. He caught up. Found us. Me. Then he went back, met the UN convoy, and they devised a rescue plan. People died saving me." Her eyes were still empty, her voice cold and soft and neutral—like reciting a shopping list, algebra, the name of a textbook. Like it was nothing.

But she began to shake again, and this time Amiri moved. He stepped over Eddie, behind Rikki, and cradled her inside his body, curling so close each shuddering breath felt like his own.

"Jaaved," he whispered. "He wants the location of that reservoir."

"Given what's happened, it's the only thing I can think of that would make me valuable. But it doesn't make sense, either. If what killed those people is part of some biological weapon, he already has what he needs."

"*Someone* has it, yes. But not necessarily him."

"So, what? Broker gave him the weapon? Sold it? And now the other guy wants to make his own?" Rikki shook her head. "We have two parties here. Unequal footing. Broker was the one in control today. Jaaved needed *him*."

"Broker was using the man."

"Not to get me. He could have snatched me off the street any time he wanted."

"He nearly did," Amiri said, thoughtfully. "In Kinsangani. He wished to make a show of it."

"Fuck that," Rikki muttered. "Why?"

Why, indeed. "Who else knows of the bats?"

She faltered. "Just one person. Larry. Not the location. Only what we discovered."

Something cold settled in his heart. "Wouldn't he have informed others?"

"He understood the dangers. We felt like the scientists who built the atomic bomb. I destroyed all the records. I filed false reports stating the area was clean. The rebels moved in soon after anyway, so we didn't have to worry about settlements becoming infected by close contact with the bats. We just . . . let the whole thing die."

"You trust Larry."

"He's the only one who knows. I'm sure of it."

That was no answer. Amiri exhaled, slowly. He thought of Max. "Larry asked us to protect you. Why would he do that?"

Rikki stiffened. "Does he know what you are?"

"No." He brushed his nose against her hair. "The agency I work for appears quite normal. It is a good cover, one that allows us an outlet to help others. To not . . . let ourselves go to waste."

"Bunch of do-gooders?"

"Oh, yes."

"It sounds crazy. All of this, insane." And then, quieter: "Broker doesn't care about the reservoir. He said I had something."

"Something in your blood."

"I have a feeling that's only part of it."

Amiri's arm tightened. "Broker is an old enemy."

"You met him before."

"No. But I have had . . . encounters . . . with his organization."

"An organization that would have an interest in people like you and Eddie? And what about me, those other doctors you said have gone missing? The refugee camp. The *disease*?"

"I do not know how the puzzle fit together," Amiri said. "Only, that Broker's interests, and those he works for—the Consortium—rest with money and power."

"And you?"

"The Consortium has a history of collecting our kind. Kidnapping us, killing us, using us. They are . . . proficient at such things."

Rikki sat up, turning. Studying his face. "They hurt you, didn't they? They took you."

He remained silent for a long time. Then, so softly he could hardly hear himself: "I was not the only one."

She squeezed his hand. "How long has it been?"

"Two years."

"Two years." She laughed, a bitter sound. "Are they part of some government? The military?"

"I would not discount the possibility of such ties, but in essence, they are a rogue corporation. Business people."

"And they find it in their best interest to keep your existence a secret?"

"To protect themselves, as well. Because they *are* us."

"I don't understand."

He sighed. "The world is far more strange than you can dream, Rikki Kinn. Monsters are afoot, every creature of legend. Hiding before your very eyes."

"And what happens when you stop hiding?" Rikki leaned close. "What happens, Amiri?"

He said nothing, but he did not need to. There were words in her face, living words breathing in her gaze, and he could hear them, already knew them by heart. She understood—the isolation, the fear—loneliness devastating as death, marching through the heart with a thunderous ache. She suffered it, too. He saw it in her eyes.

Amiri could not help himself. He touched her, his fingers gliding along the high round bones of her cheeks. She closed her eyes, leaning into his touch, and when his thumb caressed the corner of her mouth, her lips parted and the heat of her mouth washed over his skin, soft as night. Rikki barely breathed; and he could not move. He savored—so warm, so unhurried. Marveling that something so small could feel so thrilling.

He was hard for her. Hard and aching. And it frightened him.

"I am not safe," Amiri whispered, almost desperately, foolishly. "Women are not safe with me."

Rikki exhaled sharply, then smiled. "Are you sick? Grossly malformed? An *animal* in bed?"

A strangled laugh rose deep from his throat. "How can you make such a joke?"

"I have no idea," she confessed, resting her head against his shoulder. Low quiet laughter escaped her. "But it feels good."

And it did, Amiri thought. It felt too good.

HE LISTENED TO RIKKI'S BREATHING SLOW, AND WHEN HE was quite certain she slept, Amiri untangled himself and studied her face, the stretch of her pale arm and hand as it rested so carefully on Eddie's chest. She held the boy like a child, for reassurance, and the jealousy and regret that gnawed at him was shameful, indeed.

He forced himself to stand, gazing down upon Rikki's still form, and remembered from long ago an old Masai warrior, recently widowed, who had whispered in ever-so-grave tones that hearts did not meet one another like roads. Hearts fell like rain. Hearts burned in fire.

And some hearts did not find each other, ever.

Amiri walked into the darkness. He listened, but heard nothing but the buzz of insects and the distant mournful cry of some prowling leopard. Scents charged the air, none of them human. Nothing dangerous.

And nothing that felt like home. Amiri could not even see the stars. He tried, and was hit with a longing for hot dry nights and the open grassland that stretched as far as the heart could fly. For the first time in years he wanted to see his father. Just one glimpse of that old golden gaze, his grim smile tough as leather and nails.

Enough. Amiri closed his eyes. "Rictor, I know you are there."

Air whispered across his neck, this time followed by the faint scent of something rich and green, like an early spring rain—a weighty presence, which made the cheetah stir uneasily, one animal to another.

I need your help, Amiri thought, unable to say the words.

"My help," rumbled a low voice. "You want a miracle."

Amiri opened his eyes and looked into the shadows. "Eddie deserves one. He did not ask for this."

"No one asks for death. Not even the ones who think they want it."

Amiri swallowed his pride. "Help him. Please."

Rictor said nothing. Amiri's claws pushed through his fingertips, fur rising up his arms. The taste of blood still had not left him, and fury only made it sweeter. "You can save him. You can save us all. You have the power."

"I have limits. I can't interfere."

"So you say. But I have found you do what you wish when it suits you. I am certain *Elena* would agree."

"Leave her out of this."

"How can I? She is the only reason I do not call you a monster."

Something hard slammed into his gut. Amiri doubled over, caught his breath, then came up fast, claws flashing. Rictor appeared from the shadows. Caught his wrists mid-strike, holding him with a strength like mountain stone. Amiri had forgotten what that felt like.

"Good that you remember." Rictor's fingers tightened with crushing strength. "Hypocrite. Calling *me* monster."

Amiri snarled. "I never tortured anyone."

"You would have. Afterwards, you would have done anything they asked."

"Like you? Licking their boots every time they commanded you? *Little pet? Mon petit meurtrier?*"

"Do not call me those names."

"Or what? That was what we were to them. What we still are. Murderers. Animals. They are here even now, hunting us. Nothing has changed."

"You're more of an asshole," Rictor said. "Elena should have left you in that cage."

"The same could be said for you."

Rictor spat, grim-faced. "I killed the last man who went so far. Don't think I'll do any different for you."

Never, Amiri promised silently, but memories rose: the doctor, the lab, that woman who ruled them all with her black unending eyes. Too much, the thoughts were so real he could still taste the pain and humiliation of his imprisonment being shoved down his throat.

Rictor made a choking sound, and let Amiri go with a shove that sent him down on his knees. Both men stared at each other, breathing hard.

"Help him," Amiri whispered.

"And if your woman becomes sick?" Rictor asked, hoarse. "Or you? If you had to choose, who would you give a life to?"

My woman. Mine. Amiri thought of Rikki curled asleep in their camp, and his heart ached so hard he had to close his eyes to steady himself. Dangerous. He was a fool. He had to end this now before he fell too hard, too deep to run.

"Wishful thinking," Rictor whispered, with such pain it brought Amiri up short.

But he had no time to respond. Behind him a low cry filled the night, so full of terror, so heartbreakingly agonized, the cheetah burst through Amiri's knuckles, splitting skin with fur, claws cutting into his palms. Amiri did not think—he ran, tasting blood in his mouth, plowing through the tangle of jungle plants.

He found Rikki still curled beside Eddie, no guns pointed at her head, no jaws at her throat. Instead, her slender body shook with violent tremors, like her bones were trying to rattle free of her flesh. His heart died a little, looking at her—the entire world shrank to one floating spot in his swimming vision—and he fell to his knees at her side, staring, inhaling.

No scent of sickness. No fever rising off her body. Her eyes were merely closed, eyelids twitching wildly.

Just a nightmare. Amiri's relief was as painful as his grief, and he fought for breath, reaching out to touch her hand.

Rikki jerked awake, screaming. Amiri was unprepared, caught stunned, and only when her fist lashed out, slamming against his jaw, did he come back to himself. Sparks cracked behind his eyes. His head snapped back. He felt like his neck would break. Her strength was immense, uncontrollable; she moved like a caged animal, eyes open but still lost in nightmare. The scent of her fear, an all-too-familiar poison.

Amiri twisted, reaching out to haul her across his lap. "Rikki. *Rikki, wake up.*"

She stiffened in his arms, still caught in the dream—and just when he thought he would be treated to another demonstration of her strength, Rikki let out a faint sigh and sagged against his chest. Tremors wracked her body, heartbeat fluttering, wild and small. Amiri felt like a giant holding her.

He felt other things, too. A raw desire to protect her that ran so deep from his heart to the cheetah it was more than instinct: primal, in his blood, burning down, born again in fury and desire and pain. He could not have let Rikki go to save his life, and it made him realize, with a jolt of pure fear, just how entrenched his feelings truly were.

Your woman. Your mate.

Amiri closed his eyes, fighting himself. Blindsided. Drowning. Shape-shifters mated for life, and the bond went deep as the soul; inexplicable, inescapable. Once found, never lost—rare as butterflies whispering Shakespeare. His own father had never found a true mate. Never just one woman, one heart to call his own. He had fought viciously against the idea, called it weakness. Madness. And it was, Amiri realized. All of this, madness.

"Hush," he murmured shakily, pressing his lips against Rikki's short hair. "It was a dream."

"No," she breathed, and her hands clutched the front of her shirt, knuckles pressing hard against her breasts. She turned and peered up at his face; he thought he saw tears, but her gaze slid sideways, over his shoulder, and her expression shifted into alarm.

Amiri looked. Rictor stood behind him. His gaze was hooded, his mouth set in a hard flat line. Rikki began to push away; Amiri tightened his arms, holding her close.

"Rikki Kinn," he said quietly. "Meet Rictor. He is . . . an acquaintance of mine."

"An acquaintance," she echoed, sounding baffled, shaken. But she stared, and he watched her surprise slide into something sharper as she analyzed what little she could see of the man.

Rikki Kinn was no fool. She did not look happy. She did not smell relieved.

"You found us," she said, voice flat. "How?"

Rictor's mouth tilted. "No jumping for joy? No hugs and kisses for your savior?"

"You're no salvation yet—and I don't know jack shit about who you are. Answer my question."

"Magic," Rictor replied, with enough dry humor to make Rikki's frown deepen. "Something you should start getting used to."

"Rictor," Amiri said sharply. "Enough. See to Eddie."

Rictor gave him a long look. So did Rikki. Amiri ignored them both, reaching out to pat the young man's hand. His skin was hot, even more so than before—and it seemed, almost, that the air around him shimmered.

Rictor knelt beside Eddie. He began to touch him and Rikki said, "No, don't."

He ignored her. "The boy's already dead. His body just doesn't know it yet."

Rikki made a low strangled sound. Amiri swallowed hard. "You must save him, Rictor."

"And if I do? Are you willing to pay the price?"

Amiri said nothing. He had little to offer but his own life, and that was something he could not give—not unless Rictor offered to protect Rikki, as well. And he knew better than to ask.

"You're still choosing him over her," Rictor said, and studied the woman with a cold scrutiny that made her stiffen in Amiri's arms. Amiri stifled a growl, shooting the man a warning look that was completely ignored in favor of Rikki, whose scent turned hard, brittle.

"What choice?" she asked him roughly. "What are you talking about?"

"You." Rictor's mouth slanted once again into a cold smile. "Matters of the heart."

Amiri would have attempted murder, but just at that moment, Eddie's head moved; a restless jerk, followed by a twitching hand. His eyelids fluttered. Relief surged, though short-lived. Blood trickled from the young man's mouth; a small stream, then wider, thicker. His throat gurgled with an ugly wet sound that cut Amiri to the bone.

Rikki lunged, reaching for Eddie. Amiri held her back. She twisted, struggling. "Let me go. We have to turn his head or he'll choke."

Amiri said nothing, still staring. Temperatures were rising, heat washing through the air, shimmering and rolling over his prickling skin like an open roaring oven—crowding the air in his lungs until it was hard to breathe. Rikki stopped fighting him.

Eddie began to twitch. Violent, restless, eyes still closed. Another nightmare. Death, idling.

"He's losing control," Rictor snapped. "Go, now!"

Amiri was already on his feet, Rikki in his arms, but it was too late. The world collapsed into a shower of sparks, foliage crisping golden and hot with veins of fire—the air itself etched with webs of heat and light—nowhere to run, no place to go. Eddie cried out behind them, a hard wordless yell of utter misery, and flames exploded from the ground as though they stood on the surface of the sun. Rikki screamed. Amiri felt a flash of pain.

And then Rictor was there, his arms around Rikki, his fingers digging hard into Amiri's shoulders. The air became a vacuum; fire and smoke curling against an invisible shell, which turned green as sun-washed emeralds, pulsing with the same hard light that Amiri found in Rictor's eyes; burning, unforgiving, cold as the air that soothed the pain radiating from the soles of his feet. Blood roared. Rikki shouted. Rictor closed his eyes, and Amiri stared into the maelstrom, searching for Eddie.

Then, nothing. Fire, light, all of it gone. Amiri found himself trapped inside a void, senses stuffed, and the only thing he could feel was Rikki in his arms, trembling. His knees buckled; he almost dropped her, and the both of them sank to the ground. Limp, boneless, sagging against each other. He hugged her close, pressing his lips into her hair. She buried her face in his neck.

Amiri's sight returned slowly. The world was so quiet he would have thought himself deaf had it not been for the sound of Rikki's harsh breathing. Smoke curled through the air, burning his nostrils and eyes. Nothing but thick snowy ash remained of their scant belongings and the surrounding jungle. No vines, no trees, no guns. The fire had cut an incinerating swath, spreading outward in a circle at least several hundred feet wide.

And in the middle of it, Eddie. His clothes were in burnt tatters, but his skin was pink and unharmed. Rictor knelt beside him. Amiri stared, unable to speak, too afraid to know. Rikki twisted, following his gaze.

"Eddie," she said, hoarse.

"He's still alive," said Rictor. "Barely. He has minutes, at most."

Rikki broke free, scrambling across the charred smoking ground to Eddie's side. She touched his face, smoothing back his hair with a tenderness that broke Amiri's heart.

"I'll pay the price if you can help him," she said, tearing her gaze from Eddie to look at Rictor. Amiri was too shocked to protest. Rictor also appeared surprised. Both men stared, and her eyes sharpened. "Don't play dumb. Don't you dare. Not after what I've seen and heard."

"You're putting too much faith in a stranger," Rictor replied. "Not your style, Doctor."

Rikki's eyes narrowed. "I'll give you whatever you want. But that's assuming you have a cure, a way to get Eddie out of here. And if you do, then you're *shit*. Shit to let that boy die. Shit to let all those others—all of *us*—lose our lives from this disease."

"Careful," he said. "Keep talking like that and I might just begin to like you."

She gave him the finger. A grim smile touched Rictor's mouth, and he looked down at Eddie. Spread his hand over the young man's chest.

"This will cost," he said, but so quietly it was almost an afterthought.

"I will pay," Amiri said, moving close to Rikki's side.

Rictor shot him a hard look. "No. *You* won't."

He and Eddie vanished.

CHAPTER ELEVEN

LARGE fires tended to draw the eye at night: Amiri and Rikki did not wait to see who would find them. They did not talk. Just started walking, and after a time—given that she could not see in the darkness and kept falling on her face—Amiri picked her up in his arms and began to run.

Rikki could count on four fingers the number of men who had ever hauled her around like a sack of potatoes, and Amiri had the dubious distinction of being the fifth. There was an art to it. Smooth gait, strong arms, an almost uncanny ability to keep various body parts from slamming into anything hard. Her father had been quite good.

Amiri was better. He cradled her against his chest, folding her so close and tight she could have been curled in the fetal position on some hard vertical bed. His strength was immense. Being held by him felt safer than a cocoon made out of woven steel—like nothing could touch her. Nothing bad, ever.

And oh, the irony. Glowing eyes. Men who might be cheetahs, who vanished and who lit fires with their minds. Incredible, impossible; she was sensible, a scientist. Surely that meant something.

Or not. It was too weird. Hairless cat, weird. UFO, weird.
The kind of weird that showed up in the *National Enquirer,*
or those late night television documentaries her dad had
loved, the ones about singing crystals and possessed nuns
and the elusive tracks of some howling Tibetan Yeti. Oh,
her dad would think this was great. He'd be all over Amiri
like . . . like . . .

She couldn't finish the thought. It hurt too much.

The sky began to lighten. Rikki could not guess how
long they had been traveling. Amiri found an old elephant
trail—pounded earth, decades old, following a circuitous
path deeper and farther into the rich heart of the wild and
the green. It led them to a stream, and there, finally, he set
her down. He did not look tired, but she thought he must
be. His body seemed to soak in the early rays of morning
sunlight, and he stretched and stretched. Nearly naked.

She looked away, face red. She could ignore his body at
night—no light to see—but it was different now. And she
liked looking at him far too much.

The edge of the water was crowded with vines and shining leaves, the soft muddy shore trampled with fine small
hoof prints the size of her thumb. Rikki crouched, scooping
water into her mouth. It made her think of Eddie. She could
still see his face in her mind, bloody and slack-jawed; like
Frankie, like Frankie, like Frankie in the car with the glass
all over his body and her mother screaming, screaming,
screaming.

"Will he live?" Her voice was low, hoarse. The first
words she had spoken in hours.

Amiri took a moment. "If Rictor says he can make the
boy well, then he can. And he will."

"You trust him."

"No. But I trust the woman who does."

Rikki tasted something rather unpleasant at the mention of another woman—a woman who Amiri trusted. She wondered what it took to gain that trust. And what it would mean to be his friend, to have him care, truly, from the heart.

"Your friend Rictor—"

He shook his head, cutting her off. "Not a friend."

"Okay." She hesitated, considering. "So how does he do what he does?" *Vanishing, healing, stopping a goddamn inferno . . .*

"Rictor is not human," Amiri said. Like it was the most natural thing in the world. And to him, perhaps it was.

"He looks human," Rikki said. But then, she had met quite a few people in her life who wore their humanity as nothing but a veneer. Being human and having humanity were two different things—biology and a state of mind. Heart and soul.

Amiri shrugged. "There is a reason I did not want your colleague to draw my blood."

Mack. She had hardly thought of him, had not really grieved. "How do you know your blood is different? Have you done tests?"

"Tests were done on me," he said flatly. "I overheard the discussion of my results."

"Ah," she breathed, and then, with some hesitation: "Will you tell me what they said?"

He blinked once, and the mask slid into place—that cool neutrality, painful to see because it reminded Rikki so much of herself. "It meant little to me. Only, that there were recognizable differences in my DNA. Acute variations. Something even a rudimentary expert in genetics would recognize."

"Huh." Rikki bit her bottom lip. Thinking hard.

Amiri arched an eyebrow. "You would like to study me."

"Not at your expense. But I would also be lying if I didn't admit to some curiosity."

"Curiosity killed the cat," he replied, eyes glittering. "And science is a cold art."

"Science saves lives," she reminded him.

He stared a moment longer, tension radiating from his body, then took a deep breath, fingers flexing. "I am sorry. I forget you are not them."

That stung. "Thanks a lot."

He gave her a sharp look. "You have no idea what I endured."

Rikki felt the insane urge to tear off her shirt and show him just what it was she thought he had endured. God only knew it could not be worse. But she kept her hands clenched. Looked him straight in the eyes. "You went through something terrible. You think about it every day. Little things remind you. Even sleep isn't safe because you have nightmares. So yeah, I get that. I understand. But what happened to you is not my fault. Don't blame me, or all of humanity, for what you went through. I did *not* hurt you."

"But it is in you," he whispered. "The danger."

Anger stirred. "It's in everyone. Or haven't you figured that out yet?"

Amiri closed his eyes. "You could not possibly understand."

"Of course not," she breathed. "Because there's no way at all I would know what it's like to be kidnapped and humiliated, or tortured within an inch of my life. No way at all I would know what it feels like to be treated worse than an animal."

Amiri stared, and his expression was awful, naked, a

bitter thing to taste. He leaned toward her, and she held up her hand, staving him off. Scrambling backward in her haste to get away.

"Never mind," she rasped, and got to her feet. Started walking. Her eyes stung. She did not know why. He had meant nothing. He was afraid. Same as her.

Rikki heard footsteps. She walked faster, then found herself bursting into a hard run. Heard pursuit, but did not look back. It was all she could do to keep her footing, to see past the tears clouding her vision. Her heart ached so badly she thought it would burst.

A thorny vine snagged her ankle. She started to go down. Never hit the ground. Hands grabbed her waist. She glimpsed dark skin and green leaves and a gasp of sky—right before she landed hard on a long lean body that grunted and slid beneath her.

Rikki tried to roll away, but Amiri's arms tightened. She gave up without a fight. Too exhausted, sagging limp and tangled against his body. Tears leaked from her eyes. She could not stop crying, could not even think of the last time she had been this weepy. She did not want Amiri to see her. Begged herself every which way to suck it up and stay strong.

But he moved, rolling them on their sides, and he was big and warm and his hands touched her cheeks, his thumbs smoothing her skin, and his lips pressed once, twice, against her eyelids. He whispered, "Are you hurt?" and Rikki shook her head, hating herself, hating him. But hungry for his touch. Still hungry for his kindness.

"You don't know me," she finally managed to tell him, her voice raw. "You don't have a right to tell me who I am."

"And you have never done the same?" he prodded gently,

though his own voice was hoarse, broken. "You have never been judge and jury?"

"All the time," Rikki said.

"So," Amiri murmured.

"Yeah." Her tears began to dry, but her nose was disgusting. She tried to wipe at it, but his hands were still in the way, brushing tears from her cheeks. "I'm not who you think I am."

Amiri tilted up her chin, forcing her to look at him. His face swam into focus, his skin rich and dark, his features fine as a knife's edge. His eyes glowed, like amber soaked in sunlight, and the way he looked at her was just as warm and soft and sad.

"You and I," he rumbled, and then, quieter: "I am too wary. I look for problems, upsets. I anticipate. It is the only way I know how to keep myself safe."

"Yes," she said. "I know how you feel."

Amiri drew in a slow deep breath, and pressed his mouth against her ear. The brief contact made her shiver, but his voice, low and smooth, did far more, washing away the worst of the hurt as he murmured, "Forgive me. Please."

Rikki closed her eyes. "Forgive you? For what? Being honest? Protecting yourself?"

"I was foolish."

"You were afraid."

He hesitated. "Yes."

"Because I'm not like you." She took a deep breath. "You think I'll hurt you because I'm human."

"It is not that simple."

"Of course not."

Amiri remained silent, staring. There was a hush in the

way he held himself that made her think he was more on edge than she; as though one wrong move, one word, one glance, would hurt him so far down she would never find him again. The idea hurt. She had thought she knew what misery felt like, but this was something else—and God, she was a fool.

Amiri reached out, very slowly, and caressed the corner of her eye. And then, even more carefully, he leaned closer. Rubbed his cheek against her cheek. Pressed his lips once more to her ear.

"I am sorry," he said again, so quietly. "I am sorry to have caused you pain."

"You're sorry," she said. "But you still don't trust me."

Amiri went very still, his lips lingering against her ear. "And does it matter to you, whom I trust?"

Rikki said nothing. Amiri's hand slid behind her back, and this time when his mouth touched her ear, it felt like a kiss.

"Tell me," he whispered.

"Yes," she breathed. "It matters."

"Ah," he sighed. "Then I will trust you, Rikki Kinn. I will give you my trust. And you . . ."

"Yes." She turned her head, just slightly, enough to look into his eyes. "Yes, Amiri. I'll do the same."

She had little choice but to say those words—her heart gave her no alternative—and she watched in tense silence as Amiri stared, his gaze brutal, without a mask to hide his hunger and loneliness, so naked and raw it stole her breath away. No one had ever looked at her with such eyes, with so much desire, and it marked her as deeply as the scars on her body, as deep as her memories of Markovic and her father. One look, the same as a knife. One look, as strong as love.

Rikki kissed him: light, gentle, a mere brushing of her lips across his mouth. Amiri did not react, remaining so still that for a moment she felt shot with uncertainty, shame. But just as she was about to pull away, Amiri's hand shot from her cheek to the back of her head and he dragged her close.

His kiss was fire. Slow and hard, grinding her so close to the edge of pleasure she almost came apart in his arms. Warmth poured through her body, pure sunlight in her bones, and when Amiri finally broke off the kiss it was all she could do to breathe again, to see past the stars dancing in her eyes. Senses, strumming on a razor's edge.

Amiri's breathing was ragged. She swallowed hard. Focusing on the pleasure still aching between her legs. She could hardly speak. "Is it always like that with you?"

He shook his head, not even attempting a smile. "Never."

"Well," she breathed. Amiri untangled himself and rolled to his feet. He pulled Rikki with him and they stood together in the dappled morning sunlight, covered in dirt and leaves. Her hands were lost in his loose grip; just glimpses of pale skin caught in long fingers the color of rich earth; buttery, smooth, glimmering with a hint of gold. He was a beautiful man.

Amiri gave her an uncertain look. "We should go."

Rikki tried to smile, but it felt shaky. "Death and destruction on our heels."

"And more to come."

"You shining optimist."

"I will leave that to you, *mpenzi*." Amiri kissed her hand. "You, who truly do shine."

Her smile steadied. "You'll be quoting poetry next."

"If you like." He turned to look down the path, and then back at her, his mouth quirking. "This makes it easier, you know."

"Easier?"

"When I tell you the wind has shifted, and that I smell people. You will not think I am crazy."

"Just a bragger," she said. "Do you really smell anyone nearby?"

"Old scents. But it means we may be close to some kind of village."

"Finally." Rikki let out her breath, slowly. "What are we going to do, Amiri?"

"One thing at a time." He tugged her into a swift walk. "We do not know what we will find."

And that, she thought, was far too true for comfort.

TWO HOURS LATER THEY STUMBLED UPON A WIDE STREAM filled with naked women. Rikki no longer had the ability to consider that even remotely odd.

She and Amiri lay on their stomachs. Stones and branches pressed uncomfortably into her skin. Insects crawled over her arms, and the air was hot as an oven. No breeze, not at ground level, surrounded by walls of thick vegetation. Her stomach hurt and her throat was dry. She would have knocked out her two front teeth for a pizza and beer.

Below, at the bottom of the tumbling hill, the women splashed in a winding stream cut with gentle turns of white water. Some of them held babies. Several washed clothes. She heard gentle chatter, some giggles.

"Well," said Rikki. "Do you think they're dangerous?"

He looked, caught her smile, and shook his head. "Only if you believe we have stumbled upon the last living tribe of Amazons."

Rikki's smile widened. "Anything's possible."

He grunted. "And if we are contagious?"

"Oh, the irony of you bringing that up." She pressed her

cheek on her arm, thinking hard. "I don't believe we are. Despite Eddie."

"We still have not become ill."

"That, and too many people have been throwing themselves in our faces, unprotected."

"Unless they have a vaccine."

Wonderful thought. Rikki chewed her bottom lip—and caught Amiri watching, raw hunger in his eyes. Unabashed, naked. Heat thrilled.

Below, the women continued to splash in the water, laughing. Rikki imagined Amiri in that water, him taking her hard on some flat sun-warmed rock, and the flash-fantasy was enough to make her mouth dry, her lower extremities throb.

She cleared her throat. "Our only alternative is to keep on walking."

"We need help. We have no time for anything else."

"Agreed. I just wish I knew why this was happening."

His mouth tightened. "It is a game. There is no *why*. No reason. It means nothing."

"Except that people are dying."

"It still means nothing. Life is cheap, to some."

Rikki touched him, lay her fingers on his arm. Squeezed once. "Tough guy," she said. "We don't have to go down there. You could leave me somewhere. Run ahead, find a different way back to civilization. You'd be faster alone."

He gave her a dark look. "Unacceptable."

"I thought you were a pragmatist."

Amiri reached out and touched her chin. "I am the man who promised to protect you. I would rather lose my skin than be pragmatic with you. Anyone but you."

His touch, his voice: like a velvet chain, supple and binding. Rikki slowly exhaled. Amiri's eyes glowed, warm as the sun. "I will take care of you, Rikki Kinn. I will keep you safe. And someday, when we are far and away from this place, I will tell you of all the foolish, awful things I have done. And you will either shake your head at my stupidity, or be unable to look at me for shame. But we will be alive. We will be alive, and so will others."

"Cheerleader," she said, breathless. "Pollyanna."

"Indeed," he replied, and kissed her mouth. He started gentle, but she held on and he dug in deeper, kissing her as though it were the last time he would ever have the chance. It felt so good that for the first time in years she wanted to be naked. She wanted to sink her body onto his. He was resting on his stomach, but she knew he was hard. She could feel his arousal in his kiss, in the jump of his muscles as her hand trailed down his back, sliding into the crease of his ass. Rikki nipped his bottom lip.

And then he was on top of her. No warning. His body sinking between her thighs. She felt a moment of panic, but quashed it. Amiri was not trying to hurt her. He was not trying to take off her clothes. But he was pressed so tight against her they might as well have been naked. The hospital scrubs were flimsy, already torn. His erection rubbed hard between her legs and it made her so hot she found herself—despite all her caution—reaching to tug the elastic past her hips. He caught her hand, stopping her, but when her fingers made a detour from the edge of her pants to his underwear, he shook like a thunderstorm. His eyes glowed like fire.

"We must not," he hissed. "It is not safe."

"It never is," she whispered, but she had a feeling he meant something else, something more than mere discovery, and she did not care. She had spent her whole life living on the edge of disaster—her whole life pretending not to—and she was done, done pretending. She wanted this. She wanted him. The danger meant nothing.

Rikki stroked him, encouraging Amiri to move against her. He did, with a look of such agonized hunger on his face that for a moment she almost wondered if he were right, if he had his reasons, but then his hand slid down the front of her pants to touch her and pleasure rocked her so hard she arched off the ground, breath hissing. Amiri slid down her body, tugging her pants with him. His hands began to trail up her stomach toward her ribs. She grabbed his wrists, pushing away. Giving him a warning look.

He blinked, obviously surprised, but said nothing. His hands moved down again, spreading apart her legs. She was naked to him and she did not care. She was naked and she was not afraid. She was naked and there were strangers at the bottom of the hill, and she would not give a rat's ass if they saw her. All she wanted was his touch.

He gave it to her. She covered her mouth, trying not to cry out, but the pleasure was deep and hard and his tongue was firm where it should be firm, hot and wet and supple, while his fingers stroked and ebbed and sank, pressing and tightening, tearing her apart with desire. She forgot pain. She forgot everything. Writhing, shaking, building around that blinding breaking touch.

A strangled gasp escaped her that Amiri covered with his mouth, moving fast to kiss her, one hand still caressing between her thighs. She shuddered, tightening her legs around his hand, twisting with pleasure. He kissed her so deeply she almost came a second time—fingers digging into his shoulders like claws.

He was still hard. Rikki caught his erection, her grip featherlight, holding him against her damp inner thigh. Amiri trembled, his gaze hot, wild. Glowing.

"Careful," he rasped. "I have nothing to protect us."

"Then you better be quick," she muttered, hoarse. "Because I want you in me now."

He made a low, strangled sound, and began moving against her thigh. That was not good enough for Rikki. She pushed at him, and he rolled onto his back. She sank between his legs and covered him with her mouth. Her heart thundered so hard she could hardly see straight, and Amiri's harsh breathing was so desperate she wanted to make him scream. But in the back of her mind she could still hear those women bathing, and she wrapped her tongue around his head, sucking fast, fingers sliding up his shaft, and set a rhythm that sent him bucking deeper into her mouth, that made her body ache all over again to feel him inside her, pumping and thrusting, and when he came there was just enough warning to move her head, which was good because he jerked so hard she might have choked on him.

Her ears rang. Rikki collapsed on his chest. Sweat-soaked. Delirious. Like an anchor had been torn off her shoulders. She felt so light she could fly. Crazy, crazy, girl. She could not believe this. What the hell was she doing—what the *hell*—

"Wow," she breathed.

Beneath her, Amiri said, "Oh."

Oh. Not exactly the enthusiastic response she had been expecting. Rather less enthusiastic than any man had a right to be. So *unenthusiastic* that Rikki thought she might just have to rip his balls off.

She raised her head, staring. But Amiri was looking in another direction entirely.

Rikki heard a sharp cracking sound. A real knuckle-crunching flex of hard metal. She twisted, blinking hard. A row of women stood behind her. Dripping. Half-naked. Looking rather unhappy.

And carrying enough firepower to blast her ass back to the United States.

"Damn," Rikki muttered. "They really are Amazons."

CHAPTER TWELVE

THE village had no name, but it was nestled in the thick of the jungle, surrounded by deep groves of banana trees and plantains, small fields of sugar cane, and long plots of potatoes. This was farmland hacked into existence with machetes and strong backs. Bush meat smoked over open fires, and the homes were simple and small, made of mud and sticks, with wide flat leaves as thatching for the roofs.

Some children fetched water from a pump, while others kicked a dusty red ball in need of air. Several of the older boys and girls held worn books in their laps. They sat in the shade, concentrating on the pages like the world rested on their shoulders. Amiri felt a deep melancholy, seeing them. He remembered his students, and wanted to go to those children. Peer over their shoulders.

Everyone stared when Amiri and Rikki were led into the village. He saw no men, only boys in their teens. There were no elderly, though several of the women had gray in their hair, despite the smooth youth of their faces. They watched Amiri with haunted eyes, and for the first time in his life he felt like a monster simply for being a man. Carrying the sins of his gender.

Rikki stayed close. Her scent was carved into his body, deep as blood and bone. His skin tingled. He could taste her still on his lips. Feel her mouth, her kiss. Shot down, crippled, mind lost and wild—he did not know whether to be ecstatic or ashamed. Years of struggle, fighting his instincts, lust . . . and in one moment he had lost himself. He had wanted her and so had taken her.

And she had taken him. Taken him as surely as death would. He was hers now. Even the cheetah could not resist.

Some of the women from the stream—those with children—split off as they entered the heart of the village. The rest, still armed, guided Amiri and Rikki to the edge of the potato field. Another woman met them there. She carried a hoe, and wore a white blouse and yellow-checkered wrap around her lean waist. A gold cross glittered against her throat, and her skin was so dark it was almost blue. Her lips were full, her nose straight and broad. Hair shorn to the scalp. Gaze sharp as a knifepoint.

She rattled something off to the women—listened to their responses—then fixed her gaze once again on Amiri. She leaned close to examine his eyes, a furrow forming in her brow. He did not like the way her expression faltered, ever so slightly.

She spoke to him in Bantu, then Lingalese.

"I speak only French, English, or Swahili," he replied, and repeated himself in all those languages.

The woman frowned, and looked at Rikki. Studied her, then examined once again their held hands. Her scowl deepened.

"Excuse me," Rikki began, but the woman jammed her hoe into the ground and fixed her with a distrusting look.

"Who are you, and what are you doing here?" she asked in heavily accented English. Her voice was as cutting as her gaze, and Rikki's spine straightened, a stubborn light kicking into her eyes.

"We were attacked," she lied stiffly. "Near the river, several days ago. We ran, and got lost."

"Lost." The woman sucked in her cheek, chewing thoughtfully, and again examined Amiri. "You are her guide?"

She said it with some disdain, and Amiri raised his chin. "I am her protector."

She raked her gaze over his nearly naked body. "You must not be very good, to have had all your clothes and weapons stolen. Or were you too busy fucking to notice they had gone missing?"

Amiri did not take the bait. Rikki gave the woman a dirty look. "We need a phone or radio, if you have one. Otherwise, we'll leave."

"There is no phone here. Close, but not here." She tapped the handle of her hoe, still thoughtful. "You . . . your clothing. I worked in a hospital once. Are you a doctor?"

Rikki almost lied; Amiri could taste it in her hesitation. But they were obvious enough as it was, if someone came looking for them, and he was unsurprised when she said, "Yes, I am."

"And are you skilled?"

"That depends on what you need."

"What I need is competence."

"Then you'll get it," Rikki said in a hard voice.

The woman grunted, eyeing her. "A white doctor and her bodyguard, appearing from the jungle without supplies, or clothing. Escaping from an attack. I do not think I like the sound of that."

"So, we will go," Amiri said. "And you will not be troubled any further."

"Unlikely," replied the women, and said a sharp word in Bantu.

Guns lowered. Amiri did not feel much safer. The woman handed her hoe to a young girl, who carried it into the field. No one spoke. Everyone watched. He felt like he was back in Russia, sitting in the cage. All those eyes, as claustrophobic as bars and walls.

Rikki squeezed his hand. The woman said, "I am Mireille."

She led them a short distance away to a small collection of tents that had been erected on the edge of the banana grove. Made of tarps and canvas, some were adorned with small belongings; others, devoid of any decoration. Hastily built. It was eerily reminiscent of the refugee camp he and Rikki had left behind.

Seated in the shade, and on cots, were more than twenty hollow-cheeked women and children; quiet, listless, eyes dull. No energy to care for themselves, or even react to the appearance of two strangers. Compared to the bustle, the brief bursts of laughter from the rest of the camp, it felt like a death zone.

Indeed, up close a foul scent filled the air; rotten, wet, like a body had perished in some dark hole and was slowly decomposing. The women, he realized. Several were quite ill, indeed.

"What happened to them?" asked Rikki, though she looked as though she already knew.

"They were raped." Mireille gazed steadily at Amiri, as if he had been the one to inquire. "Almost all the women in this place have been degraded, often and repeatedly. Some still suffer severe internal injuries."

Rikki knelt in the dust, eyeing a little boy sitting some

distance away, his clothing ragged, his arms clutched around a brown sewn ball. "Do you have any medical supplies?"

"Some."

Rikki gave her a sharp look. "You'll have to be more specific."

"You can see for yourself, Doctor."

"My name is Rikki." She turned back to the look at the boy, her gaze drifting over the tents. "You organized this?"

"Someone had to."

"Where did you get the supplies?"

"Donations."

Rikki frowned. "And these people? How long have they been here?"

"Long enough."

"Where did they come from?"

Mireille remained silent.

Amiri said, "This camp is completely isolated. There are no roads. How did they find you?"

"People find what they need most, when they need it," she replied cagily, and then said, "You. What are you good for, beside fucking women and losing guns?"

Amiri set his jaw. "I used to be a schoolteacher. Or if you need meat, I can hunt. Take your pick. But I would like to know the location of that phone."

Rikki and Mireille stared at him.

"The phone," he said. "Where is it?"

"A teacher," Mireille said, ignoring him. "What are your subjects?"

"Literature, mathematics, history." He glanced at Rikki, and found her staring at him with a faint, somewhat amazed, smile. "I taught for seven years."

"And now you play with guns," said Mireille, and there

was a trace of sadness in her eyes that was at odds with the sharpness of her mouth. "These are bad days for men."

"The days have always been bad," Amiri replied. "It is what we make of them that matters."

The woman grunted. "Come with me. I will show you the children. They could use a proper lesson. Normalcy."

Amiri hesitated. "It has been days since the doctor had a proper meal. Do you have any food to spare?"

"All I need is water," Rikki said. "And some help if you want any progress made with these people."

Mireille nodded sharply. "I will find you extra hands. As for the rest, there is bottled water in the central tent, along with the medical supplies. You will find some food there, as well."

"Bottled water," Amiri said dryly. "Evian, perchance?"

Smart-ass, Rikki mouthed, over Mireille's shoulder.

The woman frowned. "Take it or drink from the pump at the center of the village."

Amiri inclined his head. "Later. First the phone."

"That will take time. There is a man with a phone, but he does not live here. I must send someone for him."

"How long will that take?"

"Hours, at the very least." She raised her eyebrow. "Time enough for the children."

If you are telling the truth, she might have added. Amiri was quite willing to prove his worth.

"Take this little fellow with you," Rikki said, holding out her hand to the boy holding the ball. Silver flashed around his neck: a whistle, hanging from a cord covered in American flags. Rikki looked troubled when she saw it, but she said nothing as the boy took her hand, gripping his toy in the other like it was a lifeline.

Rikki gave him to Amiri. He thought he must seem a

monster to one so small; dangerous, intimidating, unsettling. But the boy did not turn away, and after a moment, Amiri picked him up. He looked like he needed to be held.

"Your name?" he rumbled in French, noting scratches on the boy's face, the red rims of his haunted eyes. His scent was odd, almost metallic. Like he had been riding in a machine for some time.

"Kimbareta," said the boy. "Kimbareta Adoula."

"That is a good strong name, Kimbareta. I am Amiri."

"Amiri," echoed the boy, in a soft voice.

Rikki watched them. Her expression was peculiar, inexplicable. Soft. It made his throat full, seeing her look at him like that. Made him ache and feel so full of emotion he thought every breath, every word he spoke for the rest of his life would be full of his heart.

His father had been a fool. And maybe Amiri was, too, but he would take this way over the alternative, any day. No matter the danger.

Amiri leaned in and brushed his lips across Rikki's cheek. Her smile was soft, almost shy, and it made him warm like a lazy splash of sunlight on some golden summer day. Rikki was not a shy woman. This was a smile for him alone.

There were words he wanted to say. Strong words. Powerful declarations. But he held them tight, wore them in his eyes. Rikki looked deep, searching his gaze. Nodded, just once.

Amiri left with Mireille and Kimbareta, to go and teach the children.

HE WAS A KILLER, NATURAL-BORN, HAD BEEN RAISED TO AC-cept the price of blood. Not for murder, or pleasure, but survival. His father had been interested in little else, only strength, canniness, taking care. Amiri had failed him in all those things.

But his life had been his own. His path, marked by nothing but his own sweat and ingenuity. And he had loved. He had loved his choices.

Teaching felt like coming home again. It was the first time in years. Holding a book to a child. Feeling the child inside him bloom and swell. Even if he had never taught the alphabet with armed women breathing down his neck.

There were ten in his impromptu class. Varying ages, but all of them were clean, moderately well dressed. They had books. A veritable library, surprisingly new—with letters in both English and French. A diversity of choices, some quite advanced, though nothing the children could not easily handle. Someone had been working with them.

The boys and girls also presented him, with some pride, with pens and clean paper, rulers, calculators, new boxes of crayons—a treasure trove of school supplies so fresh and new they could have come straight from the aisle of an American grocery store. Amiri raised a pen to his nose and drew in the scent of cardboard and untouched plastic. New, indeed. It had hardly been unpacked from the box.

"Who gave these to you?" Amiri asked the children, in French. It was the end of their second lesson, the third hour. Mathematics. Kimbareta leaned against his leg, still tracing numbers in the dirt with a stick. His other hand held the hem of the dark green wrap tied around Amiri's waist. Mireille had practically thrown it at him, with orders to cover himself up.

Amiri still held up the pen. One little girl, her hair pulled away from her face in neat narrow braids, reached out and took it from him.

"The *mondele*," she said, twirling the pen in her fingers. "They always brings gifts."

"*Mondele*," echoed Amiri. "What does that mean?"

Even Kimbareta looked at him like he was an idiot. The girl rolled her eyes. "The white man."

"And the man with the golden eyes," said the boy, pointing. "Eyes like yours."

"*Unnatural* eyes," Mireille said, speaking over Amiri's shoulder. Her approach had been no secret. Neither were his questions. He turned, meeting her gaze. Letting her see his eyes.

"Golden like mine?" he asked, as something hard squirmed in his gut.

Mireille's mouth tightened. "I think you have taught the children enough for today. They can learn the rest on their own."

"They are gifted," Amiri said, tearing his gaze from her to look at the boys and girls. They beamed at him, shuffling their feet. "All of you, quite brilliant."

"Doctors and lawyers," Mireille said, with the first real kindness he had seen since meeting her. It did not last, though. Her face hardened, and she clapped her hands. Children scattered. All except Kimbareta, whom Amiri hefted up into his arms. The child squirmed slightly, reaching down for his ball, left alongside the numbers written in the dust.

Amiri picked it up. Handed it to the boy, who held it high. The sewn hide came quite close to the shape-shifter's nose and he caught an unusual scent. Like monkeys. Blood.

Again, something cold settled in his gut. Amiri steadied his breathing and began walking back to the tents, scanning the jungle border, which loomed impenetrable: the fields, with those long straight lines and soft soil, which he realized now had been plowed with machines; and the women, all the women, armed with guns. Watching the jungle as he did. Watching him, as well.

Mireille kept pace. She was the only unarmed woman he had seen in this place. He said, "You have foreign aid?"

"One or twice a month," she said, with some stiffness, fingering the cross at her throat. "They come with the *mondele,* their employers. They bring us supplies, protection, more refugees. And sometimes, they take women. For immigration to Europe and North America."

"They tell you this?" Amiri could see Rikki in the distance, bent over a prone figure resting on a cot. She seemed to be administering a shot. "Have they told you why they are helping?"

"Goodwill," she replied carefully. "They have interests in this region."

"Interests," he muttered, and picked up his pace. He was almost running when he reached Rikki, and when she turned and saw him the raw relief that filled her face rocked him hard.

He walked straight to her, ignoring the eyes scrutinizing him, the whispers, the child in his arms. He walked a straight line, unfaltering, and Rikki held her head high, watching him like a queen.

He walked to her and he kissed her. Hard, full on the mouth. She leaned into him, her hands crawling up his ribs, and he felt somewhat delirious, like he was running through fire, on the edge of death, on the verge of the profound. The cheetah rumbled.

Rikki broke off first, blinking hard. Breathless. Amiri's heart pounded so violently he could hardly hear himself as he murmured, "We must leave this place. Now."

She did not look surprised, which told him something. A strained smile touched her lips—a grimace—and she looked down at Kimbareta. Touched the whistle around his neck.

"Sweetie," she said, in French. "Who gave you that?"

"Doctor," said the boy. "For my friend."

"A doctor." Rikki exhaled slowly, like something was hurting inside her.

"Does that mean something to you?" Amiri murmured, conscious of Mireille listening.

She sucked in breath, eyes hard, distant. "Nickel-plated, brand new, shining like a mirror. Attached to a shoestring covered in the old Red, White, and Blue? Yeah, that means something. There was a box of them on a doctor's desk back at the camp. Never seen so many whistles." Rikki turned toward Mireille. "And your medicines. I found coolers full of antibiotics, antimalarial drugs, antiretroviral treatments for HIV . . . not to mention enough brand-new over-the-counter medication to kill a horse. You can't get that here. Even the Red Cross jumps through hoops for some of what I found."

Mireille's jaw tightened. "I will not deny help when offered."

The back of Amiri's neck prickled. "Who offered? Who brought these new refugees to your camp?"

"Ask them yourself," she said coldly.

"I did," Rikki snapped. "They don't remember how they arrived, but they sure as hell recall the camp they were dragged from. People started getting sick there. Men arrived. Foreigners. UN peacekeepers. They grabbed a handful of women and children, and put them in trucks. Administered shots. Next thing they knew, they had been relocated here."

"Were they sick at the time?" Amiri asked.

"Not from the disease. They were the only ones standing at that point. Easy to find."

"What are you talking about?" Mireille asked sharply. "What is this?"

"Don't play dumb," Rikki replied, cheeks flushed. "This place isn't just any refugee camp or hidden fucking village."

"It is a holding ground," Amiri finished, feeling Kimbareta twitch. "The men who help you are not doing so out of goodwill. They are using you."

Mireille's gaze darkened, filling with a sharp weariness that was old and drawn. "Who are you? Why are you here?"

Rikki stared. "I told you. We were ambushed."

"No," she snapped. "Who sent you?"

Amiri set his jaw. "No one."

Mireille's raised her chin. "You lie."

"So do you," Rikki said. "You knew where these people were from. You knew everything. You just didn't give a damn."

The woman shot her a scathing look. Amiri heard movement behind them. Turned, just enough to see the guns pointed at his head. Kimbareta's eyes widened. Rikki said, "Shit."

Mireille took the child. The boy resisted her, but Amiri made him go. Rikki moved close. He grabbed her hand, spinning slowly. Five guns. No escape. Everyone was staring.

"I will go and find that phone," Mireille said. "And *then* we will see."

And then we will fight, thought Amiri, squeezing Rikki's hand. *And you will die.*

CHAPTER THIRTEEN

THERE was a scalpel in her pants, hidden in the folded-down waist of her scrubs. She could feel the cold metal through the cloth. The blade was very sharp. Rikki had put it there while rummaging through the medical supplies. No one had seen her. Mireille had left a guard, a woman with a gun, but Rikki used her to administer some aspirin and that was that. She had quick hands. A bad feeling. Which was now paying off.

Two of the armed women led Rikki and Amiri to a small mud structure in the center of camp. Not a high-security outfit, but difficult to escape, nonetheless. Too much activity: children playing all around, women preparing meals, the main water pump right across from the door, not to mention guards. Four, that she counted, surrounding the hut. Mireille took no chances.

The hut had only one room and no windows. No furniture, not even a bucket for a toilet. She sat down on the brushed dirt floor, chin on her knees, thinking. Amiri did not join her. He paced, movements aggressive, so tightly coiled she half-expected him to start kicking a hole through the wall.

"What are we going to do?" Rikki asked him.

"I do not know," he replied tersely. "Escape. Gain control over the phone she mentioned."

She stood and grabbed his hands. He pulled away from her. "No. I will not go back to that place. I will not let them hurt you."

"We'll escape." Rikki was proud her voice did not waver. She felt light-headed, but a few quick breaths worked wonders to clear her mind; razor sharp, steady as a rock. Amiri, however, seemed to lose yet more of his composure. He began pacing again. Hands clenched into fists, loosening and squeezing; quick, violent.

And then he stopped, directly in front of her. Looming over her body with lethal grace, leaving her breathless and overwhelmed with nothing but his presence, which burned into her skin like fire.

"How did you cope when you were taken?" Amiri asked, voice flat, dull. "How did you control your fear?"

Rikki did not know how to answer. No one had ever asked. "Moment by moment, I suppose. Each breath, every heartbeat. I didn't think about the future or the past, just the present. Surviving, staying sane, one second after another."

He nodded, almost to himself. "I was tortured. It was not just experiments. Not only blood tests. They wanted to break me. And in a way, they did. Afterward, I gave up my earlier life. I could not rebuild it. I let fear rule me." He gave her a piercing look. "But you . . . you did not. Why is that?"

Again, she felt taken aback. "There was never a choice. I had no home, no family. If I had run, I would have been finished. I would never have owned my life. And I was . . . I was all I had."

"So you kept it. You fought for it." Amiri gave her a faint smile. "I think I envy you, Rikki Kinn."

"You could still have it back, if that's what you want."

"No," he murmured. "I came to Nairobi with nothing. No friends, not two pennies, hardly an idea of what it meant to live amongst humans. My head was full of stories, and I was too young to know better. But I survived. I made a life. And now . . . now I have another."

"Also built from scratch."

"With friends. This time, friends."

"You know how to keep your friends. You don't push them away."

"Friends who are meant to be do not allow themselves to be pushed. They stick, because they must."

"Shape-shifter wisdom?"

"Experience."

"What about family?"

His expression turned impossibly grave. "I never knew my mother. I never knew her name or where she lived. Only that she was human. My father used her to bear a child, nothing more. When I was born he stole me away and had me raised on the teats of a wild cheetah who had lost her cubs. I did not meet another human until I was three."

Rikki stared. "Those are the best parts?"

"Essentials," he replied, with a faintly bitter smile. "I have never lived an ordinary life."

No, she supposed not. "Why did your father keep you in such isolation?"

"Shape-shifter children start changing their shapes at a young age. It happens naturally, without thought. But it makes us vulnerable to discovery. Imagine a human baby sprouting fur in the middle of an airplane or restaurant." Amiri shook his head. "Isolation is safer."

"Or having a child with someone you trust."

Again, bitterness flooded his face. "My father, as you say,

was a pragmatist. Far more than either of us. He did not believe in trust. Nor did he see the point in taking the time to learn the worthiness of a mate before convincing her to bear his child. I suppose I cannot fault him entirely. It was how he was raised, as well. Those who run as cheetah are so few, it has not been safe to mate with others of our particular kind for several generations."

It was like listening to the dry recitation of a nature special on PBS, only far more alien. "Do shape-shifters . . . only run as cheetahs?"

"No. There are other kinds. Clans, if you will. Crows, leopards, dolphins, more and more that I cannot name. And other creatures that are even farther from humanity than we are."

"You could have children with them, couldn't you?"

Amiri hesitated. "With some, perhaps. But shape-shifters who are of different breeds . . . to take each other as mates . . . that is forbidden. The children would not be . . . normal."

"What do you mean by that? Why normal with humans, but not with other kinds of shape-shifters?"

He shrugged, almost helplessly. "It is taboo."

"In other words, stop asking?"

He smiled faintly. "What else would you like to know?"

"Do *you* want children?"

She watched him freeze, staring, and her heart ached so deep she had to force herself to breathe.

"Forget it," she said. "I didn't mean—"

"Yes," he replied firmly. "Yes, I would. But I never thought—"

Amiri stopped, looking past her at the curtained flap—the makeshift door. Rikki heard a scuffing sound, and then the material was pushed aside by Mireille. She held a pistol in one hand. In the other, rope.

"Fuck that," Rikki said immediately. "I'm not getting tied up again."

The woman tossed the rope at her feet. "Do it or I will kill you."

"No," Amiri told her. "No, you will not."

Mireille's eyes narrowed. Her finger rubbed the trigger. Safety off. "Orders, from you? Just who *do* you work for? A newspaper? Or with the United Nations?"

Now Amiri was calm, steady as a rock. "Who do *you* work for? Who pays for this? Who keeps you safe?"

Mireille's eyes flickered. "You talk like you know so much, but to ask these questions . . ."

"Questions *you* should ask," Rikki said.

Mireille's mouth tightened. So did her trigger finger. "I have. I know who I work for."

"Do you really?" Amiri asked, far too softly. "Do you know everything?"

She made a disgusted sound. "I am not the police. I receive what I need to keep my people safe, and that is all I care about. I do not want to know the rest. Details are irrelevant."

Rikki wanted to strangle her. "If the men helping you are who we think they are, none of you are safe."

Mireille made a hissing noise, pure fury flickering across her face. "What do you know of safety? All of us here have been tortured, thrown away by men and our country. We cannot work, because we might be raped. We cannot farm, because we might be raped. We cannot send our children to *school,* because we might never see them again. You could never understand that kind of fear. Never.

But here—*here*—we are armed and fed. And if I have to cut out my soul and bury it, I will do so if it means we stay alive."

Rikki said nothing. She understood. Had their roles been different, she might have done the same. But that was neither here nor now, and it was *her* ass on the line—hers and Amiri's. Which, as far as she was concerned, made Mireille fair game.

Amiri shifted, body coiled tight. "We have all been damaged. But what you do—"

"Survival." Voice rising, high-pitched. "Survival for all of us here. And if you threaten that, I *will* kill you."

Amiri's mouth snapped shut, body rolling with tension. But in his eyes, Rikki found compassion, boundless, something so soft she could only marvel that Mireille must be blind. Blind not to see that he understood.

Mireille gaze flickered to Rikki. "Take off your clothing."

She went cold. "Like hell."

"Do it now."

"No fucking way."

Amiri stepped in front of Rikki. Mireille's mouth flattened into a hard line. "Well-meaning fools are more dangerous than bullets. I have seen men and women die for talking freely around the wrong people. And I do not trust the circumstances that brought you both here. I want to make certain you are not carrying a recording device."

"I'm a doctor, not a plant."

"I believe you are a doctor," agreed the woman, "but I have not kept the others alive this long through carelessness. Take off your clothes."

Her scars. She felt the hidden scalpel press against her stomach. Mireille was not close enough for her to grab the gun. She wondered if she could move faster than a trigger finger.

Markovic trained you to leap over small buildings in a single bound.

Yeah. Nothing faster than a motivated gymnast. But this . . . if Mireille got off a shot and it went wild . . . if Amiri got in the way . . .

If Amiri saw her scars . . .

She looked at him, battling herself. "I don't want you to see this."

He regarded her steadily. As if Mireille did not stand there with a gun pointed at their heads. As if they had all the time in the world, just the two of them. As if he knew exactly what she was hiding.

"Do you still give me your trust?" he asked, softly. She had been expecting an offer of closed eyes, a turned back. Not that question. But she answered him, because she had to, because she could not lie, not about that.

"Yes," she said. "I trust you."

The very faintest of smiles touched his mouth. "And am I not your friend, Rikki Kinn?"

"My best," she whispered. Cut to the core by the truth of those words, how easy it felt to say them. Insidious, natural, like breathing.

Which only terrified her more. Because if not now, then never.

Rikki took off her shirt. Quick. Before she could change her mind. Halfway through she heard a hiss—but by the time the cotton touched her chin there was nothing left but stunned silence.

No one said a word. No one breathed. She could not look at them. So she gazed down, at her body. She had seen it enough times not to flinch. To be distant, even calculating. Every scar memorized. Every cut remembered. She was a doctor. She had practice.

But Rikki tried to imagine how Amiri must see her. What he must think of the initials carved deep into her breasts. Numbers and stick figures and bored little marks. Slash marks riding up her ribs, into the soft tissue. Evidence of men. Men who had sawed deep. Who had grown tired of small cuts. Men who had practice removing body parts. Trying so hard to do just that. Laughing. Holding her down. Pissing on her open wounds.

She remembered. She remembered everything. And it could have been worse. She knew that. But it was small comfort.

And here, now, Rikki felt suddenly, profoundly, afraid. What an idiot. *What a fucking idiot.* Showing herself to Amiri. As though he would not care that her body had been turned into a toilet stall, replete with graffiti. As if he would ever, *ever,* look at her the same way again—as a woman, a person. As though she would ever be able to look at *him* without wondering what he was thinking. Disgusted. Full of pity. Afraid to touch her.

And the loss of that, the idea of it, burned so deep that Rikki thought she could have been standing again on the edge of her father's grave. The pain was the same. Like death. Like losing a part of herself.

Rikki closed her eyes. Clutched her shirt so tight the cloth tore. Felt movement, a wall of heat rush over her naked torso. She held her breath, stricken. Unable to think past the memories, the scream building in her throat.

Hands touched her arms, hot and big and safe. Sliding up her shoulders, her neck, the line of her jaw. Impossibly gentle. Holding her.

"Look at me," Amiri said.

Rikki opened her eyes. Found him so close all she could see was gold and heat and fire. No grief. No pity. His eyes were bright—not with light—but shimmering and red-rimmed with something so raw, so terrible in its fury, she thought the world moved for a moment, just for him. But she realized that was her, swaying. Leaning into his embrace as he pressed her close. Gentle at first, then tight, hard, crushing her against his body.

"I know you, Rikki Kinn," he breathed into her ear. *"I know you."*

Tears burned her eyes. Behind him, Mireille made a low sound. Amiri said, in brittle tones, "Are you satisfied?"

"Yes," she replied, voice strained.

"Then get out." Quiet. Deadly.

Silence, followed by a faint scuffing sound. Light momentarily flooded the hut's interior, and then nothing but shadows. Amiri never moved, not until Mireille was gone. But when the curtain fell, he took a deep shuddering breath and stepped back, just enough to see her body. Rikki held herself still, letting him take his fill.

He was silent too long. She could not stand it. "I went to plastic surgeons. They were able to fix . . . some things. Not all."

"How could they?" he whispered. "How could they do this to you?"

It was hard to breathe. "They were bored."

"Bored," he rasped, and Rikki stifled a gasp as claws erupted from his hands. Light ran golden up his arms, like a violent mist, tendrils sucking against his skin. He saw, and turned away fast. Hiding.

Rikki hesitated, then reached around him and grabbed his wrist. Her fingers touched fur, sleek and soft. She could not fathom the difference, and held him as she slid around his body. It was dark, but she could see the variation in his skin, running from human to fur—the line so blurred she could hardly tell where one began and the other ended—only, that his hands were not human, but long and contorted with arcing black claws that jutted like hooks from the tips of his fingers. Dangerous, lethal. Inhuman.

She held his hand. She twined her fingers through his. Pale skin riding spotted fur. His claws, sharp and glinting. She forced herself to breathe, slow and even, listening to her heart thunder. Looking into his eyes. He was shaken. Unnerved. Frightened?

"So, you see," he whispered. "You see what *I* am."

"I see," she said. "But I know you, Amiri. *I know you.*"

He shuddered, inhaling sharply. Then glanced down at her breasts. Rikki did not think. She began to cover them. His hand shot out, stopping her.

"Not from me," he rumbled. "Never from me."

She fought tears, breathless. "It's hard."

He leaned close, and his hand was suddenly bathed in golden light, shifting to dark human skin. He cupped her face, gaze hot, wild. "For us both, it is hard. We are too used to hiding. But we cannot hide from each other. I could not live that way, and neither could you."

"Can you live with this?" She swallowed past the lump in her throat, pointing at herself. "Day in, day out? It will never go away, Amiri. *Never.*"

"Better to ask if I can live with your temper. Or your smile, your courage . . . your stubbornness. Better to wonder if I can love a woman who is strong, who can survive." Amiri leaned close, eyes far too bright. "What do you think I care about, Rikki Kinn? Truly. What do I care about *scars,* if you do not care about this?"

He held up his hand, and she watched again as claws pushed through his fingernails, fur running rampant down the shifting muscles of his arm. But the light did not stop, and neither did the fur. It spread like wildfire across his body, muscles fading beneath a sleek spotted coat that bristled and shone. Still shaped like a man. Only . . . not. Rikki had the distinct and unfortunate desire to start calling him a Thundercat.

She was so caught up, she almost missed the transformation of his face—bones shifting, lips fading into a cleft that was more animal than human. His forehead receded. His ears grew sharp and tufted. Golden fur, teardrop lines, spots like black roses.

Breathtaking, astonishing. And yet, she could still see Amiri in that alien visage. Not just in his eyes, but in the structure, the sharp angles and curves. The man was still there. He would always be there.

"Rikki," he murmured.

She placed her hand on his chest, fingers sinking into fur, and looked him dead in the eyes.

And then she kissed him.

It took Amiri by surprise; she could feel it. His muscles tensed, his breath caught. He did not touch her.

Rikki leaned into him. His mouth was oddly shaped, but it was warm and firm and she would not pull away. She was afraid to pull away. There were too many holes in her heart, and she was making another—another way to grieve—but God help her, because she could not help herself.

His hands crawled into her hair—trembling, light as air—and finally, finally, he kissed her back. Tentative, with heartbreaking gentleness. This man, so much the warrior, alien and primal, touching her like she was made of butterfly wings. Shifting, fur receding, bathing her in a light that tingled sweet. His mouth transformed, as did his kiss; wet and slow, so deep Rikki lost herself, hanging limp, held to him only by the strength of his arms.

Amiri broke away, slowly, pressing his lips to her throat. "You terrify me, *mpenzi*."

Rikki smiled, eyes still closed. "You the running kind?"

"As much as you are," he said, surprising her. "But I think . . . I think I am ready to stop."

She opened her eyes, searching his face—human now, sleek and sharp and wild—but before she could say a word, he turned his head to look at the curtain covering the door. She did not ask. She listened.

"Helicopters," Amiri said, eyes distant.

Rikki did not hear anything but the distant laughter of children, but knew better than to doubt. She threw on her shirt, then joined Amiri as he stalked to the curtain and pushed it aside. A woman stared back at them, stony-eyed, rifle sharp against her shoulder—standing too far away for them to contemplate stealing the weapon.

She made a sharp gesture. Amiri held his ground. Rikki touched her stomach, fingers grazing the scalpel still hidden in the rolled waist of her scrubs and took a quick look around. The other guards were gone, and several women were rounding up the playing children, shooing and dragging them into the scattered shelters.

Mireille appeared from within the maze of homes. Walking fast. When she saw them standing in the doorway of the hut, her pace faltered—and then she broke into a run toward them.

"You called them," Amiri said, glancing pointedly at the sky. Rikki heard the distant chop of rotors.

"Before our last encounter." Mireille fingered the cross at her throat, and looked at Rikki. Stared too long, her gaze dropping—just like all the others—to her covered breasts.

"Need another look?" Rikki asked.

Mireille's eyes grew cold. She flung out her hand to the other woman and snapped her fingers. Took the rifle and pointed it at them. "Walk. Walk fast."

Something hard settled in Amiri's face. He touched Rikki's elbow, and guided her so that she walked in front of him, protected from the gun. Mireille hung back, keeping a safe distance, and directed them on a straight-line path past the huts, past the makeshift refugee tents, toward a clearing at the jungle's edge. No one else joined them. Several times, Rikki thought she glimpsed movement at the edge of her vision, but when she looked, nothing was there.

The grass was tall in the clearing, though some had been flattened into narrow trenches. A regular landing pad. The distant thundering chop of the helicopters grew louder, throbbing with Rikki's blood, her terror. Sweat trickled down her back, between her breasts.

"You're sending us to die," Rikki said—truth or lie.

"I am not a sentimental woman," Mireille replied. Behind her, the grass tugged slightly apart. Rikki saw a small face watching them. Kimbareta. Spying. His eyes were large. He still held his ball. The whistle was clutched in his hand, near his mouth. Rikki did not want him to see this.

"Sentiment and compassion are two different things," Amiri replied. Rikki was certain he must see the boy. "Apparently, you have neither."

"So quick to judge," murmured the woman, her gaze flickering back to Rikki. "Too quick."

Hope flared. "Does that mean you'll let us go?"

Mireille shook her head. "I negotiated an award for this camp. Those men . . . they want you quite badly."

"You cannot trust them," Amiri said. "Please."

"Please," she echoed dully. "And if I suddenly believed

you? If I believed *her*?" Mireille looked at Rikki. "Those scars . . . what was done to you. That means something. It makes you one of us."

"One more to sacrifice."

"One life for many," Mireille whispered. "Surely you understand the alternative."

"Every night, in my nightmares," Rikki told her. "Every time I look in the mirror. But that doesn't make it right."

Mireille's jaw settled. She hefted the rifle higher against her shoulder. To their left, two helicopters flew into sight. Still far away, just toys in the sky. But too close.

Kimbareta saw them, too. He scrambled to his feet, eyes huge. Absolutely terrified. Rikki recalled what the adults had said: the refugees had been transported in by helicopter. Not good memories, apparently. Bad men. The boy raised the whistle to his lips and blew hard.

The sound was like a hundred fingernails on a dozen chalkboards—piercing, unbearable, and one hell of a distraction. Mireille whirled, and Amiri moved with her—a blur, a heartbeat, a breath of nothing but devastating violence—and suddenly the gun was in his hands and the woman on the ground, staring at him with no small dismay and fear. His hand was on her throat. His knee on her chest.

Amiri held out the rifle and Rikki took it from him. Her heart pounded so hard she felt sick with it. Stunned with the knowledge that he could have stolen the gun from Mireille earlier, had he wanted to. Amiri was that fast. Faster than human.

"Where is the phone?" he asked, voice tight, deadly.

"Given back," Mireille stammered. "The man who owns it came and went."

"Where?"

She tried not to answer. Amiri snarled and she flinched,

trembling. A different woman, smaller and more frightened. Not the person who had argued so passionately about survival, strength. Rikki tasted something bitter, and grabbed his shoulder. "Get off her, Amiri. Do it now."

He hesitated, glancing at her. Then back at Mireille. His shoulders stiffened, and he carefully, slowly, let go of her neck and stood off her body. She lay frozen for a moment, eyes wide. Amiri tried to say something, stopped, then turned away. Rikki saw him focus in on Kimbareta. Hesitate. He took two long steps and swept the child up into his arms.

The helicopters were close. Debris kicked up into Rikki's face and the grass began to flatten. Hot air blew like a hurricane around her body. She knew the passengers inside the craft could see them. And if they could see them, shoot them. Rikki knelt by Mireille. She could hardly hear herself as she shouted, "I'm sorry!"

Mireille frowned. Rikki punched her in the face. Bone crunched. Her knuckles screamed. So did Rikki, but thankfully, the object of her violence slumped in the grass, unmoving. She hoped the men in the helicopter had paid attention to that little display. She did not want Mireille to bear the burden of their escape. Which she might, anyway, but this—as Rikki was certain she would understand—was all about survival.

Amiri grabbed her arm and they started running toward the jungle. Bullets slammed into the ground behind them, barely missing their heels. Rikki tried moving faster, but it was Amiri who pushed and pulled, making them fly until her feet hardly seemed to touch the ground.

They threw themselves into the underbrush, which was thick as a wall. Rikki went down immediately and Amiri hauled her up, carrying her for several steps against his

side before her feet touched the ground. Her finger nursed
the rifle's trigger. Behind them were shouts, and, less than
a minute later, the distant crash of vines and leaves, muffled
grunts.

They ran for a long time. Late afternoon sun gilded the
canopy. Monkeys shouted. The air was hot, heavy to breathe,
like her lungs were made of stone. Rikki thought about
dying, the dead, weapons and disease. She thought about
magic, and knew that if it were just Amiri, he could escape.
Get help. She was holding him back.

She stopped running. Amiri spun around. Kimbareta had
one fist in his mouth. There was a new scratch on his cheek.

"Do *not* even say it," Amiri growled.

"What," she snapped, "you're a mind reader now?"

"I am not leaving you."

"If they get me, they won't look as hard for you."

Amiri snarled, grabbing her arm. "You will have to shoot
me first."

"Man, I will put a hundred bullets up your ass if it means
you get away from me."

"I am terrified," he said dryly, and yanked her back into a
hard run. Not far, though. Not far enough. He stopped suddenly. Listening. Kimbareta stayed very still in his arms,
still clutching his ball. Eyes huge and far too old. Like Eddie, like her dead brother.

Goddamn.

Amiri edged forward, tapping the stock of her rifle. She
raised it, aiming where he pointed. Easing out her breath,
slow and silent. Watching the undergrowth as he set down
the child, tucking him low behind the cracked damp remains of a fallen tree. Amiri pressed his finger against Kimbareta's mouth and the boy nodded gravely.

The shape-shifter reached up and tugged on Rikki's shirt

hem, drawing her down behind the same tree. She lay flat, on top of the child, and Amiri covered her in leaves. She kept the rifle at her side, finger on the trigger. The heat was intense, the sensation of insects crawling on her skin, worse. Fear burned. Her throat felt raw. Beneath, the child lay still as a corpse. Amiri mouthed, *"Stay here,"* and then he was gone, sliding sideways into the underbrush, fading from sight like a ghost.

Rikki and Kimbareta waited a long time. The child hardly breathed, was so quiet she would have hardly known he existed, had she had not been so concerned about smothering him. She did not dare move, though. Certainly not when she began to hear voices, close. Familiar.

Moochie. Talking into a radio. He was missing men. Rikki bit back a fierce smile.

Then, nearby, commotion. A shout. Rikki's heart twisted, thinking of Amiri, but she waited, listening to the crash of a body being dragged. Moochie moved into sight. So did two other men, a ruddy-faced behemoth jabbing his gun at a tall man in a tan uniform, green badge prominently placed over his heart. He wore glasses, and his dark brown cheeks were round and fit for smiles—or in this instance, a deep frown. Around his hip was an empty gun holster, and clipped on the other side, inside a black case, a rather clunky phone.

The tall man sweated outrage. Outrage tempered by intelligence. Enough to keep his head. He did not shout or demand. He stood with his hands at his sides and met Moochie's gaze. The mercenary checked him out, posture loose, easy, his arms resting on the gun slung around his body. If any of those three men turned, looked too deep into the bush, they would see her. Rikki hoped Kimbareta wasn't prone to hiccups.

"You look somewhat official," Moochie said to the man. "Name?"

"Ekemi," he said carefully. "I am the ranger for this region's conservation office."

"The park is several hours away. What are you doing down here, hiding in the bush?

"Visiting friends," said the man sternly, folding his arms over his chest. "And you?"

"Ditto," Moochie replied, and reached out to snag the phone. The Ranger tried to stop him, but all he got for his trouble was the barrel of a gun pressed against his head.

"I need that," he protested, but his voice was low, even. Controlled.

"It was nice of you to let the women use it." Moochie dropped the satellite phone on the ground. Raised his foot and stomped hard, breaking the case. He did this, again and again, until little was left but the basic components. The Ranger watched in silence, fists clenched, a faint tremor in his jaw.

Moochie eyed him, brow raised. "You know who we are?"

"Mireille's saviors." The Ranger said it with some disdain, glancing sideways at the man holding the gun on him. "Corporate security force?"

"Something like that. Big money, small armies. All the shit that comes with it." Moochie smiled tightly. "I guess you can go. If you see a white chick, short, hair like Tinkerbell—or a black dude, golden eyes—be sure to let someone know. There's a . . . reward."

"How fortunate," replied the man, terse. "Given that you've obliterated my phone."

"Morse code. Pots and pans. Sound travels." Moochie glanced at the other mercenary and nodded. The man lowered his weapon, and pulled a pistol from the back of his pants. He handed it to Ekemi. The Ranger checked the ammunition and safety—leaving it off—then slid the gun home.

"You'll be compensated for the phone," Moochie said, moving away, scanning the jungle wall. He looked into the bushes where Rikki and Kimbareta were hiding. And made eye contact.

Rikki died. Moochie froze. Just long enough for her to know the game was up. But she did not move, or lift the rifle. She held her breath. Waiting. Watching Moochie stare.

Until, very slowly, he looked away. And kept on walking.

Rikki expected him to turn, but he never did. He gestured for the other man to follow, and left the Ranger. The man—Ekemi—slumped over the moment they were gone, bracing his hands on his knees. His glasses fell off. He bent, reaching for them, taking a moment while he was down there to toss around bits of phone—collecting chips and wires, tucking them in the palm of his hand. He was shaking. Muttering to himself. Behind, Amiri emerged from the undergrowth.

The shape-shifter moved without sound, gliding, muscles made of air. Deadly. Focused. Sliding right up against the Ranger's back, while the man remained entirely oblivious. Rikki watched, breathless, unsure what she was about to witness: murder or a tap on the shoulder.

Amiri's hand shot around the man's head, covering his mouth. He jammed a knee between his shoulders, bending him back like a puppet. The Ranger bucked against his grip, twisting wildly, but Amiri dropped him so hard to the ground he bounced, wheezing.

Rikki scrabbled to her feet, leaves and vines dripping off her clothes and hair. She pulled Kimbareta with her.

The boy was filthy, his face tear-streaked with dirt, but he did not make a sound. Not one. Kid had good instincts. Or experience in hiding.

"I have no wish to harm you," Amiri hissed into the Ranger's ear, but there was no need. The man no longer appeared to be listening. Or even aware he was held captive.

He stared at Rikki. He stared like he knew what he was looking at. He stopped struggling.

Amiri gave her a long look. She hefted the rifle. Kept the child behind her as she approached. The shape-shifter, very carefully, removed his hand from the man's mouth.

"Do we know each other?" Rikki asked him, quiet.

"Doctor Regina Kinn," said the man. "Dead woman."

She set her jaw. "I'm starting to feel way too popular."

"I know Jean-Claude," he replied, and just like that, everything changed.

CHAPTER FOURTEEN

EKEMI was sturdy, lean, and surprisingly fast. Trails, cut narrow as rope, led through the jungle on an ascending path that wound and coiled up the lowland mountains, higher into the mists. The Ranger made them run. No excuses, no rest. Amiri carried the child. Rikki held the rifle tight against her chest. He watched her from behind. Days running, and her body was lean as a whip, cheeks hollow. She needed a good meal. A bed. Safety.

Kimbareta no longer had the ball. It had been lost, forgotten. He clutched the whistle instead; a lifeline. Amiri cradled the child to his chest. Light as a feather. Eyes closed, limp. Asleep.

"He doing all right?" Rikki asked breathlessly, glancing over her shoulder.

"He is a good child," Amiri replied. "No trouble."

She looked away, back up the trail. Then, gave him another quick look. "Why did you take him?"

"Do you disagree?"

"No. It just wasn't . . . practical."

"He was there, a child. Men, coming with guns. I did not think about practicality."

Rikki smiled. "Good."

Good, indeed. Amiri did not tell her that he was concerned for the child's life in other ways. All those refugees from the camp, direct witnesses—they had been saved for a purpose. Whatever it was, it could not be good. Not if the Consortium were involved.

No one from the village had followed; Amiri was quite certain. He handed Kimbareta to Rikki after the second hour and doubled back for a short time, leaving his wrap hidden in a nest of vines before shifting shape to run the trail. He found nothing. Heard nothing that should not belong. He hardly trusted himself, though. It was only a matter of time before they were discovered. If not here, then elsewhere. The Consortium wanted Rikki too badly. And based on those photographs left in Kinsangani, there was also unfinished business with *him*. No doubt painful.

Night fell. Darkness, swollen and hot. Ekemi had a flashlight. He made them keep going. Rikki began to stumble more. Her breathing was rough, exhausted.

Finally, though, Amiri caught a shift in the breeze, new scents. The low hum of voices. "There are people ahead."

Ekemi slowed. "There should be. But we are still some distance away."

"He has good instincts," Rikki said, and thankfully, the Ranger left it at that. Amiri continued to listen, though, judging and calculating. Wondering whether they could trust this man, though it seemed they had little choice. Rikki, if nothing else, seemed curious enough to take the risk. And Ekemi's scent carried no tang of deception.

Less than a mile later, they entered a wide clearing filled with several whitewashed one-story buildings. Even without his advanced eyesight, Amiri would have been able to see them. Lanterns burned, as did open-air fires, flames contained in stone pits. People sat around the blazes, talking and laughing. Amiri heard the faint wails of Jimi Hendrix drifting on the night air.

"Groovy," Rikki said, deadpan. "What is this? Jungle beach party?"

"Local volunteers," Ekemi said. "They will not bother us."

Perhaps not, Amiri thought, but their group still suffered an uncomfortable amount of scrutiny, even though the Ranger took them on a circuitous path toward the buildings. Amiri noted several smaller, cruder structures erected on the periphery. Clothes hung on lines; pots and pans and buckets were stacked neatly on low tables set out beside curtained front doors. At one of them, Amiri heard murmuring, saw candlelight burning through a window; a man reading, shirtsleeves rolled up to his elbows. At his side, a woman was painting her nails.

Ekemi began to walk past, then hesitated. "Do you want the child to stay with you?"

"Is there a reason he shouldn't?" asked Rikki.

He shrugged, pushing his glasses higher on his nose. "I have no beds, but they . . ." He hesitated, pointing at the couple in the small structure. "University students from Kinshasa. Married, working on their thesis. They brought much of their own equipment, including cots. I am sure they could make room for one as small as him."

Amiri hesitated. Part of him did not want to give the child up. He looked at Rikki and found the same uncertainty mirrored on her face. But Kimbareta stirred, eyes closed, sucking gently on his fist, and Amiri looked back through the window at the young man and woman, who were quiet, engaged, almost effortlessly normal.

"They are good people?" he asked, hugging the child a bit closer to his chest.

"Very," Ekemi said. "And it would be only for tonight, until we can find something more comfortable for you all."

Amiri shared another look with Rikki. She sighed, lifting one shoulder. A reluctant shrug.

Ekemi knocked on the door frame. The man pushed aside the curtain. He was tall and dark, his eyes quietly assessing. But when the situation was explained—heavily edited—he and his wife looked at the boy with genuine kindness, if not a little bewilderment, and Amiri began to breathe a little easier. Kimbareta hardly stirred from sleep as he was handed over.

"He's been through a lot," Rikki said to them in French, her fingers finding Amiri's wrist. "Be careful with him."

"Of course," said the woman, smiling, rocking the boy with a sway like water. She turned away and disappeared behind the gauze of a mosquito net. Rikki continued to stare after the vanished child. Brow furrowed. Still concerned. He understood exactly how she felt.

Ekemi wished the other man goodnight, and led them away to one of the white buildings, the largest, set off-center on the edge of the clearing. It was squat, with a metal roof. Painted beside the door, on the building itself, was a small sign:

ICCN: L'INSTITUT CONGOLAIS POUR LA CONSERVA-
TION DE LA NATURE.

"Congo's wildlife service," Ekemi said, unlocking the door. "This is our first outpost in this particular region. Forgive the humble circumstances."

Humble, indeed, thought Amiri, a moment later. The room they entered was hot, stuffy, and almost completely empty except for two chairs and one table, which held a

kerosene lantern and several file folders. A narrow gun cabi-
net had been nailed to the whitewashed walls. At opposite
ends were two more doors. The air smelled like sweat and
fresh paint.

Ekemi took a book of matches from his pocket and lit
the lamp. "We are lucky to have funding for guns, let alone
this roof over our heads."

Rikki made a humming sound, turning in a full circle.
"Must make your job more difficult."

He shrugged. "It could be worse. We are not like Virunga.
Their pressures are much greater. More rebels, more skir-
mishes. Over a hundred rangers dead in ten years. All for
the gorillas, the hippos, those damn ivory tusks."

"Mysteries, dying," Amiri murmured to himself. Rikki
gave him a curious look. Ekemi did not seem to hear. He
had already gone through one of the other doors.

Rikki followed him. "Tell me how you know Jean-
Claude."

"We are old friends from Kinshasa," he called back, his
flashlight beam bouncing through the darkness. Amiri
heard a rattling sound. "Both of us liked the idea of being
big men in uniform, but I had the education and Jean-Claude
did not. So. Conservation. Soldier. We are both moderately
happy with our lives."

Ekemi returned, his arms full of water bottles and small
tins, which he dumped on the table. Amiri saw peanuts,
beef jerky, and a variety of other things he was not entirely
keen on consuming. What he really needed was a good hot
cup of tea. And a nice rare steak.

He sighed. "How did you recognize Rikki?"

The Ranger smiled, cracking open some peanuts. He
handed the tin to Rikki. "Jean-Claude sent me a picture several years ago. You had longer hair then."

"I had to cut it."

Rikki's voice was flat, empty. Amiri bumped her elbow. Reassurance. She leaned into him. Ekemi did not miss the gesture, but his gaze flicked away and he cleared his throat, passing out water.

"Jean-Claude phoned last night. His old UN contacts informed him of the kidnapping attempt. Said, too, that the camp you had been working at had been razed to the ground by rebel forces. When he did not hear from you, he became concerned. Asked that I . . . keep an ear out. Listen for news."

"You called me a dead woman."

"That is what Jean-Claude was told. No survivors." Ekemi folded his arms over his chest, eyeing them both. "But you would not be running as you have, not unless there is more to the story."

"Much more," Rikki said. "You should ask Jean-Claude. He tried to warn me."

"Then he did more for you than me. Something has scared him."

"Not easy to do," Rikki said.

Amiri wondered if he should feel a bit jealous of this man, Jean-Claude, who seemed to be so concerned with Rikki's life. Trying to imagine someone else holding her heart made a worm twist in his gut, a rather ugly one, and he decided that, yes, it was quite appropriate to feel a modicum of jealousy.

"Do you have another phone?" he asked. "It is urgent."

Ekemi shook his head. "That phone the mercenary destroyed was our only. I took it with me everywhere, simply because it was so precious. But . . . you are not entirely out of luck. There is a Catholic mission, some twenty miles east.

They have a radio. Weak transmission, but it could get a message out."

Better than nothing. "I can go tonight if you give me instructions."

Rikki stiffened. Ekemi looked incredulous. "Tonight? In the dark? Sir, I do not know what your profession is, but that is suicide. The Congo has no mercy."

"Neither do I," Amiri replied. "I know what I am doing. I can be there by morning." Sooner, in all probability. He might even be able to return here by dawn, if all went well.

The problem was leaving Rikki behind. No place was safe for her. He wondered if she would ever be safe, with the knowledge in her head. Or whatever else the Consortium might desire from her.

A chilling thought. He glanced at Rikki, and she shot him a look like chewing glass. As much as he wanted to be alone with her, he was suddenly quite glad they were not.

She tore her gaze from him. "No disrespect intended, Ekemi, but why are you helping us? It's dangerous. People are dying left and right."

The Ranger leaned against the table, searching her face. Smiling, ever so faintly. "You ask that question of a man who would sacrifice his life for a gorilla? Come now, Doctor Kinn. A woman in need is far more appealing than a hairy primate, no matter how much I love them."

Rikki snorted, drinking from her water bottle. Ekemi's own smile widened, but only for a moment. He looked at Amiri, and something brittle crept into his gaze. His lips slanted into a grimace. "There is a bad spell going on. Deep in the forest. Things are happening that no one can explain, but those men who came for you today at Mireille's camp are part of it."

"Explain."

Ekemi popped a handful of peanuts into his mouth. "This park is so new it hardly has a name. Less than six months old, on the books, recognized by the ICCN. But it is huge. Vast. A gift from the government to its people, I was told."

"But it bothers you," Rikki said. "Something stinks."

"It should not," Ekemi replied. "I should be delighted. But though Zaire is now the Democratic Republic of Congo, little has changed, especially in the way of politics. So, while there are rumors of gorillas and other critical species in these forests, the recent concession of land remains . . . too good to be believed. And there is far *too* much corruption in the current government to believe in *much*."

Something hard settled in Amiri's gut. "You think the government has made an arrangement."

"A man could build an empire in this jungle and no one would know it. Men make themselves God and Country, and all it takes is money and charisma and guns."

"Those men in Mireille's camp," Rikki said. "Have you seen them before?"

"Others just like them. They stop here occasionally, ostensibly to see how we are doing. Foreign mercenaries, mostly, though some militias have come this way. Passing through. I have been given instructions to let them do just that, and not to follow as they move deeper into the jungle." He smiled bitterly. "This makes me a conservationist in name only, but I am outnumbered and outgunned, and there is no one to hear my concerns."

"So, what you are saying," Amiri replied carefully, "is that these men are established, somewhere in this jungle."

"Established and safe, with helicopters coming and going at all hours."

"What a terrible way to keep a secret," Rikki muttered. "How do the other people here feel about all this?"

"They know little of the politics. All they care is that this is a new park, with little competition for research spots. Almost all the people here are graduate students, like the couple who are caring for the child you brought." He shrugged, chewing a peanut. "Blind to everything but the wildlife. Some may be leaving soon, though. The forest has begun to . . . unnerve them. They claim to have seen strange creatures. *Bouda,* specifically."

"Bouda?" Rikki echoed.

"Shape-shifters," Amiri said, voice flat. "Members of a tribe that have been attributed with having the power to transform into hyenas. More of a western African myth than central, I would say."

"Nonetheless. The students tell me they have seen animals who walk on two feet. Golden glowing eyes." Ekemi gave Amiri a long searching look. "To be honest, when I first saw you, I wondered. I have never met a man with eyes such as yours."

"Superstitious," Amiri said, but he thought of what the children had told him, back at the village, and the hairs rose on his neck like little claws. He felt Rikki watching him.

Ekemi pushed away from the table. "I have sleeping bags you can use. I would offer you my own bed if I had one."

"I will be going soon," Amiri replied.

"Not yet," Rikki said.

Ekemi hesitated, glancing between them. "Will you sleep in separate rooms?"

"No," they answered, in unison. Amiri cleared his throat, daring the Ranger to say anything. The man was wise enough to keep his mouth shut. He showed them to the storeroom, which was mostly empty except for open boxes of canned food and water, as well as bound stacks of toilet paper and an open first-aid kit. Someone had been searching for Band-Aids.

Ekemi pulled two sleeping bags free of some boxes. "There is an outhouse just behind this building. I will be around if you need anything." He hesitated, pushing up his glasses. "Do not go tonight, sir. Wait until morning."

Amiri could make no such promises. He was keenly, almost painfully, aware of Rikki's presence, and her voice was low, strained, as she said, "They could come here looking for us. You sure you're up for the risk? All of these people?"

"Are you protecting something important, Doctor Kinn?"

She hesitated. "Yes."

"Then all will be right in the end. Besides, Jean-Claude would never forgive me. And he is a far better shot with his gun." Ekemi saluted Amiri, left them the flashlight, and closed the door securely behind him. Footsteps faded, followed by the gentle click of another door closing.

Amiri said, "Do you trust him?"

"Seems too good to be true. But . . . my gut says yes. I would assume yours does, too, given that you're planning on leaving me here." Rikki's gaze was flat, cold—but worse, disappointed. "Don't suppose you thought to ask me how I felt about that."

"I did not think. I simply . . . spoke."

"Eager to get things done?"

"We must," he said, aching. "But that does not mean I want to leave you here."

"You're afraid."

"Terrified of the possibilities," he admitted. "But I suppose you think this is little different than what you proposed earlier. That I leave you behind."

"Gee, no," she replied. "Certainly nothing along the lines of *'You will have to shoot me first.'*"

"Circumstances have changed."

"As far as you're concerned."

"And can you run twenty miles in the dead of night, Rikki Kinn? Can you keep up with me?"

"You know I can't. And I'm *not* saying it's a bad plan."

"You are still unhappy, though. I can hear it in your voice."

Rikki turned away from him, and began unrolling the sleeping bags. Amiri touched her shoulder, but she shrugged him off. He tried touching her waist, and she batted his hand away. Panic swelled. As did irritation.

When he grabbed her the third time, he did not let her push him aside. He held on tight, pulling her hard against his chest. Warm and small; her scent was raw, female. Memories filled him: her hot mouth, the taste of her body on his tongue. Lust warred with his temper.

Amiri dragged in a rough deep breath, trying to control himself. She had been hurt. Tortured. And he had already been rough with one woman today. He did not want to remember that look on Mireille's face ever again.

Monster, whispered a tiny voice. Amiri gritted his teeth, relaxing his hold on Rikki's arms. She did not move away, simply pushed deeper into his body. He closed his eyes, savoring the contact.

She turned. The flashlight was still in her hand, pointed at the floor. The ambient light gave her a ghostly pallor, her eyes huge, haunted. She tried to say something, stopped, cleared her throat.

"If you go," she said slowly. "You will come back to me."

"I will fly to you," he whispered, stooping to peer into her eyes. "My skin is your skin. All that I am, yours."

He saw her swallow hard, her gaze uncertain. "Sounds binding."

"Unto death." He kissed her gently on the mouth, and after a moment, Rikki relaxed, sagging against his body. Her fingers trailed down his spine, featherlight. Gentle, tender. So few had ever been gentle with him in anything; tenderness, rarer yet. He could not fathom what it did to him—just one touch, her acceptance. No fear. No fear, when fear had guided so much of how he lived his life. Survival begged absolute distrust—of everything, everyone.

But Amiri had trusted more than he should. He had loved more than was safe. He had broken the rule of fear, and it, in turn, had broken him—with his capture, with all the little betrayals and deaths that had accumulated over a lifetime. So much easier to be alone.

Rikki had changed everything.

And now you cannot go back to being on your own. She is home. You are home.

For the first time in his life, home.

"How do you do it?" he murmured, stirred by a tenderness that was low, deep; an ache he imagined poets must share. He felt like a poet with her.

"Do what?" she breathed.

He kissed her ear. "I am not lonely with you."

She went still in his arms. Then, carefully, she pulled away, just enough to stare into his face. Her expression, profoundly grave. No words, just that look, that glimpse of wonder in her eyes, that lovely light like the shimmer of some spring morning, first light of dawn: golden and sheer and young.

He kissed her. He wanted to be gentle, but the moment his lips touched hers, he could not help but drag her close, hard against his body. He forced his tongue past her lips and she moaned against his mouth, kissing him back with a ferocity that sank like fire into his bones. Her fingers dragged at the wrap around his waist, tearing it away from his hips, pushing down on his underwear. He could hardly think past her mouth, her hands—she slid her fingers down the crease of his backside, tugging, squeezing, and he hardened so fast and so painfully, he broke off their kiss, gasping.

"We cannot," he breathed, but he could barely think past the sight of her swollen lips and drowsy eyes, the scent of her desire pouring over him in waves. Rikki flung out her hand, reaching for the first-aid kit. She knocked it over and dropped to her knees, rummaging, and after a moment, held up a condom. Electricity shot through him. Even more when she yanked his underwear all the way down to his ankles and placed her mouth over his erection. She did it fast, in one smooth movement, leaving him totally unprepared for the sensation of her tongue caressing the underside of its head, her hot breath, the wickedness of her fingers dancing light over the shaft; and lower, to his testicles. He reached out, wild, knocking aside one of the boxes, and Rikki started laughing, quietly, with him still in her mouth.

Amiri pushed her away, sinking to his knees in front of her. He felt all bent up, crushed with pleasure, but he forced himself to hold back, to think.

"I do not want to hurt you," he said, shaking with the effort not to touch her. "I do not want you to be frightened of me."

Rikki's eyes darkened and she reached out, grabbing his penis with both hands. She squeezed, and the pleasure was so close to pain, he threw back his head, breath rattling in his throat.

"Does this look like a frightened woman?" Rikki murmured throatily, brushing her lips against his open mouth. "I want you to touch me, Amiri. I want you inside me."

He grabbed the back of her head and caught her mouth, sucking on her lower lip. Rikki sighed, melting into his body, and he reached down, breathless and hesitant, to touch her breast through her shirt. She stiffened, but he thought it was with pleasure because she made another low sound, squirming against his hand. Her hard nipple rolled against his fingers, and he squeezed gently, pulling. Rikki cried out, back arching, fingers digging into his shoulders.

Emboldened, Amiri pushed up the hem of her shirt. Slow, easy, watching her reaction. She kept her eyes closed, but he sensed new tension. A furrow between her eyes. He hesitated, then said, "Lie down."

She finally looked at him, and her uncertainty branded him to the core. Amiri touched her face, as gently as he could. "Trust me."

Rikki swallowed hard, face flushed, and lay down on her back. Amiri said, "Turn over, and take off your shirt."

She hesitated. "If you don't want to see—"

He kissed her before she could finish. "Do as I say."

Rikki did, but she started to grumble, muttering things that even he could not understand. He bit back a smile, watching as she tore off her shirt and tossed it—with some anger—at a box. She lay down on her stomach.

"Happy?" She sounded bitter. Amiri did not answer. He straddled her hips, and began to massage her back. Long strokes, following the fine lines of her spine and shoulders, tracing paths with his mouth and tongue and fingers, savoring her sighs of pleasure. He moved lower, his erection rubbing briefly against her backside, and had to stifle his own groan—and the overwhelming urge to take her right then.

He removed her pants. Slid them over her hips. Heard something metallic hit the floor beneath her. She flinched, reaching. Much to his surprise, her hand came back with a scalpel.

"Ingenious," he murmured. "I hope you were not planning to use that on me."

"Be good," she muttered lazily, and put the blade aside.

Amiri nudged it aside just a little further, making her laugh—which turned into a gasp as he began kissing his way down her lower back. Her thighs shifted, the scent of her desire so strong and rich, he wanted to bury himself in it.

So he did: slow, easy, reaching beneath her with one hand to raise her hips. He did not pierce her body, but rubbed himself against her, tight and hard, reaching out with his other hand to sink his fingers against her cleft, flicking lightly until she trembled. He moved deeper, his fingers sliding into her hot wet core; hooking, pressing. Rikki's breath rattled, and she began moving her own hips against his hand as he pressed harder and tighter against that small spot. He took her almost to the edge before pulling away, turning her, ignoring her cries of protest as he made her recline on her back. He sank between her legs, reveling in her taste and scent as he went deep with his tongue. Her thighs tightened, and so did he, sliding his hands under her body to squeeze her closer. She writhed beneath him, and while she was distracted, he reached up with one hand to touch her breasts.

Amiri felt the scars beneath his fingers. He remembered every mark, every ragged cut, each initial and brand. His fury was as strong as his lust, and the two warred together, making his heart bleed. He could not imagine what she had endured—at the mercy of sadists, men who treated her as less than human, tortured to the very edge of life. Forced to live, every day, knowing that the reminder of that pain would never leave her.

But you are still alive, Rikki Kinn. Alive and strong and unbroken.

And he could not admire her more—could not love her more—than he did just at that moment.

He moved up her body, kissing her stomach, her ribs. She began to cover herself, but he pulled her hands away and covered her scars with his mouth, dredging up every ounce of gentleness he possessed. Trying to show her, in ways words never could, how much he desired her.

She stopped fighting him, after a while. She began to relax again. But it was not until he moved to kiss her mouth that he tasted something salty, and realized that she had been crying.

Everything inside him stopped. He could hardly breathe. "I hurt you."

"No." Rikki swiped at her eyes. "No. Just the opposite."

"Rikki," he murmured, searching her face, heart breaking. But she kissed him before he could say anything else, and a moment later pushed the condom into his palm. She had to help him put it on—his hands were shaking too much—and she started laughing, sniffing back more tears. Amiri kissed her brow, and Rikki straddled his lap, sinking down on top of his body.

It had been a long time, and she was hot and tight and felt so good it was almost over on that first long stroke of her body. He kept strong, though, and fell into her rhythm as she began to move, her arms gripping his shoulders, her eyes closed and her head thrown back. She thrust hard, fast, and just when he thought she was going to climax, she stopped abruptly, gave him a breathless, wicked grin, and climbed off his body to turn so that he could enter her from behind. Which he did, giving himself over to every primal desire and raw ounce of lust, thrusting into her body as she writhed against him.

Rikki slammed her fists into the floor, throwing herself forward on her elbows. He braced himself with one foot planted on the ground, bending over her body as he ground himself into her heat. She matched him, crying out his name, her sharp sounds of pleasure as loud as his own groans, and he felt himself tightening harder and harder, feeling her body do the same, and at the exact moment she flew apart, he finally let himself go, the sensation so rippling and long, so mind-blowing, he lost himself, body jerking spasmodically, his thoughts drifting free into warmth and an undercurrent of raw lust that did not go away, but only quieted, waiting.

They collapsed together on top of the sleeping bag, and Amiri curled around Rikki's sweat-soaked body, inhaling her scent, drowning himself in her warmth. Both of them could hardly breathe, and after a moment, Rikki started laughing again; quiet, almost a giggle.

"You think anyone heard us?" she asked, still panting.

Amiri laughed, weakly. "I do not care. I think I could have you again, even now."

Rikki groaned, reaching back to touch him. He felt himself harden immediately, and he buried his face in her hair, desperately trying to control himself.

"Insatiable," Rikki whispered, turning to look at him. Tears glittered again in her eyes, but she was still smiling. Amiri's own eyes burned. His throat felt too tight.

He would have told her what was in his heart. He was ready. But behind them, outside the storage room, a door slammed open and feet pounded the floor. Amiri dragged a blanket over Rikki as Ekemi burst in, breathless, sweat rolling down his face and his glasses askew. His eyes were wild—as was his scent, bitter as acid. He hardly seemed to notice they were naked.

"There's something you have to see," he said.

OUTSIDE, THE WORLD HAD CHANGED. EVERYONE WHO HAD been sitting around the fires now stood, gazing south into the trees. Amiri and Rikki joined them, staring. Gazing deep into the tangle, where green fire burned.

It flickered and shimmered like some arboreal aurora borealis: ghosts made of emeralds and starlight, spun from darkness. A stiff wind cut across Amiri's face, carrying the familiar scent of spring rain, and on the edge of his hearing he imagined music, a pipe that was anything but cheery; instead dragging a note as old as stone through the heart of his heart, like an anchor, or pain. Amiri clutched his chest, and noted Rikki doing the same, her palm pressed tight over her heart as she stared into the jungle. No one else seemed to hear that music. Ekemi, the men and women with him, did nothing but stare, and laugh nervously.

But there was nothing to laugh about.

"Stay here," Amiri said, and ran into the jungle. Shouts followed him—everyone but Rikki, it seemed—though he felt her with him as he plunged deep into the twisting labyrinth of trees and vines.

He ran for a long time. As he did, he felt as though he entered a different world. The air smelled different. Mist rose from the ground, which was no longer cut with vines and the thick unbending jungle brush, but soft, yielding, as though he ran through a meadow, unseen. No more light, no dancing specters, nothing but the stars—and somewhere, the moon.

He ran until he found the man. A man sprawled in the thick jungle. Naked. Smoke, curling from his skin. Across his back was a sickening crisscross of deep lash marks that for one moment glowed faintly green.

"Rictor," Amiri breathed.

CHAPTER FIFTEEN

MERCY. Remorse. There was neither in the heart of the person who had hurt the man who lay on the long table in front of Rikki. She had seen a lot of things in her life, but this—even with her own injuries—was one of the worst.

Rictor's back was raw. Split open. There was not much light to see by—the lanterns hardly adequate—but even daylight would not have helped; his wounds were sickening. They were reminders of her own scars, the same determined cruelty: splitting a person open, peeling them apart, one strip at a time.

His back had taken time. Someone had enjoyed this.

"I thought he was powerful. Who could do something like this to him?" Rikki whispered to Amiri, tugging up the blanket that covered Rictor's lower body. Ekemi stood just outside the little building, talking to someone. Within earshot, if they were not careful. And they had to be. Rictor was going to raise too many questions. His wounds were fresh, wet, but there was no blood. No sign there ever had been. Just a trace of something green and iridescent against the ragged edges of his wounds.

Amiri rubbed his face. For the first time since meeting him, she thought he looked exhausted. "Only Rictor can tell us who did this. But I can say this much—it should have been impossible to make such wounds on his body. He is not like us."

"Impossible men, impossible punishments. You're talking in relative terms. No one is at the top of the food chain, Amiri."

"How comforting."

"Like a boot up the ass," she muttered, placing a hand on her ribs; feeling the lines of her scars beneath the flimsy shirt. Remembering the hot wash of blood soaking into the earth beneath her.

No blood here. No blood.

Amiri caught her hand and squeezed. Rikki closed her eyes, savoring the safety of that touch. The heat, the shadows in this room, were suffocating—as it had been earlier, in the storage room, although in a much more pleasant fashion, one that was still making her body tingle. She had never felt such pleasure, such overwhelming lust, and the way Amiri had touched her, the reverence in his eyes as he had looked at her body . . .

She took a deep breath. "Rictor said *you* wouldn't pay for helping Eddie. Do you think this is what he was talking about?"

Amiri hesitated. "That would require a selfless act."

"You don't think he's capable of it?"

"Right now, I cannot imagine what to think."

Rikki sighed. "I hope Eddie is okay."

Ekemi returned to the room. He looked unhappy. Playing Good Samaritan had come back to bite him on the ass. He sighed wearily, pushing up his glasses. "How is our guest?"

"Alive," Rikki said. "How are you?"

"Envying an unconscious man." Ekemi smiled weakly. "The others want to fetch medical help. I have managed to convince them that it will be unnecessary, that you are skilled enough to care for this man, but the complications of his presence—"

"It cannot be helped," Amiri interrupted. "He is . . . a friend."

"A friend," Ekemi echoed. "I thought you were all alone here?"

"He's been looking for us," Rikki explained, somewhat awkwardly. "We were separated early on."

"The rebels must have gotten to him," said the man, his breath whistling between his teeth. "But how he made it this far into the park, hurt as he is . . ."

Rikki frowned. "How do you know he wasn't hurt inside the park?"

"Consider it another arrangement. Rebel forces do not step foot past the threshold of the reserve's boundaries. Not for any reason."

"Were their commanders paid off?"

"If the government was, why not them?" Ekemi shrugged. "It is one thing that I am not sorry for. And neither is Mireille, which is why she puts up with so much. She knows the price, otherwise."

"Yes," Amiri said grimly. "She made the price quite clear."

Rikki's hand ached. She had tucked the little scalpel back into the folded-down waist of her scrubs, much to Amiri's amusement. "Have you heard the name *Jaaved* before? He's associated with the rebels who destroyed the refugee camp where I was working."

"I have not," Ekemi said. "But it sounds foreign."

Everything was foreign. Rikki felt like she was blind,

deaf, and dumb. Nothing made sense. Except Amiri. Her leap of faith.

Rictor's hand flexed. His eyelid fluttered. Ekemi said, "Finally, answers."

"Not yet," Rikki replied quickly, feeling Amiri's tension rocket. "In fact, you should go. The fewer people around him when he wakes, the better. In my personal medical opinion."

No one liked to argue with doctors; few ever presumed to do so. Ekemi nodded, somewhat reluctantly, and walked quickly to the door. He closed it after him with a soft click, shutting out the faint babble of voices, the buzz and chirr of night insects.

Rikki grabbed a bottle of water, upended it on a cloth. She dabbed at Rictor's cheek, the back of his neck. He was a big man, taller than Amiri. She could not imagine him submitting to any violence, and she recalled that look in his eye, the cold profound intensity that was quiet and dangerous and wild.

Just like Amiri. Even like herself, down in the recesses of her heart. All of them different, but all of them fighters. As Eddie said, it took one to know one.

A long whisper breathed from Rictor's mouth. A string of words like music, lilting and soft. Amiri knelt. Lanterns scattered the floor around the table, and Rikki shoved some of them out of the way. Just in time. Rictor's eyes snapped open. He stared, blind. Not fully awake. Caught in a nightmare. She could see it in his gaze.

Right before he attacked Amiri.

Even wounded, Rictor was fast. Rikki barely got out of the way, falling backward as the two men slammed into the floor, striking each other, eerily silent except for the harsh hiss of their breathing. Rictor fought like a man on fire—desperate, one long screaming heartbreak, agonized and terrible.

Amiri twisted, trying to wrench him off, but Rictor's hands caught his throat, squeezing, and Rikki watched in dazed horror as long black claws erupted from the shapeshifter's fingers and toes. Golden light streamed. Amiri snarled and his teeth were long, bones shifting in his face. Rage burned.

Someone was going to die. Rikki grabbed a chair and slammed it down on Rictor's head, shouting wordlessly at him. The man never budged. He turned to look at her, his eyes shining green—

—and then he screamed in pain, letting go of Amiri's throat to clutch at his back. Rikki stared, stunned, as his wounds glowed.

Amiri used the distraction to kick Rictor hard in the gut. The man rolled off his body without a fight, slumped on his side, gasping for breath. Amiri also lay still, staring. Muscles twitched in his face. Claws became fingernails scraping the hard floor.

Rikki fell to her knees between the men, heart jackhammering, sweat soaking through her clothing. Ekemi burst open the door, skidding to a stop.

"What has happened?" His eyes were wide, staring at them all slumped on the floor.

"Later," Rikki said, her voice rising. "Get out. Get out *now.*"

He blinked, and she saw his fingers twitch for his gun. But she held his gaze, pointing like her own hand was a weapon, and he slid backward slowly. Looking at her like she was someone new. Rikki wanted to laugh. Jean-Claude should have provided a warning label.

Ekemi left, shutting the door. She thought about running to lock it, but could not move. Drained, deserted, devastated; her body was abandoning her, finally. All she could do was breathe, and throw out one hand to touch Amiri's arm. He hardly noticed her. He was still staring at Rictor, wearing an expression she could not name. Rikki twisted slightly, to see . . . and felt the pit of her stomach drop away.

Rictor. His face was like some reflection in a mirror made of twisted steel—distorted, broken, gorged on agony—features slippery beneath a grief so profound it could have no name, no place, no firm fix as anything but otherworldly, beyond human. No human could feel the pain she saw on his face and survive. Her own sorrow was like some broken shadow in comparison.

The man shook. Curled around his stomach, trembling violently. She thought he might be cold, but his eyes were squeezed shut, his jaw clenched tight. Fighting to keep it in, she realized. All that anguish, swallowed.

Rikki almost touched him. She stopped herself, though, remembering her father, Markovic. Those months she spent in the hospital, forced to face the endless trail of doctors and nurses and visitors. Torn down, again and again, but always able to stand. Too proud to let anyone see her suffer.

Pride and stubbornness, all she had left.

She looked at Amiri. He stared back with a sharp clear gaze; furious, burning, primal as death. His lip was cut. Blood dotted his cheek. Beside him, Rictor turned over on his back and opened his eyes. Green, bloodshot, red-rimmed. He glanced sideways at Rikki, and then Amiri. His gaze lingered.

"Oh," he said, slowly. "I am so fucked."

A sentiment reinforced only a moment later when Ekemi

slammed open the door and flew inside, gun out, glasses askew. Rikki's stomach dropped so low she almost expected to see it hanging between her legs.

"They are here," he said.

Amiri stood fast, taking Rikki with him. "How many?"

Ekemi looked as though he wanted to throw up. "Too many. Ten armed men, perhaps more. They must have hiked up the trail in the dark. They are at the edge of the camp. Coming in slow."

"Rictor," Amiri said. "Do something."

"I can't."

"Rictor—"

"I can't," he snarled, staggering to his feet. "I've been neutered, Amiri. For helping you. *I put myself back in the cage.*"

Amiri stared. Ekemi threw up his hands. "You should be running now, not fighting. Go, *go!* I will try to stall them." The man dashed through the open door.

Rikki grabbed Amiri's arm. "Go. You still have time."

"I won't leave you. Not like this."

"Screw that. They want me *alive.*" Rikki shook him. "Run. Get help. Come back for me. You know where to search now."

"If I lose you—"

"Never," she interrupted harshly. "You will never lose me."

Amiri gave her a look so fierce she felt as though it would melt her bones. The golden undertones in his skin intensified, like an aura of sunlight burning from his body. He snared the back of her neck, dragging her close. No words. Just his heat, his calm steady eyes, filled now with lethal promise. She stared, lost in the power of his gaze, and hardly noticed as light poured off his skin, followed by a wave of spotted fur. His face began to transform, and he leaned close, pressing his shifting mouth to her ear.

"I love you," he rasped, and then his hand fell away and so did his wrap, and she watched, stunned, as Amiri fell on all fours, his human skin, his human body absorbed and molded and liquefied, until all that remained was the cheetah.

But his eyes—his eyes were the same—and the look he gave her was grave as death. He turned that stare on Rictor, who stayed silent. Implacable.

Amiri ducked his head, backing away. He padded to the door, looked back once—holding Rikki's gaze—and then he was gone, into the darkness. She stood for a moment, staring at the open door, straining to listen to shouts, gunshots—anything—but all she heard was silence, not even the approach of those men who wanted to harm her.

She turned to Rictor, studying the hard chiseled lines of his face. Enigma. Magic. Finally regaining his composure. "Why did you come back?"

"I had no choice."

"Eddie?" Her heart ached, thinking of the young man. And of her brother.

"Safe. Alive. I left him with his friends."

"It cost you."

"Everything but my life."

"Then you have everything you need," Rikki replied, and grabbed his arm, yanking him toward the storage room. He was twice as big as her, but she caught him by surprise. That, and Rictor was much weaker than he was letting on. He could hardly stand straight, let alone fight her off, and the look he gave her was so ridiculously incredulous, she wanted to laugh.

"At least *try* to hide," she said, and she shoved him inside and slammed the door in his shocked face.

Rikki took a deep breath, swallowed down her terror, and ran from the building. It was pitch dark, most of the pit-fires having died down. She heard muffled cries all around her, and thought of Kimbareta and his babysitters. She stayed away from their home, though, angling toward the farthest edge of the camp, where Ekemi had said the men were coming in. She ran, because she thought it might look more suspicious if she walked, but she made no effort to hide herself—and sure enough, strong arms caught her up around the waist, hauling Rikki against a broad hard chest.

She thought about using the scalpel, but a rough voice said, "Lady, you should have kept running," and she could not bring herself to stab that hand.

"Moochie," she said, proud her voice did not quaver. "Where's the second Hardy boy?"

"Right here," Francis rumbled, out of sight. Rikki hardly heard him past the chaos that suddenly filled the night: men, women, voices high and frightened—pots crashing, the tear of paper and fabric. Ekemi's voice, ringing out in protest. And somewhere, a whistle blowing.

She strained against Moochie's arms. "Call them off. You've got me."

"You're not the only one we want," Francis said. "Where are the two men you were traveling with?"

"Eddie's dead," Rikki said, and this time she let her voice crack. "If you didn't find his body, that's your fault."

Moochie's arms tightened. His breath smelled like watermelon gum. "And the other dude? The woman at the camp said you weren't alone."

"He left. We split up."

"Right," Francis said, sighing. "Of course."

Rikki heard the distant chop of helicopter rotors—a far too familiar sound—and all around the periphery of the camp, lights began flaring, bristling with sparks. She caught the outline of Francis's face, watching as he pulled off his night goggles. Moochie let go of her and did the same. Neither man commented on the fact that she did not fight, or try to escape. Nor did they ask more questions about Amiri or Eddie. They simply stood with her, hands resting on their guns, as they waited for the helicopter to arrive.

And it did. Landing lightly, its rotors spun a windstorm through her short hair. Francis and Moochie each took an arm and guided her to the side doors, which slid open to reveal a very bristly Marco. He smiled, smug, and grabbed her arm, yanking her inside—throwing her down into a wide leather jump seat.

In front of her, wearing a tailored gray suit, sat Broker.

Rikki stared, utterly speechless. He smiled, and tapped his head. "Thick skull."

"Not *that* thick," she retorted, finally finding her voice. "I saw your brains."

"As have many," Broker replied easily, revealing a rather large gun. "But I never let anyone make the same mistake twice."

And he shot her.

CHAPTER SIXTEEN

For much of his youth, until the age of ten, Amiri knew only one human, an old woman named Wambui, who lived alone at the base of Nyiru, a remote and sacred mountain located on the edge of the Great Rift Valley.

Wambui was the only human his father trusted with his life, and Amiri spent a great deal of time with her, learning what she had to teach. In the old colonial days she had been the nanny for a British family. She spoke English. She could read, had command of numbers. She also possessed a remarkable memory that allowed her to see something only once and remember every detail in its most minute form.

She used that memory to recite, word for word, all the books she had ever read in her employer's library: Dickens and Shakespeare, Longfellow and Stevenson, Twain and others. Little of Africa—though Amiri did not understand enough to rectify the loss until he was much older.

Not that Wambui lacked her own stories, her own tales of the land and its people; of gods and magic.

Mwirigo juri iraa, whispered her voice across the years. *Road of clay.* The Road of Light, the spiritual road con-

nected to the Creator, to honey and milk. A road of kindness. A road without anger. Or fear.

No such thing here. Amiri ran. He ran upon the road of
the forest with all his heart driving him, flying through the
undergrowth as though the world lay open before him, un-
encumbered by nothing but the strength of his soul. Dying,
breathing, fighting—blood thundering—and all he could
see in his mind was Rikki.

Rikki. And him, running. Running away. Running to
the possibility of help, but still running. Leaving his woman
within the mouth of a lion.

I will find you, he promised. *I will save you.*

Find that radio. Get the word out. His only goal.

Ekemi's directions to the Catholic Missionary—
reluctantly explained while Rikki tended Rictor—were
simple: Go east along the old woodcutter's trail, which led
from the park to a larger track, formerly used by loggers and
their trucks. Follow that for ten miles to an actual road. And
then keep on running.

An easy enough plan to follow, even at night, but sometime after Amiri left the base camp he began to wonder if
he was being followed.

It was a small feeling: a prickle at the back of his neck, an
involuntary hunch between the surging muscles of his shoulders. He remembered, too, what Ekemi had said: *Bouda.*
Men who were animals, seen in these woods. Golden eyes.

He was not, therefore, entirely surprised when every hair
on his body suddenly stood on end, and a pulse not unlike
the throb from a very loud crash of thunder rolled through
his chest. It was a shape-shifter call, one animal to another.
Amiri was not alone.

He had no time for subterfuge. None for stealth. But he

stopped running. Held himself very still, listening. Even so, he almost missed the approach, the soft pad of careful feet. He caught a scent that was old and dry—so familiar, Amiri had to take a moment to wonder if he was losing his mind.

A cheetah emerged from the undergrowth. Large, scarred, golden eyes bright as sun-fire. A lethal gaze. Familiar as his own spots.

Amiri stared, feeling his world burn. Pieces falling together in ways he could not bear to contemplate.

He shifted shape, flowing into his human skin. As did the other cheetah, though with much greater reluctance.

"Abuu," Amiri whispered, when he finally found his voice. He stared at the man who emerged from the cheetah's body. Tall and sinewy, with blue-black skin like old leather. Straight nose, high cheeks, narrow jaw. Imperious stare. It had been fourteen years, but his father was exactly as he remembered.

"Cub," said the old man. "Finally."

Amiri could hardly hear him. His ears rang. "You are here."

"Business," said his father, staring—as though soaking in the sight of his son. Amiri could hardly let himself imagine the old man might have missed him. The possibility, far too remote; the chance, far too painful.

"You mean the Consortium," said Amiri heavily, following his intuition.

His father's expression never changed; inscrutable, cold. "That is one name. But yes. We have . . . an arrangement."

Amiri wanted to bend over and be sick. "Then you are no better than a butcher."

"Not a new sentiment, coming from you."

Of all the ways he had imagined seeing his father again,

this was not it. "Are you aware of what they did to me? And others? The torture, the experiments?"

The old man's eyelid twitched. "Bottom line, cub. It all comes down to survival."

Not the answer Amiri had been looking for. "You have never trusted humans."

"Those in the Consortium are not human."

"And did they send you here to bring me back? Will you betray me?"

"Will you come without a fight?"

"No," Amiri said. "I will not."

Which was enough. His father attacked. Faster than the wings of a hummingbird—faster than Amiri—his fists pounding his son's stomach like a punching bag. Amiri managed to slip away, claws pouring from his fingertips. He swiped at his father's chest, then higher, across his face. He nicked skin, and when his father stumbled, he dropped down and ran, throwing himself into the body of the cheetah.

His father followed. Chasing him. Jaws snapping. Eyes hot as fire. And had the circumstances not been so dire, so *incomprehensible,* Amiri would have taken fierce pleasure in running with his father again.

Unfortunately, that was not the case. Unfortunately, his world was going insane. Everything he thought he knew, betrayed. And by the one person who, though his methods had been abhorrent, had always protected him.

Claws sank into Amiri's haunches, dragging him off balance. He snarled, spinning, lashing out at his father. The two cheetahs rolled, mouths seeking each other's throats. Screaming. His father left several openings that Amiri did not take—part of him, despite everything, afraid of the injuries he might cause—and the old cheetah sprang away, landing light in a tangle of vines. He shifted shape, just enough to regain his use of speech, spotted fur idling down his long lean body in a sheer golden mist. Humanoid, barely.

"You have grown weak," rasped his father, flexing fingers that were mostly claws.

"Do you *want* me to hurt you?" Amiri replied harshly, also shifting. "Why are you doing this? It goes against everything—"

"The woman," interrupted the old man. "What is she to you?"

Cold entered Amiri's heart. "She is mine."

"She is human."

"As was my mother, and yours."

"But she *knows*. You have shed your skin for her."

Never mind how his father had discovered that. Amiri leaned close. "She loves me still. She *loves* me, *Abuu*."

His father waved his hand, disdainful. "Women always say what men wish to hear. She is no different. She will betray you."

"No."

"Fool." The old man raised his chin, eyes blazing. "You never had the stomach for survival. Is she with child yet?"

"*Abuu*—"

"You have no time. Ride her hard and fast. Get yourself a cub and then I will kill her for you."

Amiri struck his father. An unthinking act, but the pure raw fury that filled him was a heady wild thing; utterly satisfying. "*You will not touch her.*"

His father's lower lip bled. "Would you kill *me* for her?"

"In a heartbeat."

"Ah." His mouth slanted into an odd bitter smile. "That is something, I suppose."

Amiri stood back, staring. "I will not let you take me back, *Abuu*. Not before I find help."

The old man raised his chin, tufted ears swiveling against his head. "The Catholic Missionary. Their radio. That will be inadequate to reach your friends."

He wanted to hold his head and scream. "How much do you know of my life?"

His father ignored him. "You have another option."

"And what could that possibly be?"

Again, a smile. "Follow me."

IT WAS AN ODD TRUCE, BETWEEN FATHER AND SON. AN UN-spoken promise not to kill each other.

Amiri kept stealing glances at the old man. Fourteen years since they had stood in each other's presence, and that last time had been ugly, as well.

No stomach. Too soft, whispered his father's voice. *Angelique would have betrayed us all.*

"No one would have believed Angelique," Amiri said, before he realized that his father had not spoken.

But the old man's gaze stayed steady and straight on their path, and he brushed lightly on the fur of his arms as he said, "She was terrified of you. A small heartless woman. But she was beautiful and people liked her. They would have listened. Asked questions. Made your life . . . difficult. I did what had to be done."

"Murder is never the answer."

"You know better than that," said the old man, giving him a sharp look. "It is not murder when you are defending your life. Even *you* said that you would kill for your woman. You would kill your own father to keep her safe."

Pain bloomed in Amiri's heart. "Will it come to that?"

His father said nothing, but his pace quickened, and a moment later he dropped into the body of the cheetah. Amiri followed suit, and the shape-shifters ran, keeping low to the ground, moving through the night maze of trees and water and vines. The world burned inside Amiri's ears—burned with the roar of his blood—and he was so caught up in his own private hell, he could hardly differentiate the sounds that poured into his ears.

Until, quite suddenly, he heard men talking. Accompanied by a small sharp clicking sound.

Amiri and his father crept through the twisting undergrowth, dragging stomachs over sharp rocks and snapped limbs, until they crouched on the edge of a small clearing. In front of them, men. At least thirty, gathered around scattered cook fires that cast a glow over their rough-hewn olive uniforms, bodies bristling with weapons. Much like the men he had killed and questioned.

Standing in their midst was a man who wore no uniform, but lightweight clothes drenched in sweat, clinging to a lean body. Amiri glimpsed long hair, a silver pendant hanging against a dusky-skinned throat. A sharp, angular face; and sharper eyes. He watched the man's jaw flex, and every time it did, he heard that clicking sound. Too metallic to be bone.

The old cheetah shifted shape, melting into his full dark human skin. "Your other option, cub."

Amiri shifted as well, digging his fingers into the dirt. "What option? The man is likely a terrorist."

"But he hates Broker."

"Broker is dead."

"Broker never dies," said his father grimly.

Amiri studied his face, struck with an odd feeling. "You tried?"

"I had an irresistible opportunity."

Realization stung. "You are with them against your will."

His father ignored him. "Broker had Jaaved's wife kidnapped not one day ago. He sent pictures of what was done to her. What is *still* being done. Jaaved is not taking it well."

"You want to strike a deal."

"He knows me."

Amiri hesitated. "Why now? What hold does the Consortium have over you?"

Again, his father did not answer. He stood, and began walking down to the gathered men. Exposed, head held high. As though he belonged. Amiri followed his example, focusing on Jaaved and no one else—not even when a shout went up, and thirty guns of varying sizes and pedigrees were suddenly aimed in their direction.

Jaaved met them halfway, carrying himself with rigid precision. He held a gun in his right hand. His jaw was tight, and he smelled like blood and smoke. He placed the tip of his weapon against the old man's forehead. Amiri held his breath.

"I have a fantasy," rasped Jaaved, without preamble. "About cutting out tongues and slicing testicles. Perhaps serving them for supper. Recording the whole affair. Sending it to family members and young children."

"How vivid," said Amiri's father. "Any guests in mind?"

Jaaved snarled, revealing a great deal of metal in his mouth. "I should kill you on principle. What do you want, Aitan? And why does Broker send his messengers to me *naked*? Another reminder of my wife?"

"Hardly. Though I am certain my employer would be gratified to know you followed his instructions so . . . liberally . . . by crossing into his land with all these armed men."

"He asked me to come."

"Indeed. But I am not here to pass along his message."

Jaaved grunted, eying him . . . and then Amiri. "You are?"

Amiri kept his expression flat, cold—though part of him was still shocked at hearing his father's real name spoken out loud by this man. "I am someone with an offer. If you have a taste to kill."

"That depends."

"I will give you Broker," said Aitan.

Jaaved raised his chin, staring. His jaw flexed—clicking—sharp and violent. Gun still pressed to the old man's forehead. "Why would you do that?"

Aitan gave him a long steady look. "Because we have both been hurt in similar ways."

Amiri managed not to react, but it was difficult. He kept his gaze focused on Jaaved, who stared into the old man's eyes for quite some time.

"You can promise Broker?" he said, slowly.

"I can promise many things," replied Aitan, "but Broker, I can deliver."

Something dark and frightening passed through Jaaved's face. "He has something else of mine."

"Your wife."

"Another woman. A doctor," the man said.

"She is dead."

"Is she?" Jaaved's eyes narrowed, and he looked at Amiri. "What do you get out of this?"

"Satisfaction," Amiri replied shortly, forcing himself not to tear the man's throat out.

Jaaved held his gaze, and grunted. He lowered his gun. "Come. Let us talk business."

CHAPTER SEVENTEEN

B EING kidnapped had, of course, its disadvantages. Complete and unremitting terror was one of them, as well as the certain promise of an untimely and, most likely, ugly death. Neither of which Rikki was entirely keen on experiencing.

But when she opened her eyes, hours after first being tossed into that helicopter, and found herself nestled on a soft downy bed of raw white silk, she had to wonder what, exactly, she had been running from.

Her head hurt. Her chest ached. She hardly wanted to move, but she touched herself, fingers sliding up her naked body, over her scars, to a tender spot just above her right breast. There was a bandage there. She remembered the gun, the sprout of a dart against her body. Her inner elbow was sore, too. She found needle marks.

Rikki took a deep slow breath and turned her head. Past the bed, she saw creamy walls and dark wood trim, polished floors of the same kind and color. The air smelled sweet and cool, filled with the soft ambient glow of gentle lights shining from the ceiling. On the other side of the bed, on the nightstand, she found an artful arrangement of orchids. And beyond that, a large window that overlooked the jungle. It was light out, but only just—dawn or twilight, there was no way to know.

Rikki sat up, clutching the sheet to her breasts. At the bottom of the bed she saw a folded set of soft clothes, also white, as well as a set of tennis shoes. And on top of those, much to her surprise, was the scalpel. Her precious little blade. It made her think of Amiri. She hoped he was safe.

She slid out of the bed, looking for cameras. Found nothing, but that meant little. She dressed quickly. Located a bathroom, dark and rich with wood and marble and glass. Opulent. She stood inside, looking at herself in the mirror. Her face was gaunt, eyes glassy. Every bone stood out.

Taking a hot shower would have probably made her high, but she did not feel comfortable exposing herself like that. She felt vulnerable enough, just using the toilet.

She splashed water on her face, smothered herself with a soft clean towel, and went back out into the room. She thought about trying to break the window—a chair might do the trick, or there was always the lid from the toilet. Even her own body, if she got really desperate.

Try the door first, stunt girl.

So she did. And it opened. Rikki held her breath, listening, but when no one raised the alarm, she poked her head into the hall.

It was empty—except for some magnificent decorating. Rikki wasn't sure whether she wanted to live in this place forever, or find some matches and burn it all down.

She stepped into the hall and closed her door. Started walking—listening hard, moving on light feet. She held the scalpel in one hand. Passed many doors, all of which had electronic locks and security pads set into the wall.

The hall was long. Rikki began to worry she might

never find the end of it, but after several minutes of rising panic, she heard the gurgle and churning bubble of water. A fountain. The air began to smell like orchids again.

Rikki entered a large cavernous room, at the center of which was a magnificent stone sculpture that looked like nothing more than some mountain cliff torn off its edge and then planted, perpendicular, in the center of a rock pool. Water flowed down its ragged sides, the crevices of which were filled with dangling moss and orchids, occasionally shrouded by delicate ferns. Below, inside the deep waters of the pool itself, swam monstrous koi as long as she was tall, parting the waters beneath lily pads and flowers.

She heard giggling, took a step back, raising the scalpel . . . just as two children ran into view. One of them to her shock was Kimbareta. Still wearing that whistle, though his clothes were different. Like Rikki—white, easy, a jogging outfit.

The boy skidded to a stop when he saw her, and she dropped to her knees, holding out one arm. He threw himself against her body, clutching her neck. The kid might not know her worth beans, but Rikki was gratified that he seemed so happy to see her face.

"You okay?" she asked him, her French rather poor. The boy nodded against her shoulder, and she rose slowly, holding on to his hand. In front of them was another child, one Rikki had not see before. A girl, no older than eight or nine. She was lovely—brown skin, high cheekbones, and hair that curled and flowed, shot through with gold.

Her eyes were gold, pale and rich as metal.

Rikki stared. "Hello."

"Hello," said the girl, first in French, and then English. Utterly composed. "Who are you?"

"My name is Rikki. And you?"

"I am A'sharia." Spoken with the dignity of a young queen. Rikki thought she could see a resemblance to someone she knew, and it made her light-headed.

Kimbareta stiffened. Rikki turned. Broker stood behind her, flanked by Marco. Terror clawed up her throat, but she took a deep breath, and then another, forcing herself to stay calm, sharp—in the moment, second by second. She could do this. She was going to survive.

"Already awake and about," said Broker. "I gave you enough sedative to leave anyone else unconscious for three days."

Rikki shrugged. "So?"

He raised his brow. "It's only been ten hours."

"Good metabolism." She squeezed Kimbareta's hand. "Why are these children here?"

"They are my guests."

"People don't keep children as guests. Not unless they have a good reason."

"Ready to fight for them?" His smile widened. "Never fear, Doctor Kinn. I may *hire* perverts, but I can assure you, my proclivities do not run any younger than the age of good intellectual discourse."

Which was not a terribly satisfying answer, but as good as she could hope for. Rikki swallowed hard, squeezed Kimbareta's hand one more time for good measure, and then gently pushed him toward A'sharia.

Broker said, "Go on. Both of you play."

The children looked at Rikki with some pity, and gave Broker stares of incredible distrust. He made a shooing motion. A'sharia grabbed Kimbareta's hand and tugged. They ran away. Very fast. No longer laughing.

"Smart kids," Rikki said dryly.

"Most are," Broker replied, and held out his hand. "Please join me, Doctor Kinn."

Rikki did, though she refused to take his hand. Indeed, she still held the scalpel—though she failed to see any use in stabbing Broker, as crushing his skull had done little to hinder him. Nor did he seem at all troubled that she was carrying it around in such an obvious manner. She was not much of a threat, apparently.

She held the scalpel tight though. Felt better for it. A nice, sharp accessory.

Marco smiled. Rikki wanted to set his eyebrows on fire. She ignored him and kept pace with Broker. He led her down another hall, this one considerably shorter. At the end of it was a large dining room, finely appointed, mostly empty. Moochie and Francis sat at the far end, eating. They looked up when she walked in, but only briefly, and showed nothing on their faces.

Broker held out a chair for Rikki. She sat, facing a long line of windows overlooking the jungle. Marco took a seat nearby. A small round woman emerged from behind a swinging set of doors and looked at them enquiringly.

"Tea or coffee?" Broker asked.

"Arsenic," Rikki said. "Lighter fluid."

"Bring both," he said to the woman, with discomfiting ambiguity.

"I was expecting a house of horrors," Rikki told him, her palm sweaty around the scalpel. "This feels more like a resort."

"I prefer luxury to cold sterility," Broker replied. "It makes my work easier."

"Kidnapping, torture, the manufacture of biological weapons . . ."

"High enterprise. Very lucrative."

"Money isn't the reason you do it," she said, searching his eyes. "Not in the slightest."

The woman returned carrying a tray laden down with coffee and a pot of hot water, with tea bags, lemon, and sugar. No chemicals or poison. Not now, anyway. Broker took coffee. Rikki began steeping her tea. Such a normal thing to do. So mundane.

"What do you want from me?" she asked him. "What is the point of all this?"

"Why did your father go to prison?" Broker asked, watching her over the rim of his cup. "Why did he die?"

Her breath caught. "That's not relevant. Or your business."

"Answer the question."

She cut the tip of her thumb on the scalpel. "No."

Broker smiled coldly. "He went to prison because of you. Because he was *protecting* you. Voluntary manslaughter. Murder, in the heat of passion."

She felt Moochie and Francis watching. Saw Marco's greasy-lipped smirk on the edge of her vision. Ignored them all, staring into Broker's cold, cold, eyes. "You already know."

"I know about the child molester who moved into the neighborhood. A man whom your father found standing outside your window in the middle of the night. And I know about the baseball bat he took to that man's head, pounding it into pulp." His lips thinned, and he stroked his temple. "Apple doesn't fall far from the tree, does it?"

Rikki could hardly breathe. "Why are you doing this?"

"Ask instead why your father reacted as he did. Instinct? Need? Because it was the right thing to do?" Broker tapped the tabletop, smiling idly. "We all have reasons for our actions, Doctor Kinn. All of us righteous, even at our most abhorrent."

"He was a good man," she whispered. "The best."

Broker raised his brow, that ugly smile flitting across his mouth. "He would have been free by now, isn't that correct? It was a three-year sentence. Three years, and he was dead after only twelve months. Stabbed twice in the gut. All because he committed himself to protecting you."

She threw her cup of tea at him. He knocked it aside. Hot water sprayed everywhere. Chairs scraped back; Marco was ready to jump across the table, but Broker held up one hand, and with the other, wiped water from his burned cheeks.

"Wildcat," he said. "I like that about you."

"You must like something more than that," Rikki replied shakily, heart racing. "One woman out of six billion, and you choose to make my life your business. What have I got to offer someone with your connections?"

Broker stripped off his jacket and laid it across the table. His body was trim, well muscled beneath the damp spots in his fine white shirt. "Your description is apt. Six billion people in this world. All of them different. No two alike. Why is that, Doctor Kinn? What makes each of us unique?"

"Our DNA," she said, after a brief pause.

Broker smiled. "Exactly."

Impossible, ridiculous. "I don't understand."

"Oh, I believe you do."

Rikki wrestled with the idea, and her opinion did not change. "You want something in my DNA?"

He did not confirm or deny, but the answer was there in his silence. Rikki sat back, studying his face, those cold dead eyes that could not hide themselves, no matter how much he tried to smile.

Tread carefully, Rikki thought, clutching the scalpel

under the table. She said, "Assuming I believe you, how the hell do you know I have what you want?"

"As I told you, Doctor Kinn, I make it my business to know many things."

"But in my case?"

His eyes narrowed. "There was a man, once, who was very powerful. He lived a very long time. And he had many children. He left behind a strong bloodline, Doctor Kinn. Many lines, all over the world. And it was once my job to track them."

Rikki had to wrap her mind around that concept. "You're implying I'm a descendant."

"I am implying nothing."

"This is crazy," she retorted.

Broker stood. "Come along, Doctor Kinn."

Rikki did not want to move. She wanted to fight. To take the scalpel still gripped tight in her hand and make her own slasher flick.

But a little voice told her to move, and she got up. So did Marco, Francis, and Moochie. One big party. In the Congo. In the house of a psychopath. She hoped Amiri got here soon.

Flanked by the mercenaries, Broker led Rikki down the hall, past the stone fountain, and down another passage that was less decorated, the halls wider. They passed no one else, and she heard nothing but the sounds of breathing, the rustle of clothing. And yet, there was nothing empty about the facility she moved through; she could feel the unseen presence of others, suffered that weight as she passed doors, and curtains covering sections of wall beside those doors. The air smelled like a hospital, cold and sterile.

Broker pulled aside one curtain as they walked, letting

it fall back almost immediately. Long enough to reveal a window. Long enough to show a woman sitting on a cot in a white padded room. Mireille. Cradling her face.

Rikki started to stop. Francis nudged her. She said, "It wasn't her fault."

"I know," Broker said, and stopped. "Here we are."

Rikki hesitated. Marco grabbed her arm. Broker opened the door and she saw an examining table inside. Straps. Stirrups.

She swung with the scalpel and caught Marco in the shoulder. He roared, slamming her into the wall. She hit it hard enough to bounce, but she ignored the pain and tried to run. Francis caught her around the waist. Moochie grabbed her arms. Marco wrenched the scalpel from his shoulder and lunged. Francis side-checked him with his hip.

Broker said, "Get her inside."

She kicked. She screamed. She tried to bite, but Francis was quick and Moochie stayed out of range. They got her on the table, just barely, taking her blows with soft grunts. Marco tried grabbing her feet. She clocked him in the face and his nose spurted blood.

Broker sighed, and hit the intercom by the door. "Ajax, report to this location, please."

Rikki did not miss the look that passed between Francis and Moochie. She kept fighting, but she was watching their faces, too. They would not look her in the eyes.

A new man appeared in the doorway. He looked like he ate steroids with his Cheerios. His arms were oiled monoliths—chest broad, straining against his too-small shirt—his legs thick and bowed at the knee. He had hairy knuckles. A thick brow.

Broker said, "Ajax? If you would."

Ajax reached behind the door. Pulled hard. A man stumbled into view. Bloody, broken, hardly able to stand. His face almost too swollen to recognize.

But she did. Because he was a friend.

"Jean-Claude," Rikki breathed, and Broker leaned close to her ear.

"Everyone who protects you suffers," he whispered. "This man saved your life, Doctor Kinn. He wrested you from blood and pain and death. Look at what you give him in return."

Jean-Claude was so quiet, Rikki wondered if he hardly knew she was there. Or if he even cared. His eyes were swollen shut. He smelled like blood. He smelled like her memories. She remembered his warnings at the ferry, his fear, and wanted to kill Broker. Again. "You son of a bitch. You could knock me out, easier."

"Yes," he replied smoothly, "but sedatives contaminate several of the tests I need to run. Otherwise, my dear, you would be quite unconscious, and this poor man safe at home with his wife and children. Unfortunately for him, I know how sentimental you are."

Broker flicked his finger at Ajax. The big man hauled Jean-Claude away, leaving behind a smear of blood where he had slouched. Tears burned Rikki's eyes. "Tell me what you want."

"I want you," Broker said softly.

Rikki looked at him. Hate filled her throat. Hate lodged in her gut. Her heart ached with hate.

She stuck her feet in the stirrups. She held her breath and gazed up at Francis and Moochie, who stared back, impossibly grim. They released her shoulders and arms, and she lay down. She thought of Amiri, what he had undergone at the hands of these people. If he could survive, so could she.

If she could survive what had been done to her, she could handle anything.

Broker stood over her. "You are a very strong woman, Doctor Kinn. To break you would require almost killing you, and I do not want that."

"Why are you doing this?" she whispered. "Why?"

"Because someone must," he said, and for one moment something came alive in his eyes, something that was not warm or soft, but hard and vital. "Because otherwise, Doctor Kinn, we are all going to die."

CHAPTER EIGHTEEN

T HERE was no need to travel with Jaaved. The man had his instructions—indeed, he already held some inkling of where Broker kept his facility. He had been in the region because he'd been summoned, but he'd had revenge on his mind. Revenge and, perhaps, one Doctor Kinn.

Amiri and his father left Jaaved in the wee hours of morning and ran. Ran fast, ran hard, right up until they reached the base camp where Amiri had left Rikki and Rictor.

Chaos had spit on the land. Amiri saw no dead, smelled little blood, but the miasma of fear and anger coated the air, thick as rotting soup. Ramshackle homes had been torn apart, with clothes, pans, books—anything not tied down— now spilled onto the grass. Men and women were trying to clean away the destruction, but they did so with movements that alternated between sharp, furious and exhausted. Ekemi was amongst them. He no longer wore his glasses, and his nose looked as though it might be broken.

Amiri did not want to speak to him. Guilt twinged, but he had to know. Had to be sure.

He shifted shape. His father remained a cheetah, and flopped down on his side, eyes closed. Resting. Amiri watched him, feeling lost in another, far stranger world. Heart aching. But staring did no good, changed nothing. He left the jungle to find out what had happened to Rikki and Rictor.

People saw him coming. Few recognized him from the night before, given the spike of fear and uneasiness that marred the already devastated faces. His nudity walked almost twenty feet ahead of him—which, for the first time in quite some while, made him regret that he could not carry clothes while running as a cheetah.

Someone ran to fetch Ekemi. Amiri was close enough to see the man's expression change. It was not terribly pleasant. Not that Amiri blamed him. Of late, he felt rather like a bad charm.

"Rikki," Amiri said, as soon as Ekemi was in earshot. The man's uniform was stained with blood, as was the skin around his nose and lip. He glanced down at Amiri's nudity, but showed nothing on his face except stricken concern.

"They took her," Ekemi said. "There was a helicopter."

Amiri's jaw locked. His entire face frozen—a cold mask, revealing nothing, though beneath his skin he screamed. He had left her. He had known what would happen, and had gone anyway.

You did what you had to. As did she.

His father's whisper. Still inside his head, even though the man himself was a stone's throw away. The irony was sickening.

"Did they harm her?" He had trouble getting the words out.

Bitterness stole across Ekemi's face. "Not to my knowledge, but I was . . . otherwise occupied. They took the boy, too. The child you brought with you."

"Kimbareta?" Amiri frowned. "What of Rictor?"

"Your friend is gone. He asked for a rifle, took some clothing and ammunition, and disappeared into the forest." Ekemi shook his head. "I believe he was trying to follow the helicopter."

He forced himself to breathe. "I will rectify this situation, Ekemi. I will make it right."

"No." Ekemi backed away from him. Not unkindly, but with a finality that cut, nonetheless. "We will be fine on our own."

Amiri tried to argue, but stopped. Ekemi had every reason to be wary. Later, maybe. When this was all done. He would find a way.

He held out his hand. Ekemi shook it, briefly.

"Thank you," Amiri said. "For everything, thank you."

"Go," said the man, gravely. "Go and do what you must."

Spoken as though he believed Amiri were capable of saving Rikki. As though he had no doubt.

A small comfort. Amiri turned and ran.

His father was not waiting where he had been left. Amiri tracked the old cheetah around the border of the camp, finding him crouched above a bent sapling, mouth open, inhaling a scent on his tongue. Amiri knelt beside him, and touched the broken plant. Brought his fingers back to his nose. He tasted rain, the weight of a thunderstorm.

His father shifted just enough to speak, still more animal than man. "The one who passed here is not human."

"No," Amiri said. "None of us know what he is."

"Old blood," Aitan rasped. "Gods and monsters."

An appropriate description. Perhaps even for themselves.

They continued on, embraced by the cheetah, and though they were made for open plains and dry winds, the jungle held no secrets, no barriers. Amiri slipped through the morning shadows, relentless, and inside his heart he sensed a pulse that was only Rikki—as though he could feel her heartbeat closed tight within him, reaching and pulling him near.

His father's motives remained more elusive.

Time passed. Amiri's throat burned. He thought about finding water, and was close to doing so when a gunshot blasted the heavy mid-morning air. He heard shouts, branches breaking.

Power poured into his muscles. He surged ahead of his father, cutting a streak through the tangle. Sunlight danced through the leaves into his eyes. He caught the scent of thunder, blood, men . . . and found Rictor, who was pressed on his side in a mass of ferns, using a fallen tree as cover, a rifle balanced and braced against his shoulder. He wore pants, but no shirt. The gashes across his back were livid, raw, etched in green. Nothing, from his upper shoulders to the base of his spine, had been spared.

Men were firing on Rictor. It was difficult for Amiri to see how many, but the scents were thick and the harsh tones of heavy breathing gathered like the wind in his ears. He followed the sounds to their source—found three mercenaries, men in black staying close to trees and the ground. He crept behind them and they never noticed. He felt his father join him, staring.

Broker's men, Amiri imagined the old man saying; the words were in his eyes. Cold eyes, calculating. Amiri saw no remorse—none—and watched his father lunge from the underbrush, slamming one of the gunmen sideways into the ground. Amiri followed suit, moving so fast the second man could hardly react to his partner's death before he himself tumbled into the leaves, screaming. Amiri sank his jaws into that soft throat and ripped. Blood gushed into his mouth.

He heard the creak of the last man's gear as he turned,

heard a muffled gasp. A gun went off—a thunderous blast. The mercenary flew sideways, a hole in his chest. Amiri turned. Found Rictor walking toward them, rifle poised. His eyes were like cut glass, sharp. Even before, in the lab, the man had never looked so uncompromisingly lethal. Amiri wondered, briefly, if he was going to die.

"Took you cats long enough," Rictor rumbled, pacing over to the dead mercenary. He glanced around, scanning the undergrowth, then set down his rifle and started stripping the corpse of weapons. Amiri shifted shape. Rictor glanced up and said, "Your guy doesn't have bullet holes in his vest."

It was not an actual request, but Amiri had no desire to sting another man's pride. He stripped the man he had killed, unbuckling his vest, and tossed the clothing to Rictor. Rictor slipped it on, wincing just slightly.

"What happened here?" Amiri asked, glancing at his father. He found the old cheetah sitting on his haunches, watching Rictor. Blood covered his muzzle. The air smelled thick with death, and was just as still. No birds sang. No monkeys rattled through the canopy.

Rictor met Aitan's stare, and held it. "Ambush. My hearing's not as good as yours."

"I am surprised you are so proficient with a gun," Amiri murmured. "I cannot imagine you ever had a use for one."

"Not before now." Rictor finally tore his gaze from Aitan. "Go ahead. Ask."

Amiri inclined his head. "Who hurt you?"

"That's not what I wanted you to ask."

"And?"

"And I did it to myself," he replied darkly. "The moment I got stupid."

"From birth, then?" said Aitan, shifting into his human

body. Rictor gave him a hard look and traded his rifle for the AK-47 and a pistol.

Amiri rose smoothly to his feet. "Interfering, Rictor?"

"Do not talk to me," he said harshly. "Do not."

"I simply want to be clear. Are you here to help us?"

"You fuck," Rictor snapped quietly, and there was enough grief and rage in his eyes that Amiri felt ashamed of himself. But it was brief, because this was survival, and the question had to be asked.

Aitan looked to the east. "We are close. We should hide the bodies. Someone might have heard the fight."

Rictor's mouth tightened. He bent down, grabbed ankles, and started pulling. Pain twisted his face, but he made not one sound. Amiri moved to help him, taking the brunt of the burden. Neither man looked at the other.

A radio crackled. Rictor snatched it up and clipped the device to his pocket, turning the volume down low. Amiri glanced at his father. "How close?"

"Less than an hour's walk, even in these bodies."

Rictor straightened. "You have a plan?"

"I will tell you on the way," Amiri said.

"Wow," Rictor said, some time later. "You're screwed."

The three men stood on the edge of a ravine. Below them, nestled in the cleft of the rolling mountain forest, jutted the edge of a large octagonal structure, constructed of glass and concrete. Amiri could not imagine the cost and manpower to construct such a facility in the heart of this isolated place. Everything, flown in. Indeed, he saw several clearings filled with helicopters, as well as a landing pad on the roof of the structure. Arrogant, obvious, exposed.

Amiri exhaled, slowly. "Do you have a better plan, Rictor?"

A grim smile touched the man's mouth. Mists rose around them; the air was hot, but with a damp fresh scent that provided an illusion of something cooler. Amiri heard voices. Far away, near the bottom of the ravine. Nothing dangerous.

"Broker is going to kill you," Rictor said, looking him straight in the eye. "Broker dreams of you dead. I'm on that list, too. Artur. Elena. Everyone who was there in Russia."

"Why?"

"Why does any man murder?" Rictor looked away, down at the facility. "We killed someone he loved."

Aitan crouched, palms open, hovering close to the ground as though soaking the warmth of the earth into his skin. It was an old gesture, one Amiri had seen a million times—though not in years. It made him hurt. It made him remember good times instead of bad.

"It is the only way," said his father quietly. "They expect me to bring him in. And Broker will not wish to immediately kill Amiri. He will torture him first. That will give me time to take down the security protocols for Jaaved and his men."

"Ah," Rictor replied. "Hope he's not quick with the hot irons, then."

Amiri set his jaw. "How long until Jaaved is in position?"

"Six hours, at least. We moved considerably faster than him."

"Rikki might not have that much time."

"She is more valuable to him alive," said his father coolly. "She will survive."

"Why?" Amiri snapped, choking on fury and fear and heartache. "Why do they want her?"

Aitan hesitated. Rictor said, "Blood. The blood of the Magi, to be specific."

Amiri stared. He knew little of the Magi, only stories told

by fellow shape-shifters and other members of the agency:
A sorcerer, two thousand years old, had cursed himself and
another with immortality, a long life that had not offered
respite from death, but only the desire for it.

"I do not understand," he said. "How does that involve
Rikki?"

"The Magi was a baby factory," Rictor replied. "He had
loads of children. Buckets of children, for two thousand
years. Right up until this century, when he finally died. He
has babies scattered you still don't know about."

Aitan looked intrigued. "They are all similarly gifted?"

"Some. Depends on how diluted their blood is." Rictor
gave Amiri a bitter smile. "Would you like to guess how
many members of Dirk & Steele are his descendents?"

"I would rather not," Amiri replied, rather troubled by
the whole idea. "But even if Rikki *is* related to him, then
what do they hope to achieve by having her? She is an extraordinary woman, but she has no otherworldly gifts."

"Not that you know of," Rictor muttered.

Aitan rose slowly. "Enough. I will scout the perimeter.
Both of you stay here."

Amiri wanted to protest, but remained quiet. Being
around his father made him feel like a child again, a stranger
in his own skin. He hardly thought he knew himself or the
old man. Nor did it help having Rictor near. One had raised
him. The other had tortured him. The two were not so different.

Aitan slipped away. Rictor said, "Enjoying your reunion?"

"Read my mind."

"Go to hell."

Amiri studied him, unaffected by his anger. "Are you
truly powerless?"

"You think I like your company that much?"

"I think that you are, and always will be, a stranger. I do not know what to think."

"How heartening," Rictor muttered.

Amiri sighed. "I am sorry. Is there *anything* that can be done for you?"

"No." The other man's gaze turned distant, thoughtful. Edged with hard memory. "I'm alive. I have everything I need."

"Indeed," Amiri murmured, surprised by his answer. Suffering an odd pang of conscience. "Rictor. Why *did* you come to us? You said Elena, but—"

"She never asked me."

"You said she did not have to. What does that mean?"

"It's none of your fucking business." Rictor stood. The radio crackled on his hip. He turned up the volume. Voices hissed. Amiri heard comments about transport times, supplies, more men . . . and then, at the very end, a mention of one Doctor Regina Kinn.

You should see what she did to Marco, someone laughed. *Son of a bitch wants to kill her ass.*

Amiri stood, heart pounding. Staring blindly at the facility. Desperate enough to slam himself against those walls.

"Don't," Rictor said, watching him. "Don't even think about it."

"And what would you do for Elena?" Amiri asked sharply. "I *cannot* wait for Jaaved. Not when she is down there waiting for me."

"Then do not wait," said a new voice, soft and cold as ice. Amiri whirled, stunned.

Broker. As though materialized from air. No sound of his approach, and hardly a scent. He stood as though carved from stone—perfectly still, his gray suit smooth as bone. His eyes were flat, dead.

Further back, some distance away, was yet more movement. A cage closing in. Men rose from the forest floor like an army of ghosts. Camouflaged, weapons held high. Amiri tried catching their scents, but all he found was the faint musk of leopard scat. The mercenaries had used a spray to cover their odors.

And they had been in place for a long time, if Amiri was any judge. He had heard *nothing*. Of all the foolish, stupid, *senseless*—

"Amiri," Broker said, and his gaze flicked to Rictor, who had his gun pointed strong and steady at the pale man's face. He smiled, but it seemed forced. Uneasy. "You know better than that."

"I know I could slow you down," Rictor replied. "I know I could tear you apart with my bare hands."

"You could do more than that, but only one man can kill me." Broker tapped his skull. "I've foreseen it. But he's not here. You are. And what strange irony that is. *Mon petit meurtrier.*"

Green light flashed through Rictor's eyes. Power. But only for a moment, and then it was like watching a man be struck by lightning, or hit in the spine with a dozen hammers all at once. Rictor's eyes glowed, and in that same instant his back arched so deeply Amiri heard his spine crack. A scream of pure agony choked free of his throat. He fell on his knees, coughing, gagging.

No, Amiri thought, watching Broker. *No.*

But the damage was done. Broker stared, pure astonishment cutting through his gaze. "What is this? What has happened to you?"

Rictor spat. Broker crouched, peering closely. Eyes finally sparking with some vital, dangerous light.

"A man like you needs no gun," he said, and then, even softer: "You are mortal."

Amiri stepped in front of Rictor, dropping low, fingers digging into the dirt. "Stay away from him."

"Or what?" Loose laughter tumbled free of Broker's throat. "Oh, my. If only Artur and *Elena* were present—"

Rictor reached around Amiri and fired the gun. Broker caught the bullet in his head and flew backward, slamming into the ground. Rictor scrambled to his feet, shoving Amiri aside. Running. He emptied the gun into Broker's chest. Then kicked him.

Amiri kept expecting one of the watching mercenaries to stop Rictor, but none did—except for a single individual, a familiar face. From the airfield. His eyebrows thick as a rug. He looked from Broker to his attacker, and his eyes darkened with outrage. His finger tightened on the trigger of his gun.

Amiri knocked Rictor out of the way, hearing a roar in the air, feeling a roar in his body as pain snapped through his shoulder. He fell down hard, swimming in agony. Rictor fell on his knees beside him, handgun tossed aside in favor of the stolen AK-47, held tight and steady, aimed at the mercenaries as though his one weapon could kill them all. His face was grim as death, and he wore a cold hard resignation that was, for one brief moment, unreservedly bitter.

"It's a flesh wound," he said of Amiri's wound, glancing down for just a moment. "Took a slice out of your shoulder, but nothing else. No smashed bones."

Amiri had suffered from flesh wounds and this felt incredibly more painful. But he rolled to his knees, clapped his hand over the injury, and felt a tear in the meat, gushing blood. A quarter of an inch lower and his entire shoulder would have been destroyed.

Not that it mattered. Not when Aitan walked free of the forest.

He moved as though he owned the men around him, as though he was Broker and the man dead on the ground was the servant. Amiri searched his father's face, but all he found was something aloof and pitiless, a quiet indifference, as though Aitan might watch the world burn and feel nothing: no love, no anger, no passion at all to live.

This was not the man Amiri remembered, even at his worst. The man who stood before him was a stranger.

This was not our plan, Amiri thought, and he had the sudden, terrible feeling that this had never been his father's plan.

"I am certain you would rather die than be taken alive," Aitan said to Rictor, with hardly a glance at Amiri's bleeding shoulder. "Consider, however, what will happen to those who take your place when Broker awakes."

Amiri stood, staggering. Rictor moved with him, catching him with his shoulder. Gun still raised, ready to fire. Behind Aitan, the mercenaries moved free of the forest, wielding a considerable amount of firepower.

At their feet, Broker stirred.

"In or out?" Rictor whispered. "Are we doing this?"

"In," Amiri breathed, thinking of Rikki. Sweat soaked his skin; the pain was immense. He wanted to vomit.

The bullet in Broker's forehead wiggled free, rolling into the grass. Amiri had never seen such a thing, and watched, steeling himself for the inevitable.

Broker opened his eyes and sat up. His face was still wet with blood; a red mask. All around them, silence. His men showed no reaction to their employer's resurrection. Not even when he stood, and bullets rolled out from under his shirt and hit the grass.

Broker looked at Amiri. He looked at the blood, and the wound. Extreme displeasure filled his face. "Someone shot you."

An unexpected response. Not the first thing Amiri had thought to hear. Though it made sense. Broker wanted him dead, but only by his hand. His revenge.

Broker looked at Rictor, then Aitan. "Who was it?"

"Marco," said the old man.

He nodded, as though unsurprised. "Kill him."

Aitan turned without hesitation. Marco stared, incredulous, then backed away with arms raised.

"No," he gasped, staring at Broker. "Please—"

The shape-shifter's hand lashed out, sweeping across Marco's throat, leaving behind a hole so deep that Amiri imagined he saw the man's spine. Marco scrabbled at himself, blood gushing. Eyes rolled up with horror. He collapsed on his knees, writhing, twitching.

Aitan shook his hand. Blood spattered the grass. His fingers were thick with claws, spotted fur riding up the sinewy muscles of his long forearm. Amiri could only stare, disgusted and astonished: His father, killing on the order of another—partially shifted in front of witnesses? This was a man who had murdered to keep such secrets, to keep himself safe from such a future. Who had raised his son in virtual isolation, simply to protect their bloodline.

I do this for you, whispered his father, inside Amiri's mind. *Anything for my children.*

Amiri stamped down that voice, the terrible echo of his father that would not leave him.

Broker straightened his jacket—a ridiculous gesture,

given the blood soaking through his clothes, still shining on his face. He gave Aitan a cold look. "Jaaved is coming?"

"As you requested," replied the old man, without a glance for his son. "He believes he will kill you tonight."

"And Amiri believed you were offering him a way to do the same." Broker smiled, faintly. "You were right about the lure. Nicely done. Very . . . poignant."

Amiri clenched his jaw tight. Slid a mask over his face. Calm, steady, hiding the storm in his heart. Erasing his rage. His fear.

No fear. Not when Rikki still needed him. All he had left was her. No one else mattered. And if she got hurt, or worse, *died*—

—he was going to kill his father.

CHAPTER NINETEEN

THE door was locked. Rikki had tried forcing it open more times than she could count, but all she had gotten for her trouble was a sore shoulder.

The window was made of unbreakable glass. Rikki had tried opening that, too. With a chair. And the lid from the toilet. And the pillow that now lay on the cold hardwood floor, next to her body.

She thought about her father, how he must have felt in his prison cell. Of the letters he had written her, saying it was okay, that he had books, that he thought of her all the time and when he got free, when he was paroled for good behavior like his lawyer said he would be, that every day would be like a Saturday, and he would make his flapjacks for breakfast and she would make her omelets, and nothing would be different. Nothing ever again. Just the two of them against the world.

She missed her dad. She missed him with all her heart. She missed him like she missed Markovic, who'd had nothing but given her everything he could, raised and nurtured and loved her as much as he was able, helping her survive and become what she had: strong and educated, but mostly just strong.

And she missed Amiri. She missed him like she missed her father and Markovic, and that was silly because she hardly knew him, but she missed him like there was a hole in her heart the size of those big Kansas skies, and she wanted him. She wanted him like she wanted home. Like she wanted her childhood back. She wanted him like she wanted everyone she had ever loved to live again, to rise from the dead, to tell her they loved her back, and always would.

Amiri, she thought. *Please find me.*

Her body hurt. Bone marrow extraction usually left an ache. Broker had taken blood, too. A lot of it.

And he had injected her with hormones. Specifically, to induce the development of multiple follicles. No secrets from Broker. He wanted to harvest her ova. Not all of them, he had said. But enough.

Stem cells. Actual children. God only knows what he wants to do with them.

Rikki did not plan on sticking around long enough to find out.

She forced herself up. There was a closet. She went to it and found more white jogging outfits. She took out a set, tossed it on the bed, and went to the bathroom. Looking at herself in the mirror, she stripped off her clothes. Her scars glared at her. She glared back, tracing each cut with her finger, pretending it was a knife. Drawing it in. Savoring.

I am going to fuck you over, Broker. I am going to ruin you. I am going to own you because you sure as hell won't own me. Not as long as I'm breathing.

Rikki turned on the shower. She stood under the scalding

water, skin burning. She did not cry; she planned. She always thought better in the shower, and this was no different. She gathered herself in the heat, in the scent of soap, and when she turned off the water, she was ready. She wrapped a towel around her body and went back into the bedroom.

Moochie and Francis were there. They stood by the window. A tray of food was on the nightstand.

The men stared at her chest. The towel covered all the important bits, but the scars were extensive. She looked like the love child of Freddy Krueger and Edward Scissorhands.

"Jesus," Moochie said. Francis grabbed his elbow, giving him a warning look.

Rikki no longer cared—Amiri's gift to her. That, and her priorities were straight as hell in this place. She wiped away the water that dripped from her hair into her eyes. "Why are you both here?"

"We wanted to make certain you were all right," Francis said.

Rikki laughed out loud. "You've got to be kidding."

Moochie nudged the tray. "We brought you dinner."

She stared, incredulous. "I have been kidnapped by a psychopath. He is running experiments on me. Who the hell knows what else he's going to do. You think I want to eat? You really want to know how I'm doing?"

"Do you want to escape?" Francis asked quietly. Rikki's mouth snapped shut. Moochie turned slowly to look him.

"Yo," he said. "Maybe we should talk about this."

Francis gave him a long steady look. "Do you feel like murdering children for money? How about women? Last I checked, that's not what we signed up for. In fact, I don't think we signed up for any of this, Moochie-boy."

"He'll kill us first," said Moochie. "This man has a long

arm. He'll find us and he'll kill us. And even if he doesn't, we won't ever be able to work again."

Francis looked at Rikki. "He's sending us away tonight. New assignment for his organization. He wants us to go to Morocco and kill a family. Mother, father, two little boys. No reason given. He just wants them dead." He turned again to Moochie. "It's a test. You know it as well as I do. He thinks we're soft."

"Why does he care so much about what you are?" Rikki asked, unable to help herself. "Why not replace you? Kill you? He does it so easily with everyone else."

Moochie's jaw tightened. He shared a long look with Francis. "Broker recruited us. He found us. Paid us big money. We were flattered. His outfit is big, has a reputation. He could have had anyone."

"But he wanted you two. Why?"

Francis raised his eyebrow. "Maybe it has something to do with what he wants from *you*."

"Now you're talking shit," Moochie said, but he did not sound entirely convinced.

Rikki studied them. Both were big, with similar raw-boned features. Blond hair. "Are you related?"

"Cousins," Francis told her. "Our mothers were sisters."

"And the rest?" Rikki held his gaze. "The supernatural? Broker, able to rise from the dead? Doesn't that surprise you?"

Both men went still. Moochie cleared his throat. "We, um, saw . . . stuff . . . growing up."

"Stuff."

"Doesn't matter," Francis said shortly. "Moochie? Dead or deader?"

Moochie looked rather ill. "Dead."

He smiled faintly, and looked back at Rikki. "Do you want out, Doctor Kinn?"

"Yes," she said. "But you have to help me do something first."

BROKER, THEY SAID, HAD LEFT THE BUILDING. RIKKI refrained from making an Elvis joke.

Moochie went to find the children—there were only two, he confirmed—while Francis led Rikki to the room where Jean-Claude was being kept.

"Security cameras?" she asked him, as they ran down the halls. "Guards?"

"The former, but unmanned. Used just for record-keeping. This facility is supposed to be secure. Prevention versus preparation."

"Not your style?"

"I don't ask questions, and I don't make suggestions unless I'm personally invested."

"How many other prisoners?"

Francis hesitated. "We can't take everyone, Doctor Kinn."

That was a bad sign. "How many?"

"At least thirty," he said heavily. "Mostly women. Some of them pregnant."

Rikki stopped in her tracks. "Holy crap. Did they get pregnant here?"

"Don't know. Moochie and I have only been with Broker for a month. But the women came from that camp at the bottom of the mountain. The one you ran from."

Rikki thought of Mireille, and forced herself to breathe. "He's harvesting them."

"It could be worse. They're treated well."

"Only a man would say that."

Francis held up his hands. "Don't get sanctimonious on me. I'm not saying these women aren't scared, but they're precious cargo—the only reason this place exists, if you ask me. Wouldn't be a surprise if Broker had a dozen of these facilities set up across the world."

And you could be next in line for the honor of being Golden Goose. Lay some fucking eggs, kiddo. Breed and be happy.

"Shit," she muttered, feeling ill. "How were you planning on getting us out of here?"

"Helicopter. Take one, sabotage the rest. There aren't so many men here, Doctor Kinn, and the scientists usually stay on the lower level. Right now, most of the paid guns are with Broker."

"Why? What's he doing?"

Again, hesitation. "He's bringing in your friend. The Kenyan."

Rikki died. Part of her just flat-out died, standing there. No more world, no way to breathe. Her heartbeat felt like a drum in her chest, thudding and thudding. Francis gripped her arm. She placed her hand on his chest, steadying herself.

"Amiri," she said. "When were you going to tell me?"

His expression never changed. "I wasn't. You have a window of opportunity, and he'll be too heavily guarded. If all of us are going to make it, someone has to stay behind."

Rikki sucked in her breath and pushed away from him. "Then take me back to my room. Take me back, or find another way. But I won't leave without him. Not on my life."

Francis stared, and she was suddenly reminded that this was a dangerous man, no matter how polite or concerned he acted toward her. No matter how helpful. He was a hired gun. A paid killer.

"You ask a lot," he said, in a voice far calmer than his eyes.

"But you don't have to give," she replied, forcing herself to stay steady.

Francis showed nothing. He did not blink. He regarded her with the same intensity a snake might give a mouse: flat, cold, utterly heartless. Finally, slowly, he unclipped his radio and held it to his mouth. "Moochie, you read me?"

The radio hissed. "Loud and clear."

Francis held Rikki's gaze. "Never mind what you were sent to do. We need to prepare for the boss. Got that?"

The silence was longer this time. "Got it. See you soon."

The radio clicked off with a finality that felt like a bullet in her heart. Rikki forced herself to breathe, stifling a desperate aching disappointment. But she kept her chin up, her expression calm. No regrets. No regrets, not where Amiri was concerned.

But to wish for a helping hand was not such a bad thing.

"We're still leaving tonight," Francis said. "Moochie and I will slip away in Morocco. We can't stay in this job."

"Deader worse than dead?"

"Depends on whether you want to lose your soul, or just your life."

Rikki heard a commotion down the hall. Shouting. Francis hesitated, but she had nothing to lose, and began running toward the uproar. He caught up in moments, grabbing her elbow. Not before she rounded the corner, though. Not before she saw a man in handcuffs slammed down, face first, Ajax riding him to the floor with a knee in his back.

Not Jean-Claude. Someone new. His pale face was bloody, his hair brown and long enough that it covered his eyes. He had a remarkable gaze—intense, defiant—and when he suddenly looked at her, his bloody cheek pressed to the floor, she felt captured, pinned, as though he could see right through her.

Ajax looked up, too. Francis said, "What you got there?"

"Bait," said the big man, in a surprisingly soft voice. His gaze flicked to Rikki. "Another tool. Friend of the Kenyan. Asking too many questions. Made a hard catch. We lost five men taking him down in Kinsangani."

"Sedatives?"

"Broker said no. Said he wanted his mind good. Said he had things to talk about."

Francis grunted. He tried to drag Rikki away, but she dug in her heels, staring at the man. Friend of Amiri. Of Eddie, too. And if he was just like them, with similar powers . . .

She watched as the man squeezed shut his eyes as though in pain. Ajax noticed, hauled him up, wrenching the man's shoulder so hard he should have cried out. His lips only tightened, though; he did not make a sound. He simply pivoted suddenly, off his right foot, and slammed his forehead into Ajax's nose. Rikki heard the crunch from ten feet away.

Ajax shouted, but he did not let go. He slammed his hairy fist into the man's head, and Francis yanked Rikki around the corner. She hardly noticed. All she could see was that man's eyes, his intensity.

"They work for the same agency," she muttered, mind racing.

It was crazy. She was insane. "Francis, can you get in there to talk with that man?"

"You're not serious."

Rikki shook his arm. "Just . . . take a leap of faith. Go in there. Get that man alone. See if you can get a phone number from him, a name, anything. You must be able to call out of this place."

Francis briefly shut his eyes. "Should have minded my own business."

"Please," she begged. "You said you wanted to help. A phone call is a hell of a lot easier than breaking me out of Fort Knox, and that man has *friends*. Maybe friends who can help."

He took a long deep breath. "I'll take you back to your room first."

"No time. You said it yourself. Window of opportunity. Besides, no one here will touch me. Broker cares too much."

Francis shook his head. "Fine. Stay here. If anyone finds you, just . . . just lie, Doctor Kinn. Lie like your life depends on it."

He stalked away. She listened hard. Heard him say a few sharp words to Ajax, who inquired about her sudden disappearance. "Stashed in a room just down the hall," Francis responded easily, and Rikki thought that if anyone should give lessons in lies, it was him. He was too smooth.

Rikki peered around the corner. She did not see the captive—Amiri's friend—but there was a door open, and she watched as Francis stared down Ajax like a swatter would a fly. Made her wonder about who the real scary sons of bitches were in this place, especially when the big Neanderthal backed off and leaned against the wall, hands folded behind his back.

Francis moved into the room. The door clicked shut.

After a moment, Ajax pushed away from the wall and began to amble down the hall. Right toward her hiding place.

Crap. Rikki turned and ran. Silent, careful, on light feet, trying to hear if anyone was ahead of her. The halls, however, were empty. This place, with all its doors, was like a tomb. And yet, if Francis was correct and there were at least thirty other women . . .

She heard water up ahead. Children playing.

A'sharia and Kimbareta sat on the edge of the stone fountain, dangling their feet in the pool. The giant koi, which looked quite capable of performing amputations with their massive mouths, instead nibbled the children's toes, sending the boy and girl into fits of giggles.

Rikki had to take a moment. Their innocence, their sweetness, was effortless, unthinking. And so out of place. She could not imagine why Broker kept these children here, how it was possible that they should act so normal. How anyone could be raised in this place and still laugh.

A'sharia noticed Rikki first. Her back stiffened, and she turned—quick, with the grace of a cat. Golden eyes searching. She tensed when she saw Rikki, and nudged Kimbareta. The boy grinned, clutching his whistle. His eyes were still old, but less haunted.

"Was there a man here not long ago?" Rikki asked them, speaking French. "Blond, with a picture on his neck?"

A'sharia nodded. "He said to stay here and fish."

"Ah. What a good suggestion." Rikki sat between them. She was no longer concerned about anyone finding her. There was nothing less innocuous than a woman—even a prisoner—talking to small children. No one could accuse her of sneaking around and causing trouble. Not really.

Kimbareta leaned against her arm. After a moment, so did A'sharia, but her intention seemed less to do with relaxation, and more with inhalation. She ran her small nose over Rikki's arm, sniffing loudly.

"You smell like my *Abuu*," said the girl, finally. With great approval.

"*Abuu?*"

"My father," said the little girl. "You carry a scent just like him, all over your skin."

Amiri, she thought. But that was impossible, no matter the resemblance. "What is your father's name?"

A'sharia never answered. Behind them, Rikki heard the lumbering hiss of a large man breathing, and turned. It was Ajax. He was standing in the corridor, just outside the main hall. Watching her.

Kimbareta clung just a little tighter to Rikki's arm. She tried to free herself from him, but he refused to let go. When she stood, she had to take him with her, balancing the boy on her hip.

Ajax continued to stare. Rikki said, "Yes, I know I should be in my room, but the door was unlocked so I—"

He started walking toward her, fast, swinging those massive arms like the pendulums from some mighty clock. His knuckles were bloody. So was his nose, swollen and crooked. Not that it seemed to bother him. Rikki backed away, stumbling, trying to set down Kimbareta, but the boy whimpered when he looked at the approaching man and he hid his face against her breast. She could not blame him. She wanted to hide, too.

Ajax grabbed her arm and hauled her close, squishing the child between them. The big man's breath smelled like his skin: blood and meat, rancid.

"How's your nose?" she asked, unable to help herself. "Enjoy getting sucker punched by people smaller than you?"

"Fuck," he said. "You're all freaks." Like it was something he had been waiting to get off his chest. Rikki was not impressed.

"Look who's talking," she retorted. Ajax's eyes darkened. His fingers squeezed. It hurt, but Rikki never let her expression change. She took it. Thinking about knives—and how she did not want these children to see violence.

Rikki said, "You got something else you want to say to me?"

Ajax looked at her breasts. "You're here to die. Everyone dies here. Eventually. And when the boss man is done using you, he'll give you to me. He gives them all to me."

"Big man," she replied, hiding her fear. "I don't know if you should be bragging about leftovers."

Heat flared in his eyes. He laid his other hand on Kimbareta's head, fingers and palm engulfing his skull. The boy flinched. So did Rikki. Ajax's fingers began to squeeze.

Rikki was too short to adequately knee the man in the groin, but she jabbed her leg upward and his reflexes kicked in. Ajax bent over, protecting himself, and as soon as he let go, she scrambled backward, fast, and put the boy down, shoving him into a run. Ajax shouted, red-faced.

Rikki was ready when he came at her. She could hear Markovic in her head, shouting at her to be *quickquick-quick,* and she darted sideways as those massive hands tried to grab her. It was an odd dance, and the only reason she did not run like hell was because those kids were there— watching, eyes huge, just out of range but still too close.

Ajax tried to land a punch. Rikki leapt away. He tried to sweep her legs; she executed a tumbling roll. He was fast, but he was no gymnast. Just mean. But then, Rikki thought of Jean-Claude and Kimbareta—that bloody man in the hall—and she suddenly felt a whole lot meaner, herself.

She let him get in close, then slammed her fist up into his face with all her strength. It hurt like hell, but it felt good, too, as she hit his broken nose square on. His head rocked back so hard she heard something snap.

But she was too cocky. Ajax staggered, shouting, but he still managed to swing low and catch her in the gut with

one massive fist. Rikki doubled over. He grabbed the back
of her neck. Dug his thumb into a tendon. The pain was
crazy. She went down on one knee, choking.

An animal screamed. Wild, so high-pitched it broke
into a squeak. Ajax jerked, crying out. His hand loosened.
Rikki stumbled away, looking up. Stunned.

There was a cheetah cub on his back, scratching and digging in with tiny claws. Its golden eyes glowed, and its fierce
determined sounds brought gasps as the cub sank its teeth
into the thick muscles of the big man's neck and bit down,
hard.

Ajax snarled, reaching back to grab at the cub. Rikki ran
and jumped, scrabbling, grabbing his ears in her fists and
letting herself hang from them. Her feet touched the ground
and she brought her knees to her chest. Ajax howled. He
grabbed Rikki around the ribs and tore her off, slamming
her down onto the floor. Reached back to do the same to the
cheetah cub.

A'sharia. The little girl. Rikki fought to stand.

A large golden blur passed between her and Ajax. Another cheetah. Screaming. Suddenly standing on two legs
with black claws whistling through the air. Ajax grunted,
eyes bulging. A wet sucking sound filled the air, and the
cheetah—the man—dragged his claws from that muscular
gut, leaving a hole the size of a football. Ajax staggered,
falling.

Rikki swung away, sick. Heard a low noise, a sharp intake of breath behind her. Looked up and found herself staring at Amiri.

The hard desperate relief that passed through her body
almost took her down to her knees. This was a sight for sore
eyes, a sore heart, and a sore soul. Like coming home.

And then she saw the bigger picture. Amiri had a gun pointed directly behind his head. His shoulder was a bloody torn mess. Rictor was cuffed, hands behind his back. The two men were flanked by mercenaries—and Broker.

Rikki heard a soft mewling sound. She turned, and found a lean, lithe dark-skinned man gently peeling the cheetah cub off of Ajax's still back. The cub began to transform the moment it was in the man's arms, fur receding into smooth brown skin and a slightly chubby body that was again human and young and fragile. A'sharia clung to the man, and the man—older, with some gray in his hair—clung to the child, making soothing noises.

A small hand found Rikki's fingers. Kimbareta. She dragged him close and looked back at Amiri. Found him watching that other shape-shifter with the most peculiar look on his face: disbelief, confusion, incredulity, and a pain that struck her deep for its loneliness.

Rikki hardly looked at Broker. She walked to Amiri. Knowing she should not, that she could *not* let on how much she cared. It would be turned into a weapon against her. But she had to let him see her eyes. She had to be close to him, if only for a moment.

I love you, she told him silently, imagining he could hear her, that he could feel it. And she imagined, too, that what she saw in his eyes when he looked back was the same. Still wild and dangerous, filled with that lethal grace that made his every movement poetry. It would not matter what Broker did to him. Amiri was, and would ever be, a man beyond capture. Elusive. Magic.

Rikki looked at Rictor, then Broker. "The whole gang is here, I see."

"And you've been having adventures," he replied crisply.

His face was covered in blood, as was his shirt. She saw bullet holes.

He waved at his men to flank the room, and then looked past Rikki at the second shape-shifter. Rikki turned. Found herself recognizing a man who was Amiri, only thirty years older. Tall, lean, whipcord thin; a chiseled face, steady gaze.

But cold. So cold. Aloof, calculating. The only thing that made Rikki think it might be a mask was the way A'sharia clung to his large, bloody hand, as though it were a lifeline, her most favorite thing. Rikki remembered holding her father's hand like that. Feeling like he was the best person in the world. And no kid felt that way about cruel sons of bitches.

"Aitan," said Broker. "Is A'sharia well?"

"Well enough," rumbled the older man, and his gaze flicked to Amiri. "Your sister, cub."

Amiri lifted his chin, but said nothing. Kimbareta wanted to go to him. Rikki held the child back.

"Ah, well," Broker said. "I have my own family reunion to attend to."

"Will there be picnic baskets?" Rictor drawled. "Apple pie and pink lemonade? Maybe your *sister* will attend?"

Broker suddenly had a gun in his hand. He placed it against Rictor's forehead. Neither man blinked. Rikki held her breath, and shared a quick look with Amiri, who looked equally concerned.

"My sister," Broker whispered, with his first real emotion she had seen thus far: something like grief, something in his eyes like a hard stain. "Little Miss Graves. I do not think, Rictor, that you should speak of her."

"Something finally cut you, Broker? Broken man not so broke?"

Broker's gun hand twitched; a tremor touched his jaw.

Then, quick as a thought, he reached back and slammed the butt of his weapon against Rictor's face.

Rikki bit back a gasp. Kimbareta buried his face in her stomach. Amiri surged toward Rictor, catching the man against his ruined shoulder as he staggered, head bowed. Blood dripped from his nose.

Broker leaned close and whispered something in his ear. Rictor straightened so fast his spine cracked, and he looked at the other man with such hate, Rikki took a step back.

"Something finally cut you, Rictor?" Broker smiled, and looked at the surrounding men. "Remove these three to the lab. Aitan, take the children back to your chambers, then prepare the men for Jaaved."

Kimbareta's fingers had to be peeled off Rikki's body. Amiri's father did the work, coming nose to nose with her. Their eyes briefly met. She saw a crack in the cold, filled with something raw, wild.

And then, nothing. Aitan pulled the boy away, and he was replaced by men in black, mercenaries, none of whom had even the slightest shred of compassion in their eyes. They grabbed Amiri, pushed Rictor, shoved Rikki— packed the three of them so tight together, they walked on each other's heels. Rikki was fine with that. Her hands were free. She grabbed Amiri's hand, clinging to his body, soaking in his heat, his scent, savoring the contact as though it might be their last. He squeezed her fingers and it was a touch she felt down to her soul.

"Mpenzi," Amiri murmured.

"You and I," she breathed, and kissed his shoulder.

And then, because Rictor had no one at all, she reached behind him and grabbed his hand. He looked at her, surprised. His nose was crooked, beginning to swell.

She squeezed his fingers and gave him a faint, sad, smile. Rictor swallowed hard and looked away.

Rikki did not let go of either man. She held them together.

She held them tight until they reached the lab.

CHAPTER TWENTY

THE lab in the sublevel of the facility was too much like the one in Russia for Amiri's comfort: cold, sterile, coated in the scents of men and women starved for sun. A wide open space, it was divided by counters and tables and bookshelves—thick with chemicals and glass, the hum of electrical instruments, the smell of blood.

His shoulder throbbed. He wanted to tear off Broker's head and bury it under six feet of earth and rock. Let him try growing one of *those* back.

The mercenaries pulled Rikki away the moment they entered the lab. He tried to fight them, to stay close to her, but something sharp pierced his neck, and his knees instantly wobbled. He lost all feeling below his chin. Dropped hard to the tile floor. He expected his mind to follow his body, but he stayed conscious—and painfully, furiously, aware.

"Put him on the table," Broker said, somewhere from behind. Men reached under Amiri's arms, hauling him up. He could not fight them. He tried, with all his strength. But all he received for his trouble was ruined pride and a glimpse of Rikki's pale face. She was staring at him with such strain,

such terrible focus, he thought she might break apart if someone touched her.

The men slammed him down on a cold steel table. He
remembered Russia. The cattle prods, the scalpels, the needles. Bars and electricity and voices in his head. He shut his
eyes and focused on his breathing. On Rikki.

"You play too many games," Rictor said, somewhere
near. "You arrogant fuck. You should kill us now, if you
know what's good for you."

"As if you should talk," Broker replied, stepping into
Amiri's view. "Though even if your threat was not idle, I
have, quite literally, nothing to lose. Nothing, anyway, that
you can take from me. All of this, that surrounds you, is a
well-oiled machine."

He turned back to Rikki. "On your own table, my dear."

"And if I tell you to fuck off?" she shot back.

Broker raised his brow, pointed at Amiri, and pulled a
hacksaw down from a shelf above his head. He smiled.
Rikki gave him the finger. But she got on the table. Amiri
did not bother telling her to remain defiant, to let Broker
carry out his threats. He was quite certain she might give
him the finger, too.

He could not turn his head, but he heard movement behind him—a creaking sound and the rattle of metal links. A
sharp click. Rictor said, "Hope you brought your camera."

"To help savor old times?" Broker set down the hacksaw.
His men ranged around the lab, keeping to the shadows
while their employer stayed within the light—the harsh fluo-
rescent light that made his skin match the color of his suit:
bone gray, bone cold. Dashed dull with dark blood. He
looked from Rikki to Amiri, gave a frown. "No. Consider
this a moment of reflection. Everything, I planned so care-

fully. But I did not account for Rictor. Nor for the both of you."

"Could have fooled me," Rikki said. But Amiri knew their presence was not what he meant.

"You care for him," Broker said. "You might even love him. I saw it in your eyes."

"Feeling compassion?" she asked.

"Not hardly. But it does make things more interesting." Broker paced to Amiri's side, and peered down into his eyes. "Tell me, Doctor Kinn . . . are you aware that every woman this man has loved has died a painful and horrible death? *Murdered.* Did he tell you that?"

Rikki said nothing. Amiri could see her face. She plainly did not believe Broker, but then her gaze flicked down, and she met the shape-shifter's eyes, and there must have been something on his face, because a trace of doubt crept into her expression. Not fear, but a question.

"Did you tell her?" Broker asked him, leaning even closer. His eyes, cold and bright. "Did you explain the price of your secrets, Amiri? Why you are a danger to this woman?"

"Rikki has nothing to fear from me," Amiri rasped, speaking for her, to her. He tried to see her eyes, but Broker stood in his way. "What happened—"

"What happened is that you participated in murder." Broker glanced back at Rikki, shifting just enough that Amiri finally saw her face. Which told him little. Her expression was flat, carefully neutral—disturbingly so. "All those women did was love you."

"Only one." Amiri struggled to move. "You are telling lies."

Broker smiled. "Beast. Animal. At least your father accepts that part of himself, but you . . . you cling to that idle fantasy of humanity that has no place for you. There *is* no home for your kind. Not amongst humans. Not with *her*."

Amiri had excellent hearing, which was the only reason he knew Rikki was going to move before Broker did. He heard her shift, and then she was in the air, lunging at the man's back. She wrapped her legs around his waist, grim and utterly silent, and dug her fingers into his eyes. Broker grappled. Men moved. Amiri tried his best to do the same, shifting as he did, fur pouring through his skin as his muscles rolled and twisted. It was like a metabolic burn, coursing through his veins. His hands twitched, his leg jerked, and though he could not move well, he forced himself to remain in a state of perpetual shifting—very slight, very careful, with a mix of disappearing fur and skin and claw. He began to regain strength in his limbs.

No one noticed. The men finally peeled Rikki off Broker's back, and slammed her again on the table. Amiri bit back his outrage, though he watched every man who touched her, memorizing their faces and scents.

Broker's eyes were red, bleeding. Fresh blood, mixing with the old. Behind, Rictor laughed softly—but only until Broker took a step, stood between Rikki's legs, and backhanded her across the face. The crack of his hand meeting her cheek sounded like a gunshot, and Amiri would have rather taken a bullet than seen that.

Rikki did not make a sound. Her cheek burned scarlet. Her lip bled. Amiri said, "I am going to kill you."

"Idle threats are amusing only up to a point," Broker replied, moving to the sink. He turned on the water, testing it until steam rose. He washed his face. One of his men handed him a towel, and after a good scrub it came away pink and brown and crusty.

Broker glanced at Amiri. "I am going to train you all, shape-shifter. All of you, my pets."

"Go to hell," Rictor replied, and there was rage in those words. Killing fury, wound so tightly it made Amiri's skin crawl to hear it. But only because it was too close to what he himself already felt; his skin was crawling with anticipation and not fear. He kept his focus on Rikki. Plotting, in his head, every possible path he could take to her, every weapon he might use, when he finally regained use of his body.

Rikki looked from Broker to him, her gaze defiant. He saw her take in the faint ripple of his fur, and he let his finger twitch, for her benefit. She blinked, and tightened her jaw.

"Broker," she said. "This is not where you produced the weapon that killed all those refugees. This is no Level-Four containment lab."

She was stalling. But it was an interesting observation, nonetheless. Broker continued scrubbing away his gruesome mask of blood. "What makes you think, Doctor Kinn, that what occurred in that camp is the product of a weapon?"

Rikki frowned, gingerly touching her lip. "One thousand people lost their lives."

"But twenty survived. And they are the entire point of the matter."

"What the hell does that mean?"

Broker tilted his head, and threw down the towel. "Tell me, Doctor Kinn . . . what do you know about gene therapy?"

"Gene therapy?" She seemed taken aback. "I know enough. The point is to cure genetic diseases by replacing targeted genes."

"And the problems with it?"

"The immune system can reject the therapeutic DNA as

foreign. Almost like it would the common cold. It's a faulty process. Unpredictable."

"That it is." Broker smiled, faintly. "Especially when one uses a *virus* to implement alterations to the genetic code."

Rikki stared at the man—stared for such a long time, even the mercenaries began glancing at each other.

"No," she whispered. "No, you *wouldn't*."

"It is effective," he replied. "Not contagious, contained as well as a disease can be. But in this case, inelegant."

"It's the same as butchering people." Rikki's bloody fingers curled against the table. "What could possibly be worth that?"

Broker remained silent. Amiri growled, "What is it?"

Rikki gazed at him from across the room, and her distress was so apparent, so mixed with horror, he felt the cheetah begin to rise through his skin with even greater ferocity. "He's implying that the Consortium used a virus to introduce new genetic material to those people at the camp." She flashed Broker a hard, incredulous, look. "Why would you even think to do such a thing? On a mass scale?"

"Pure altruism, I can assure you."

Rikki looked as though she wanted to dig her fingers into his eyes again. "*Tell me*."

"Wildcat," he said, almost to himself. "We conducted the test to confer a biological advantage. To make people strong."

That makes little sense, Amiri thought, but he stayed quiet, unwilling to draw attention to himself. His muscles were gaining strength; the paralyzing agent burned away. Few of the mercenaries were watching him. They focused on Broker, on Rikki. *Wildcat.* Apt name. She leaned off the table—a sharp movement that made several of the men touch their guns.

"Those people did not need an *advantage*," she said, voice low, deadly, "*whatever* you might perceive that to be. They just needed to be left alone."

"Like you?" He smiled, coldly. "Poor little Regina Kinn. Lost her daddy. Her coach. Her friends. Lost her integrity by covering up a major biological find. Lost her body to knives. Lost her life. Nowhere to turn, no place to hide."

"How do you know about . . . my find?" she whispered. "How does Jaaved?"

"How does anyone discover secrets?" Broker began unbuttoning his bloody shirt, his fingers slow, methodical. "Friends, my dear. Friends who did not die quite fast enough. Who thought they could bargain with rebels while sprawled in the dirt with a gun to their heads. Something I am sure *you* didn't think of, even when being cut." He stripped off his shirt, and tossed it into the sink. Scars lined his chest, what appeared to be words, but in no language Amiri recognized. Ugly, thick and curling. He had seen such scars before, on another friend. A former immortal.

Rikki stared. Broker said, "Jaaved has ears in low places. As do we. It was only a matter of time before rumors spread our way. And it was perfect. Everything was lining up just as it should."

"You didn't need Jaaved," Rikki said.

"We required his name, the distance he could provide us. Jaaved is simply one more buffer, another set of hands. Albeit, well-connected ones. And all we needed to promise him in return for his cooperation was a demonstration we had already planned . . . and you. His reservoir queen."

"And what of us?" Amiri inquired, finally daring to speak. "You knew we were coming."

Broker flashed him a hard look. "We took doctors. We spread rumors that made their way back to Larry Coleman.

We knew of his connections to Dirk & Steele, and his sentimental feelings towards Doctor Kinn. His call was inevitable."

"Arrogant," Amiri said.

"Manipulation is an art. But then, your Dirk & Steele is also quite proficient at such things." Broker moved toward Rikki, and Amiri watched the tension gather in her body. He very carefully tried to flex his leg. Feeling had almost returned. His muscles obeyed.

"You keep staring at my scars," Broker murmured to Rikki. "They *are* quite special. Gave me a new lease on life. Would you . . . like to touch them?"

Amiri almost leapt off the table, but he kept himself steady, still as stone. Heart thundering. Rage building. The cheetah was turning over and over inside his chest, begging for release. He watched Rikki, the defiance in her eyes, those thrown-back shoulders and raised chin. He could smell her fear, but he could not see it. Not even a trace.

"Why did you hurt those people?" she asked Broker, making him look at her, and only her.

"A drop in the bucket." Broker continued to close in, leaning over Rikki in a way that was disturbingly intimate. "You are looking at the small picture, Doctor Kinn. The world is changing. Not for the best. And I have . . . seen things. Up here." He tapped his head, the intensity of his words and voice curling a path up Amiri's spine. "*Other* people have seen things. And we all agree on one simple fact: that we are living in the last twilight of man. Sometime soon, in ten days or ten years, this world as we know it will end. Billions will die."

Rikki stared. Amiri stared. He could not imagine what Rictor was doing; the man was so quiet he might as well be asleep.

"You're insane," Rikki said.

"Yes," Broker replied. "Perhaps, even, about this. But I will do what must be done, Doctor Kinn. I will try now to prevent such deaths. I will try to save lives by taking some."

"You care nothing for humans," Amiri said, regarding him carefully. "You have told others they are less than our kind, less than those who have power in their blood. So why . . . why try to save them? Why go to such lengths?"

Behind, Rictor began to laugh, quietly. A sour, grim, sound; bitter as poison. Everyone but Amiri looked at him. "You can't have babies with the air, Amiri. Broker is saving him some good future breeding stock. That's all he cares about."

Cold ran down his spine. He thought of his own mother; his father's attitude toward women. Rikki said, softly, voice tinged with horror: "That's why you're collecting all those ova."

Broker closed his eyes, revealing, for one moment, a weariness that was weakness, a flaw in his composure that ran down to the bone. "As you saw for yourself, the process for strengthening human DNA is a flawed one. Indeed, quite by accident, the reaction to the current gene therapy process was violent enough to mimic most symptoms of Ebola. Fortunate *only* in that it will prevent people from asking too many questions."

Amiri tugged against his restraints. "That is why you had the rebels burn the camp. You truly *were* getting rid of evidence."

"And me?" Rikki swayed forward. "How do I fit into this?"

"We need to improve the process. We must make it . . . more efficient. It is guesswork, experimentation, but your genetic material confers upon you a unique strength that has, based on our research, saved your life innumerable times. It is, in fact, like finding an individual who is one immense CCR5 mutation."

Confusion passed fleetingly over Rikki's face. Amiri watched Broker, too. Felt keenly that they were treading on unsteady ground, that this was the beginning of the end, and that the man would lose patience soon. Still, he had to ask. "What is that?"

Rikki never took her gaze from Broker. "It's a gene that has been found to confer a natural immunity to certain diseases, such as HIV. Even the plague."

"But imagine something on an even larger scale." Broker's eyes narrowed, became pale specks in the paler mask of his hollow face. "Imagine a genetic makeup that prevents total illness, that keeps bones strong, that makes your flesh heal faster than the norm. That is you, Doctor Kinn. And it is valuable because it makes you strong . . . and because good health is something *no one ever notices.*"

Rikki exhaled slowly. Controlled, steady. "You're full of shit."

"And your blood is full of antibodies for the virus. You contracted it, my dear. And you were immune. As is Amiri, I suspect. Shape-shifters seem to be resistant to so much."

"And Eddie? He got sick. He . . . died. That seems to defeat your purpose."

Broker smiled, faintly. "Tinkering is required. Again, you will help with that."

"You've killed so many," she said tightly, almost desperately. "Someone will catch on."

"More than four million have died in this region since 1998. What is a handful more compared to that? No one will notice, Doctor Kinn, but even if they do, it will simply become another statistic. And we will continue, here or elsewhere. We always do."

A radio crackled; one of the men answered it, speaking softly. And then: "Sir, Jaaved is nearing our location."

Broker showed no reaction. He gestured at the men surrounding Rikki. One of them grabbed her arm, yanking with a roughness that made Amiri see red. Broker watched his reaction, and dropped his hand to the fly of his pants. "I wonder, perhaps, if I have time to use you for sport, Doctor Kinn. Right here, right now. Just to drive Amiri insane."

"You will *not* touch her," he snarled.

Broker smiled. "What if I already have?"

Enough. Amiri finally moved. Shoulder throbbing. Sluggishly, but still fast enough. He launched himself at Broker. Body-slammed the man so hard they flew. Amiri's fangs dropped. He could smell blood, already taste it.

Hands grabbed his body, hauling him off before he could rip out Broker's throat. He heard Rikki screaming his name, but he lost her as fists and boots and weapons pounded his body. Rictor was silent—except for that hoarse, choking gag—and still on the floor, Broker began to laugh. Amiri could not hear Rikki. She was gone. *Gone.*

"Where is she?" Amiri rasped. "What are you going to do to her?"

"Anything I want," Broker whispered, sitting up, looking at Amiri with cold amusement. "I own her. *I own you both.* Remember that, Amiri. Rikki Kinn is mine until she dies. Mine, in every way. And you will never see her again."

He stood, looking past Amiri at Rictor. "And you. The same will be true of Elena. I promise you that. But I think I'll let you watch when I play my games."

Rictor said something in a language Amiri did not understand, but it made Rictor cry out again, as though every bone in his body was being crushed. Broker laughed, and kicked Amiri in the shoulder, right in his wound. The pain made him scream, made him want to vomit up his guts.

Broker kicked him a second time, then dug his fingers into his shoulder wound, tearing it wider. Amiri had never passed out from any kind of pain, but he could feel himself riding close to the edge of darkness, and he made himself stay focused. He tried to bite Broker's hand, and got cuffed in the head for his trouble.

Broker crouched. His fingers were wet with fresh blood. "For my sister," he said. "You might not have pulled the trigger, but you were there in Russia for the beginning of the end. And you will suffer."

"No," Amiri whispered, staring into his eyes. "For every hurt you give, that will only make me more joyful that she is dead. Dead like a coward. Beating out her own brains because she went *insane*."

Broker snarled, slamming his fist into Amiri's bleeding shoulder. He pounded the wound, grunting with the effort. Somewhere, Rictor shouted.

Darkness curled. Amiri drifted into his own twilight. He closed his eyes, searching for Rikki.

The pain went away.

CHAPTER TWENTY-ONE

RIKKI fought the mercenaries every step of the way as they dragged her from the lab, squirming, biting, kicking. Not one of them fought back, but they pinched and squeezed and finally just hauled her off the ground and carried her like a sack of flour.

Halfway to her room, she heard a familiar voice say, "You pussies can't even handle one little girl? Jesus Christ. You shouldn't be allowed to carry guns."

"Moochie," said the man holding Rikki. "Get the fuck out of my face."

"We'll take her from here," said Francis, his voice far calmer. "Unless you like having her ass in your face."

"It's not a bad one." The mercenary slapped Rikki's backside.

That, when he put her down, required a very precise kick in his balls. Rikki had a good leg. The man doubled over, groaning. His friends tried not to laugh.

"Right," Francis muttered, and grabbed her shoulder. He steered her away, fast, Moochie taking a position on her left.

"Thought you were leaving," Rikki said, when the other men were out of sight. She tried not to feel a thrill of hope.

"Thought so, too," Moochie muttered, but shrugged when Francis gave him a dirty look. "So I like to complain. Shoot me."

Rikki peered into their faces. "What's the reason you changed your minds?"

"Had an interesting conversation this afternoon. Put some things in perspective."

Moochie grinned. "What he's saying is that we got a better offer."

"And here I thought you both had hearts of gold."

"And Swiss bank accounts."

"Cha-ching," Rikki said, just as they reached her room.

Francis hesitated before opening the door. "Things are going to move fast now, Doctor Kinn."

"Amiri, Rictor, the kids—everyone in this building. I won't go unless they do," she said.

"Understood," he replied. "But that's not what I meant."

He opened the door. Inside stood Aitan.

Rikki stared. The shape-shifter tossed a set of keys past her head. "Francis, Moochie. Go free my son and his friend. Take them to where I've put the children. No detours. Doctor Kinn and I will handle the rest, and we will meet you as soon as we are able."

"Broker?" Francis asked.

Aitan hesitated. "We must move fast. Now go."

The men left. Rikki shut the door. Stared some more, into those golden eyes.

"You're his father," she said.

"I am." His voice was dispassionate, cool. "From the look on your face, I suppose my son has been telling stories."

"No," she said. "But I'm not blind. You're here, working for Broker. You betrayed him."

"And I saved a daughter," said the old man, his gaze piercing, without remorse. "I will save Amiri, too, if I can."

Rikki hesitated. "I don't trust you."

"Nor I you. But my son . . . loves you." Aitan raised his chin. "And I will not take that from him again."

Again. Such an ominous word. Rikki thought of what Broker had said, down in the lab, and resisted the urge to rub her arms. "Fine. Where do we start?"

Aitan gave her a sharp look. "Just like that? You are willing to fight for my son, no matter the cost?"

"We're wasting time."

"You are not even the same color," he mused, in a surprisingly contemplative voice. "Let alone the same kind. How do you expect to make this last?"

"True grit," Rikki ground out. "Or maybe I'll just hit him over the head if he tries to leave me."

Aitan grunted. "I want many grandchildren."

"What an optimist," she muttered, and held out her hand. He looked at it for a moment, and then clasped it tight. His grip was dry and warm, and his eyes flared bright.

"You will do," he said; and then, quietly: "Yes, I think I will like you."

Rikki had no words for that. Based on what Amiri had said, his father didn't like shit about anybody, least of all humans. But she nodded, and he let go, and reached behind him on the table for two handguns. He did not take a weapon for himself, but gave both to Rikki. They felt heavy in her hands. A good solid weight.

She and Aitan left the room. He followed a path not unlike the one Francis had taken her down earlier, and for a moment she thought they were going to Jean-Claude. But Aitan made her take a left at a different corridor crossing, and they ran lightly to a set of wide double doors that were locked with a security pad. Aitan's fingers flew over the keys. He pressed his thumb to a blue touchscreen.

The doors clicked open. Inside, Rikki found a dark room full of switchboards and monitors, blinking red lights ... and a rather grumpy-looking man sitting at a keyboard. He made a low sound when he saw Rikki, but then Aitan was there, and he hit the man hard over the head. A good blow. The man tumbled out of his chair like a dumpy-armed teddy bear.

Aitan opened a panel in the wall. He held out his hand for a gun. Rikki handed one to him. He hammered the butt against the wires and chips until sparks flew and smoke curled. The dim lights flickered, just once.

"Security grid is down," he said. "Jaaved will be here in moments."

"Broker's men will fight."

"The men who were supposed to guard the periphery are dead." Aitan handed back the gun. "I did it myself. All of this ... it was waiting for the right moment. I made the arrangements, manipulated Jaaved and Broker in an appropriate fashion, and now, the culmination. Both are too arrogant to consider failure. Or betrayal."

Maybe you are, too, she thought. "There's still going to be a fight."

"Are you frightened, woman?"

"My name is Rikki," she said in a hard voice. "And yes, I'm frightened."

"Good that you are not a liar," he replied simply. "And yes, there will be blood and bullets and pain. But it is still less than what my son would do for you. Much less, even."

"I didn't know we were competing."

"Competition is the same as survival. Nothing else matters."

"No surprise you said that," she said, and followed as he led them back into the maze of halls. Rikki lost track of everything but those lean shoulders, that swift gait. The sound of his breathing. He reminded her so much of Amiri. Father and son. She could not wrap her mind around it.

"There are too many people imprisoned here," Rikki said, as they passed numerous locked doors. "How are we going to save them?"

"We are not," Aitan replied. "Not yet. Those kept here are safer where they are, until the fighting dies. My own daughter and her friend are in such a room. Jaaved's men will not be able to enter, and the doors and walls are bulletproof." He glanced at her. "There are, however, several more hands we need."

He stopped at a door. Blood stained the floor nearby. Aitan keyed in the code and pushed inside. A man stood in front of them. The man she had seen earlier. Dressed in black, with loose brown hair that covered his eyes. His familiar face was cut, swollen, but he looked at the both of them with perfect lucidity, those eyes still cutting through her, and nodded once.

"I'm Max," he said, and Rikki handed him one of the guns without saying a word.

The second door that Aitan opened, minutes later, made her gasp.

There was another man inside, but he was not human. He was tall, almost seven-foot, and the backs of his muscular arms were covered in long sheaths of golden feathers. Feathers, everywhere. Dotting his chest, his hard stomach, jutting from a mane of long brown hair that framed a face so angular and sharp, it alone might have made her question whether he was human. His eyes were golden, piercing; his skin was almost the same color. Rikki could only guess that he was a shape-shifter, but the sight still boggled. Beside her, Max went still. Staring.

"Kamau Shah," breathed Aitan, and for the first time Rikki saw hard emotion—a stricken shock that seemed to rattle the old man to the core. "My friend. What has Broker done to you?"

"Bad-shift," rasped the other. "He induced it. I cannot find my way home to one skin or the other."

Aitan briefly closed his eyes. "We will find a way. We are free now, brother, if we can fight for it."

"Broker?"

"Soon."

Kamau—if that was his name and not some language Rikki was misinterpreting—cracked some very impressive knuckles. She danced back out into the hall to give him room, and just around the corner one of the mercenaries appeared: the man she had kicked in the balls.

He was not expecting Rikki and was slow on the draw. She raised her weapon fast—but a blast broke the air and a bullet slammed into the man's chest. Not from her. She turned, found Max with his gun raised.

"Doctors shouldn't have blood on their hands," he said.

"And you?" she asked hoarsely, but all Max did was shrug, and hide his eyes behind his hair. Somewhere nearby, a shout went up. She heard the sharp *rat-tat-tat* of machine guns. Aitan slipped into the corridor, Kamau close behind.

The old cheetah flashed his claws. "Jaaved is here. He is making good on my promise."

Max's eyes went distant. "We need to keep Doctor Kinn from him. We need to go."

"No," Rikki snapped. "Not without knowing Amiri is safe."

"Agreed," said Aitan, and they began to move again. Toward the fight.

THERE WAS A RED HAZE INSIDE AMIRI'S BRAIN, A SHADOW OF pain he fled from, sinking deeper into his dreams. Dreams of Rikki, and then his father. His father's voice was whispering inside his head, telling him to wake, that it was time, that soon he would have to run. Amri did not want to listen. His father was a bad man.

But he opened his eyes. Found himself in a cage.

It was a large cage, made for a man and not a cheetah. There were bars and a bucket for a toilet, but nothing else. No bed, just hard concrete. The air smelled like the lab, recently cleaned with bleach. No light. It was pitch dark, but his eyes adjusted, and he found another cage nearby. Inside, Rictor. Sitting up, staring blind into the dark.

"What happened?" Amiri asked, his voice slightly echoing. He glanced around the cavernous room for cameras or guards. Found nothing. They were alone.

"What does it look like?" Rictor shot back, voice dull. "Cages, for animals."

Amiri made no reply. His throat was raw with thirst, and his shoulder throbbed. The rest of his body was still sluggish. But he thought of Rikki alone with Broker, and he could not help the sound of rage and frustration and fear that broke from his throat.

"You're thinking of her," Rictor said.

"No doubt you're thinking of Elena," Amiri retorted.

"No doubt," Rictor agreed.

"Why do you bother? She loves her husband."

"I know."

"And yet, you think she could love you just as much?"

In the darkness, Amiri saw Rictor turn to look in his direction. "You owe me the price of a life. The least you can do is not be an asshole."

Amiri lay on his back, staring at the bars of his cage. "You never answered my question, about you and her. How you knew to help us."

"Fuck you," muttered Rictor.

"And the rest? Are you certain you would not like to talk about that, either?"

"Not with you."

Amiri thought for a moment, perversely driven to irritate the other man, and recited, softly, " 'Give sorrow words . . . the grief that does not speak whispers the o'er-fraught heart and bids it break.' "

Rictor grunted. "I can't believe you just quoted Shakespeare at me."

"It seemed appropriate."

"He was a mouth breather and his farts smelled like onions."

Amiri closed his eyes. "You just ruined me."

"My pleasure."

Behind them, Amiri heard a rattling sound. A lock being turned. The door opened and light flooded the room. He squinted, found two silhouettes just standing, staring. Only for a moment. Those bodies ran into the room, and he heard keys jangling. Saw blond hair, the glint of a diamond, the pattern of a tattoo. He smelled gunpowder and cigarettes, the faint whiff of orchids, and deeper yet, Rikki.

He was on his feet in a moment. "Who are you?"

"Dumb and Dumber," said the man with the tattoo. "We are so fucking dead."

"Shut up," said his companion absently, unlocking Amiri's door. Rictor's cage, too.

Amiri said, "What is this? Who are you?"

"Doesn't matter now," said the man with the earring, giving him a long steady look that was old and cold and deadly. "That woman upstairs won't leave without you. Or everyone else in this goddamn building."

"Morality is the fucking plague," said the tattooed man.

"Damn straight," Rictor muttered.

Amiri rubbed his arms. "Take me to her."

The man with the earring hesitated. "I have a message first. Max is here. Held captive on the upper level. Broker brought him to use against you. *And* because he was causing trouble with our people in the city."

Amiri froze, then forced himself to take a slow breath, listening hard to those words. "That is not the message."

"No. Max asked me to patch a call to your boss in America. Help is coming. Couldn't understand it all, but the gist is that you'll see a familiar face in either ten minutes, or twenty-four hours. Whichever comes first."

"That's a lousy offer of help," Rictor said. "Fuck. I bet he's going to get Dean to come here. What a little turd."

Amiri ignored him. "You work for Broker. Why are you helping?"

The tattooed man passed a gun over to Rictor. "We already covered that. Morality. Plague."

"Money," added the other man. "Survival. Do you really need anything else?"

"Names," Amiri told them, and the mercenaries shared a quick look.

"Moochie," said the man with the tattoo. "And that's Francis."

"How cute." Rictor checked the gun clip. "Let's go shoot people."

The men ran from the room, Amiri sinking down on all fours to run within the skin of the cheetah. His shoulder hurt, but the pain lost strength against his focus on Rikki, Max and the rest of his friends. Help was coming. Ten minutes or twenty-four hours. Either way, he had to make certain everyone stayed alive long enough to see that moment.

Outside the lab, in the long hall, men and women in long lab coats were dashing into rooms, hauling paperwork, laptops. Hair wild, glasses askew, they were babbling and shouting to each other in various languages. A red light strobed against the walls. Amiri smelled fear. It reminded him too much of the escape from Russia, and he glanced at Rictor. Found a troubled frown on the man's face. From memories or something else, he could not tell, but the whole thing made him cold, angry.

How many such facilities exist? How many are suffering? And the people who involve themselves, all in the name of science . . .

He stopped himself. Concentrated on running. Listened hard as they took the emergency stairs, rattled up the metal steps. Above them, shouts. Moochie and Francis shared a look, and then the smaller, tattooed man climbed ahead, leaving the rest of them behind. Amiri heard him whistle a greeting, then receive a few sharp words in reply—something about soldiers, rebels. Somewhere not so distant, gunfire blasted. Amiri flinched. Rictor grabbed Francis's arm and hissed, "What the hell is going on?"

"Diversion." He indicated Amiri. "His father set it up. A terrorist is in the compound, shooting the living shit out of Broker's people. Jaaved. All we have to do is reach the assigned meeting place and wait out the fight. Pick off the winners, if we need to."

"Rikki," Amiri whispered, shifting shape. "Where is she?"

Francis hesitated. "With Aitan."

Fury rolled through his chest. "He will betray her."

"No." That diamond earring glinted as Francis turned to look up the stairwell. "You've got it all wrong."

She is safe, whispered his father's voice, loud inside Amiri's ringing head. *She is a fighter. She fights for you.*

He wanted to slam his fist against his skull. Footsteps rustled on the steps. Moochie appeared. "I sent them in another direction. Come on. We have to hurry."

"Where would Broker go in a time of danger?" Amiri growled, as they sped up the stairs.

"Helicopters," Rictor said, before the other two could respond. "He'll search out his most valuable assets, and then try to run with them."

"Rikki," Amiri said. "Us."

"And some others," Francis added, giving Rictor a hard, keen look. "The children."

Sister. Amiri felt a pang strike through his heart at the memory of that little girl, so much like him, a twin in everything but gender. He had never imagined such a thing—*a sister*—but he felt the rightness of it at first sight, knew the truth. He'd suffered an odd and petty jealousy, just for a moment, as he watched that child hold her father's hand—a father who welcomed such a gesture, when Amiri had never been offered the same affection.

She is blood. Your family. You must protect her. She is yours to protect.

A growl rolled from his throat. They reached the landing

door, and edged into the empty hall. Amiri smelled violence, listened to shouts and screams echoing off the walls.
Close, dangerously so.

"Aitan moved the kids to a new room. That's where we're
supposed to find each other." Moochie's gaze darted down
the corridor, and he took the lead, running smooth, silent, on
light feet. Amiri smelled blood, and around the bend they
came upon three bodies swimming in a pool of red—two
in the black mercenary gear that Broker's men favored,
and one man who wore a torn olive uniform. Rebel. Militia.
Jaaved's hired soldier.

Francis passed the dead without a second glance. "We're
close."

Unfortunately, so was everyone else. They found a firefight near the room where the children were being kept.
Broker's mercenaries were pinned down ahead of them,
just at the intersection of several different halls, peeling
out of hiding to shoot at some unseen target that every few
moments chewed the plaster with a rain of bullets.

"Hide your gun," Francis hissed to Rictor, and stepped
in front of him as Moochie dropped to the rear, aiming his
weapon at Amiri. He winked, just once. Which was no comfort at all. Francis waved at the men ahead of them, one of
whom slid sideways, away from the corridor intersection.
His face was ruddy, sweat-slick, and he eyed Amiri and Rictor with suspicion. Francis snapped his fingers at him. "Broker wants me to bring these men to a special holding room.
Is he already up at the helicopters?"

"Fuck, no. He insisted on going into 4B. Got company
right afterward. Never did get a good look, but the boss is
pinned down, and so are we. We can't leave him behind,
and there's no way to circle around in this spot."

"4B?" Francis echoed, voice slightly strained. Amiri's

stomach dropped, and he shared a quick troubled look with Rictor. Was that where the chidren were? If Broker had taken them . . .

"What about the others?" Francis asked sharply. "How many of us are left?"

The man gave Amiri and Rictor a wary look. "Enough."

"And the other side?"

"No way yet to be sure. Feels like an army, though."

Francis glanced at Moochie. "Got our little Avalon?"

"On it." He moved forward, tattoo pulsing as he reached inside his vest and pulled out a small brown cylinder that looked suspiciously like a cigar-shaped grenade. He pulled the pin with his teeth, pushed aside some of the men manning the corridor intersection, and tossed the device down the hall. Amiri heard a sizzling sound, then several large pops that whistled and burned.

Thick white smoke began pouring into the corridor. Francis grabbed Rictor's arm, and he gave Amiri a hard look. He guided them toward the smoke. The man they had been speaking to tried to stop them. "What the hell are you doing?"

"Our jobs," Francis snapped. "You've got temporary cover. Use it to blast those guys to hell and give *us* some cover. We'll be with Broker."

"You won't make it."

"Give us some goddamn *cover*," he hissed, with such force the other man stumbled back against the wall.

"We got thirty seconds," Moochie said, and Amiri had no time for second thoughts before the four of them passed into the smoke screen, keeping close to the right side of the wall as bullets rang down from behind them on the left. No one shot back. The sudden silence was eerie, almost as much as being blind. Amiri could hardly see his hand in front of his face; the smell of the churning smoke was bitter, acrid. Beneath it, though, a familiar scent. His father.

I am here, he imagined the old man whispering, and just ahead of them, a low crooning whistle rose from the mist. Amiri faltered. He knew that voice. Max. He grabbed Francis's arm. "Those were not Jaaved's men shooting."

The mercenary froze, but he was already standing in front of a white door. 4B. He held up his finger to Amiri, and keyed in a code. The door clicked. He opened it a fraction and said, "Mr. Broker? It's Francis. I'm here to escort you to the helicopters."

Amiri wished for silence—that Broker would be elsewhere, and not with the children who must be hidden inside this room—but a heartbeat later he heard that soft cold voice say, "Come in," and Francis did. But only for a moment. A gun went off. The mercenary flew backward into the mist-shrouded hall, slamming into the floor. Moochie shouted. Amiri darted into the doorway.

Broker was there. Shirt still missing. Scars puckered. Kimbareta was in one hand, gun in the other. Its muzzle was pointed against the child's head. A'sharia—*my sister*—crouched on the bed, claws out. Making high-pitched hissing sounds.

Broker took the gun off the boy's head and pointed at Amiri. He was too close to miss. Had no intention of missing. His eyes were cold, dead, done. No more games. Amiri prepared to lunge, ready to fight, to die. He thought of Rikki.

Something hard hit his shoulder just as Broker fired his gun. Amiri felt heat burn his skin, but nothing hit him. He heard a thud, though. A grunt. Smelled blood and spring rain and thunder. He turned and found Rictor—Rictor sliding backward, hard against the opposite wall inside the corridor. Rictor, falling down. Crumpled. Eyes closed. Chest gaping.

It happened in moments, heartbeats, hardly a breath of time. Amiri watched Rictor die.

He could not fathom it. He could not believe. He looked back at Broker, who even seemed stunned. Staring. As though he had just murdered the unthinkable; a myth, a god.

Rage poured free; Amiri saw red, heard Rikki's voice somewhere distant behind him. He threw himself at Broker, and this time the man was too slow. The gun went off again, but wild—the bullet struck the wall—and Amiri tore into the man, disarming him easily, ripping Kimbareta away and tossing the child on the bed.

He held down Broker's pale straining throat. He began choking him.

Broker smiled. A terrible grimace, the crack of a rattling laugh. A hand touched Amiri's shoulder. He looked up. It was Rikki, tears in her eyes. And just behind her was Max. His face torn, beaten. But good to see.

"I need that man's mind," said his friend. "Don't kill him yet."

"It hardly matters," Amiri replied, but he eased off Broker and leaned back, letting the man push away from him, hands clutching his throat, wheezing. Wheezing and still laughing.

Amiri could not bear to look at him. He stood, wrapping Rikki in his arms, breathing in her scent with such desperation that part of him thought she might be the only reason he still wanted to be alive. He saw his father gathering the children off the bed, pushing them into the massive arms of an extraordinary creature—another shape-shifter, with feathers and muscle and golden piercing eyes. The man picked the children up and took them into the corner.

Moochie crouched in the hall, one hand pressed against Francis's wounded side. His other held the radio. He was talking fast. Tears ran down his face. Rictor sprawled nearby in a spreading pool of blood.

The smoke from the grenade was beginning to clear. Any moment they would have more company. Nothing was going according to plan.

Amiri looked again at his father. Met that inscrutable, cold, gaze. But the old man glanced past him, at Broker, and the hate that twisted his face was so shocking, so visceral, Amiri turned Rikki away, shielding her.

"Where is it?" Aitan growled. "Where have you hidden the device?"

"No taste for watching your daughter die?" Cold words. Everyone stopped, staring. Broker smiled. "You didn't tell them? About the chip in your child's brain? The detonator? What I did to her *mother*?"

Amiri felt sick. He watched Aitan begin to shake with fury. Pure rage. "*Where?*"

"Anywhere," Broker said, calmly. "And should I . . . fall out of circulation for a certain length of time, I have left instructions for the device to be used. Not just on your daughter, but others. So. Let me go, let me take Doctor Kinn and your son, and I will tell you where it is."

"Max," Amiri said.

His friend closed his eyes, dark hair falling over his face. "He's closed up tight."

Aitan flowed forward. "I could give you to Jaaved. Imagine his delight when you do not die from his torture? When you heal before his eyes? I doubt anyone would see him again, for all the time he will spend lavishing his love upon you."

"Then your daughter would die. Nor would she be alone. Kamau Shah would follow her. And Rikki Kinn."

Amiri's heart lurched. Rikki stared. "You're lying."

"Touch the base of your skull. You'll feel a hard bump."

Amiri could taste her reluctance, her fear, but she did as Broker said, and when her fingers rubbed the back of her neck, words were unnecessary. Her face paled. Behind her, the avian shape-shifter also examined his neck, and a snarl of rage passed over his face. The children, huddled in his arms, winced.

"Fail-safe. If I cannot have you, no one can." Broker stood. "Do we have a deal?"

"What of the others?" Amiri asked, struggling with himself. "Those we leave behind?"

"Jaaved's men rule this facility now. They are on their own."

"Then take me," he said. "Leave the woman out of this."

"I need her more than I want to kill you."

"Then *me*. Only me," Rikki said. She pulled herself out of his arms, but Amiri stayed close, grappling with her hand. Refusing to let go. Fighting for options. But he could not think; his thoughts were crazed, random—focused only on Rikki and death and the little family he had never known existed.

Broker's gaze traveled over them all, proprietary, almost triumphant. Amiri heard a commotion out in the hall. Men. Moochie shouted, but no guns fired—even though, somewhere distant, Amiri heard the renewed spark of a firefight.

"Both of you," Broker said. "We go now. The rest of you will not follow. If you do, I will give the order to kill the child. And if that still does not dissuade you, then the eagle and the doctor will die as well."

He walked past them. Arrogant. Giving Aitan a long look that had the old man drawing blood from his palms. The sweet spot of his spine gleamed like a row of jewels. Amiri wanted to sink his teeth deep there.

Max grabbed his arm, shaking his head. "Stall him," he mouthed.

Right. Friends were coming. Ten minutes or twenty-four hours. Amiri wanted to laugh. And then, perhaps, go a little mad.

Rikki grabbed his hand, pulling him after Broker. He shared his own look with his father—again inscrutable, showing nothing of his heart—and Amiri wondered how it was possible he could hate and love one person so much, both at the same time. He heard a voice inside his head, a whispered, *Forgive me, I am with you*, and his father chose that moment to nod. As though it *was* him, in his son's thoughts, speaking softly.

Amiri frowned, but there was no time. Out in the hall stood men: four mercenaries and Moochie, his hands covered in blood. He tried to draw his gun on Broker, but was stopped instantly. He fought the hands that restrained him, shouting obscenities, grief making his voice raw, hoarse.

"Stick him in the room with the others," Broker said. "Lock the door. And take the doctor's gun, if you will."

Amiri had not noticed Rikki was armed. She had a small gun in her jacket pocket, which she handed over with a grimace. Behind them, the door was locked. Moochie's shouts were instantly cut off. On the floor was Rictor. And Francis, breathing shallowly, bleeding out. Rikki made a sound low in her throat, and Amiri pulled her close against him. His heart felt numb. No grief. He could not feel grief. Not now.

He looked away. Hands nudged him. They started walking down the hall. Two mercenaries were in the lead, two bringing up the rear. A convoluted path, down halls that smelled of disinfectant and orchids and fear.

Straight into the arms of another enemy.

CHAPTER TWENTY-TWO

IT seemed to Rikki that she would never breathe normally again. Her heart was going to need therapy. Medication, maybe, if she survived this. Meditation, too. A nice long vacation in some boring American town. Give her the Midwest. Indiana. Ohio. Iowa. Rolling fields of corn and old folks driving pickups at thirty miles an hour on a state freeway. Cotton candy, Saturday morning cartoons. Omelets and flapjacks and big fuzzy slippers. Anything but more men with guns or psychopaths obsessed with controlling her life. Rikki was done proving how tough she was, even to herself. Enough. She believed it. She had the scars to prove it. Badass, be thy name. Yippee-ki-yay.

She stood in the main hall, Amiri at her side. In front of her, the fountain had been turned into a monument of death. Bodies were in the water. Puddles glistened on the polished floor, water mixed with blood. The dead, everywhere. She felt as though the miasma of violence covered her skin, filled her lungs. It made her remember years past, seeing her friends in the dirt, bodies shredded by knives and bullets.

And here, more rebels. More of Jaaved's men. Dressed in olive uniforms and thick black boots, weapons held with grim pride. Broker's small group was vastly outnumbered. Rikki felt like a sardine about to be stabbed with a hundred different forks. Nowhere to run, nowhere to hide. Broker had led them into the main hall, the only way to the helicopters. Such bad planning. Broker was obviously not paranoid enough for secret exits and entrances.

Which was terrible. Because his foes had found him. Eight men. Two to one, when it came to firepower. Rikki supposed it was inevitable. Forget Shit Creek; she was going over Shit Niagara Falls.

A man pushed through the gathered soldiers. Dusky skin, long dark hair. Strong features and a compact muscular body. Hairy knuckles. His jaw flexed, and she heard a loud metallic clicking sound. She remembered, with painful clarity, the sight of a man being stabbed by a pen.

"Broker," said Jaaved. "Attempting to escape?"

A cold smile touched Broker's mouth. "It crossed my mind."

"I secured the helicopters. Your security center. No one was able to call out for help. You are alone here. You are mine."

"How titillating," Broker replied. "And if I offered you a deal? Perhaps the lives of your family?"

Jaaved narrowed his eyes. "They are safe. I had them moved."

"You had your children moved." Broker tilted his head. "Not your parents. Or your sister. Or your brother and his children. Quite shortsighted, if you ask me. I took precautions last night."

"You lie."

"Did I lie about your wife?" Broker snapped his fingers. One of his men reached slowly inside his vest and withdrew a small envelope. He tossed it at Jaaved's feet. "More for the photo album. Feel free to send them around for any holiday you celebrate next."

Whatever was in those pictures made the blood drain from Jaaved's face. His hands shook. And he only looked at the photo on top; the rest he shoved back into the envelope. He took a deep, shuddering breath.

"I am going to kill you," Jaaved said.

"Of course you will," Broker replied. "But if you do kill me, you will never see any of those people again. Ever. Can you live with that?"

Rikki was seeing all kinds of hate today, and most of it was directed at Broker. Jaaved had a particular twitch, though, a flutter in his eyelid that kept perfect time to the precise clicking of his jaw.

"What do you want?"

"Free passage."

"I require the woman."

Amiri tensed. Broker said, "I suppose you think you could take her from me."

"It crossed my mind," Jaaved replied, with a cold smile.

Broker also smiled. "There is a device implanted at the base of her skull. If you take her, I will order her death. If you kill me, eventually the same will occur. And no . . . do *not* accuse me of lying."

"Even if you are . . ." Jaaved looked at Rikki. "You could make this easy on us all. Tell me what you know, and I will let you go. Give me the location of the Ebola reservoir."

"Sure," Rikki said. "It's up your ass."

Jaaved's jaw clicked, and somewhere behind them, in another part of the building, men began to scream.

Rikki flinched. It was a distant, blood-curdling sound,

wet and dripping with terror, and it had been years, years since she had heard anything so horrible—like men were having their souls ripped from their flesh.

Jaaved tensed, and glanced at the men beside him. "You four, go check it out."

They looked at him like he was insane, but they went—more afraid of their boss than the unknown, she supposed. The mercenaries in front of Broker shifted, just slightly, fingers tightening around their guns. The screaming continued, getting closer, broken by the chatter of gunfire. She thought she heard a familiar voice mixed with all that shouting. Moochie.

Hope flared. She glanced at Amiri. Noticed Broker watching her, in turn.

"Enough," Jaaved muttered, sweat beading on his forehead. He looked at his remaining men. "Kill the guards."

Rikki had no time react. Amiri grabbed her around the waist, slinging her into his arms. Guns thundered. From the corner of her eye, she saw the mercenaries fling themselves to the ground, rolling, firing back on the rebels. Both sides caught bullets, blood spraying.

And there was Broker, his body jerking as Jaaved pumped him full of lead, making his choice.

Amiri ran, carrying her, but only as far as the fountain. Too many bullets were flying. He threw them both into the water, dragging her up hard against the stone. Shielding her body, pressing against her so tight she could hardly breathe. The firefight seemed to intensify. Rikki heard more shouting.

Amiri grunted. It was a terrible sound, terrifying. A scream built in her throat. Rikki wished she could see. He made another low groan, and then, quite suddenly, was pulled from her.

Jaaved was above her. His eyes were wild and he was

covered in blood. He held a gun in his hand . . . but when he pulled the trigger, it made a clicking sound.

Amiri snarled, swaying. He bled freely from a hole in his back, and blood flecked his mouth. He lunged at the man and they both went down in the water so hard that a koi was knocked free of the pool. It flopped wildly on the floor, suffocating. Rikki knew exactly how it felt.

Jaaved pulled a hidden knife from the small of his back and slashed at Amiri . . . who moved too slowly. The blade cut deep. Amiri staggered, and golden light rose from his skin. Shining like the sun. Jaaved blinked, taking a step back. Raising a hand to his eyes.

Amiri lost his human body. He melted, he transformed, he flowed like liquid gold into a skin that was spotted and lean and hungry. Cheetah. Eyes blazing, body bleeding. He lunged. Jaaved stumbled, horror in his eyes—too shocked to defend himself. Amiri snapped his jaws around the man's throat and ripped it out.

Rikki stared, breathless. All around them the gunfight was dying down, and then it stopped completely. She hardly noticed. All she could see was Amiri. She rose to go to him. Amiri turned to meet her gaze. Blood covered his mouth.

One more gunshot split the air. Amiri jerked, blood spraying from his shoulder. Rikki gasped, lunging toward him, and saw Broker, resurrected, gun in hand. Finally going for the kill.

Rikki no longer had her gun. She did not think, she did not look. She ran, throwing herself directly in front of the danger, shielding Amiri's body. Broker had already begun to pull the trigger again; she saw it on his face as time slowed down.

The gun went off. It nicked Rikki in the side and pain crushed through her. She kept running, though. She could not stop, and Broker let her come—he did not want to kill her. That was his mistake. She threw herself at him in a long sweet dive, and slammed him so hard into the floor she heard his skull crack. She wrestled for his gun, nearly passing out from the pain, but she remembered knives and laughter and Amiri, and pried the weapon from his fingers, jamming it under his chin.

She hesitated. Broker looked her in the eyes and very gravely said, "Until we meet again, Doctor Kinn."

Rikki pulled the trigger. His brains splattered. She kept pulling the trigger until the clip was empty. Numb, horrified, unable to stop. His head was pulp, almost gone. *Murderer.* She was a murderer, for a second time. Cold-blooded.

Then, suddenly, she was not alone. A man fell beside her. A man with strong shadowy hands that reached into that bloody mess, pulling and twisting until Broker's head was all the way gone. She heard a thud as the remains of his skull landed somewhere near. She wanted to vomit, but held it together. Peered up. Looked into a familiar impossible face. Rictor. Living and breathing. Green eyes staring back with something that could have been grim pleasure.

"You're alive," she whispered.

"I guess I didn't lose everything," he rumbled, and helped Rikki sit up. She could hardly move. Her side hurt like hell, and her head pounded. Dazed, almost delirious. She looked for Amiri. Found a lump of spotted fur crumpled on the tile floor. A sob tore from her throat.

"Rictor," she breathed, choking. He said nothing. Simply picked her up. She hardly saw the rest of the room, but she was dimly aware of the silence, the incongruous sight of men in olive uniforms bleeding to death and staring with pure horror, in their final moments, at a man with the head of a cheetah, his upright body covered in sleek spotted fur.

And at his side was a golden chiseled giant, talons sprouting from his fingers, his arms rippling with long shining feathers. Gods and monsters. She was living inside a legend.

She glimpsed Moochie, who was covering those men with his gun, eyes hard as stone. But that was all she saw, because Rictor set her down beside Amiri, and she curled her body around his, pressing her cheek into his fur. Clutching his paw. She could not feel him breathing. She could not hear his heart beat.

Rikki closed her eyes and died.

Just a little.

AMIRI HAD A VERY TERRIBLE DREAM WHEN HE DIED. IT WAS of his father, and the old man was inside his head, screaming, holding up the body of Rikki Kinn, who was also dying. His father was weeping. There were tears on Rikki's face as well, and it was awful, murderous. Amiri could not stand it. He could not stand to die that way, to have that as his last vision.

So he woke up. Swam into pain. Glimpsed a woman above him, but not Rikki. He wanted Rikki, even if the face he saw was welcome. Brown hair, those round cheeks.

"Elena," he whispered.

"Hush," she murmured, and from behind, a large hand touched her shoulder. A man, pale and dark, lean as a hard winter. Artur.

"Sleep," said his friend, his Russian accent thick. "Go back to sleep. We are here now."

"Rikki," he breathed, his eyes falling shut.

"Safe," Elena said, and he felt the heat of her healing hands course through his throbbing body, burning to the bone. "Rest, Amiri. You're all safe."

Safe. A myth, he thought, but he fell away into sleep. Deep, dreamless. Aching for Rikki. Needing her with all his heart. Wishing so much for her presence that when he next opened his eyes it felt as though hardly any time had passed.

But he was in a bed with white silk sheets, and there was a woman beside him who was small and warm and smelled like vanilla and spice.

Rikki. Breathing. Alive.

Amiri touched her. He saw a new scar on her side, but the flesh had knitted. His own body was sore, but he reached around and touched a rough patch where he knew there had been holes. The cut in his chest was gone, too.

Elena. Elena had saved them with her magic hands. Ten minutes or twenty-four hours. His friends had arrived.

Amiri smiled to himself and kissed Rikki's shoulder. She stirred, and opened her eyes. Stared at him for a moment, like he was a ghost . . . and then, ever so gently, with almost more tenderness than he could bear, she touched his cheek, the corner of his eye, and said, "Hey, there."

"Mpenzi," he whispered. "Rikki."

"Amiri," she breathed, smiling. Tears leaked from her eyes. Tears dripped on her chin, but those were from him and he wiped them away with his thumb.

"You are my home and my heart," he murmured. "Let us not ever frighten each other this way again, Rikki Kinn. No more. My soul could not stand it."

A breathless teasing smile filled her face. "Scaredy cat. I thought you knew what we are."

"Dangerous," he replied, laughing softly. Covering her mouth in a long deep kiss that journeyed down her throat, to her lovely beautiful scars.

"I love you," she breathed in his ear. "I love you so damn much."

And that was the last thing he let her say for quite some time after.

CHAPTER TWENTY-THREE

T HERE was a crematorium in the basement. Aitan knew all about it. Rikki supposed it made sense.

There was quite a gathering when they incinerated Broker's body, and his head: strangers and familiar faces alike. They threw in Jaaved for good measure. The process took two hours. They sat outside the room and waited. Grim. Quiet. Making sure he was dead. Even Francis was there—who, apparently, had been one of the first people that the woman, Elena, had been persuaded to work her magic upon.

All of which was quite confusing to Rikki. Healing gifts aside (and she did not give a rat's ass if it made Amiri squeamish, but she was going to talk to that woman about running tests) there was no physical way Elena or anyone else could have arrived so quickly at the facility. San Francisco to the Zairean Congo, in less than three hours? *Like hell.*

Rikki had tried asking. She'd received, for her trouble, words and names, things like "Dean" and "teleportation" and "Oh, God, he really screwed that one up." Which made no sense, but then neither did men who transformed into animals, or fellows who could resurrect themselves from the dead with hardly a burp. Life was strange. Her daddy would have loved it.

"You think he's *really* gone?" Rikki said, to no one in particular.

Rictor grunted. "He said only one man can kill him."

"That would be me," said one of the strangers from the agency, one more silent witness who had joined them in the basement. He was a tall and handsome man, dusky-skinned, with black hair and intense eyes. He called himself Blue. Rikki had no idea what his connection was to Broker, just that he had been more than happy to help shove the headless corpse into the cremator.

And he had also shorted out the detonator placed at the base of her skull. Done the same for A'sharia and Kamau Shah. Just with a thought. Rikki never felt a thing, not until they dug it out of her skin and placed it in her palm. Like a grain of rice—if rice exploded inside heads and killed people.

"So," said Moochie. "Does this qualify as dead? I mean, he's being incinerated. How the fuck is his body going to heal *that*?"

Until we meet again, Doctor Kinn.

"Whatever," Rikki said, battling a chill. "I give up. My life is going to be an endless array of sequels to bad horror films. I'll pull back my shower curtain sometime next summer and Broker will be there, naked, with a knife in his hand."

Amiri frowned. "That is not amusing."

No. And neither was the idea that an organization was making biological weapons that could change the structure of someone's DNA. Something Larry needed to know about—the military—the world.

But what then? Betrayal, exposure? The risk of opening

Amiri and others like him to the unrelenting scrutiny of strangers? The idea terrified her, in the same way those damn bats and their veins full of Ebola had. Because she knew some would panic at the truth, just like she knew some would want to use those bats—that disease—as a weapon. And who was to say that any government, any military, would not feel the same about shape-shifters and psychics? Who was to say that Amiri and friends would not be locked up for life, or coerced into untenable positions, if the truth was known? This was not some television special with a man claiming to speak to the dead—even if he could. This was blood and guts and magic.

And how . . . how was she supposed to weigh the lives of potentially millions of victims over what her heart desired?

"Because we'll take care of it," Max said softly. He sat beside her, and his voice was for her ears only—though she knew Amiri heard him as well. It was slightly disconcerting that he had read her mind. "We will stop them, Doctor Kinn. It's a dirty war, but it's *our* war, and we won't let the Consortium continue."

"I don't know you guys," she said. "You're asking me to abandon my responsibilities on a leap of faith."

"Have you not already done that?" Amiri asked.

"More or less," she said. "But this is something else entirely."

"Fair enough," Max said. "But give us a chance first. Help us, even. We'll need someone with your training. There aren't too many doctors and scientists in our organization."

"I'm no psychic," she said.

"We're not prejudiced," Max replied with a smile. "But let's face it . . . you're not entirely normal, either."

Who is? Rikki wanted to ask him. But he had a point. And the idea of helping hunt the Consortium—and perhaps studying that virus—made a hot bolt of anger-fueled excitement pass through her gut.

"I'll think about it," she said, and glanced at Amiri, savoring his quiet smile that was not triumphant, but instead humbling in its reassurance, its support. As though he trusted her. As though he had faith as well.

It made her breathless. She had to blink hard and look away, finally focusing on the discussion going on around them: a somewhat grim and humorous argument about slasher flicks, and about how being hunted by crazed chainsaw-wielding serial killers compared to being hunted by crazed megalomaniac serial killers who hired men to carry the weapons for him.

"We are such tools," Moochie said, nudging Francis. His cousin smiled, but his face was pale, and he looked like he still hurt.

Rikki caught his eye. "Was it worth it?"

His smile gained strength. "Better than being dead."

"And now? Have you guys decided what you're going to do yet?"

"Still working on that better offer," Moochie replied, glancing at Max. "Isn't that right?"

Max rubbed the back of his neck. "I think we can come to an agreement. Though there is a certain question of loyalty. Some things can't be bought."

"You can trust them," Rikki said, giving Francis and Moochie long steady looks. "Isn't that right?"

The men hesitated. Rikki rolled her eyes.

The cremator clicked off, a sound so loud they could hear it in the other room. Rikki tried not to think about how many lives had been tossed into that thing since the construction of this facility. Ashes to ashes, dust to dust. All the beauty and joy and pain of a human life, reduced to nothing. Less than a memory. Broker's legacy to the world.

They gathered the ashes and left. It was a long walk upstairs, through the facility. Rikki tried to memorize every step, the scent of the air, the crisp cleanliness of the floors. Amiri touched her hand. Rictor walked on her other side. Blue held the box of ashes. They were all suspicious that way.

Ahead of them all walked Aitan. At his side, Kamau Shah. Immense, striking, powerful. He wore only slacks. Still caught between man and bird, with long golden feathers running up the lengths of his arms, meeting between his shoulders like an odd cape. His hair was tangled with feathers, his fingertips ending in black talons.

No remedy, or so Amiri had told her. If Kamau were to find his way back to one body or the other, it would have to be on his own.

And if he has family? Someone he was taken from? How will he return to the life he had, looking like that?

Questions. Always more questions.

Rikki glanced up at Amiri, and found him watching his father. She tugged on his arm and he bent down, just enough for her to whisper in his ear, "He loves you."

Amiri took a breath, hesitating. "He is my father."

But that was all he said, as if the words were caught in his throat. Rikki understood. She squeezed his hand. Sometimes silence was all you had.

UPSTAIRS, CONTROLLED CHAOS. PARTS OF THE FACILITY STILL looked like a war zone, but it was a war zone that now belonged to Dirk & Steele, and Amiri thought that made it somewhat lovely indeed.

The scientists had been rounded up, locked away, while their experiments—more than thirty women, most of them pregnant—now roamed free, even if they had been asked to stay within the west wing.

He thought he saw Mireille across the main hall, talking to the one of the pregnant women. No doubt preparing an insurrection. He and Rikki had been the ones to release her. She had not been pleased to see them, though the look in her eye had been more of shame than anger. A feeling he shared, when he thought of how he had frightened her. And what might have happened to her, in this place.

"So," Rikki said, holding his hand. "Big powerful detective agency. What are you going to do about all those people? This facility, even? Are you going to tell anyone, or just . . . sweep it under the rug?"

"I do not know," Amiri said, glancing at her. He found the other men doing the same, with troubled frowns.

Aitan gave them all sharp looks. "You must make up your minds. The unborn those women carry. . . . none of them are human."

Everyone stopped. Moochie said, "What do you mean, not human?"

Kamau Shah rumbled, golden eyes glinting. "They took sperm samples from me. Aitan, as well. No doubt others. And if not shifter blood, then their scientists tinkered in other ways."

No one else said a word. Amiri went very still inside his heart, trying to wrap his mind around such a thing. He could not. The problems, the questions, were too vast. They all stared at each other, disbelief and a terrible dawning comprehension cutting across their faces.

"What do we do?" Max said. "Do they know what their children are?"

"No," Aitan replied. "They were never meant to raise them."

"And if we explained?"

"They will not understand."

"They might," Blue said. "My wife is a shape-shifter."

Aitan's eyes narrowed. "And would you be willing to risk the safety of your children on the whim of another?"

Blue said nothing. Max ran his hands through his hair. "How do we handle this? We can't just . . . return them home. Even if they weren't carrying those children, they've been through too much. They need help. But to have *shape-shifters* as babies? That affects us, too."

"They will be called demons," Aitan said grimly, glancing at Kaumau. "The women *and* the babies, once they begin shifting. They will be killed or turned over to the authorities. You cannot allow that. You must take the children. Raise them with those who will welcome their existence."

"But where?" Rikki stared. "You'll have to keep the women here until they give birth. And then what? You'll steal their children? Are all of you kidnappers now? You'll be no better than the Consortium!"

"That cannot be allowed," Amiri said. "You must give the mothers the choice."

"Are you still naïve?" snapped his father. "Even if you explain, even if by some miracle those women understand and are not frightened, they cannot be trusted. Not in the long term. Not when the child becomes difficult. *Inhuman.*"

"It is not just one life at stake, but all of the shifting kind," Kaumau said. "I abhor the idea of stealing children from their mothers, but what choice do we have? It is not the same as having a mate who loves and protects your young. These women were forced, and even if they wish to keep them, they believe their babies will be human. Like them. Not . . . different."

"Oh, my God," Rikki said. "You realize what you're saying, don't you?"

Amiri could not speak. He kept thinking of the mother he had never known, his anger that he could not know her—his fear that even if he had, she would have rejected him.

"They must be given the choice," he forced himself to say, the words cutting him. With terror, with heartache, with the sudden piercing knowledge that he finally understood why his father had made his choice. Feeling inside himself the desire to do the same. Take the children, run and hide. Protect them from the world.

"But if they choose yes," hissed his father, "what will you do? Keep them prisoners so they do not betray their children, even by accident? Send them far away? And how will the children learn? Will they grow up thinking they are freaks? Monsters?"

"There must be a way," Blue said. "A better way."

The old man's face twisted with disdain, and Rictor began to laugh, very quietly. "You poor fucks. Forget turning this shit over to the government. You need this facility, just like you need to step in where the Consortium left off. At least until you have a handle on all that supernatural spawn."

Max closed his eyes. "I'm going to go look for Elena and Artur. We need to call Roland and talk about this now."

"Talk all you want," Rictor said, his smile fading into something dark, serious. "But there's no right answer. You know that, don't you? Someone is going to pay. You just have to decide if it will be the children or their mothers."

Blue balanced the box of ashes under his arm and pinched the bridge of his nose. "We're forgetting that the Consortium may want this place back. We've got their scientists, their experiments. Do we prepare for a siege?"

"No," Aitan murmured. "That is one thing you need not concern yourself with. Except for the unborn, little of value was kept in this facility. Notes were electronically transmitted, and biological samples—sperm, genetic material, blood—were regularly flown out. Even the viral weapon was imported."

"That still doesn't explain why they would just abandon this place," Rikki said. "They put so much into it."

"And it was exposed. Tainted. The Consortium prefers to hide, to avoid direct confrontation, though it occasionally engages in it. Abandoning facilities is not new to them. The Russian lab was destroyed after my son escaped."

"We tried to go back there," Blue said. "It had been filled in with concrete."

Aitan shrugged. "The Consortium has other facilities. Unfortunately, I do not know their locations."

"You know quite a bit," Max said, carefully.

Aitan tilted his head. "As Broker would say, I made it my business."

"And they will not want the women?" Amiri pressed. "Can you be certain?"

His father hesitated. Max gave him a long hard look, then turned away, started walking. Francis stopped him, and glanced at Moochie. "We'll go with you. We also have some insight into the running of this place."

"Aitan?" Max glanced over his shoulder. "We could use your help, as well."

Amiri watched his father hesitate. He expected the old man to say no, but found himself surprised once again. Aitan spared him a quick look—steady, without emotion—

and followed Max and the others as they walked off. Kamau joined him, and there was a camaraderie, a friendship between the two shape-shifters that Amiri could not look away from until the men crossed out of sight. He had never seen the old man have a friend, or work with anyone—not until coming here.

Fourteen years. So much had changed. In himself, as well. He was a different man. All the pain, all the hardship—worth it, for bringing him to this point, to be with these people.

He brought Rikki's hand to his mouth and kissed it. Savored her slow worried smile, her thoughts still clearly on women and babies and impossible questions.

"Come," he said quietly, his own heart knotted. "We have men to scatter."

But in the end, all they did was dump the ashes of Broker and Jaaved over the edge of the ravine. Rictor spit on the ground. Blue sighed. Amiri watched Rikki watch the sky, and said nothing at all. Words were inadequate for the uneasiness he felt. The fear that none of this was over.

Of course it is not over, whispered his father. *Not until you die, cub.*

A disquieting thought. Amiri watched Rikki walk ahead with Blue. He caught snippets of conversation—Eddie's name. Blue said, "He's resting, but he's still not well. He's having trouble . . . controlling things."

"Eddie was changed," Rictor rumbled, beside Amiri, too quietly for the others to hear. "Broker's virus. It altered the boy. Not something I could fix."

"You did what you could," Amiri said, concerned. He slowed his pace, deliberately putting distance between themselves and the others.

"Ah," Rictor said. "I sense a Deep Conversation coming on."

Amiri glanced at him. "You are not alone. You have . . . friends."

"Do I now?"

He smiled faintly. "Do not push your luck."

Rictor also smiled, but it faded, fast. "About why . . ."

"Excuse me?"

"Why I came to help you."

"Oh."

"Yes. Elena freed me from the Consortium. You know that."

"She spoke of a circle made of sand and light. She passed through it, and . . . something broke. You were free."

"Free," Rictor rumbled, as though the word meant something different to him. "Not many could have done what she accomplished. Takes a certain kind of blood. Different from the Magi, from anything mortal. She doesn't know."

Amiri felt cold. "And?"

He looked down at his hands. "Her blood, the act of freeing me, created a bond. I don't know how or why. I tried to get rid of it, but I never could. I . . . felt her with me all the time. Ever since that moment. It didn't matter where I went, in this world or others. She was always with me. It was how I knew she was worried about you." Rictor stopped, and looked at him. "You don't know what it was like. How much it hurt. To love her and feel her and not . . . be able to touch her."

Amiri tried to keep his voice steady. "You speak of the past. What of now?"

"Now," Rictor whispered, and the pain that entered his gaze was livid, raw. "Now I feel nothing. She's gone."

"She is your friend."

"She belongs to Artur." Rictor closed his eyes. "I have nothing left of her. And for all the pain it caused me, that is what I miss, Amiri. Nothing else, not even the power. Just that. Just her. Inside of me."

Amiri tried to imagine loving and losing Rikki in such a way, and the thought was crippling. He would not be strong enough to bear such a burden. But Rictor . . .

"You are still immortal," he said. "You are still what you were, even if you are powerless."

"I suppose," he said, and gave Amiri a hard look. "If you ever tell anyone what I told you—"

"You will kill me. Yes, I am quite clear on that."

"And you owe me."

"We will argue about that some other time."

"Already scared?"

"With you, always," Amiri said—and found himself, several minutes later, living within an odd bitter irony when they entered the main hall and found Elena and Artur, pale and dressed in blue, heads bowed close, talking without speaking. Memories surged: the four of them, together, in Russia, depending on each other for their lives.

Elena waved when she saw them, but her smile widened only for Rictor. She smiled at him like there was a rainbow in the sky. Rictor, on the other hand, showed nothing. Heart of stone. Implacable. Dangerous. Master of lies.

Elena hugged him. And Amiri watched Artur watch Rictor, and he knew there were no secrets between the men. Not when it came to her.

"Rictor," she said.

"Elena," he said.

Amiri wandered away. He looked for Rikki. Found his father instead.

A'sharia and Kimbareta were with him. He was teaching the children to track. Amiri felt some surprise that the old man was including the boy in the lesson, but his father looked at him and said, "I am not the man I used to be," which was enough of a shock that Amiri found himself sitting down on a fallen tree, watching his father teach the children with a gentleness that Amiri had never been shown. It made him jealous, but only for a moment. Mostly, it made him sad.

"I thought you would be with the others," Amiri said.

"I gave them the truth," replied the old man. "What more is there?"

"Much more," he said.

Aitan sighed, and looked at the children. "Go and play. Stay close."

A'sharia smiled—sweet, breathtaking—and led Kimbareta deep into the bush. Leaving the two men alone.

My sister, Amiri thought, staring after her. Still marveling. All of this, remarkable. And painful.

"Life is painful," said Aitan, again surprising Amiri. "And yes, I betrayed you. But not in my heart. I had to play a careful game with Broker. He murdered A'sharia's mother, and then took the child as a way of controlling me."

Amiri had to struggle with that. "How did he find you?"

Aitan closed his eyes. "When I killed Angelique and drove you away, I went back home to visit with Wambui, your nurse. I believed you kept in contact with her, even after you left."

"Of course," Amiri replied. "She was the closest person I had to a mother. It grieved me greatly when she passed away."

Aitan sighed. "We were not on the best of terms, even at the end. I told her what had transpired between us, and she was so cross with me, so bitterly angry, she cursed me."

"Wambui?" Amiri frowned. "She was no witch."

"We kept it from you. She had gifts, powers. That is why I knew she could be trusted with rearing you. But I never expected her to turn on *me.*"

Amiri grunted, not entirely sympathetic. "What did she do?"

His father grimaced. "She put me inside your head as punishment. I experienced everything you did. All your thoughts and fears. Fourteen years inside your mind, cub."

"Impossible.

"So naïve." A bitter smile touched his mouth. "If it makes you feel better, I learned a great deal. You . . . raised me . . . to be a different man."

It was difficult to breathe. "You did not search me out."

"But I did. When you were captured by the Consortium, I went to find you, to rescue you." His gaze turned distant, his voice dropping to a whisper. "They caught me, cub. And when I refused to cooperate, they took my woman, and they took my daughter." He held out his leathery hands. "But now, freedom."

Amiri could not stand this. He could not bear to hear more. But he looked into his father's eyes and said, "Do you hate me? For what you endured?"

"No," breathed Aitan. "You are my son, and I love you."

Amiri looked away, stricken. His father clapped him on his leg. "Those friends of yours are good people. I will work with them, for a time. And then, when I am done, I will take A'sharia back to Kenya. Perhaps the boy, too. Your sister is fond of him. He makes a good pet for her."

Amiri gave him a sharp look. His father laughed, standing. "Come home to Kenya, cub. When your heart can stand it again. There is no need to fear. Not with me, or that woman at your side."

"I know," Amiri said. "I know what she is to me." *And what you are now, as well.*

Aitan sighed. "I am glad you never listened."

And that, combined with declarations of affection and mind-reading, was enough to leave Amiri quite rattled, as though the world had teetered and fallen, leaving him still floating in the sky, casting for an anchor.

He went to hunt for Rikki.

THE ODD THING WAS, RIKKI FELT SAFE—EVEN HERE, WHERE bullet holes still riddled the walls and blood smeared the floors. She could mark death in footsteps, track where lives had ended, but she felt no fear.

No lingering desire to make it a summer vacation home, either, but still. No fear.

She passed pregnant women standing in the doorways of their new rooms. Talking with each other, holding hands. Laughing. Sweeping away with their voices the miasma of all that was dark and wrong with this facility. As though pain had never existed here, and that something new was in its place. Possibilities.

Rikki did not know what to make of that. Women stopped her in the hall, bellies round and large. They wanted to ask her questions about these new people. Whether they were truly safe. Rikki answered them as best she could, given that her French was rusty and she had little to give. Safe, yes. She was certain of that. But nothing else.

And that felt wrong to her. She wanted to be in the thick of it. She was a doctor; but more, she was one of these women. They had been her future. Broker had promised that, more or less. Just another experiment. What affected them, would affect her. And their children.

So what now? You give up your career? Everything you've worked for? To do what?

Rikki was not sure. But she knew one thing—she could not go back to the way things had been. Not after everything she had seen and done. Moving backwards never did any good. There was no such thing as time travel, and clinging to the past just made the heart sore.

So you help, she told herself. *You make a difference. Same as always. That much won't change.*

No. Not on her life.

She found Jean-Claude in the cafeteria. He sat by the window. She thought Elena must have done something for him. Nothing major, but the swelling had disappeared, and his nose appeared less broken. Rikki kicked out a chair and plopped herself down. Stared, for a moment, at the plate of half-eaten rice and beans he had pushed aside. Her stomach growled. He nudged it toward her. Rikki grabbed his spoon and took a bite. It was good.

"So," she said, after several minutes of strained silence, "you did try to warn me."

"I had no idea it would be this," he said, his eyes still bloodshot. "Just rumors. Doctors going missing. Corruption."

"And then they came for you." Rikki put down the spoon. "Your family?"

"Safe. They wanted only me."

"Jean-Claude—"

"I know," he said.

"I'm sorry."

"I know," he said again, gently, reaching out take her hand. "But I am your friend, Rikki Kinn. I saved your life once, yes?"

"Yes." She squeezed his fingers, and a faint smile touched his mouth. He raised up his arm, and settled his hand more securely over hers. Dug his elbow into the table.

"You will not beat me this time," he said. "And if I win, you will tell me what this place is. All of it. I am so very confused. And if *you* win, you will do the same."

"A girl has to have some secrets, Jean-Claude."

He hesitated. "How good it is to see you smile."

Good to have a reason to smile, she thought, and slammed his hand—very gently—into the table. At which point he cried foul, laughing, and they gave up the arm wrestling for quieter talk, which was censored and careful and gave nothing away that could prove dangerous to her new acquaintances. She did not like lying to Jean-Claude, though. Not when he seemed to know she was doing just that.

Rikki eventually excused herself. Her heart hurt. She went to find Amiri.

And she did. Soon after, walking fast down the hall. He smiled when he saw her—almost, she thought, with relief—and grabbed her hand, tugging her close for a hard long kiss that took away all her pain and confusion.

"Come," he whispered in her ear. "I want to run away."

"Where no one will find us?"

"We will be ghosts," he breathed, kissing her mouth. "We will feast on sunlight and the hearts of shadows."

He led her outside, and she felt like a kid again as he pulled her into the forest. The world was safe with Amiri; the danger, the horror melted away into something small and distant that could not touch her, that had never touched her.

They ran until they were breathless, and leaned against the trunk of a fat tree, impossibly ancient and thick with bulging branches and twisting vines. Good climbing. A better place to hide from the world. Rikki kicked off her shoes, took a deep breath, and jumped, grabbing the low branch. It bent under her weight, but not much, and it was easy enough to swing up, just like the high bar. Markovic and his training. She missed the old man. Almost as much as her father. But the pain was easier now. The loneliness was gone.

She looked down only once, and found Amiri chasing her. Graceful, easy. Fast. He passed her easily, but it was still a race, and she danced up the tree, scaling it like the colobus monkeys screaming at her, or the full-throated birds flashing wingtips in the corners of her eyes. Her body moved entirely by instinct, and when Amiri looked down and met her gaze she could not fight the fierce grin that spread across her face. Laughter bubbled up her throat.

"You," he said, smiling. "You are such a surprise, Rikki Kinn."

He reached down and pulled her up until they stood together in the canopy. Her bare feet dug into the smooth bark of a wide branch, thicker than the bumper of a jeep. Better than any balance beam.

Amiri stood in front of her, perched with ease near the trunk, his face half-hidden in shadows and leaves so that when he looked at her it was, for a moment, like seeing the face of some golden-eyed apparition: too elegant, too wild, to be anything but magic. The heat of his gaze made her dizzy, and she had to glance down, away, so that she felt like she was flying, hovering, caught in a web of air and light. The view was incredible; lush, rolling.

When she looked back at Amiri, she found his gaze unflinching, warm and golden and so full of life she could not help but reach out. Her fingers grazed his chest—his smooth, perfect chest—and he gathered her close, his hand slipping around her back; a gentle vise, an anchor. Forty feet above the ground and he made it seem like they were standing free and easy with the earth hard beneath their feet. She forgot to breathe, but managed enough of a voice to whisper, "You're the first person in years I've been sure of, Amiri."

His chest rumbled. "Who were the others?"

"My father. My brother. My coach. All of them dead now. The only people who ever loved me."

"I love you." Amiri's arm slid up the trunk of the tree, gripping the branch above their heads. "Shape-shifters only take one true mate. Something the heart knows. And it knew you, Rikki. From the start."

Words to fly by, words to live by, like riding a rush of pure energy, straight from the sun into her heart. But for a moment—just one—it felt almost too good. It made her afraid.

"My mother left," she found herself saying, very quietly. "I don't know where she is. If she's still alive. My father was murdered, Markovic . . . lung cancer. My brother, Frankie, killed in an accident." Rikki stopped, closing her eyes. "I thought I had found him again, you know. When I saw Eddie for the first time. It was like having my brother back . . . and then losing him all over again. And I couldn't do a thing to save either one of them."

"Eddie is fine," Amiri said quietly. "He *will* be fine. You helped save him."

She shook her head. "Everyone I've ever loved has been taken from me. If anything ever happened to you—"

He placed his hand over her mouth. "And me? How do you think I feel?"

She tugged his hand away. "You've lost, too. In the lab, what Broker said . . . about the women you've loved . . ."

Tension strained his body; his expression flattened, far

too neutral. "Only one woman. Her name was Angelique. She was the first woman I ever loved. Our affair was casual to her, but not to me. I wanted her to be mine, and I thought if she knew me, all of me, that it would . . ."

"Awe her?" Rikki supplied, when he said nothing else. "Make her realize just how special your love is, because of the man you are, that you aren't the kind to trust your heart lightly?"

Amiri stared. "Am I so transparent?"

"No." Rikki kissed the corner of his mouth. "But that's how *I* feel."

"Ah," he breathed, smiling. "So you like me, just a little?"

She shoved at his chest, laughing. "Don't change the subject."

His smile faded. "There is little to change. She rejected me. She called me a monster, a demon, even a sorcerer. She threatened to expose me. I was heartbroken, frightened. I turned to my father for advice. He went out that night and killed her."

Rikki felt sucker punched. "What?"

"He murdered her. Then threatened to do the same to any woman who ever learned the truth about me. I believed him, and I ran away. And though he was not near, I . . . took the lesson to heart. I stayed far from women, and if I kept a female friend, she was always old or married. I did not want the temptation. I did not want to suffer such heartache again—or the possibility that another woman might die because of me."

She was still trying to wrap her head around the idea that his father—Aitan, that man who had helped save them— could do something so cold, so ruthless. "How long ago was that?"

"Fourteen years," Amiri said. "A long drought. I hardly understand how I survived, knowing what I do now."

"And what's that?"

Soft hunger filled his eyes. When he smiled, she could feel the predator in him, the danger. That sweet, hot, danger. He grabbed the back of her neck, his fingers sliding into her hair, and he pulled slightly, just enough to tilt her head so that her neck lay exposed.

He kissed her throat. He kissed her jaw. He lay his mouth over hers and kissed her tenderly, so soft and light she pushed against him for more. But he kept her hungry, aching, and whispered, "You ask for an impossible answer, Rikki Kinn. Better to pretend you have been blind all your life, and now can see the sun."

"I *can* see it," she said, and pulled back just enough to look at him, and marvel. A light sheen of sweat covered his brown skin; his limbs were loose, powerful; and when she met his gaze his eyes were bright, so intense her breath caught. He stared back at her with naked pleasure, as though she was a wonder, a mystery. And she felt like one; the entire world was her own private fairy tale, scattershot with magic.

The sun was setting, casting shadows etched in silver. Amiri held her close, and they stood on the branches of the ancient tree and watched the world swallow fire, followed by the hush of twilight, the first gasp of stars.

And though for years she had convinced herself that nothing was more important than a lonely heart, the thought of going back to that, even in the face of terrible loss, was a cruel and indefensible joke. Rikki had been living without living. She had been passing through life with her soul in a cage.

And Amiri, she realized, had done the same. Lonely hearts, frightened of their shadows.

But now they were free.

"It's a whole new beginning," Rikki said.

"Indeed," Amiri replied, and they stood above the world, and watched the twilight gather life.